Patsy,

I hope you enjoy the ride!

Pat

The Talisman Effect

A Novel
by
Patrick Rowlee

The Talisman Effect

Published by Patrick Rowlee

First printing, Spring 2018

Paperback

ISBN 9781980957966

OTHER NOVELS BY PATRICK ROWLEE

Varrick's Disturbances

Two Faces to No One

Blackballed

He Plays Like Cobb

COMING SOON

Colleen Street: Slices of the Sixties

DEDICATED TO

My Early Musical Influences:

father Robert Emerson Rowlee “The Music Man”

sister Diann Rowlee “The First Flautist”

brother Keith Kennedy “The White Miles Davis”

Preface

This story's life began just moments after the last one finished, when my wife pointed out, "You love music, Paddy. Why don't you write your next one about music (rather than sports or politics)?" She was right. The person who knows me most knows how much I love to talk and think about music – both the music I love to share with others and the music I love that others share with me. Music has played many roles in my life – my entertainer, comforter, cheerleader, supporter, and confidante - and those roles add up to make it my dearest of friends. You see, music has not only been *with* me all my life, but *inside me*, as I traverse the course spread before me. But, if I could distill music's value in my life to just word, it would be passion. It is best spelled P-a-s-s i-o-n. If you look carefully at how I punctuated it, you'll notice I did not place a hyphen between the second 's' and the letter 'i.' So, what I've done is isolate 'passion' from 'ion.' I wondered: What if music literally transmits or *passes* negative *ions* through not only our ears and brain, but throughout our entire beings – our ears, brain, muscles, pituitary, heart, liver, lungs, and – last but never least – our psyches? This musical passion inside me has always existed – learning songs ("Mary Had a Little Lamb" and "Twinkle, Twinkle Little Star"), hearing my favorite TV show themes, listening to 45 records on a turntable and my trusty transistor radio, buying my first LPs, attending my first school dance, watching my first concert, reading and memorizing the liner notes on all my albums, and - later - considering a career as a music critic. And, as I've matured as a person, my passion for music has grown each passing year. After watching my 45 rpm treasures spin around our family record player at age nine, hearing my first FM rock radio program at fourteen, having friends and family in bands (some obscure, some not), writing dozens of top ten lists (songs, albums, lead guitarists, singers, etc.), and then conceiving and completing the story you're about to read, I've come to realize music has not been a *part* of my life. No, this passion can't be reduced to such a limited role or mere portion of my life, but music is rather a major source of my inspiration, happiness, and joy. It is as fundamental to my being as blood is to a body's health and life. There are many things I love that I'd be willing to live without – TV, travel, recreation, comedy, and maybe even the game of baseball – but there is no way I could exist without music. Music helps me feel, taste, savor, and digest life; and it courses through my veins and arteries and arrives where it first began - in my heart. Music is *that* vital to me. I don't think it's an over-reach to say that music is my life's blood. And, if it *is* for you too, then buckle up as we begin a musical journey through the life of a person whose very existence he owes to music.

The music of his early life – from the early 1950s through the ensuing three decades – is the soundtrack for all the ups, downs, dreams, nightmares, tragedies, and miracles he will encounter, go through, and exit – all the while dancing along to his soundtrack. This art form called music is his passion, his friend, his refuge, much more even than music has been for me. So, I hope you enjoy the ride and maybe even reflect on your own musical journey. Who knows? Your ride and his may take parallel routes to similar destinations with perhaps kindred results. What I know for certain is what a musician once said about the transformative value of music: “All it takes is a three-minute song to change someone’s life.”

The ride you’re about to take has many three-minute life-changers. The soundtrack in this story is as important as the story. In truth, this man’s soundtrack *is* the story.

Foreword

Before all this stuff happened, I could hardly scribble a simple sentence; much less string together a series of paragraphs like I'm doing now. And, now that I've been on this project awhile, I've produced a slew of paragraphs which will beget a bunch of chapters, which will comprise the bouncing baby of a story dealing with thirty-three years of a man's life. Even though I've only been part of this story for the past few jam-packed months, we both will tell the story of his last three years, but only he can describe his first thirty years in any detail.

Since it was his idea for me to help tell the story, the least I can do is my best. I promise to give this story the *old college try* with every fiber of my being. And, now that you have some idea what I'll do for his story, I'll reveal the other side of my nature. Truth is, I'd never do half this much work for anyone else's story, including my own. But, if someone else *had* asked me to do even a fraction of the work I've done on this project? Why, I'd have told him or her in no uncertain terms to "stick it where the sun don't shine." Which, shows you how much I used to hate writing. Used to. So, the deal with me helping this man you know nothing about is that he's as vital to my existence as the sun is to our planet's. As we say down South: you're darn tootin' I promise - no, *pledge* - to do whatever Ross Man asks - even when I have no idea how to do it.

My part in this story started while I worked at a convalescent hospital in Alpharetta, Georgia – close to Atlanta. And though I was just a janitor on the graveyard shift, I liked my job. A lot. In fact, it was the only job I'd *ever* liked; and the only job that lasted me past the first day. You may ask, "Why did you never keep a job before the one at the hospital?" The simple answer: People didn't get along with me.

Now, don't get me wrong. *I* get along with anybody (even Ma, my *un-dearly* departed, never-happy-in-her-life maternal parent). But! Hardly anyone tried to get along with me. Why? I don't know for sure. But, I do know that back then everyone either ignored me or treated me like a household pet, but I never found out why. And, maybe I never will. Who knows? Maybe it just doesn't matter, after all.

Hold on, for Pete's sake. I haven't even introduced myself. My birth certificate says *"Pammy Lee Wertzhog"* across the middle of it, but no one ever called me any of those names. Not family, nor friends (if I'd had any), nor classmates, nor any of my co-workers at the hospital. I don't have the stomach to mention the nastiest names people called me, but feel free to use your imaginations if you want to guess what they were. The names I *will* mention weren't nice at all, to hint at the garbage I was called. The ones I can tell you about were these: Fatty Worst Hog, Pammy Fart Hog, and - what folks called me most - Hammy Wart Hog. Yeah… I was called "Hammy Wart Hog" so much by people in Alpharetta that I'm sure many of those idiots thought I liked that stupid, lame name so much I had to have it legally changed and now – look at me! – I'm signing all my flippin' checks using Hammy Wart Hog. Yeah, some folks *are* that ignorant… or stupid. Feel free to pick which option resonates with you.

At the facility everyone called me Hammy or Miss Wart Hog, but I never corrected them; not once. Why? Because, as I told myself more times than I care to count, "At least they called you *something*, Pammy; names without any cussing or farts in them. Look at it this way. It could've been worse, maybe much worse." So, once I made that concession, I was 'good to go,' like folks say nowadays.

I'll stop here a sec to say something in case you might already have a false notion about Ross Man: The man never called me *any* of those names... ever. And if he ever heard someone call me some name other than my own, he never let on. But, if he *had* heard someone reference me any other way than by my given name? You can rest assured Ross would've put his own end to that and nipped any trouble in the bud. So, that's enough of Pammy Lee telling you how good a man Ross is. But, if I told you more? I'd bawl like a baby and never find the time to finish my part of this project. Please remember as you follow along that the story you're reading or hearing, isn't mine at all. It is, pure and simple, Ross's story.

Just so you know what to expect, I'll stay out of the way when I can, but I'll jump in here and there – either because Ross asked me or it's the right thing to do, which is the same thing.

Chapter One

Dr. Regina Speckman assumed the patient she'd been tending for twenty minutes would be the last of her shift, but that was before she flipped over the single-page report on her clipboard to discover a new sheet inserted among her case files. Resisting the temptation to slam the board down, she asked herself: "*Why does kind of this crap happen to me*?" Clicking her tongue, she sat in the room's one chair.

She scanned her new patient's file: *"John Doe: Head trauma. Possible auto accident - as driver, passenger, or pedestrian on 11/7/1982. No dental records; No ID. No vehicle found."*

What the Hell is going on here? This must be someone's idea of a cruel, sick joke.

Looking down the hallway in both directions to possibly catch the perpetrator of this prank, the neurologist refocused and returned to reading:

"Patient Status Report - 4/2/85: Comatose since 11/7/82. Released from Alpharetta Memorial Hospital 4/1/85 to Alpharetta Convalescent Hospital. No known family."

"What the hell is this - The Twilight Zone or the worst April Fool's joke ever?" she sputtered, while standing in front of a comatose patient's bed - the one she'd presumed was her last for the night. However, she had no cause to worry about being heard since there wasn't another conscious soul in the entire wing. At 5:25 a.m., the only other conscious person in the head-trauma ward was a woman she'd never spoken to, either a nurse's aide or a night janitor.

What room is Doe in? One seventy-three. Oh, good news! At least he's close by. After a short shuffle down the waxed white linoleum hallway to room 173, Regina peered inside. "There he is, in all his glory." She approached the lone bed in the darkly lit room and grasped the man's wrist. After staring at her diamond-studded Rolex fifteen seconds, she jotted down his pulse before taking his temperature. "Ninety-six, point two. Close enough." After filling in the information required on his chart, she took a chair and dragged it to the bed. Getting a good first look at Doe, she realized both his eyes were not just open, but wide open. *Gorgeous gray eyes, but no life in either one.* Seeing 5:48 a.m. on her watch, she sighed, *Another day, another goner.* Speckman padded out to the hallway and headed to her office, where she put away her clipboard, gathered her purse and lunch bag, and left the facility.

Chapter Two

Hi, it's Pammy Lee again. So, as I said before, I loved that job. Partly because I didn't have to deal with other staff and partly because I went at my own pace & did my duties in whatever order I felt like doing them. But this one night, as I proceeded to clean room after room on the ground floor, mopping and wiping everything that might've been touched in the past twenty-four hours, I saw him for the first time. All by himself and looking dead, except for both his eyes being not just open, but wide open. The man (I didn't know his name then) had the prettiest gray eyes I'd ever seen, but not a single speck of life in either one of them.

I stood gazing at those eyes for the longest spell while I started guessing what his story might be. I called my little game with myself "The Story of Mr. Gray Eyes." I first tried imagining the basic facts - who he was, where'd he come from, and how he'd fallen into his coma. Not to brag, but I've got quite a vivid imagination. In fact, Ma told me that all the time when I was a kid. She'd say, "Hammy, you have one vivid imagination; I'll give you that. Know what vivid is, Wart Hog? More real than TV. Your imagination is more vivid even than Mr. Huntley and Brinkley's Nightly News show."

I decided Gray Eyes couldn't be from the South, but somewhere far away and exotic – like France, England, Alaska, or California. Somewhere the opposite of here. So, guess what? I started picturing Mr. Gray Eyes (what I called him before I learned his name) driving in this handsome convertible sports car with the top down and the Georgia breeze flowing like silk through his beautiful wavy black hair. In my mind, Gray Eyes looked relaxed and happy – contented as a cow, as folks say. The clothes I imagined on him were real nice: a white silk shirt with sky-blue lines running through it, which highlighted those dreamy eyes on his gorgeous face. I also pictured a pair of fancy beige slacks without a single wrinkle but a big crease running down the middle of each leg, like some butler had ironed them. And then, the best part of my 'internal movie' was the pair of fancy loafers I conjured that were the color of wine. (Red wine, of course.) And socks you'd die for that looked like the ones rich men wear when they're golfing or dining at some fancy restaurant with candles, chandelier, and caviar.

And right when I felt like the life inside me had been sucked into the head of this new man with the beautiful eyes, I heard footsteps coming down the hallway. I ducked into the john, shut the door, and start scrubbing the sink like all get out. I heard a chair drag over the floor followed by lots of paper shuffles and scribbling. After, oh, twenty minutes, I couldn't hear anything anymore, so I figured the coast had cleared. I finished cleaning the toilet this patient had never used, before rejoining him at his side. I lingered long enough to wish him a good night. He didn't look at me, of course, but I imagined he did. So, I said real sweet and familiar-like: "Good night, Handsome'" before leaving room 173 to finish my shift.

Chapter Three

Dr. Speckman, after filling in the date (1/26/1985) and all of John Doe's vitals (good to excellent), wrote the following comment at the bottom of the form: "Vital data - all nominal with no significant change. Patient unresponsive to all stimuli. Comatose status unchanged. If status remains 30 days, stimulus therapy and brain-function monitoring will cease. Prognosis - poor."

It's Pammy Lee again. So, a month passed without any change in Mr. Gray Eyes. There *was* one change having to do with him - his care. No one checked on him anymore, except for the nurse's aides – and then just to change, wash, or dress him. He had an IV, so he received all his nutrition without being fed by anyone. And, the fancy doctor lady who used to check on him late at night? She quit doing that a coon's age ago.

I got to thinking about this whole situation and it seemed very sad. This poor fella had no name, no family, no friends, and no visitors, plus now he had no help, therapy, or contact with anyone. I choked up thinking about it and wished I could do something, but then I wondered - what could that something be? Since I'm not a health professional, I had no clue what to do for him; but he was awfully lonely-looking sitting there with no one to help him with anything. So, I decided I'd visit him more and check on him every night, which is exactly what I did.

Since that fancy doctor lady wasn't around anymore, I decided to take up the slack and be Mr. Gray Eyes' nurse. I began by touching his forehead every hour to see if he felt hot. If he did, I'd get a paper towel from the john, wet it from the cold water in the sink, and place it over his forehead to bring his temperature down. I did that each night on duty (six nights a week with Sundays off). That worked fine for a while, but then I started thinking I ought to do more. Know what I did? Started playing music for him.

I'd found this device called a Sound-About in his bed stand that had to belong to him. It said Sony on the cassette player and had a pair of headphones. I placed one headphone on one of his ears and played the cassette. (Note: two years after Sony introduced the Sound-About, they changed its name to Walkman.) I'd listen with the other headphone as I sat next to him, leaning in and humming along when I knew the song.

I did this ten to twenty minutes every night during my breaks. I had two short ones besides my half-hour lunch break. So, every night but Sunday, I'd put one headphone on Mr. Gray Eyes' ear and listen to his music with the other.

One evening, soon after I'd started my new nursing routine, something happened that frankly freaked me out. A patch of blanket on his bed began moving. I could barely see it at first, but then it got so much clearer that I started believing my own eyes. Both his arms were tucked under the top sheet and blanket - probably to keep them from moving. But, his right hand kept moving.............. up and down, up and down, up and down. So, I pulled back his covers till I uncovered his right hand. Guess what? Gray Eyes' right index finger continued bobbing up and down, even after I lifted it off the bed. He wasn't moving his finger to the music's beat at all.

His one finger kept tapping away. I'd never seen anything like it, so I just sat there - watching him tap away on his bed, all to his heart's content. I watched him till a brain storm hit me like a ton of bricks. Gray Eyes wasn't tapping his finger like you or I do to a song when we like it or want to keep the beat. No. It reminded me of something I hadn't thought about for twenty years – since my Girl Scout days. It seemed like he was tapping out some sort of message. So, after my shift ended I went straight home, found my Morse Code chart inside my Girl Scout duffel, and brought it to work the next night.

During my first break, I rewound the Sound-About to the beginning and pushed 'play.' As soon as I placed a headphone next to his ear, that same index finger started tapping away again. I got my chart and began writing down every letter he tapped out. I know you're thinking I'm either lying, crazy, or both, but I started jotting down groups of words that became sentences, and those sentences made up the start of a story - Ross's story.

Chapter Four

Here's word for word what I wrote down from his finger-tapping. You judge for yourself whether I'm lying, but you'll see how different his writing was from mine.

Throughout my life, people have entered it and people have left it. Likewise, various jobs came and went. I've moved in and out of countless residences – some houses, but mostly small apartments. But, throughout my lifetime, only one constant or single element has been a part of my core existence. This component, which transcended everything else, has been the blessing known as music. I know that many people claim music is a huge influence in their lives, but I want to emphasize that in my case, it hadn't just been in my life; music **is** *my life. And, it will always be my life's blood and the primary force in my existence.*

I can't think of an event, person, or place in this existence that hasn't been represented in some way or other by music. More specifically, a certain song, jingle, or symphony. Music has always provided the soundtrack for the movie that is my life story.

All the way back to infancy, music has touched me, uplifted me, or knocked me flat. The first song I ever knew, the one that came to define my early years was a huge hit the year I was born: the super cute, hard-to-forget "(How Much Is) That Doggie in the Window?"

Sung by Patti Paige, "Doggie" came out the previous year and sold over two million copies in the early Fifties. Whenever I heard the tune in my mother's presence, she'd brighten, flash a winsome smile, and say: "You used to love that song. Whenever it came on the radio or TV, you'd mimic the dog barking in it. You were so cute, Ross. Oh, how you loved that song!"

And whenever she regaled me with that memory, I felt soft and squishy while envisioning Miss Paige's stroll down a busy boulevard peering in a pet store's windows while singing the little ditty. Yes, it's awfully cute, almost to the point of being sickening sweet, but I can't deny that "How Much is that Doggie in the Window?" has never ceased to provide me the body memory mixture of warmth, "squishiness," and a soothing sense of safety. How three minutes of music can accomplish that profound of an effect on one's life is beyond my comprehension.

After several minutes of non-stop decoding and writing, this first part ended. At first, I didn't connect it with the story because I'd focused only on getting down the words he'd tapped out. It took me a spell to decode this first message because I was out of practice, although it had been a specialty of mine in Scouts. But, what might seem weird is that I found nothing strange at all about Ross telling a story. I admit to knowing nothing about seizures, comas, or other states of unconsciousness, but at that moment I deemed it the most natural, weirdest thing I'd ever witnessed. It's hard to explain what I mean by "most natural, weirdest thing," but I think you'll get the idea after what I'll tell you next. As Gray Eyes continued tap-tapping during the second tune on his tape, I paused the player and started it again. Here is what he 'said' and what I wrote:

Another early music-related influence was not a song, but an artist – the late, great Nat King Cole. During my boyhood, he was one of my favorite vocalists, even though Cole wasn't considered a singer, but a pianist par excellence – especially in the jazz community.

Since I first remember, even more comforting than the childlike melody of "Doggie in the Window" was the voice of Mr. Cole. I always associate the man's dulcet tones with comfort, love, and safety. In fact, I've never not felt any of these three sensations any time I've heard him sing. Eventually, at age twenty, I confessed to my mom the effect Nat had had on me since I could first remember. Her reaction at first was disarming, but then a smile spread across her face. "I used to rock you at night for fifteen minutes, during Nat King Cole's TV show, and you'd always lay there and listen intently as though listening to an important message."

And sure enough, my research revealed Cole had, for a time, his own network show at night that lasted just fifteen minutes. Because no major company would sponsor his show, NBC subsidized the program and kept it on the air. Since I was eighteen months to three years old during this period, Mom rocked to calm or comfort me. Nat's soothing voice, even today, is inextricably linked to the peace and safety I felt whenever Mom rocked me. I'll never forget this classic song for those reasons.

This part of his story I worked hard to write correctly. I then checked the label on his player for the second cut, which had been labeled "'Unforgettable' - Nat King Cole."

I then played the next two songs back to back, and here's how Ross responded:

Every Christmastime as a boy, there was a song that wouldn't just cheer me, but perk me up considerably. It didn't matter if I was sick or well, because whenever I heard this cowboy's voice on the radio, my entire being brightened. A sense of hope raised my spirits and I couldn't help but feel wonderful. I don't know whether it was his voice or the story of a little creature overcoming overwhelming odds to save the most important night of the year, but I can think of no more uplifting song for any time. I always feel aglow as I envision the singer with his cheery smile singing about the night before Christmas and the magical trip Santa and his eight reindeer made that fateful night.

The other tune that still stirs me today is Nat Cole's classic composition about campers roasting one of my favorite treats over a campfire.

Sure enough, the last two songs had been "Rudolph the Red Nosed Reindeer" and "The Christmas Song." Even though we were months away from the holidays, I still loved hearing them both. I don't know about you, but Christmas music makes me feel like everything's going to be all right. It gives me a snug-as-a-bug-in-a-rug feeling, providing a glow that warms me all over. It's possibly the best sensation I've yet to experience.

Chapter Five

I'll be honest here, but then I always am. In fact, I can't carry this burden any longer, so here comes a confession: After I'd read those words tapped out by my new friend, I was…… bumfuzzled, to borrow one of Ma's words. (May she rest in peace, even though she doesn't deserve it.) "Bumfuzzled" describes to a tee how I felt at that moment: I was *freaked out beyond belief.* In fact, I'd never seen anything like it. And the first thing in my brain was a question: How would the rest of the staff respond if they saw a plain Jane graveyard-shift janitor like myself scribbling away on a pad while staring at a comatose patient's finger? They surely would report me to one of the administration's Big Wigs; like the doctor who'd given up on Ross.

The more I thought about it, the more scared I got. I jumped up and took a long, hard look in every direction; not just in Gray Eyes' room, but up and down his hall, at the nearest nurses' station, and anywhere else I could think to look. And guess what? Not a single soul in sight. So, I felt better about the whole deal and decided to continue my 'experiment.' I placed a headphone next to Ross's ear again. (By the way, he called himself "Ross" in his first story, so I started calling him his name right away.) I took his Sound-About off "pause" and was about to play a couple more songs for us, when guess what? Lo and behold, that finger started to tap. I got excited, but not so much I forgot what I was doing. I sat there maybe ten minutes while getting this all down:

For as long as I remember, there has never been anything I've enjoyed doing quite as much as listening to man's greatest talent......music. But, since we were poor – just my mother and I – my main source of musical enjoyment was our little black and white Zenith TV in all the fourteen funky little apartments we rented somewhere in the San Bernardino area during my childhood. On Sunday evenings, there was only one network to which our set was tuned – The Columbia Broadcasting System (aka "CBS"). And the Ed Sullivan Show was the only program on the Sabbath I ever watched from eight o'clock till my bedtime at ten.

My first memory of watching Ed's show happens to also be the first time I laid eyes on my favorite musician, my first "Soul Brother," the beaming, balding, sweating, dark-skinned man gripping a gleaming golden trumpet in one hand and clutching a white hanky in the other – all the while singing in the most impossible voice that might best be described by applying the frog-related word 'croak' instead of the usual 'sing.' Of course, you know I refer to none other than the legendary musical genius Louis Armstrong, who in every performance on Ed's show played either a classic jazz number or a Broadway hit.

However, the first tune I ever heard him sing was a Negro spiritual. His performance of the little ditty is more memorable and perhaps more enduring than any other image engraved in the American consciousness at the time. Looking directly into the camera & grinning his million-dollar smile, Louie's bulging brown eyes locked with mine. So, according to my little boy mind, no one else on Earth maintained eye contact with Satchmo besides me and me alone.

I noticed his oval face, beaded in sweat, began expanding more & more, as the song progressed to its climax. His energy level surged to such a degree that, along with his saucer-shaped eyes, the veins on his neck swelled exponentially. I'd never witnessed a single person transform so much in three minutes. I can't single out a specific detail of Mr. Armstrong's performance that did the trick, but this master musician mesmerized me so much that my very perception of the world metamorphosed that night. And, my goal has been about staying seated atop that puffy cloud high up in the atmosphere ever since.

Changing the subject from the fabulous Satchmo back to the little kid named Ross. (Not "Ross Man," as many call me today.) Let me try to capture in words the ridiculously detailed 'movie in my mind' of those three minutes way back in 1956. No, I won't do the scene any justice by attempting to describe it, but I will – at the very least – try to summarize what transpired. Standing at first next to my mother in her rocker, I made my circuitous way to our TV by circling each of the pieces of furniture squeezed into the room. Raising my pajama-clad arms toward our ceiling and kicking my feet forward, then backward, and then forward again, I discovered the phenomenon known as an adrenaline rush, which I've re-experienced a multitude of times since. And by the time I reached the metal 'rabbit ears' setting atop the Zenith, I'd scuffed my cloth slippers across the green 'hairy' rug I later learned is called 'shag.' As I "cut" that poor, old cheap rug, I alternately danced and marched in curlicues on the only carpeted floor in our place.

My mother got so tickled by my performance she began calling me "Little Louie." She'd say, "Sing it, Little Louie. Sing your song and blow your horn, Little Louie!" And I'd command my little voice to croak harder and harder until I did start sounding like King Louie. I'd hold one of my fists to my mouth and blow, making a tooting sound that, to my naïve ear, replicated Louis Armstrong's style of playing that shiny trumpet - note for note. Oh, how I loved "Satchmo."

Even though he's regarded the most influential jazz musician of all time, I loved his singing the most. I know Louis played a bright and sometimes mournful horn like no one else, but his singing was so heartfelt and so sincere that it's what I remember most about him. To me, his instrument showed his musical talent, but his voice revealed something more – a positive, effervescent spirit and a sincere, loving heart.

Another song I loved to hear him 'croak' was an open letter to humanity; a plea for all inhabitants of Earth to treat each other with love and respect. He likened the various hues of people's skin with the colors of the rainbow. The message, at least to me, was clear: God made humanity for the same purpose He designed the rainbow – to enjoy the beauty of His creations. And, Louis Armstrong's outstanding trait was that he meant every word he sang.

I'm not religious, but Louie's style of performing was as spiritual as any man or woman's I've ever observed; and, for that, I'll be eternally grateful. If I could picture in my mind pure joy, it would be the sight and sounds of Louis Armstrong singing on Ed Sullivan's Show.

The last two songs were "When the Saints Go Marching In" and "What a Wonderful World," both performed by Satchmo. I'd always liked Louie, but – boy – did I love him now. Just knowing what Ross thought about the man's singing and how he'd been like a messenger telling us how we ought to treat one another was inspiring. Another wave of tears swept my face, but not because of sadness. They were tears of joy; joy as pure as the music of Louis Armstrong.

Chapter Six

After those songs finished, I realized how late it was. I rushed out of Ross's room before anyone seeing us 'listening to music' might also wonder why I, a lowly janitor, sat at a patient's bedside instead of performing my assigned duties of mopping, dusting, cleaning, and so on.

The next night went the same. With no other conscious souls around, I visited Ross on the hour to check his temperature and then during my two breaks. (I would love, love, love to have seen him during lunch, but me scribbling notes over a patient's bed while eating my lunch didn't sound wise, so I ate in the break room by myself – as I always did.)

I sat down, switched on Ross's doohickey, and again shared its headphones with him. But this time I played the same tune twice in a row, just to see if that would help me keep up with his fast-paced tapping. It ended up working darned good… er, I mean "darned well." (Slowly, but surely, I started learning to write right.) Here's word for word what Ross 'said' next:

Saturday mornings back then were magical for many reasons. Since there wasn't school, there was less chance of getting hassled, chased, or beaten up. I didn't have stomach aches and didn't worry about being late to school or conflicted about whether to ditch or not. But, the main reason I loved Saturdays was because of the programming on TV. They were the types of shows I liked most: cartoons, adventures, and shoot-em-up westerns.

My favorites were "Mighty Mouse," "Sky King," and "The Roy Rogers Show." I'd harmonize with Mighty Mouse whenever he sang about "saving the day" and then cheer on Sky King, niece Penny, and his nephew whose name I forgot ages ago. During the opening credits I'd join the announcer booming the unforgettable phrase "Out of the Western sky... comes Sky King!" And after Sky flew away from his newest adventure, I'd get hyped up for my two top heroes - Roy Rogers and Dale Evans - as they launched into yet another nail-biting, nerve-racking exploit. And Roy's sidekick, the irrepressible Pat Brady with his trusty Jeep Nellie Belle, always provided much-needed comic relief not only for the show, but for me as well.

But, first and foremost, were Roy and Dale, the famous & fierce pair of crime-fighting love birds who always saved the day and put the bad guys in their rightful places in half an hour. And though I was a young boy who hadn't discovered girls or romance yet, I was impressed by the love flowing between Roy Rogers and his winsome wife Dale Evans.

At the end of every episode, Roy and Dale smiled brightly at us, their adoring audience, and sang their familiar theme song, bidding us all good-bye until we'd reunite soon. And that moment was always the high point of my week, showing me that anything could be possible.

Pammy here. Even though I'm too young to have watched "The Roy Rogers Show," I'd heard about it from Ma, who'd immediately fall into sobs whenever she talked about it. The theme song Ross described was labeled "Happy Trails" on his Sound-About's tape.

Chapter Seven

You can see for yourselves Ross can tell one heck of a story at the drop of a cassette tape. Whenever his Sound-About blared out a tune, I was ready with my trusty Morse code chart, pen, and pad to record whatever story originated from his brain, navigated itself to his lovely right index finger, and onto my arm. Up to that point, every song had come up in order on his playlist, so I was tempted to fast-forward the player and see where we, Ross and I, could go from there. (I confess those last nine words do sound wonderful: "and we, Ross and I, could go from there." As if he and I - "we" -could *ever* go anywhere relationship-wise or any other way. But, I must also confess what you might've already suspected: Pammy Lee Wertzhog had the biggest crush of all time on Ross McInerney. I can't tell you why but did I ever!)

My fear of messing up this 'experiment' kept me from changing my recipe for success, so instead I just continued with the next tune, just as I had been.

I had an extensive record collection back in the early and middle Sixties. Most were 45's, which I stored in shoe boxes by my bed. (I never had my own room since we couldn't afford more than a one-bedroom apartment; in fact, sometimes we had to settle for a studio flat.)

Since my father left when I was three, I hardly remember him. However, I do recall what he looked like. Dad had thick, curly reddish hair that stuck out, literally and figuratively. Being an Irishman, he had fair skin. For some reason, I can still picture my father's arms in detail: long and lanky with reddish-rust hair and clusters of brown freckles. And, a tattoo on each arm which he'd gotten while serving in the Marines during WW2. What I remember about Dad's tattoos is that not only did their glaringly artificial bluish-green ink clash crazily with his pale, freckled skin, but were both 'GI' (general issue); tattoos you'd see on virtually every other veteran serviceman in those days. Beyond their color and predictability, I can't remember anything else about them.

Dad was on the tall side, but not quite six feet. What enhanced his stature was his rail-thin build; so thin he couldn't have tipped the scales at more than a buck-fifty.

Robert McInerney was a man of music. It wasn't just his stock and trade, but his chosen vocation, avocation, field of expertise, lifestyle, and maybe even a "divine calling," as my mother would say with tongue firmly planted in her cheek. She claims he was the most musical person she'd ever known. "Your father ate, drank, and slept music," she'd utter when discussing Dad, which was more than often (daily and some days more than once). I don't believe she ever got over him, but that never stopped her from baring & bearing the rawest brand of contempt for the man. Musically, he is best described as a jazz man who also played blues, rock, and whatever else paid the bills. (Meaning, HIS bills; not ours. Mom says he never paid a light, gas, or water bill of ours, not to say she never tried.) Although Dad was proficient on piano, drums, various horns, and flute, his main instrument was the saxophone. From the pictures we have of him either playing or posing with an instrument, he mainly played tenor with a series of combos, all famous. (If I said the front men's names, you'd accuse me of name-dropping or plain lying.)

The man with whom Dad performed most is a household name not only in jazz circles, but in the pop and R & B worlds even more. I know you've heard of him. Unfortunately, he was a womanizer and a junkie. He probably tried treating his bandmates well, but when anyone is constantly chasing his next skirt or fix, he won't be trustworthy with his bandmates, and this iconic legend was no exception.

One night, Mom and I had dinner at a nearby grill. Before you think we could afford to dine out, we were only there because it was free. Mom waitressed there days but often the owner would invite 'us' to visit him at night, when my mother made sure we both ate until our stomachs filled to the limit. Rich was sweet on my mom and wanted more than an employer-employee relationship, but she wasn't having it, at least not yet. "Never poop and eat in the same place" was the nugget of wisdom she'd quote to explain the foolishness of mixing business with love.

So, on this night Rich gave me a bunch of quarters to feed his jukebox while he and Mom "talked business," meaning he'd be making moves on her, hoping she would take the bait. So, I sauntered over to his new Wurlitzer and decided to play my favorite song from the womanizing dope fiend for whom my father worked.

Since Rich had said, "Play anything, Ross, long as it isn't polka," I loaded up on R & B, and this one tune I selected five times.

Before that number came on, though, I heard the opening strains of Nat King Cole's "Unforgettable." After pivoting away from the juke, I saw Rich pull Mom onto his little dance floor, where they commenced dancing slowly. I could tell by the way he whispered in her ear he was putting the moves on my mother.

Immediately after my beloved R & B tune came on, I hardly heard it because of all the screaming. I turned toward Mom and Rich, thinking she was yelling at him for putting his hands somewhere she didn't want them, but it wasn't that at all. What she screamed about was the tune I'd selected. "Ross McInerney, why on Earth did you put that thing on? I can't stand that song, and you should know that by now." Turning to Rich, she said, "Please stop it!"

"I can't, Mary," he said sheepishly.

"WHAT DO YOU MEAN YOU CAN'T? Stop it right now or we leave!"

The man turned white as a ghost. Whatever fire burned in Rich a moment before had been fully extinguished by my mother. She'd always possessed a 'talent' for putting out men's fires, but her considerable gifts were now at maximum capacity and on full display.

Turning from Rich and stomping directly toward Yours Truly over by the jukebox, Mom demanded with as shrill a voice as I'd ever witnessed, "Why did you play that thing?"

"I-I had no idea you didn't like it, Ma."

"Oh, you had no idea I didn't like it, huh? Well, first off, who's singing it?"

All I could think of as a response was, "Yes, ma'am."

Grabbing me by the sleeve, she yelled, "Don't you dare to 'yes, ma'am' me! Turn that infernal thing off before I break Rich's stupid machine. You hear me? Figure it out... now!"

All I could think to do was unplug it, which I did after shoving the massive box with all my might and managed to move it just enough to unplug it. Being a callow eleven-year-old, it took all my strength and resolve to move it, but I managed somehow. (It's amazing what miracles have been performed throughout recorded history by weakling boys when their mothers screamed demands at them.)

"Okay, it's off, but..."

"But, what?"

"I still don't see why--"

"Why a song sung by that loser boss of your father's is so objectionable? Well, let me put it plainly enough for you to understand. The stupid song is...... all about losing! And, I don't ever, EVER want to hear that poor excuse for music again! Do you hear and read me?"

"Yes, ma'am" was again the only thing I could think to say.

Mom grabbed me again by the sleeve and tugged me over to our table, where she picked up her purse. Pushing me by the back to force me to lead, I did – all the way out of Rich's packed restaurant and three long blocks to our apartment without a single word spoken by either of us.

As a result, I never played or mentioned that song in my mother's presence again.

After finishing my transcribing, I jotted "Born to Lose" by Ray Charles and returned to cleaning toilets, floors, and who-knows-what-else.

Chapter Eight

Well, Lord have mercy; I can't believe what happened there. I had no clue Brother Ray's "Born to Lose" could cause Ross to write a story like that, which is the first time he got into any real detail about his mother. I guess she really *did* hate music.

I started getting freaked out about this game I was playing with him and hoped it wouldn't backfire somehow. After all, Ross could have a seizure, stroke, or fit if he heard the wrong song. So, as a result, I resolved to stop playing music for him. But, after two days, the little voice inside started up again. She said something like, "Pammy, you've got nothing to worry about. Look at it this way, Hon: you're communicating with the man, unlike that brain specialist lady - or anyone else, for that matter. Without you playing him music, which he's already said is his life blood, you'd be depriving him of life itself. Besides, what could be worse than being in a coma for years? Nothing, not even death. So, why not find out more about him while also giving him things to think & talk about? Ain't nothing worse can happen to this man."

So, after our break, I played two songs by the same band, and here's what he wrote:

As important as Saturday mornings were to me as a boy, one night in history stands higher than all those Saturdays stacked together – the Sunday night featuring an appearance by four Brits who became my greatest musical heroes. Sunday night, February 9,

1964, was the first U.S. appearance of the Beatles on "The Ed Sullivan Show." Practically every TV in America tuned in to see, hear, and witness John, Paul, George, and Ringo. And, even though the audience – all teenage girls screaming, sobbing, and jumping around – was at first a distraction, the Fab Four sang as loudly and lively as their Liverpool voices could muster. And, did they ever deliver!

I sat in the living room / kitchen watching our 10-inch Zenith, but it seemed like I saw them live, in person. The screen, empowered by their incredible performance, grew larger and larger during their performance. My mouth must've also grown larger while I watched the four of them performing skillfully while looking like no other humans I'd ever seen.

And though I sat there by myself, I didn't feel alone. How could I? I now had four new heroes/friends who showed me in three songs that life could be much more than this existence I'd known for eleven years. Although I was young, it felt like the future opened wide like one of those gigantic eyeballs in science displays - showing me that anything was now possible.

Though only a kid, I saw the Beatles' influence on the fairer sex, and the implications were obvious even to me at my tender age. The Fab Four's message was lovely, straightforward, and relevant, but not what old-timers would call 'girly.' In fact, it was universal – cutting across geographical, cultural, and even racial barriers. Who among us with a personality couldn't relate to The Beatles' words and music? Who under the age of thirty couldn't understand their truth? And yet, their message was as old as life itself: love. Present in most of their songs, it was the motif of at least two songs they played that night: "All My Loving" and "She Loves You."

Although I hadn't a clue what love was, I knew it made the world go 'round. I saw people's eyes light up whenever the word was spoken. Not the love a mother has for her son or a son has for his mother, no; but something not only elusive, but exciting and maybe dangerous.

All I know is the Beatles' use of this four-letter word possessed the force of a bulldozer. Not only did power surge through my every nerve, I witnessed the same force affecting every member of the audience throughout that history-making show. The possibilities and implications were so seemingly limitless that I couldn't possibly think of anything else besides The Beatles.

Sometime between their second and third songs, Mom came home from an event. (A date? Maybe. Church? Never.) None of that crossed my mind. In fact, I remember celebrating the fact we'd be together, to witness this amazing onslaught of....... L-o-v-e!

Instead, time slowed to a virtual crawl. Every commercial and guest appearance morphed into a pace best described as 'ultra-slow-mo.' And when I couldn't imagine things going any more south, they did. After Sullivan re-introduced the boys, my mother shrieked: "What in the Hell is this?! Oh, my God! Turn it off, Ross, for crying out loud!"

I tried filtering out her drama & hysterics, but it was nigh unto impossible.

"Ross Robert, I'm talking to you! I want to know... What the HELL IS THIS CRAP?"

I made a quarter turn, a token gesture of obeisance, but never strayed my eyes from the now-shrunken screen. As the Beatles dove into "She Loves You," Mom started up again. "Are you seriously watching this crap? Ross Robert, I am speaking to you."

I can't exaggerate the level of 'being torn' I felt at that pivotal moment. Here I was, stuck between the most important person in my life demanding my full attention on one side and the most important musical event of my lifetime on the other. The combination of not wanting to miss a note of the Beatles' performance while not desiring to pour grease on the fire already raging inside my mother conflicted me beyond measure. So, I did what millions of young people must've done that night when their parents protested what unfolded in their living rooms: I ignored her. Two-thirds through the song, at the fourth "ooo," a door slammed. And then, slammed again; and then...a third time. Yes, Mom had one of her vein-popping anti-music rampages, to which I expected seeing no end anytime soon.

I immediately adopted a not-too-rare-case of acute tunnel vision and deafness. I focused my entire being on soaking up every warp and woof of the final strains of "She Loves You," committing every sensation to memory. I had no reason to think this event could ever occur again, at least not in my lifetime. After all, CBS rarely reran Sullivan episodes during the show's lengthy run, and videotaping for personal use was still more than a decade away.

When the show finished, I knew I had to face 'the music,' which my dear, loving, hysterical mother controlled. I had no clue what to do or how to approach her, so I came up with a new way to communicate with her. I wrote a note, mainly apologizing for not listening to her, and slipped it under our bedroom door. I can't remember what I wrote, but I'm certain "sorry" made multiple appearances along with a couple "forgives" and a slew of "I-love-yous."

I lay there on our sofa for what seemed forever, awaiting her response. It became a vigil for me, but soon after midnight I felt a tap on my shoulder followed by a kiss on top of my head. "Here," she said, laying a blanket over me. "I don't want you catching cold. Night, Honey."

Chapter Nine

I'll bet you figured out the two cuts I played, which were my favorite Beatles songs, "I Want to Hold Your Hand" and "She Loves You." And since Ross hadn't spasmed, drooled, or frothed from the mouth, I figured hearing his favorite music must suit him. That night, after going home, I thought a lot about what to play next, but decided to experiment and go with the same two songs - to see what might happen a second time around. Here's how Ross responded:

The next several months seemed filled with almost nothing but Beatles. Beatle music. Beatle magazines. Beatle boots. Beatle wigs. Beatle posters. Beatle wallpaper. You name it and a Beatles version of it existed. Untold numbers of products on the market featured the Mop Tops on their wrappers, boxes, or cans. Or, so it seemed, because all that occupied my mind was The Beatles. I could not get enough of them. To support my newfound obsession, I got my first job - throwing the morning paper from my bike's banana seat six days a week.

Every nickel, dime, quarter, and dollar earned from my route I dropped into the big glass jar next to my bed. I'd drawn a black line one-quarter of the way below the lid marking what I thought was enough to buy a pair of Beatle boots. Ever since I spotted them sitting in the window of Melchor's Men's Shop, I knew I had to have them. I even saved a bit of cash by skipping my monthly haircut. Fortunately, Mom didn't notice, but that didn't surprise me since she hadn't been noticing much of anything lately. In addition to her waitressing at Rich's Bar & Grill, she took on another job. I wasn't sure where or what it involved, but we saw each other even less than before. (That wasn't exactly a bad thing either. Mom had become moodier and – looking back – I realize it had nothing to do with the Beatles' history-making appearance on TV.)

I knew nothing about her other job because I would've had to ask if I'd wanted to know. She seemed to be sleep-walking through life, like the zombies on Creature Features Friday and Saturday nights. When I look back - usually with sadness - at that phase of our past, I realize Mom had too much with which to contend. After all, being untrained and a woman in a time when being either was not optimal, might be spelling financial doom for the both of us.

So, I took solace in The Beatles. My Beatles. Every week, I bought their newest 45 record, a pack of Beatles bubble gum, and a set of Beatles trading cards. But, that was all I would spend because I so very much wanted to buy a pair of Beatle boots; the sooner, the better.

However, as much as I'd yearned for them to encase my feet and make not only fashion history, but a significant social statement, my plans flew out the window on the day of my first school dance. Since our school in the poor part of town suffered from declining enrollment, fifth graders were now invited to all middle school dances. I wasn't merely excited by this unexpected news, I was in a state I call 'Beyond Stoked!' Not only because we fifth graders had achieved middle-school status a year early, but because an actual band would perform at this first-of-a-kind event. I told myself that since I'd never heard live music, this dance could prove exciting.

Since it was slated for four pm on Friday (an hour after school), I ran home to change clothes. My dance outfit consisted of the white shirt I wore to Sunday mass, my only pair of dress pants, and my trusty PF Flyers, which I naturally assumed would help me dance like those cool kids I'd watched for hours on end on "American Bandstand," "Shindig," and "Hullabaloo." It never occurred to me that I'd never busted a single move in my life or that I might be suddenly seized by a bad case of nerves.

After slicking my hair with Bryl Creem and donning my duds, I made myself a fried baloney sandwich, which I downed between gulps of milk. I scribbled a note to my mother, informing her the dance would last till six and that I expected to be home shortly thereafter.

Reaching McKinley School, I paid 35 cents to enter the cavernous confines that make up our gymnasium and adjoining cafeteria. Since it was almost black inside, it took a second or more to get my bearings. I could then see - on the stage at the other end - a band or combo comprised of seventh- and eighth-grade boys tuning their instruments. Once my eyes adapted, I passed between a clump of boys on the right and an equally large clump of girls on the left before getting as close as possible to the stage and the band. For some reason unbeknownst to me since this was my maiden school-dance voyage, two rows of folding chairs had been placed right smack-dab in front of the stage. Since not a single soul had claimed any of them, I had my pick. Choosing the dark brown metal chair on the right end of the first row, I sat in front of the bass guitarist and studied the whole scene on stage. The bassist looked semi-conscious, bent over his axe like The Hunchback of Notre Dame. Next to him, at stage center, stood a tall black-haired Latin kid with an impressive, almost solid moustache. I could tell by his smug grin and deft way of tuning his guitar that he had the command necessary for a front man of a band not a minute older than its audience. He was, to be sure, the hippest human in the room, including the tanned, smiling Boys PE teachers flirting with their female counterparts near the entrance.

Back to the band, the rhythm guitarist had large, thick glasses mostly hidden under the cascade of his dark brown wiry hair combed straight forward. Only when he threw his head back in a show of rock bravado would his larger-than-Buddy-Holly frames be revealed. Otherwise, he was the shortest of the bunch and the only one who might possibly pass all his classes with a grade better than a C-. And finally, I check out the outfit's drummer. This guy was for sure the only athlete in the bunch. Muscularly toned better than ninety-nine percent of America's seventh graders, this kid was the motor of the band. I could tell he was raring to go and ready for anything at, even three or four straight sets with hardly a break if asked. Yeah, I came to find out later the dude had many similar counterparts all over. He was, of course, the drummer.

Maybe a minute after my inspection of the band's membership, they lurched into an instrumental I didn't recognize.

Turning back to check out the boys and girls still clumped behind me, I could see they were all engaged in either: a.) staring across the laminated floor at the opposite sex on the other side or b.) trying their best not to be caught looking at the opposite camp. That tableaux seemed strange or awkward to me: two hundred kids looking forlorn and unengaged on a Friday afternoon while gathered together in an environment of friends, live rock and roll music, and possible future 'steadies' or even spouses.

After that first song concluded, the lead guitarist stepped to the lone microphone on the curtained stage and announced, "I think you'll all recognize this next song." Their launch into "She Loves You" changed everything – the crowd's collective energy, movement, and volume. A demi-clump of the five or six boldest (all 'greasers' and 'hard guys) headed across the scuffed tile floor before diverging in all directions. Each kid strode toward a specific girl on the opposite side and, in every case, spoke briefly before the girl nodded her head, smiled, and followed him dutifully to the spot he chose to stop on the floor. Stepping stiffly side by side or back and forth, none of them seemed to know what to do with their hands. But, despite their insecurities, it was a vast improvement from moments before, when the Beatle stand-ins hadn't begun to play.

I turned back around and faced the band. The guitarists, bass player, and drummer managed decent impressions of the Fab Four, especially when they got to the chorus and sang "oooooooo" with pure gusto. When the tune ended, the crowd exploded with applause, howls, yelps, and a flurry of wolf whistles. I took mental notes of the transformation before me. A gathering of uptight, clumsy kids had metamorphosed into a screaming, clapping, whistling throng of spirited music fanatics. Every song after that was either by The Beatles or another British band, each eliciting a rowdy, appreciative response. I knew at that exact moment I wanted to be up there on that stage, too, playing rock & roll to hundreds of adoring girls and admiring boys. My number-one goal in life had shifted. No longer did I desire to buy boots that would immediately scuff and eventually fall apart. No. Instead, I longed to learn to play an instrument and write songs like Paul McCartney or John Lennon. (Who knows? Maybe someday someone will get the name 'McCartney' mixed up with 'McInerney.' Wouldn't that be bitchen?)

Chapter Ten

I continued playing Ross's tape six nights a week while transcribing his messages arriving by way of his right index finger. It became easier for me, but I still managed only a song or two each shift. Although I feared getting caught and losing my job, I had an even bigger fear. I figured I could always get another job, but I didn't want to lose my new, *only* friend.

You may think it sounds crazy that I consider a man I'd never spoken to as my friend. And, you might be right; that might be crazy for some people. Some of us aren't surrounded from birth to death with lots of family – brothers, sisters, first cousins, second cousins, uncles, aunts, grandparents, for example – and friends (classmates, neighbors, fellow Scouts, Sunday School classmates, etc.). But, that does not in any way take away from how much I cared for him and wanted to do right by him, no matter what. Ross was basically all I had because I had no family, no friends, and no pets. So, Ross Gray Eyes was all I had in this big old mean world. And, with each *successive* song came more information about him and an additional reason to love him.

I kept playing his songs, all of which so far had been arranged in chronological order. Which means 'in time order.' (Yep, *chronological* is a word I learned while studying Noah Webster's dictionary for this project.) The next songs were from that next year, 1965. I tried picturing how Ross might've looked or behaved as he grew older and learned how to make friends; a skill I hadn't yet acquired. Who knows? I thought. Maybe I can learn a thing or two from him. Just because he can't or won't talk or walk doesn't mean he doesn't know something I can learn. In fact, I realized right then how much I'd already learned from Ross.

After that first McKinley Middle School dance, everything for me changed, especially my goals. I realized I wanted more than anything to play music, but not the corny music the school band played that sounded... you know, sad and outdated. What I yearned to play was newer, exciting music that could not just help me cope with life but might become my message or 'calling card' to the world around me. So, rock and roll it was. This was, after all, the mid-Sixties, a time when people started saying what they believed or needed to say. And, I began realizing I was no different than anyone else when it came to understanding the importance of being true not just to one's self, but to one's unique story as well. But, here's the bonus part of the whole deal: I learned the best, most successful mode of communication had been and would always be the writing of music.

So, as fifth grade ended and sixth began, I spent all my free time outside of school working. Working so I could save up enough bread to buy a bass and amplifier to play it through. You name it and I did it for work: raking leaves, mowing lawns, delivering two different newspapers – one before & one after school. "You're a working fool, Ross; just like me," Mom used to say, with equal parts pride and sadness. Between the two of us, she and I must've logged ninety hours of work every week (not counting my thirty hours of classes at school). As a result, my big glass Mason jar filled to the brim and then several more containers and compartments. In fact, I rolled up all my pennies, nickels, dimes, and quarters and took them to the bank a month after the dance. As it turned out, I'd already made ten bucks; and that was just the beginning.

"Not bad, but nowhere close to what I need for my instruments and amplifiers," I told myself. That's right – instruments, plural; and amplifiers, plural. I'd decided to not only buy myself a bass guitar like Paul McCartney's, but a couple of electric guitars, too; plus, an acoustic guitar and drum kit. Why? I realized I could make more money playing several instruments than just one. And, I figured I'd buy a bunch of instruments and rent them to other kids in town for a nominal, but profitable fee. That way, I wouldn't be 'putting all my eggs in one basket' as Mom often warned me not to do.

Working hard like that made me forget about the passage of time so, before I knew it, the summer of 1965 - between sixth and seventh grade - arrived. I finally bought that bass (imported from Japan) and a small amplifier to go with it. Those Beatle boots I'd dreamt of for so long? No longer a priority. And besides, as much as I loved the Fab Four, there were other musical fish in the sea, too. I started playing along with practically every song I heard on the radio – rock and roll for sure, but lots of soul and jazz, too.

I played along with anything and everything – first the Beatles, then the Beach Boys, and then the 'second tier': Gary Lewis

& the Playboys, the Supremes, Four Tops, Gerry & the Pacemakers, The Four Seasons, Temptations, and – of course – 'the bad boys of rock and roll.'

There were two artists then that seemed evil. Well, 'forbidden fruit' is perhaps a more apt descriptor. But whatever their attraction, I knew the Rolling Stones and this one man who could dance like no one else were getting tons of attention. Yes, the artist who was one lean, mean dancing funk machine; the musical force of nature with the conked 'do; and the leader of a huge band with two drummers and lots of sexy women singers grabbed my attention bigtime. We knew him as "The Godfather of Soul," - the one and only JB – Mister James Brown. The first few times I heard either the Rolling Stones or Mr. Brown, I changed the station. There was something dark, perhaps sinister about them that disarmed me, but – on the other hand – they appealed to my curiosity, too. After I'd heard a complete song or two of theirs, I became hooked.

I became familiar with JB because he appeared on lots of TV shows, both as a musical act and talk-show guest. Although I was impressed by the chain of radio stations he owned and his vowed desire to make the world a better place, what struck me most was the man's raw power, talent, and magnetism. Elvis might be thought of as the king of rock & roll, but I considered James Brown the king of live performance. No one else I'd heard or seen had his style, his precision, or his one-of-a-kind moves. So, whenever he appeared on TV for even five minutes, the show seemed to stop altogether. His band, the Fabulous Flames - as amazing as they were in precise tightness - wouldn't have been nearly as great without their fearless leader.

So, after practicing hundreds of hours on bass, I began developing a style all my own. I can't describe it, but I'll admit my greatest influences had become three – The Beatles, Rolling Stones, and the fabulous James Brown. "Eclectic" and "funky" were the words people used most when attempting to describe my playing style. I never knew how to process those words or labels and arrive at some understanding of what they thought of me, but I didn't need or care to know what that was. I knew who I was as a musician and even though I played off other musicians, I played within my own constructed style and was known for my 'walking bass.'

Soon, one local band after another started asking me to jam. At first, they were rock bands made up mostly of white kids, but word got around I could also play soul and funk, so some bands of the black persuasion asked me to jam with them, too. My earliest influences - Nat King Cole, Louis Armstrong, and Ray Charles - served me well because I soon found myself in demand among the soul community. And living downtown, we were part of that circle anyway.

Every day, rain or shine, I either practiced or performed somewhere around town. Since my bandmates were much older, they had their licenses and drove me and our equipment to wherever we played. Hence, my lawn mowing, leaf raking, and paper routes fell by the wayside, and I began earning dough exclusively playing gigs: junior and senior high school dances, community sock hops, and restaurants. My first mainstay band was The Ruffians, a rock outfit leaning heavily on the Stones, Zombies, and Kinks. We were in demand every Friday night at one school or another. The second group, The Groove Thang, played three teen centers (YMCA, Boys Club, and a black church) along with a couple soul food hangouts.

What's especially odd is that not only did my mother not know I was playing these gigs every weekend, she never asked what I was up to. She had 'another life' I knew nothing about because I'd never asked. A strange way to grow up? Well, since it was the only lifestyle I ever knew, it didn't seem strange at all. I was busy making a steady income, enough to save a lot of dough; enough dough to invest in several musical instruments.

By the end of seventh grade, in June 1966, I played all kinds of songs from the radio: the Beatles' "Ticket to Ride," "I Saw Her Standing There," "Paperback Writer," and "Help"; The Temptations' & Supremes' hits; James Brown's "Papa's Got a Brand-New Bag" and "I Feel Good"; and the Rolling Stones' "(I Can't Get No) Satisfaction," "Under my Thumb," and "Get Off of My Cloud." Life was good. I was making money and friends through playing music while keeping up with my studies, so what could go wrong?

For some unknown reason, Ross stopped tapping mid-song, so I'll just report the songs to which we'd been listening were the Stones' classics "Satisfaction" and "Under my Thumb."

Chapter Eleven

One Friday night, The Groove Thang played at Doctor Feelgood's Soul Kitchen, located in a red brick two-story building in the part of town known as The Gauntlet. Years before, there'd been a slew of taverns that workers from nearby factories frequented after their shifts. The term "bar crawl" could very well have originated in 'The G' because what you would've seen back in the Forties and Fifties were scads upon scads of riveters, machinists, and pressmen (all with light complexions) stumbling or crawling from one tavern to the next until either passing out or being transported home by a buddy, fellow worker, cop, or - God forbid - wife.

Starting in the Sixties, one bar after another began catering to black patrons. Doctor Feelgood's was The Gauntlet's only bar also serving soul food – chitlins, ham hocks, collard greens, beans & rice, and sweet potato pie - to name just a few. And since it was a licensed restaurant, under-age musicians could legally play there. Although the dining area took up the ground floor and the bar dominated the second, we musicians of minor-age status were allowed on the upper floor stage. Tucked into the corner farthest from the street-side windows, the slightly elevated platform accommodated our large band, which numbered anywhere from seven to ten musicians. Our core unit consisted of Cozmo Warner on drums; me on bass; Terrence Wolf on piano; Bruno Carston on tenor saxophone; Hefty Lewis on alto sax; Dorothea Durst on you name it - flute, clarinet, various saxes, percussion, and vocals; and Bunny Braxton on vocals, harmonica, and congas. Bunny might've been our leader, but he always received lots of help from the rest of us, especially Terrence and Bruno.

We rarely made much dough, but we did okay because the owner, Harold Cookman, reminded patrons to tip us. In fact, he did a lot more than remind them. He pleaded, begged, cajoled, and demanded they "let loose of not just your change, people, but your folding bread, too!" "Otherwise," he'd warn, "I can always start charging cover, beginning right now!" Since Mr. Cookman (we called him "Cookie") was large and super dark, he intimidated patrons, even in sizeable crowds, to donate cash for our cause. And our audiences always came through.

One night, Cookie didn't show up. Folks thought he'd either come down with a bug or blown town to avoid an ex-wife in search of child support. Regardless, Mister C's considerable influence and authority were sorely missed that evening. Although most of the crowd were regulars (local drinkers, families eating out, and teens from the local youth centers), there was a group of shady characters we hadn't seen before seated in a back booth who surveilled the room for something or someone. Most of us thought they were on the lookout for Cookie, wanting to collect money for his former wife. At any rate, as this clique consumed more and more liquor, they became progressively more aggressive – physically and vocally.

Three or four of the half dozen began yelling requests - current hits and old R & B tunes. We didn't normally take requests, mainly because we were a young group building a repertoire. But, the requests became so loud and constant that Bunny announced between songs during our second set: "Okay, we'll do our best to play your requests, but our catalog isn't extensive, so we hope you understand if we don't play every tune we hear you yelling out. So, please bear with us." The band dispatched a few of their requests, among them some current James Brown hits ("Papa's Got a Brand New Bag" and "Cold Sweat"), the Temps' "My Girl" along with oldies like Eddie Floyd's "Knock on Wood" and Jackie Wilson's "Lonely Teardrops," but we hit the wall with the other requests - Frankie Lymon's "Why Do Fools Fall in Love?" and Ray Charles' "What'd I Say?" We simply didn't have the personnel or the chops to play them.

So, after we'd exhausted our repertoire of oldies and the yelling continued, Bunny announced: "I'm sorry we can't play any more of your requests, but we do have a couple new numbers we'd like to do for your dancing and listening pleasure." Midway through the second tune by the Rascals, it seemed like all hell might break loose. And since Cookie hadn't left anyone in charge of security, it fell to us skinny teenagers to somehow maintain the peace.

The biggest and oldest dude led his gang of ne'er-do-wells to the stage, where he again demanded we play the two songs we didn't know. While Bunny and Terrence tried reasoning with him, the other five decided to step up on stage and inspect or intimidate the rest of us. When a couple of the thugs discovered that beneath the veil of long curly hair resided Yours Truly, they started in. "Hey, White

Boy. Whatcha doin' here? Whatcha tryin' to do – integrate our club?"

When Bruno and Hefty stepped over and tried to verbally defend me, things became a bit scary. Then, one interloper – a gangly six-foot, six young man in a knit cap – began to fondle Dorothea. And, since Cozmo our drummer was Dorothea's boyfriend, things got heated. Fists flew, bodies fell, and instruments became weapons. I had the presence of mind to keep my bass strapped on and even used it to shield myself from objects flying from seemingly everywhere. Bottles, glasses, dishes, music stands, and more flew toward me and my bandmates.

Luckily for us overmatched teens, two of San Bernardino's Finest had been patrolling nearby when they received the call. Unfortunately, with the ongoing chaos, they could neither make heads nor tails of the brouhaha and called for a paddy wagon to haul us all downtown.

As a result, my mother received a call awaking her around 11:30 pm to the effect that her son was in the city jail and could be released only into her custody. Yours Truly needed to appear in juvenile court the following Monday. I wasn't charged with any kind of infraction, but there were negotiations around what kind of penalty I might have to pay just for being there in such an inflamed situation. So, in lieu of community service, it was deemed by the juvenile court judge that I would not be permitted to perform in a club in The Gauntlet for two years. That quasi- or pretend sentence brought my brief, but eventful stint with The Groove Thang to an end. While it lasted, I enjoyed every minute of being a part of that amazing outfit. We all listened, respected, and understood each other extremely well. Yeah…… I was beyond bummed I couldn't hang with the Thang anymore because we were family. I'm sure that familial bond was an ingredient in the recipe of success we collectively created and enjoyed, but I had no choice in the matter. I wouldn't have the pleasure of seeing and performing with them for a long, long time.

All I can say is "wow." The songs stirring his memory were "Groovin'" and "Good Lovin'," both by the Young Rascals. I can only guess the unhappy soul-music fans probably didn't want to hear songs recorded by an all-white group like the (Young) Rascals.

Chapter Twelve

Although I'd started playing Ross's music for him only ten days before, it seemed I'd known him all my life. Why? Because I knew him better than I'd known anyone, including Ma. See, I'd learned a lot about the man's past, his upbringing, his passions, his victories, and his defeats. I knew what made him tick, but only up to age thirteen - so far. Thus, I was glad to see the next song on his tape labeled 1967. I played two songs, and here's what Ross tapped out.

Middle school ended and "The Summer of Love" began. I had no idea it was going on at the time nor did I know anything about the "counter culture" starting to take hold in places like San Francisco, Los Angeles, and New York City. In fact, I hadn't heard the word 'hippie' until the final week of eighth grade when my teacher Mr. Ledbetter, who hailed from Texas, used the term: "Remember, students, you will all be representing not just yourselves at our graduation ceremony, but also your parents, grandparents, and your entire families. So, don't dress up like a bunch of hippies Friday night. Dress like the respectable young people I know you all are."

I didn't give that word another thought until I enrolled at Theodore Roosevelt High School in the fall and discovered I was surrounded by people (mostly upperclassmen) wearing all kinds of weird, different clothes – headbands, hats, and bandanas; the latter were tied everywhere - around necks, arms, and legs. And, it seemed every notebook or Peachy Folder I laid eyes on had a peace sign drawn, printed, painted, or somehow affixed to it. I remember thinking on my first day, "This must be whom Mr. Ledbetter warned us about. I better see what these hippie people are all about."

Well, it didn't take me long to find out because a dance had been scheduled for the first Friday. And since The Groove Thang disbanded after the Feelgood gig and The Ruffians broke up because they all graduated from Roosevelt High last spring, I was a lone wolf. Since I'd spent the last two years playing music on stage, I hadn't befriended any of my classmates. In fact, I hadn't a single friend in any of the six classes I attended the first week of fall semester.

I stood in a long line and paid higher admission because I had no student body card. The Welcome Back Dance was already underway. Held in the fieldhouse, I could barely find an empty space on the hardwood floor to sit. I scrunched down between two groups and tried my best to blend in. I couldn't shake the notion, though, that I was a loner, a loser, a social pariah. The music, however, drew my focus, so my concerns fell away immediately.

A band of five men in their late teens clad in maroon sport coats, black slacks, and black turtlenecks were playing the heck out of a song that had come out a month before by a new band called The Doors. This local band's lead singer – a tall, chubby blonde – crooned "Come on, baby, light my fire" while colored lights danced behind him on the back cinder-block wall. Although I'd been hearing about this phenomenon for quite some time, this was my very first light show. I sat there entranced by the whole scene: a professionally dressed & sounding band, The Pharaohs; the amazing light show itself; and the scores of kids dancing wildly on the gym's hardwood floor. And when I thought it couldn't get any better, a bank of white fog escaped from both wings of the stage. I discovered that no rock music show could be considered complete without a dry-ice machine. Surprisingly, the stage crew had two at their disposal, so I found myself in 'fog heaven.' (Now you know why I don't make a habit of telling jokes... to anyone.)

This version of "Light My Fire" must've lasted twelve minutes, but no one in the audience appeared the least bit bothered or bored by it. In fact, we all seemed to be inhabiting an altogether different reality. Kids with long, flowing hair & clothes swirled or twirled everywhere. Then, the clump of kids behind me stood and began their own swirling and twirling maneuvers. And, right when I felt compelled to join them, a tap on my right shoulder diverted my attention. Turning around, I saw a being with long, fluffy blonde hair. Because of the darkly lit gym and something covering the person's facial skin, it took me a few seconds to realize it was a girl, perhaps wearing face paint, who stood before me.

Smiling mysteriously, she grabbed my hand & beckoned me to follow, so I did. We wended our way a couple hundred feet to the farthest corner from the stage. In an area just below the old-fashioned elevated bleachers we stopped and faced each other. There wasn't another soul within fifty feet. She smiled, raised both hands, and began dancing in a mesmerizing way reminiscent of

Middle Eastern belly dancers. Until then, I hadn't noticed her clothing, but as she moved and swayed, I saw various see-through layers of cloth swirling about her. I was, in a word, spellbound.

When the song ended, the silence lasted long enough for her to say "Salome" and point to herself. Not feeling at all like an idiot, but probably sounding like Tarzan the Ape Man, I tapped my chest. "Ross McInerney." A second psychedelic song began, which I discovered a week later was another Doors song, one from their just-released album titled "Strange Days." Salome grinned and held out both hands. Not knowing precisely what to do, I hoped she wanted me to join hands with her. We held our joined arms out, turning slowly one way and then the other for the entirety of the tune. I was relieved I didn't have to bust any dance steps, but just follow this beautiful creature's lead, which I did gratefully.

The next song sounded like a slow dance, so we embraced and instinctively rotated in a counter-clockwise direction. As the song progressed, though, my dancing improved. I felt myself limbering up and moving not only to the music, but to Salome's body as well. I found myself ensconced in a state I can best describe as Cloud Nine. We moved as one, first one way and then the other. It was mystical, mysterious, and mind-blowing, like Salome herself. I was thrilled the set extended forty more minutes and the lights remained dimmed throughout. I was afraid this would all end and, as magically as this creature had materialized, would disappear into the night; and I'd never see her beautiful form & face again.

After the slow song ended, Salome put her hands on my

cheeks and looked deeply into my eyes. Since it was dark, and she wore a wide band of eye shadow, I wasn't sure what I saw were her eyes. I couldn't even tell what color they were, to show you how dark it was. But - at that moment – eye color didn't matter; I couldn't care less if they were blue, brown, or pink. What mattered was that Sal looked at me like I was all that mattered to her. I'd never felt that way before because no one, not my mother nor my father nor anyone else up to that moment, had ever looked at me with such regard, such respect, such... love. And, boy, did that make me feel good. All I could do was continue locking my eyes with hers and match the same level of regard. "I love you, Salome" I kept sending out silently, but strongly. She moved in close, looking strangely sad, parted her lips, and said: "I love you, too, Ross. With all my heart." Which blew me away, totally. This vision of loveliness, this creature of rare, amazing beauty, this angelic being had received my silent statement and responded in words, the perfect words. Wow, wow, wow...

And that is how I met my first love - Salome Stephens.

I noticed my heart pitter-pattering when I finished transcribing the last part, so I told myself, "Ross had at least one love in his life." Although Salome sounded amazing to me, I realized not only did I admire her, I envied her, too. The songs I played that night were both by The Doors – their monster hit "Light My Fire" and a smaller one called "People Are Strange." I couldn't help but think both were perfectly suited to this part of Ross's story.

Chapter Thirteen

We – Salome and I – danced while locking eyes with each other the rest of the night. Then, after the lights rudely came on, we had a short, awkward conversation before going our separate ways. She told me she'd find me at school the next week before wishing me a "groovy weekend" and disappearing into the smoggy, gray San Bernardino night.

All I thought about all weekend was Salome, even while I slept. In one dream she appeared from nowhere wearing two sets of angel wings, but it wasn't as wonderful as it sounds. She wasn't swathed in white, but in shades of black and gray. And that's not all. Her whole vibe was more demon-like than angelic, and I remembered there are supposed to be bad angels, too. I learned in Vacation Bible School that Satan had been expelled from Heaven and banished with one-third of all the angels. That Salome was some type of other-worldly being sent to mess with my life was one of many thoughts entering my mind for inspection all weekend. But, as quickly as that notion entered my conscious mind, lovelier, more positive images of the girl replaced it.

Mom noticed something different about me Sunday morning. While sipping her coffee at the kitchen table, she looked over at me on the couch, where I lay curled up. I felt her stare before she set her cup down and declared: "Someone is awfully mopey." Giving me the once-over, she continued. "What is happening with you, Ross?

You're not in puppy love… are you?"

Not in the habit of lying to my mother and knowing we had too little to talk about between us as it was, I decided not to 'BS' her. "Yes, Mom. I am in love. But, please don't call it 'puppy love' because that makes it sound like it doesn't count or isn't real."

"What's her name?" she asked as she approached.

"Salome."

"Really?! Huh. Well, scooch over a little so I can sit with you."

Bending my knees to give her space, I looked away.

"Wow, you do have it bad, Hon. Did she jilt you or something?"

"No, we just met Friday night."

"Oh," Mom said as she patted me on the knee. "What are you afraid of?"

I was so head-over-heels I didn't bother hiding it. "I'm afraid… of not being with her."

"I see. Well, actually, I don't, but I'm trying, Ross."

"I know it sounds strange, but guess what? It's because it **is** *a strange situation - the way we met, the way she is, and how we communicated without talking most of the night." I then gave her a blow-by-blow account of the dance, leaving out nothing.*

"Wow" is all she said at first before sitting in silence for a long while. Finally, she patted me a few times, which was weird

because she rarely touched me (and vice versa). "Well, I wish I could be with you this week, Ross Honey, but Rich and I are going away for a few days. He wants to open a second restaurant up north somewhere, so we're checking out some locations. We won't return 'til Saturday or Sunday. Do you think you'll be all right?"

As I lay there thinking about Salome, Mom smacked me hard on the leg.

"Ouch!"

"Did you hear what I said?"

"You asked if I'll be okay without you. Yes, I'll be fine. Will you leave me some money?"

"Really? You - Mister Money Bags - asking me for cash? Heck, I was tempted to ask you for some bread. That is the term – bread - you kids use for money, right?"

"I guess, Mom. You mean, you can't leave me a twenty for food?"

"I already stocked the fridge and cupboards Friday night, but you didn't notice."

I thanked her and kissed her on the cheek. It was the first time I'd kissed her in years. She deserved it, though, because she genuinely cared about me and my 'new crush,' as she called her, Salome. Soon after, she left with Rich her boss – her very own 'new crush.'

⁂

I spent Monday thinking about Salome or asking other students about her. Since all my classes were freshman level, no one knew her. I even wondered if she attended my school at all, but I looked for her at lunch, standing outside the girls' room in hopes of spotting her. No luck.

Nearing my building on the way home, I spotted her on our stoop wearing a different outfit, but still adorned with some type of face paint. Boy, it sure looked odd in the daylight.

"Hey, what're you doing here?" was my clever opening.

"Hi, Handsome" is all she had to say to show how she felt about me. It did the trick because I bent down and planted a kiss right on her rose-colored lips. (Was I bold or what?)

"How did you find out where I live?" was my second clever ad lib.

Laughing, she replied, "I have my sources; all secret ones, of course. Can I come in?"

"Of course," I said, trying my best to sound casual. The problem was that though my mother had hardly established any rules, her number-one edict was to not let anyone inside our place when she wasn't home. It was a reasonable request I'd always abided by, but this time was... different. Why? Because Salome and I were different. I know that sounds strange, but it's how I felt. Everything in life had changed or become different because of this girl of mystery.

After I put my books away and used the bathroom, I found

her cuddled up on the couch, in the same position I had been in the day before while I'd talked with Mom. I sat in front of her on the floor, which I figured was a great location in case she might want to kiss again. She gazed into my eyes and said, "I've got a proposition for you."

Well, now she had <u>all</u> my attention. Those six words are the answer to every guy's dream, especially when spoken by a girl he likes, lusts after, or loves. "Okay; what is it?"

"What do you think about going to San Francisco with me?"

"How?"

"Hitch hiking."

"When?"

"How about tomorrow morning?"

"How about now?"

Salome laughed, parted her lips, and kissed me. Then, she said, "Now's good."

⁂

An hour later, we stood on a corner with our sign fashioned from a round piece of cardboard from a pizza Mom bought recently. With a thick black marker, Salome printed 'SF' on it, which worked because soon a soft-spoken old preacher-looking man stopped to pick us up. We rode down Highway 138 to a Mojave Desert town called Lancaster, right where its two main drags, Sierra Highway and Lancaster Boulevard, meet. With the sun setting, we decided to grab a bite to eat and spend the night somewhere nearby. We walked south on Sierra until seeing a neon sign, "Swedish Smorgasbord," beckoning and persuading us to cross the highway and have dinner. "Smorgasbords are always cheap," Sal said before grabbing my hand and leading me on the run to the single door entrance.

The place, although Spartan inside, was popular because not only did we see twenty people standing in line, but the tables were full of diners. Salome and I decided to share three dishes - macaroni & cheese, a green salad, and the cafe's specialty dish - Swedish meatballs. The whole meal cost $1.35, which left me with $48.65 since I'd taken two twenties and a ten from my big glass jar at home. Finding out the location of a nearby park, we strolled a half mile to a strip of green on Avenue J named after Jane Reynolds, a longtime resident & philanthropist.

We set up camp on the north side of the park, not far from the fence protecting the swimming pool. Spreading Salome's bag on top of mine, we zipped them together, slipped between them, and laid together - holding each other until sleep overcame us.

The next morning, we rolled up our bags, freshened up in the cinderblock restrooms, and returned to Sierra Highway, where we resumed hitch-hiking. A gold miner in a rusty Studebaker truck stopped and let us ride up front with him all the way to Visalia. We stopped in Mojave for breakfast at one of the cafes along Sierra. I must've been awfully hungry because biscuits and gravy never tasted so good. It was around two when the old guy dropped us off on Highway 99 and cautioned: "You kids be careful in Frisco now.

That can be one mean town. I remember how it was back in my navy days. Good luck."

We made good time on 99, passing through Fresno, Merced, and Modesto in a semi-blur. Now ahead of schedule, Salome made a call on a pay phone to someone, maybe family. (I didn't ask.) After I-205 became I-580 West in the summer darkness, we decided to sleep on the side of the road. Snuggling up in our combined bag, we again fell asleep in each other's arms.

Hitch-hiking the next morning was tough, with all the trucks blowing past and no one stopping, but eventually a long-haired guy in a gray and white VW microbus stopped. "Where you headed?" he asked in his 'too-cool-for-school' voice.

"Haight Ashbury," we responded in unison.

When he began laughing, I thought he was laughing at us, but he soon gave his reason. "That's really a trip, because that's where I'm heading. Jump in and put your gear in back."

I suggested Salome sit up front before I put our bags and knapsacks on the seat next to me in back. I extended my hand for the driver to shake. "I'm Ross and my friend is Salome."

For the second time in less than a minute, he laughed. "Salome. Really? Were you named after the chick who danced in the Bible and got John the Baptist beheaded? My name's Rusty."

Instead of flashing her usual smile, Salome glared at Rusty. "There was only one Salome in the Bible. Herodias' daughter, the one who asked for the head of John the Baptist, was never identified by name. I'm named after Salome, mother of the apostles James and John and the wife of Zebedee. She was at the tomb of Jesus the day He raised from the dead."

"Groovy. Well, since you know so much about the Bible, I have to ask: You aren't one of those 'Jesus freaks,' are you?"

She looked down at her hands. "I'm not sure about any spiritual labels, but I do know the historical origin of my own first name."

Rusty laughed again. "Well, let's consummate our new friendship by smoking the peace pipe. How does that sound to you two?"

I heard myself say, "A peace pipe sounds great." After all, I'd seen Indians smoking peace pipes in Western movies with cowboys. I assumed the pipe would have tobacco in it, which would be a real first for me.

"Far out. Here, Salome. Want to fire it up?"

"Okay," she said. Taking the pipe and lighter from Rusty, she flicked the tiny metal wheel on the plastic gizmo, igniting the pipe's contents. Inhaling vigorously and appearing to know what she was doing, Salome tried handing the pipe back to Rusty, who held up his hand. "I'd like my man Ross to have the next toke."

Handing me the dark brown pipe expelling curls of gray smoke, Salome smiled at me with the most sublime grin. I took it, sucked on the plastic mouthpiece, and held my breath, basically copying her. I continued assuming we were imbibing tobacco. But, right after I handed the pipe back to Salome, my lungs expended this huge cloud that shot out like a circus cannon and then broke and filled the entire front section of the high-ceilinged van. When I tried inhaling air to keep from choking, my lungs rebelled and insisted on exhaling to get all the smoke out. For a long minute, I coughed and hacked; hacked and coughed.

Rusty, who'd taken his turn, blew a stream of smoke out the lowered window before laughing. "First time smokin' dope, Ross?"

I had no idea what he was saying or asking. Sure, I'd heard the word 'dope' before (mainly in health classes), but thought the term only applied to hard drugs - morphine, opium, and heroin. I soon realized we were smoking marijuana... grass... weed... cannabis sativa.

Salome turned to look back at me. "You okay, Ross?"

"Yes" was all I managed before resuming my fit of coughs and chokes.

Without laughing, Rusty said: "Yes to what - your first time, smoking or you're okay?"

Again, I answered "yes" and, for some reason, my response struck our driver as hysterical because he laughed for the next two minutes. His laughter seemed to shoot out in all directions, like sparklers of every color imaginable, creating a comedic fireworks exhibition of impressive proportions. Salome and I, of course, were hit broadside; neither of us dodging the incoming rockets of levity bursting and ricocheting in every direction inside the bus. Then, a life-changing cannonball hit me at the core of my conscious mind. Something was happening here, and I didn't even know what it was, though I am obviously **not** *Bob Dylan's scorned-upon Mr. Jones. I'd been bowled over by an attack from a planet heretofore unknown to me; an entirely different reality as colorful as it would prove strange. Consequently, the slow-motion, black & white, two-dimensional show that had played continuously for my fourteen years on the screen inside my brain, had transformed into this full-speed, gorgeously technicolor, 3D extravaganza. And, unfortunately or not, I have two hippies & a bowl of cannabis to thank for that 180-degree turnabout in the script that guides my life.*

⁂

Arriving in San Francisco, we became one more enlistee in the armada of vehicles - cars, pickups, vans, and semi-trucks - on 101 North, otherwise known as Mission Street. Moments later, we entered an outcropping of Victorian houses, many painted in various colors of the rainbow and some colors I hadn't seen before. Rusty sat up and grinned at us like the Cheshire Cat of "Alice in Wonderland" fame. "Well, we're in Haight Asbury, kids. What do you think?"

As I gazed out both back side windows and then out the rear, my senses became …… mesmerized. Sights & sounds slowed by half. A splendid, sunshiny late summer day, the skies reminded me of a Maxfield Parrish painting I'd seen once in a large art book at the public library back home. The turquoise sky was amazingly brilliant, partly because the air was so pure by the Pacific Ocean and because of the contrast with the bleached-white puffy balls of clouds. Lowering my gaze back to Earth, I saw sets of waves of people - kids as young as eleven or twelve intermingled with teens and college-age young men and women everywhere. The scene reminded me of the crowds during my only visit to Disneyland. Groups of delighted, happy people traipsing here, there, and everywhere. The entire neighborhood looked, smelled, and sounded like a carnival or county fair instead of a suburban enclave of a major modern city. Like the Happiest Place on Earth, every passerby possessed high levels of anticipation & joy. As far as I could tell, the Haight surpassed Disney's world-famous park in terms of the happy quotient. More than anything I wanted to bail from Rusty's metal transport and join the multitudes of happy, gentle, free people outside. I realized I'd spent my existence up to that moment in an alien land that had never felt like home. But now, here I was... 'home' for the first time, surrounded by kindred spirits, comrades in arms, and free spirits...... in other words, family. How could anywhere in the world be better than right here, right now? It must've been how John Smith felt when he explored Florida, believing himself to be on the verge of finding the centerpiece of myth and legend – the fabled, rumored phenomenon known as "The Fountain of Youth."

Turning from Masonic onto Haight Street, it was six blocks before we turned onto Staryan, then a right on Page. Four house-lengths later, Rusty spun his outsized steering wheel to the right and pulled his Microbus to the curb. "Well, we're here. Want to come in, Salome?" As she turned to me and raised both eyebrows, I waited for him to ask me as well, which he did. "Ross?" I nodded yes.

Salome's glance traveled from my eyes to her nails. "Sure. Is this big house your pad?"

"My old lady and I rent the second floor, but – yeah – all three stories are open to me, to you, to anyone who enters with... the right energy. Grab your stuff, kids, and follow me."

After getting our gear and hoisting most of it onto my back, I walked hand in hand with Sal to the porch of the gray three-story Victorian with purple trim. As Rusty held the door for us with one hand, he pointed to two rows of shoes with the other. "You can park your footwear there and follow me upstairs. I smell something groovy...... probably Faye's famous lentil stew. Hope you're both hungry."

At the mention of food, I heard major rumbles and growls emanating from my belly. And, Faye's renowned soup did not disappoint at all. Then & there, I thought life couldn't get better.

It sounded like the first time Ross had ever traveled away from home. The song playing several times in a row had been "San Francisco (Be Sure to Wear Some Flowers in Your Hair)," sung by Scott Mackenzie and written by John Phillips, founder of The Mamas and The Papas. (I read in a People Magazine once that the Phillips named their first child Mackenzie after Scott.)

Chapter Fourteen

I didn't want Ross's trip story to end, but I'd grown sick of the Mackenzie song, so I figured the next tune might also relate to his & Salome's time spent in 'Hippie Heaven.'

Psychedelic - a word I'd recently heard that year but hadn't understood its meaning... yet. After hearing it spoken for the first time, my impression was that the term's creator smashed an actual prefix into a made-up suffix. Also, I didn't think it had a meaning, but over the span of '67, the so-called Summer of Love, the concept began revealing itself piece by piece, bit by bit. And today when I hear or read 'psychedelic,' I immediately think of kaleidoscopes. I guess because they consist of bits of brightly colored shards of glass smooshed together, which always create something new & strange with each viewing. San Francisco was just like that; made up of crazily colored buildings and inhabited by colorfully attired humans in all colors, shapes, and sizes – smooshed together, but 'copasetic' (agreeable) to everyone.

The short time spent in "The City" was magical, psychedelic, and full of strangeness – reminiscent of Lewis Carroll's literary classic "Alice in Wonderland," which I remember reading as a boy and having two opposite simultaneous reactions. Part of the fable was exciting, joyful, and fun while the other part could be described as scary, dark, and confusing. San Francisco, to me, was just like that.

That first night, though, was beyond exciting. Just walking up and down Page Street and its four parallel neighboring streets was revelatory. Sal & I walked, skipped, and traipsed down the most famous of the five streets, Haight, at dusk before beholding quite a scene at 710, a three-story Victorian not unlike its neighbors, but having a je ne se quos ('certain something') that set it apart from the rest.

First reason, a sizeable troupe of motley characters had gathered on its ornate woodworked canopy of a porch and a long succession of wooden steps. Each person - boy, girl, man, woman - wore a unique ensemble, costume, or uniform. At first, I thought a Halloween party had broken out six weeks too early. Most of these folks weren't wearing masks, but the two-dozen did sport both strange and familiar headwear, historical long coats, vests, and an array of combat boots, high heeled sneakers, rope sandals, ruby slippers, and wooden clogs.

Right when I'd become convinced we were passing a costume ball, Salome exclaimed, "Look - the Grateful Dead!"

Boy, was I confused. I thought she literally told me the assemblage on the porch & stairs were recently deceased, had arisen from their graves & tombs, and were displaying, en masse, a noticeable amount of gratitude for their new states of being. Salome's second question began to address my confusion. "Haven't you heard of this band? They're so groovy, Ross. I saw them play last time I was here, in Golden Gate Park. Check it out. See the guy with the kinky hair and funky wire-rim glasses wearing an Uncle

Sam hat? That's the Dead's leader Jerry Garcia. And that tall, groovy-looking blonde cat wearing wire-rimmed glasses? That's their bass player Phil Lesh. Hmmm... I don't see Pigpen anywhere, but there's Bobby Weir - the young-looking kid with the super long hair. He's their rhythm guitarist and third lead vocalist."

I hadn't thought of Salome possessing a strong streak of extroversion before, but it manifested itself fully right then. She gripped my hand and lead me up the tall set of yellow, purple, red, and blue stairs. Acting as though she'd just arrived at a party given in her honor, Sal nodded to everyone who looked in her direction before sitting & pulling me down to the purple stair with her. Although my 'date' was dressed like a San Francisco hippie, I was outfitted more like a junior high boy model for JC Penney's Spring Catalog than someone belonging at this legendary rock group's communal residence.

No one looked askance at us as interlopers (which we certainly were) but they did pass us three different joints during our short stay. The music swirling out of the open windows was a hit at the time that was psychedelic in every respect. After inhaling the sweet-scented smoke from each of the joints, the music began sounding better and better. I realized my previous time smoking weed had been in Rusty's van when I hadn't felt much of anything. I guess it's a well-known phenomenon in which first-time smokers rarely experience a high or sensation of euphoria. My first time could best be labeled a 'contact high' since both Rusty and Salome were veteran smokers who clearly felt the effects of the THC. This time, though, I experienced the euphoric and psychoactive properties of the plant known to botanists as cannabis sativa.

Immediately after the crazy song ended, a ranch-style triangle clanged, signaling supper time inside the Grateful Dead residence. We remained seated and nodded goodbye to everyone - including Jerry, Phil, and Bob - who ventured inside for their nightly meal.

Taking leave, we skipped down the stairs and headed back to Rusty's pad on the next street. Welcomed warmly by his 'old lady' Faye and a coterie of residents & guests we'd met earlier, we joined the large circle on the Persian rug, propped up by an assortment of various pillows. All the prepared dishes – mostly platters of cooked & raw veggies and salads – sat atop a telephone-cable spool table in the center. Rusty, clad in an all-white outfit of loose, drawstring pants, linen vest, and cotton band-collar shirt, entered with a bit of pomp & ceremony before announcing that everyone should join hands. He raised his eyes to the open-beam ceiling and said: "Great Spirit, thank You for bestowing this abundant feast upon us. Thank You for the plentiful harvest caused by the great rains You have sent from the Great Above. May Your gift be lovingly accepted by those gathered in Your midst." He then spoke a couple sentences in another tongue before lifting his head and arms to address us: "Consider this food to be blessed by the Great Spirit & please be sure to serve your neighbor on the right." After following his directive, we all dug in. The meal was noteworthy for several reasons, but most notable was that our group was the largest I'd ever shared a meal with – a radical departure from my usual arrangement of eating alone or with my mom, almost always in silence.

⁂

The next morning, we awoke in the tiny, single-window room Rusty had issued us. Sleeping for the third time together with our bags joined, we'd gotten the hang of our new routine. (In case you're wondering whether Salome and I had had sex yet – no, we hadn't.)

As it turned out, Rusty's pad was part of a commune comprised of the residents of the three-story house. Everyone who stayed there more than two nights was obliged to pitch in for rent, the cost of food, and other incidentals, according to our host. And, everyone spending even one night in the house was required to do chores. Sal and I were assigned the task of washing the laundry that had accumulated over the past four days, which may not sound like much until you realize twenty-six people resided there. Using two round metal tubs on the back lawn along with lots of soap and brushes, we scrubbed everyone's clothing – shirts, pants, dresses, and underwear. Another couple, Lenny and Hope, rinsed what we scrubbed before hanging everything on the trio of clotheslines behind us.

The process took no more than an hour & a half. So, after packing a picnic lunch, we walked to Golden Gate Park for the 'Love-In' scheduled for eleven o'clock. Since it was early September, the park looked resplendent: all the trees and shrubs were verdant in color and the flowers colorful in their full bloom. When I think of that day and how everything looked, I can picture how the Garden of Eden must've appeared to Adam and Eve.

It was a perfect day for an outdoor event like this, with the sun shining brilliantly and the temperature in the seventies. A breeze blew in from the west and several puffy white clouds punctuated an otherwise azure-turquoise sky. If you ever saw the cover of the album "It's a Beautiful Day," you'll know exactly what kind of day it was. Again, a Maxfield Parrish kind of scene – as brilliantly colorful and bucolic as it ever gets anywhere.

At the edge of the park's ten-acre lawn, a group of long-haired males labored at setting up various musical instruments, amplifiers, speakers, monitors, you name it – on a stage that had been constructed earlier that morning. A large group of bizarrely dressed folks began dancing, swirling, and skipping around the entire area. "Those are the Merry Pranksters," Salome explained. "They're good people, so don't worry about their appearance. They only mean to act. They never act to demean." We both thought of what she'd just said - "They only mean to act. They never act to demean" – and burst into laughter, rolling around together on the lush lawn.

Then, while we spread the folksy handmade quilt our host Rusty had lent us, a guy with long, shiny black hair appeared. "You want some help with that?" he asked.

I wanted to ask why but instead muttered, "Sure, if you'd like."

"Nah, it looks like you got it. Hey, would you two like something to make today perfect?"

I tried hiding my confusion. First, how could today get any better? And secondly, what could possibly be so great that it would improve this already perfect day? However, I had to settle my curiosity. "Okay... and, what exactly would that be?"

He began, "Well, if you've got to ask... No, I'm just jivin'. You look too young to be a pig; you know, a cop. Here, tell you what. Each of you take one of these and I promise today will be the most amazing day of your earthly manifestation." Using a set of tweezers, the guy placed into my open palm two tiny squares of white paper, a quarter of an inch wide or long with a purple blob roughly the size of a dot left by a marker pen. The items were so tiny that if I hadn't closed my hand around them after Guy with Black Wavy Long Hair let loose of them from his tweezers, the slightest breeze or misplaced exhale would've swept them away.

Mr. BWLHG said, "Enjoy your purple haze," before moving on to the next picnickers.

After Salome and I settled onto our quilted lawn of a bed, we laid down facing each other, and looked intently into the other's eyes, just as we had the night we met. It was time, I guessed, to commune……… soul to soul. From inside, I heard "Do you want to do this?"

"If you do," I responded, also without words.

Looking at me for a beat, Salome whispered, "I do," as

though saying a wedding vow.

Sobered by the sudden vibe of solemnity manifesting, I said softly, "I do, too." That brief ritual, culminating with us placing the acid dose on the other person's tongue, is the most endearing memory of my time spent with Salome that weekend.

Unfortunately, thanks to the Purple Haze adult dose, I don't have many memories of the rest of that day and most of that night, except a montage of images darting, dancing, and dipping in my head. What began as the most remarkable daydream of a day became my worst nightmare.

***

Sometime in the middle of the night, I awoke with no idea of where I was. In fact, it took me who-know-how-long just to figure out who *I was. The darkness and patterns of contour lines swirling in front of me masked my surroundings and thus, my whereabouts. Laying my head down and closing my eyes, I used body memory to sort things out. I said aloud, "I'm in San Francisco, with Salome, in this little room Rusty let us use."*

"Shhh," a voice in the dark replied. "Don't worry…… about anything. Just rest."

So, I did.

It wasn't 'til waking to broad daylight that I realized the 'voice' hadn't been Salome's.

In fact, it would be years before I'd hear my angel's voice again; and I don't mean Sal.

I waited for more tapping from Ross's finger, but that was it. Even though I played the song three more times, no more taps descended on my forearm. And since the third time wasn't the *proverbial* charm, I vowed to never listen to "Incense and Peppermints" by Strawberry Alarm Clock again. The song became synonymous with Ross's nightmarish experience.

Chapter Fifteen

In every way possible, I was a mess. My girlfriend was gone, my bearings were gone, and my sanity might be heading for the door, too. No one to help me and nowhere at all to go… except home, where I'd be alone for several days, possibly even for a week. The morning after the 'happening' was the strangest in my life, even more than the one preceding it. Although I no longer suffered the side-effects of a hallucinogenic drug - as far as I could tell - I suffered even more. Why? Because the love of my life had split. To where? I had no clue. And no one else seemed to know either. Plus, I was in a locale unlike anywhere I'd been before. 'The City' no longer resembled the magical kingdom I'd considered it twenty-four hours before. For only the second time in almost fourteen years, besides Alice in Wonderland, I could identify with a fictional female character, the iconic teenage heroine Dorothy in "The Wizard of Oz."

Also, in a physical sense, I was royally messed up. My head seemed separated from the rest of me. Not only was I dehydrated, but food scared me. I didn't relish the thought of putting anything down my throat for fear I might throw it right back up again. Oh yeah, I didn't mention I'd also been stupid enough to drink beer & wine the day and night before. So, as you can imagine, I had a physical / emotional / spiritual / psychological hangover of the nth degree.

After I scraped myself off the floor of that little room at Rusty's, I found a bathroom down the hall and doused my head in ice-cold water. I stumbled back to my cell, rolled up my sleeping bag, repacked the knapsack, and ventured as far as the front porch. I didn't see Rusty, but I did meet a guy named Jerry or Larry (or maybe Gary), who knew the location of the bus station and scrawled a crude map on a scrap of paper for me. "Go straight up Haight a mile, veer left onto Market, right on 11th, and right to the Greyhound Stable... Peace!" I know those words by heart because I kept that little map and memorized those words on the trip back home. That little hand-drawn map is my only souvenir from the trip to and from San Francisco. I call it my 'talisman' because whenever I handled this scrap of paper, it reconnected me with that time and the first love of my life. Sadly, I eventually lost the thing, just as I'd lost the woman of my dreams.

⁂

The bus trip, mainly down Highway 101, took way longer than expected, but since I wasn't in the least bit of hurry to return to our apartment and be solitarily alone for several days, I didn't mind the plodding pace. When I wasn't looking out the window, I slept. And, when I slept, I dreamt. Of Salome, kaleidoscopes, and music. But mostly, I dreamt of Salome.

I arrived at San Bernardino's Greyhound terminal sometime after midnight Friday morning. Walking home with my knapsack & sleeping bag, this one old guy must've felt sorry for me because he picked me up in a green Mercury. "You look like you've been to Hell itself and back," he said as he let me off. (So long as I live, I'll never forget that description of me.)

Because I slept so much on the bus I felt rested on my return. So, Friday morning I got up and went to school. I didn't need a late pass but hid in the restroom until ten minutes into first period when I slunk over to the Attendance Office to get one. While there, a thought occurred to me, resulting in me asking an old lady if she could tell me which class Salome Stephens had.

"Oh, we don't give out any personal student information to other students," she replied.

"I understand, but I'm worried about her," I said, before breaking down. When the pain in my throat began to subside, I managed: "She's my... my cousin and I'm worried about her. Her dad said he'd kill her if she ever ditched school, and she ditched this whole week."

The lady bit her lip and looked around a moment. "What's your cousin's name, Honey?"

"Salome Stephens."

"Does Salome's last name have a 'v' or a 'ph' in it?"

"'Ph,'" I answered confidently, yet I had no idea.

"Let me check, Sweets." Less than a minute later, she returned. "I'm sorry, Hon, but there is no Salome Stephens registered."

"But, that's impossible," I blurted. "I know she goes here."

"Well," the lady began, "not anymore. She withdrew last Monday."

"What do you mean 'withdrew'?"

"She checked herself out after class on Monday. She's eighteen, as you probably know, and withdrew herself from school since she is legally her own guardian."

"I see" was all I could think to say. It made me sound mature, which I suddenly wanted to be in the worst way, especially now that I knew Salome was an adult.

I returned to the restroom to wash my face because I didn't want anyone to see I'd been crying. Walking to my first period, I felt both lonesome and nauseous. I don't know how I did it, but I managed to attend all six classes that day. The worst time was lunch because I had nothing to distract me from thinking and worrying about Salome.

Not only that day, but throughout the weekend, all I could think of was she. And whenever I'd see a head of blonde hair, I assumed it was Sal. I kept expecting to run into her somewhere on campus or around town. Hence, for the next month, wherever I went, I looked for her. I even thought of her when I'd hear a song about a girl whose name begins with 'S.'

I cried so hard while scribbling this part of Ross' story it took me a spell to clear my head and turn off his Sound-About, which had been playing "Suzy Q" by Creedence Clearwater on repeat. Whenever he hears that song, he thinks of her. Now, you tell me, how sad is that?

Chapter Sixteen

I felt so bad about Ross losing his sweetheart that I *implored* (another new word of mine) the Hands of Time to move ahead on the Clock of Life, and luckily the next tune was from 1970.

I've always had vivid dreams; I'm not talking life-like, realistic dreams (though I do dream in Technicolor, with every single image crystal clear). 'Surrealistic' is the word that best describes my nightly mind movies. However, they rarely have any new plot. In fact, I've only had a handful of different dreams in my life and most I'd classify as nightmares.

For years now, I've had a dream where I move through these super rough waters, out in the middle of an ocean. I wouldn't call it walking because I slosh through an unending series of whitecaps and it takes all my energy & effort to make any headway. Eventually, the waves become so difficult to walk through that I hardly make it past each whitecap. And, it's not what I'd call a walk but a trek - an endless journey that increasingly threatens to consume me. The freezing saltwater splashes into my eyes, blinding and jabbing them like daggers.

After a seemingly interminable time, I arrive at a massive bridge, which lowers for me to enter. So, I begin climbing it like a ladder. But - as I traverse this curved, mountainous span with white hard ropes on either side - the bridge transforms into the figure of a woman; a woman with two white fluorescent arms. The ropes beckon me to continue onward. After a long spell, the bridge-like woman becomes Salome, her face shining like an effervescent moon and projecting bright, blinding light beams into my eyes. As I reach toward her, a massive throng appears on the rolling, curved structure. Thousands & thousands of human-like creatures approach as they half-float and half-walk. Each talks, but none make a sliver of sense. I recognize them all; and each voice grows louder as its body reaches me, but I'm still unable to interpret their words at all. They never look me in the eye but move under a hypnotic trance and continue jabbering until eventually exiting the scene altogether.

Soon thereafter, the massive bridge vanishes, replaced by a wall of water & light heading directly for me at a terrible speed. And right as I sense I can't bear to face it a moment longer, the wall falters. Right before it can crash upon me, I try the duck-and-cover method of self-protection learned in elementary school during civil defense drills, protecting my head by shielding it with my arms. And every time I arrive at this point, I wake up drenched in my own cold sweat. I always rise, shower, and wash my sheets. This dream (well, nightmare) happens at least twice a week, and sometimes several nights in a row.

The song I played was Simon and Garfunkel's song "Bridge over Troubled Waters."

And right then I had the oddest sensation. I thought I noticed something lifelike about Ross, but I couldn't put my finger on what it was. Maybe I'm just hoping so much for Gray Eyes to awaken, that I imagined he had. Who knows for sure? Even I don't......... at least not yet.

Chapter Seventeen

Another dream I've had over the years, but not nearly as often as the bridge one, is also disturbing and involves turbulent waters, but I gain solace from this one. Plus, even though there's an explosive profusion of water cascading everywhere, I'm always left with a profound sense of peace. I started having it three years after the week I'd spent with Salome. Until then I'd been plagued only by the bridge dream. I say "plagued" because her likeness would embrace me and then promptly disappear. I'd awaken not only drenched in my own liquids but be left with a tangible sense of loss & abandonment that would remain with me throughout that day. This dream, though, gave me hope in the throes of my worst despair. It always started the same way – with a fog bank comprised of bright, soothing light that ushers me, as one person would another, toward a brighter, even more spectacular light. This second light is a massive column. 'Monolith' - although not a completely accurate descriptor - is the closest approximation of one. It's the brightest light imaginable - one emanating not only outward but upward and away so far that eventually I cease seeing it altogether. And then, a palpable sense of comfort descends and envelops me. Flying doves and angels in flowing gowns of diaphanous clouds encircle me in a soundless, noble parade. The six-winged seraphim smile knowingly, imparting such incredible levels of love and acceptance that I hope the scene lasts forever.

I have no idea how long this dream of fog and beacons lasts, but it lingers in my mind for days and serves a positive role by counterbalancing the bridge dream. Sometimes I wonder if it's God's way of drawing me to him. In fact, it's even occurred to me that perhaps God IS drawing me to him, to pull me out of this realm, but I choose on each occasion to refuse the invitation. Maybe I'm afraid of this light that's both... magnetic and troubling. And perhaps it's his way of displaying grace for me to experience and partake. Sometimes this part of the dream is the only thing in life that provides me solace, which I seem to desperately need.

I only had to play the song once because when it ended, Ross kept tapping his story out on the top of his firm-as-a-board bed until his retelling concluded. The song is "A Whiter Shade of Pale" by a group with the strange name of Procol Harum.

Chapter Eighteen

My third recurring dream, similar in theme to the others, is predominately white. Not your everyday shade of white, mind you, but one with a sleek texture. And, instead of being surrounded by the usual, sky-blue air in my boyhood dreams, the atmosphere consists of soft, slick fabric-to-the-touch whiteness. The closest word I can conjure to describe it would be 'satin.' White, silky satin. Billowy ribbons of it - several yards wide and infinitely long - decorate the setting. When a brisk breeze starts to blow all around, the multitudes of ribbons rise, billow, and descend for the duration of this dream I call a 'mini mind movie.'

Besides the gigantic ribbons, another major motif is masks. All kinds of masks, but each simple and stylized, like the ones in Poe's "The Masque of the Red Death"; the oval kind that covers only the forehead and areas around the eyes, cheeks, and nose. These masks, though not attached to faces or human forms, have anthropomorphic qualities. They grimace, smile, frown, and do whatever faces do. Dozens of them glide with majesty in the sleek, white atmosphere as I pass through a gauntlet of satin replete with human-like movement.

The only mask standing out among the three dozen or so is the one with a full head of human hair, almost identical to the spun angel hair I remember setting atop our Christmas trees in my childhood. Its tint can be likened to the hue of blonde tresses that

Jean Harlow, the long-ago Hollywood movie star, wore in her day. Of course, I've always interpreted this mask with its attached wig as signifying the personage of my long-lost Salome. As she(?) progresses toward and then past me, the mask exudes an interest in me, but when I begin to look at it in earnest, it becomes aloof and hurries off. I reach out, but am unable to touch it/her, despite my compelling desire to touch, hold, embrace, and engage with this flowing ethereal entity that may possess no gender or an identity of any form other than whatever my imagination can create.

When I again find myself inside this all-white dream, I never reach an ending or even a hint of closure. I never discover the truth and therefore never truly understand this fabric-and-mask-filled realm. This third dream doesn't leave me nearly as bereft or forlorn as the others do, but nonetheless keeps me wanting for something - or, better yet, someone - more.

I clicked off Ross's Sound-About and wrote down the titles of the pair of songs that *evoked* his third & last dream. These tunes recorded by the Sixties British rock outfit The Moody Blues were titled "Tuesday Afternoon" and "Nights in White Satin."

Chapter Nineteen

Since Ross's tape player is organized in order, the next song also came out in 1970.

Although my life moved on and I gained experience both at living life and playing music, there was always a void inside that nothing, not even music, could fill or dispel. At first, I figured it was the loss of Salome, but eventually I realized that: a.) she really hadn't been my girlfriend, even though I absolutely consider her my first love; and b.) my life could not revolve in any way around another human being. If it did, it would be living a fool's paradise. Fortunately, I discovered early on that one cannot live for someone else; but, if one did, one'd eventually become disappointed and probably hate that person or, at the very least, become embittered toward her. As I grew older and gained some self-awareness, I discovered a gaping hole inside me yearning to be filled, but not by any person, drink, or substance. And, yes, I'm more than grateful I had this realization before becoming an alcoholic, addict, or a codependent.

During the fall of 1970, around the beginning of my senior year at Theodore Roosevelt High School in good old San Berdoo, I tried to fill that inner void. I tried weed, alcohol, or a combination of the two, which usually resulted in my getting violently sick at parties – in either the host's backyard or restroom - where I'd inevitably be found draped over or snuggled around their only toilet, worshipping the proverbial porcelain god. After repeatedly making a spectacle of myself and earning a reputation around town and school as a 'lightweight,' I came to realize I'd been placed on this earth for a reason grander than becoming another addict of something.

So, I did what millions did in the Sixties and Seventies: I turned to spiritual things to assuage the yearnings of my spirit & quench the hunger for something meaningful raging inside me. The options available included attending some kind of church or synagogue, participating in an alternative form of worship like chanting, or going on a months-to-years-long religious pilgrimage, but I eventually chose meditation, which seemed like a peaceful, healthy, reasonable alternative to drinking, smoking dope, or using harder drugs. Plus, meditation was in vogue enough or cool enough to draw my attention just long enough to sign up for three beginner sessions of Transcendental Meditation, supposedly created by Maharishi Mahesh Yogi.

A couple years before, TM came into prominence in the Western world because a handful of celebrities studied it under the tutelage of the Maharishi. Some of my rock heroes visited the venerable man in his home country India – all four of the Beatles, Mike Love of the Beach Boys, folk singer Donovan – and sang its praises publicly for the next decade or more. What drew my interest was a friend at school – actually, a 'locker neighbor' in the hallway of the 240-244 classrooms all four of our years at TRHS, who'd stopped taking drugs and begun meditating. In just a matter of weeks, I saw a dramatic change manifest in Tim Bunch. Not only did he stop getting high, he became super healthy and underwent a dramatic personality change. Or, should I be more specific and say Tim 'underwent a dramatic reversion back to his real self'? The guy who had been happy, bright, and peaceful the first twelve years of his life until adolescence in a studio apartment with an unhappy mother of one overcame him like some dread disease. So, based on my witnessing this transformation in him, I thought maybe TM could improve me, too.

I paid thirty-five bucks for what they called a 'student membership' and received three one-hour sessions with a local guy who'd been into TM for years. I knew Dennis from a nearby music store where he'd been a salesperson. Probably twenty-one or two and wearing his hair long, I thought of Dennis as a 'quietly cool guy.' One of those guys who exudes a positive, nonjudgmental spirit; a dude no one has anything bad to say about. My new mentor also became a role model for me. After all, Dennis was hip, rode an Indian motorcycle, worked at a store selling rock records and musical instruments, and had more to live for now than simply getting and staying high. In short, I wanted what Dennis had. I wanted younger kids to look up to me because maybe I had most of my act together, but I also wanted people to see the gentle and humble me. A tall order, I admit, but I chose it as a goal for myself in the not-too-distant future.

So, one brisk November morning I visited the small house Dennis shared with a couple musicians, who'd also forsaken getting high for meditation. He and I faced each other in straight-back chairs while he explained in a whisper the history & philosophy of Transcendental Meditation before going over its many physical and mental benefits. He then shared the fundamentals of the technique and gave me my mantra. "Now, don't tell anyone your mantra because - if you do, Ross - it could lose its power. No one else has your mantra, so you want to keep it secret. Nothing good can happen from you revealing it to anyone. Always a chance that revealing it could result in bad karma for you and with whomever you share it."

"I understand," I said before closing my eyes and saying my mantra (a two-syllable phonetic word or phrase) to myself. I continued repeating & hearing it in my head until I began experiencing new, interesting sensations in my body. The best way to describe them would be to call them 'low-volt' streams of energy flowing first in my extremities and then, eventually, throughout my body, even down to my toes and - yes - there, too. When Dennis softly told me to begin to finish, I started to consciously slow the mental recitation of my mantra. And, after coming to a complete, full stop, I opened my eyes and felt as though I'd emerged just a moment ago from ***the*** *most refreshing, inspiring nap imaginable. I felt relaxed, calmer than I could ever remember feeling, and at total peace with myself & the universe. Dennis handed me a cup of hot tea, which I sipped while he instructively explained I shouldn't imbibe alcohol or mind-altering drugs of any kind, because the power of meditation wouldn't be nearly as lasting or effective.*

I had two more sessions with Dennis and both went like the first. After the third one, Dennis officiated a short initiation ceremony that a group of us graduates went through. At the end, everyone was blissed out, enjoying all the positive energy & experiencing the benefits of meditation – physical, mental, and spiritual.

For the rest of my senior year I stayed on the straight and narrow path. No more partying, no more cutting classes, and no more having those huge highs and lows. My life leveled out and I began hanging out with kids who either meditated or attended some type of faith-based events. I even began visiting this one church, at first just for youth group gatherings on Wednesday nights, but eventually for Sunday morning and evening worship services. It was a non-denominational independent church focused on two things – Jesus and the Bible.

Since I was new to both Transcendental Meditation and Christianity, it didn't occur to me the two might not exactly be complementary. To me, they were. So, as I meditated each evening, I began having these dream-like images, in which I'd picture a gigantic, diaphanous bearded figure with long hair levitating in the sky among an array of both puffy white clouds and darker, grayer, more threatening clouds. These images were like the dreams I'd been having the past couple years, but there was no plot and they didn't feature multitudes of people. Instead, there were just images of a God-like entity high in the sky smiling at me with nothing but love emanating from him. No white fog, no blonde woman, no troubled waters; just a presence with a capital P. And biblical images from my childhood Sunday School lessons began flooding the movie screen in my head: a burning bush, the hem of a giant's garment, a wheel in flames rotating inside a larger wheel in flames descending from the sky in frightening majesty; a pillar of smoke & a pillar of fire; and a burnished face; the whitest, purest one possible.

A song called "Spirit in the Sky" by Norman Greenbaum played throughout this story.

Chapter Twenty

For the next few months, things went great. I graduated from Roosevelt High, got a job at Vince's Music Emporium giving bass & guitar lessons, continued staying on the straight and narrow, and met my second 'girlfriend,' Delilah Jones.

A year behind me at TR, Dee was a girl who tirelessly pursued me during my last semester there. Wherever I looked on campus, there she'd be – in the halls during passing periods, in the cafeteria during snack break & throughout lunch, and even near my car in the parking lot before and after school. And my response to all this attention? At first, amused, then annoyed (I mean, who likes being followed?), and eventually… flattered. Very flattered. No, 'Very Flattered' times……a hundred. You see, never had a girl pursued me as long or aggressively as Delilah had all those weeks. And, it didn't bother me that she was - unlike Salome - younger than I (although slightly). Salome Stephens was my 'gold standard.' More than that, Sal was the woman to whom I compared every girl. But even I - Mr. Denial - noticed time passing and realized the chances of Salome Stephens returning were two……… slim and none.

The truth is, when I first met Delilah I wasn't exactly taken with her. Dee was a foot shorter, wore her blond, silky hair down past her waist, and had a disproportionately large head, which – at first glance without any judgment - made her look more like an androgynous member of the Seven Dwarfs than a babe, but that was all on me. Delilah Jones had plenty of attractive qualities, to be sure. She possessed the most beautiful, piercing blue eyes, with hair that truly did look like the proverbial spun gold, a keen wit, and a delightful sense of humor to go with it. That girl cracked me up every time we met and, even more importantly, laughed at practically all my jokes. So, in a sense, you could say we were perfect for each other. I was chronically insecure, and she built me up. Delilah Jones was by no means a beauty queen, but I soon stopped comparing her with Salome and discovered she had a definite beauty all her own.

For our first date, Delilah invited me over to her family's 'home' - a large, modern mobile home in a trailer court, three or so miles from where we lived. What she had in mind for our date was cooking dinner for me... along with her family of six. "What do you think of Stroganoff?" she asked one day during lunch in the cafeteria.

"As what – a concept? Or a dish served by the world's greatest chefs and you?"

She threw her head back and laughed the hardest I'd ever heard anyone laugh before. After she blushed & giggled a little, I gave her my real answer. "I've probably never had Stroganoff, but I'll try just about anything as long as the recipe doesn't call for dog or cat."

After a second outbreak of amplified giggling in the center of the lunch room, Delilah said: "Silly, there won't be any dog or cat in it. We're out of both, so you'll just have to settle for boring, old, manly meat – a pretty low grade of beef."

The thought of someone preparing a meal for me intrigued me, so whatever resistance had tried tugging on my sleeve, gave up. "Okay, we're on. If you give me directions and a time, then it's an official date... or fig... or kiwi – or some other obscure fruit no one eats." I left her laughing in the very center of the Roosevelt High cafeteria laughing her little, cute butt off for two reasons: 1. The bell ending lunch had rung a while ago and 2. I love leaving a room hearing laughter resulting from one of my rare, but brilliant comedic gems.

⁂

That Friday night, on my way to Delilah's mobile home, I stopped off at a florist. When the stainless-steel front door of her trailer opened - a tall, chubby man answered: "Yes? Oh, no! That beautiful bouquet of flowers better not be for me because ...... I only accept red roses."

Struggling to keep the smile I'd conjured for Delilah, I responded with, "I'll have to remember that next time, sir...... but - alas -these are for your lovely daughter."

"I figured. You must be that Ross McInerney we all have been hearing about awhile." Sticking his hand out0, he said: "I'm Dee's stepfather Barney Wilkins." After we shook hands, he turned and yelled: "Dee-lilahhh! Guess who and what's at the door? Some guy & flowers!"

Barney let me in as Delilah came rushing out of what I assumed was the kitchen. Smiling first at the bouquet, then at me, she said: "Dinner will be ready in a few minutes. I'm putting the finishing touches on dessert right now. Oh, thank you, Ross! That is so sweet."

"You're welcome" I managed after noticing we had a sizeable audience. Along with her stepdad were her siblings Ariel, Abbey, and Burl and mother Dolores. Introductions were conducted by Delilah, who took a big whiff of the bouquet before disappearing with it into the kitchen to presumably place it all in water and finish preparing her five-star dinner.

Speaking of five, her five nuclear family members all sat in silence until Barney spoke up. "I understand you're a musician working at a music store, Ross. You do know you can't support yourself (much less a family) doing that kind of work for a living, right?"

Taken aback by Stepdad's observation, it took me a beat or two to respond. "We'll... have to see. I've done pretty well playing for the past several years, ever since I was twelve."

"I see. I see another musician with stars in his eyes and both feet way off the ground. Well, if you ever want a real job - a <u>*man*</u>*'s job - let me know, kid."*

Dolores, Dee's mother, cleared her throat. "Barney, you're laying it on awful thick. We just met the poor boy." Turning to me, she asked, "Are you planning on college, Ross?"

Delilah announced rather loudly from the kitchen: "Mom! Barney! Could you both please stop? Thank you both!" The door swung open, revealing my date toting a large metal platter bearing some type of covered delicacy & two bowls of uncovered steaming food. "Dinner is served, everyone!" she announced.

After we all sat down at the table, with Barney on one end and me on the other, he said with a smile, "Well, normally I'd say, 'dig in,' but our special guest tonight gets to go first."

Fighting embarrassment, I smiled. "Oh, okay... thank you!" Before I could lift a finger, Delilah - seated to my immediate right - served me from the large dish. She then lifted the large platter, stood, and proceeded to serve her stepfather, mother, two sisters, and little brother before helping herself to a quarter portion of what she'd dished out to me. I'd never seen someone my age cook, much less serve everyone else first, so I felt equally impressed by and sorry for my very first date.

Dinner went well, thanks to Delilah buoying the conversation with her wit and laughter. "Why the great mood?" Barney asked. "Oh, yeah. I forget. You have a boyfriend now."

Her mom interceded, "For heaven's sake, Barney. Don't scare the poor kid away."

After dessert was served (by Delilah, naturally), Dolores said: "I'll do the dishes tonight, Dee. Why don't you show Ross your room? I'm sure he'd like to see your record collection."

⁂

Sitting together on Delilah's bed, we looked over and listened to some of her new records, including the recently released three-record live album of Woodstock. I was impressed by the size of

Delilah's bedroom, given it was bedroom # 2 in a trailer. The walls were covered with various rock posters featuring Jimi Hendrix, Eric Clapton, Joni Mitchell, Janis Joplin, and The Doors. While I scanned the wall across from us, two-and-a-half-year-old Burl toddled in. Smiling at me and pointing at a large poster of James Taylor on the same wall I'd been surveying, he smiled, then yelled: "Ross!" at least seven times.

Delilah laughed. "My little brother's right: you do favor James Taylor. In fact, that's what attracted me to you when we met that first time." After Burl left, Dee locked the door. Sitting close enough to me so our knees touched, she looked up and smiled. And, although I was romantically inexperienced, I knew an opportunity for a kiss when I saw one. We not only kissed, we - I guess you could say - made out. When we stopped, I felt dizzy... and the most sexually excited I'd ever been. And from the look on Delilah's face, the feeling might've been mutual.

***

For the next seven months, Delilah & I dated heavily, which meant I had a dinner reservation at her family's rather modern and spacious mobile home every night of the week. She always cooked, served, and cleaned up. I thought she was an indentured servant in her own home, entrusted not only with all the cooking, cleaning, and laundry, but taking care of her three younger siblings as well. I wondered how she could work me into her schedule, but she always somehow managed. Our nightly routine crimped my social life to such an extent I lost contact with all my friends, including my fellow local musicians. When September rolled around, I could be found at one of two places every day – Vince's Music Emporium or Delilah's trailer; er, mobile home, as she always corrected me to say.

She had Saturdays off from her servanthood duties at home, so we'd usually see the double bill at one of the local drive-in theatres. However, I couldn't tell you much more than the titles of any of those movies, what with Delilah & I practicing our respective 'night moves' three years before Bob Seger's song could be heard across the airwaves. My Mustang's windows would fog immediately and remain that way until I placed the metal speaker back on its cradle after the last show had concluded and the giant screen went dark.

In October, Dee's mom started working lots of double shifts at the furniture factory. Because Delilah still attended school, Dolores shipped her three younger kids off to their grandmother's, on the other end of the mobile home court to be watched every afternoon. Barney the stepdad had begun a project three hours away in Tehachapi clearing forest land, so he stayed there five or six days & nights a week. Consequently, Delilah and I had lots of free time alone, which resulted in us doing more than making out on her bed, resulting - yes - in the loss of our respective virginities. Her mother, after discovering the onset of our newest activity, insisted Delilah take The Pill, but I can't tell you which one. (Like it matters, right?)

Around Thanksgiving, the two of us began experimenting in a second realm besides sex – drugs. More specifically, we started smoking weed and soon supplemented it with uppers, Benzedrine.

Since we had free reign of the house & no one knew of our new experiment, our drug use escalated faster than either of us would've predicted.

Just after New Year's, on a Saturday night during winter break, we decided to drop acid together with a couple of her friends, Molly and Lizzy. It was the second time I'd taken LSD, but the first time knowing what I might expect from the experience. Instead of Purple Haze, the acid this time around was called 'Orange Sunshine,' a tiny clump of orange matter reminiscent of Play-Dough. Making darned sure I'd be tripping enough that night, I took an extra clump for good measure, which ended up being not a good idea; more precisely, I hallucinated enough for everyone there. Within an hour, I recall watching the Marlboro in my hand undulate and pulsate as though the thing knew how to breathe. My hand - not normally veiny - displayed a network of never-before-seen veins of all colors, but mostly blue, green, and a shade of brown.

As the hallucinating spiked, I walked down the hall to Dee's parents' master bedroom. Entering their bathroom, I became transfixed by what I saw in the medicine-chest mirror. Either my vision had improved over night or my complexion had dramatically worsened the past five or possibly twenty-five minutes because I discovered dozens of previously-unobserved blemishes, patches, and dots just below my yellowish skin's surface. I became afraid when I discovered how mottled & bizarre my face had become... so suddenly. As I stood there staring into that mirror, I heard the music blaring down the faux-paneled hallway from the living room space where Delilah and her girlfriends were.

As each song began, I'd be drawn into its narrative while still staring at the image of the upper half of my body in her parents' 'looking glass.' And although each song's lyrics couldn't have been all that profound or noteworthy, under the influence of lysergic acid diethylamide every line seemed prescient, ominous, even frightening. I remember one song about a guy's eye color. The tune, seven or eight minutes long, appeared to last an eternity and deliver some sort of esoteric message. And, for reasons unknown to me, the girls saw fit to play the now-famous song three more times in a row. So, for at least half an hour, I remained frozen in that one spot of that manufactured box of a home staring at my image, while mesmerized by the different phenomena I thought I could see in my skin as well as the new color of my eyes.

I don't recall much else about that night in early 1972, but I will always remember in minute sensory-blowing detail the lengthy tableaux of gazing into my own eyes while trying to decipher the unspoken, profound message I thought I received during my, not Lewis Carroll's, version of "Through the Looking Glass."

Ross's finger stopped tapping after a tune I recognized. After I jotted "Behind Blue Eyes" by The Who, I tucked his arm back under the covers, kissed him on the forehead, and dashed out to finish my shift. Only later, at home, would I realize or remember that Ross's beautiful, handsome eyes were colored not blue, but his own unique hue of gray.

Chapter Twenty-One

Delilah and I continued seeing each other but, after our episode of dropping acid together, something changed between the two of us. I can't tell you what exactly, but I discovered the closer I tried to get to Dee, the more she pushed away. She began expressing some new needs: wanting "time with my friends," "my space," and "more time to think." All of which was not only a big lie, but a blatant irony of the first degree because it was Dee who'd pursued, chased, and even stalked <u>me</u>. I was the one whom any reasonable observer would label 'the Pursued,' 'the Chased', or even 'the Stalked.' But now? Now she acted like I'd been chasing or smothering <u>her</u>.

This girl – and she certainly was still a girl – who, only months before, wanted nothing more than to own me like the most precious of possessions, was suddenly no longer interested in even being around me. I don't think it's an exaggeration to say she'd idolized me weeks before, but now she yearned for my absence & abhorred my presence. And, since this was my first full-blown relationship to date, I had no context or experience about what I could or should do. It seemed the more she pulled away, the more I wanted her, needed her, and even pined for her. Weird, right? So, I still haven't quite figured it all out, but I sure couldn't make any sense out of it all back in the summer of 1972.

I decided I needed to find my own way, to go back to making myself my number-one priority. I know it sounds selfish, but I had no clue what else to do. So, what I did – ironically – was to start looking for a band to join and be with; but, a band with promise; a band that might go somewhere with their music. I asked around at the other music stores, called my old bandmates from the Ruffians and The Groove Thang, and even placed a classified ad with the heading 'Looking for the Right Band,' but no luck. None of the strategies I tried bore any fruit.

On the bulletin board in the back of Vince's Music Emporium, I found a three-by-five note card announcing: "New band forming in need of multi-instrumentalist. Bass AND guitar skills a MUST! Interested? Call 947-2650. Ask for Allen."

I called the number, got a cute-sounding woman, and asked for Allen. "Oh, Al's not here right now. Can I help you with something?" After I explained the nature of my call, she replied: "Oh…… OH! Do you play bass AND guitar? Because that's what we're really looking for."

We? I wondered. "Uh, I play bass, six- and twelve-string guitars, drums, and keyboard."

"Perfect. You sound like you might just be the man we need. I'm Julie, Al's sister, and I'm one of the singers in the group. Plus, I write our songs and play keyboard."

Wow, I thought, this sounds too good to be true. "Okay, is Al the leader?"

The most delightful giggle I'd ever heard tickled my ear. "Is

Al the leader? Uh, in his own mind, maybe. No, I'm sorry to be so bold as to admit this, but our little band has no head... yet; but – hey – it's beginning to sound to me that if you have the right chops at bass, guitar, and so forth, you might even fit the bill as our fearless leader. Plus, you sound cute, which is too good to be true. Hey, I don't even know your name yet…um, sir." Her giggle sparkled - and sparked me - through the telephone line a second time.

"Ross, but you can call me anything you want."

"Okay, I might just take you up on that offer and call you something different, just to shake things up a bit with you. Do you like and need a little shaking up, Mister Ross?"

All I could think to speak, was the truth. "Too late. You've already shaken my world."

After another interlude of giggles, Julie said: "Wow! That was the coolest line I've ever heard a boy think up before. Seriously, congrats…… okay, let's just meet you at Vince's Music Emporium tomorrow night at eight; and then we'll get acquainted, Benito Rossolini!"

"You're kidding, right?"

"I'm kidding about your name, yes; let's just call it a 'work in progress,' Rosso."

"No, no... I meant that you <u>are</u> kidding about meeting at Vince's, right?"

"I couldn't be seriouser, Roscoe." (Another peal of laughter on the other end.)

"Huh, that's weird. I work there, and we've never had a band rehearse there before."

"Didn't you hear the news?"

"What's that, Julie?"

"There's a first time for everything, Ross-a-Roni!"

"So I've been told. Okay, cool. It's convenient for me. See you tomorrow night, Julie."

"Later, Tater," Julie said, followed by a last round of electric giggles.

⁂

Even after a long day of work, I could hardly wait for eight o'clock to roll around. I told Vince I'd gladly close the shop, so he could leave early for a change. When he asked why I'd want to do that, I told him I'd be auditioning for the band rehearsing in the store that night. He laughed. "Well, make the band and you'll become family. Al & Julie are my brother's kids."

"Huh" is all I could think to say.

"Well, if it works out, Ross, congrats will certainly be in order… for you and them."

"What do you mean 'for them'?"

"Well, I never told you this, Ross, but you are a very talented musician and any band who can land you will be damned lucky." Patting me on the shoulder, he turned and went back to his office, the one next to the bulletin board. I had no idea Vince had a high

opinion of me, but it felt encouraging, which is what I needed more than anything else back then – encouragement.

I decided to stay at the store instead of wasting gas driving home & back again, so I gave Mom a call to let her know what was going on.

"Oh, dear. It sounds like you're going to be a working musician, Ross."

After a beat or two, I bit on the bait. "And, what's wrong with that?"

"Well, look what it did for your father. We haven't seen him for years and word has it he's still on the road three hundred or more days every year since he split."

For the second time that day all I could say was "Huh." I didn't dwell on what she said, but later wondered how she knew about any of my father's goings-on. "Okay. I'll be home late."

"That's fine, Sweetie. Just be careful."

"Always."

⁂

At ten minutes to eight, I heard metal tapping on glass. Looking up from my Rolling Stone Magazine, I saw a pretty blonde rapping the door with what looked like a key, smiling and waving with her free hand. I hoped against hope it was You Know Who.

Unlocking the door, I asked, "Can I help you?"

"Can you? I sure hope so. Otherwise, this band might never

get off the ground."

"You must be Julie."

"I am she. And you must be Ross."

"I am."

"I know I'm early, but I hoped we could talk before the others get here."

"Sure, come on in. We can sit on that couch and chat."

"Thanks, but..." Looking around a bit, she pointed toward the rear of the building. "Is that Uncle Vince's office back there?"

"It is."

"Can we rap back there before the boys arrive? I told them eight-thirty, so that might give me enough time to catch you up to speed on our little band."

"Okay. Well, let me lock this and we'll use Vince's office. I'm sure he won't mind."

Turning out the lights in the big front room, so shoppers wouldn't think we were still open, I led Julie to her uncle's office.

After she sat on the love seat in front of Vince's desk, I settled into the chair behind it.

"Ross, could you do two things for me, please? Would you mind closing the door and sitting here with me?" Julie patted the space on the seat right next to her.

Wow, I thought. This might get interesting. Very interesting.

⁂

My time with Julie did certainly prove interesting, but for reasons different than I'd anticipated. She was all business once I sat practically in her lap. "Okay, I'm going to give you some background on us, and if you still want to audition after that, you're certainly welcome to."

"That sounds fair."

Julie was straightforward about herself, her brother Allen (whom everyone called "Al"), and their drummer Stu. It turned out that the band, dubbed "Dow Jones & the Above Averages" by Al, was leaderless. No one wanted to take up the mantle. "We're the opposite of every other band: None of us wants to be the leader nor do any of us have any mandates or preconceptions on how the band should run, but we all know we need a 'head.' So, Rosko, you're not just auditioning tonight as a bassist and guitarist, but as a leader... **our** *leader. None of our present members has had a strong parental figure, but instead of being rebellious or naysayers, we're seeking someone to tell us what to do. However, that doesn't mean we want to be bossed around either. What it means is we desire someone to organize, manage, and lead us; oh, and play bass... and guitar... and keyboards... and... maybe sing a little, but then...that's it."*

Then, she sat quietly, waiting for me to respond, but not in a pressing or demanding way. So, I sat and contemplated what she'd said. I processed what she'd told me. And, she was right in saying it was a problem diametrically opposed to any I'd ever encountered in any band I'd either been in or even knew about, where there were too many chiefs and not enough Indians; too many chefs and not enough waiters. What was so super ironic about this scenario? I, too, hadn't received any strong parental leadership. My father had been absent forever, and my mother? Well, her parenting approach might best be described as laissez-faire because "Whatever you want, Honey" had been her rejoinder to almost everything I'd ever asked.

I mulled over everything Julie told me, concluding with the conviction that there was only one true solution. "Well, Julie... I understand what you're saying and - even though I don't need to be the leader of this or any other band - I won't shy away from the role either. But, I'll need to meet the others - to see if we jibe well - and then have everyone vote for whoever the band wants to lead. How's that sound?"

It was Julie's turn to think. After looking at the ceiling and wrinkling her brow, she proclaimed with a snap of her fingers: "Yep, let's go with your plan. You know what? I thought from the moment I heard you on the phone you will be exactly what and who we need."

I laughed. "And how did you figure that all out - just like that?" (Snapping my fingers.)

"Hon, I could tell while you unlocked the front door and greeted me that you're a gentleman who nevertheless doesn't suffer fools gladly."

"Wow" was all I said, but it was enough to seal the deal, at least for the time being. We sat quietly & comfortably on Vince's

loveseat together, and I enjoyed every moment because it happened to be the first time I'd felt comfortable around someone in an instant. I'd recently discovered in my daily ritual of studying the dictionary that there exists an actual word for this state of mutual comfort between people in quietude, and 'propinquity' is what scholars call it.

Several minutes later, I met Stu and Al. After shooting the breeze a bit, we took up our instruments and jammed on three Doors songs ("LA Woman," "Riders on the Storm," and my favorite "Love Her Madly") from their "LA Woman" album, their last with Jim Morrison. But, back to us... boy, did we sound good! It was as though we'd played together for years, even when I moved from bass to guitar to keyboard, switching with Al & Julie once each. When we were played out, around 11:30, I asked: "So, what do you all think? Do I pass the audition? Do I make the team?" Without anyone looking at the others, all three nodded, but didn't speak a word. So, I did, "Okay... I just have one question."

"What's that, Ross?" Al asked.

"How do you all feel about keeping the name 'Dow Jones & the Above Averages'?"

No one spoke, so I began to regret bringing it up. Julie looked at Stu, still sitting at his kit, and then Al, standing next to him, and asked: "Well, what do you have in mind?"

"How about 'Propinquity'?" After explaining what the word meant and why it appealed to me as a concept, everyone voted yes. And, that's how the first band I ever led was named.

I was super tired from copying down all the words for this part, especially that crazy name Ross proposed for his band, but I was starting to get pretty good at decoding his taps. The song playing over and over had been "Love Her Madly." Gee, I wonder why it's his favorite. Just kidding. I could tell he'd fallen in love with Julie and already 'loved her madly.'

Chapter Twenty-Two

Boy, did my life's circumstances change after that audition. Propinquity would start gigging as soon as we could gel as a unit. Al and Julie already had lots of connections – club managers, restauranteurs, and casino owners. They'd performed at all kinds of venues in the past, back when they played for their father. Pops, whose name was Victor, had played in and/or led a band consisting of mostly family members since he'd been a kid. You name it and he'd played there: the Catskill Mountains, Poconos, Las Vegas, Burlesque, Vaudeville, Nashville; basically, wherever music was performed live in North America back in the day.

Then, during our third rehearsal, Julie blew my mind with some news. "We can play a hotel on the Strip as soon as we say we're ready. The Hacienda Hotel will put us in their lounge for a month to start and if we generate lots of bar sales, they'll extend our stay indefinitely. Plus, they'll put us up in two of their suites, so we won't be paying any rent or having to buy any furnishings, linens, towels, etc. We also have Flamingo and Stardust connections. We know the managers and owners; and, for whatever reasons, they all like us."

Immediately, we began building and rehearsing three sets to play each night. Since most of the casino patrons would be our parents' age, we would need to play quite a few numbers from "The Great American Songbook." The other members had played together for a couple years, so they already knew all the songs. I'd heard many before but hadn't played more than a couple, so we decided to play a mini-set of three or four songs each from eight composers, following this list: Harold Arlen ("Over the Rainbow," "Stormy Weather," "Let's Fall in Love," and "That Old Black Magic); Hoagie Carmichael ("Stardust," "Georgia on my Mind," and "Lazy River"); Dorothy Fields ("On the Sunny Side of the Street," "The Way You Look Tonight," "Big Spender," and "If My Friends Could See Me Now"); Cole Porter ("I've Got You Under My Skin," "Let's Do It, Let's Fall in Love," What is This Thing Called Love?," and "I Get a Kick Out of You"); Rodgers and Hart ("My Funny Valentine," "The Lady is a Tramp," and "The Most Beautiful Girl in the World"); Rodgers and Hammerstein ("You'll Never Walk Alone," "Some Enchanted Evening," "I Enjoy Being a Girl," and "A Wonderful Guy"); Jule Styne ("Diamonds Are a Girl's Best Friend," the Christmas classic "Let it Snow! Let it Snow! Let it Snow!" and "The Party's Over"); and - last, but least - Jimmy Van Heusen ("Swinging on a Star," "Come Fly with Me," "Call Me Irresponsible," and "Ain't that a Kick in the Head").

It was agreed, for our first residency at the Hacienda, Julie would select the set list nightly, with input from the rest of us that would tell a story about life & weave in many of these numbers. It was quite touching and not as corny as I'm making it sound. She promised to select a different signature tune for each night. Even though Al and I sang lead on three songs, Julie sang the lion's share.

After a month of rehearsing at Vince's, Julie proclaimed us "ready to play for a bunch of drunks out in the desert." We'd stay at the Hacienda Hotel for the run, where each suite featured two bedrooms. She said Al and Stu would share the first suite while she and I would take the other, which caught me by surprise. But, I didn't try to read more into it than the fact she and I would share not a room or a bed, but an entire suite. We'd each have our own bedroom and, since we weren't romantically involved, that would be the extent of our proximity to one another offstage. "Oh, and one more thing, Roscoe. We have a fifth member, a horn player already in Vegas. You'll meet him when we arrive."

Since I was the new guy, I didn't want to push my luck and ask about this heretofore unmentioned guy, but I did make generic reference to him: "I'm glad we'll have some horn support because most of our Songbook tunes were written for at least one horn."

Julie began laughing; I had no clue why. Between giggles, she asked: "Don't you want to know who our mystery horn man is?"

"Well, sure. Who is he?"

"Horn Man is none other than our pops. He already knows about you and is stoked to meet you and welcome you aboard our musical ship."

"Julie, that's amazing. I can't wait to meet your father."

"Well, don't look too forward to it or expect too much. He is... let's just say he's--"

"Well-traveled," Al interjected.

"Yeah, well-traveled. That's a good descriptor. Let's just say Pops has been around."

Al asked, "Ross, have you ever heard the expression 'Rode hard and put away wet'?"

"Yep."

"Well, that's Pops.... in spades," Julie said with a wink. "He's a true professional whose peak years might soon be behind him, but he'll still deliver the goods, that's for darned sure."

And, with that, we began polishing the other two sets we'd been working on – a rock and roll one plus a blues set. So far, we'd worked up a number of Doors' tunes along with some Beatles ("Get Back," "Let it Be," "The Long and Winding Road," "Hey Jude," "Something," and "While My Guitar Gently Weeps"); Rolling Stones ("Satisfaction," "Under My Thumb," "Honky Tonk Woman," "She's a Rainbow," and "Gimme Shelter); some Rascals ("Good Lovin'," "Groovin'," "Beautiful Morning," and "People Got to be Free"); plus both Crosby, Stills, and Nash and CSNY ("Carry On," "Marrakesh Express," "Teach Your Children," "Helpless," "Wooden Ships," and Stephen Stills' hit "Love the One You're With".) Of course, we couldn't play a gig in the heart of Vegas without featuring some Elvis Presley: "Don't Be Cruel," "All Shook Up," "Blue Suede Shoes," "In the Ghetto," and - of course - "Viva Las Vegas." The latter tune I sang lead, with Julie providing dancing & backup a la Ann Margret.

Our blues set consisted of "At Last," "It Hurts Me Too," "The Thrill is Gone," "Statesboro Blues," and "Tell Mama;" some

Allman Brothers ("Whipping Post," "In Memory of Elizabeth Reed," "Trouble No More," and "Cross to Bear"); and "Mystery Train." We would've worked up more, but Julie advised against it, asserting that the Songbook classics would be most in demand, followed by rock and roll. That was fine with me, even though the blues is my favorite. After all, my top priority in this gig was to please an audience, not myself.

⁂

A week later, we packed our gear into Al and Julie's van, said goodbye to our friends and family, and drove our little two-vehicle caravan to "Lost Wages." Stu and Al took turns piloting the Econoline van while I drove my Mustang with Julie occupying shotgun. It was a good time for her and me to get to know each other better. In fact, we talked so much during that first long stretch we didn't bother to turn on either the Philco radio or my eight-track tape player.

I was glad the van, weighed down by all our equipment, lumbered along so slowly because it gave Julie and me more time to become better acquainted. It turns out we had a whole lot in common. She'd hardly known her mother just as I barely remembered my dad. And, the parent who did raise each of us had occasional difficulty caring for themselves, much less us. Although I didn't have any siblings, Julie only had Al, with whom she'd never been especially close. We both played music from a young age and shared many of the same influences. The only thing different about us was our age. Julie was almost twenty-two whereas I'd just turned eighteen, but if you saw us together you'd never guess we weren't the same vintage. Lastly and maybe most importantly, neither of us had much experience in the romance department. "I was too busy either trying to keep Pops on the straight & narrow or making sure he and Al had a hot meal to eat and clean laundry to wear."

Since we didn't leave San Bernardino until late afternoon, we decided to stay the night in Baker. After eating at Denny's, we checked into a Travelodge on the main drag. Again, I was surprised by the arrangements, with the guys sharing one room and she and I the other. What had me perplexed was that Julie, who'd flirted with me that first night at Vince's, hadn't tried since. In fact, we hadn't kissed or even hugged yet. Although I wondered what might happen between the two of us in the coming months, I honestly had no clue.

Once we parked both vehicles in front of the motel office and said good night to the boys, Julie and I toted our suitcases to the room. Looking around, I noticed just one queen-sized bed. I was about to ask Julie where I should sleep when she said: "Ross, you're probably wondering why I chose to have us room together. Well, here's the deal. You don't know this, but Stu and I were a couple for over a year; but we haven't been together since the last time we played Vegas. And, Al and I really don't get along in close quarters. So, I figured this would be, well, the least of the three evils. Now, don't get me wrong. I like you and I hope you'll like me, but this arrangement isn't what it might seem."

She continued. "One thing I like about us is we're really getting to know each other. And so, to figure out where our heads are at, I thought we'd try something that might seem strange at first, but it could be a good litmus test as far as our compatibility. Come here." She took me by the hand, flipped off her shoes, and sat cross-legged in the center of the bed. I followed suit and faced her. "Okay, here's what I'd like for us to do: To truly get to know one another, let's simply gaze into each other's eyes. After all, you know what they say… the eyes are the windows of the soul. I thought if we - you and I - spent time doing this, we might each learn who the other person, in truth, is. Does that sound okay & is that agreeable to you?"

"Sure," I said, taking the exercise as seriously as I could. So, we began gazing in each other's eyes. I was really digging looking straight into those amazingly beautiful baby-blue eyes, but it wasn't more than a minute before the both of us busted up…… bigtime, and then started rolling around on the bed tickling each other and finished our frenzy with an all-out, old-fashioned pillow fight. When we'd beaten each other breathless & senseless, we fell onto the bed and tried to recover our sobriety before sitting up again, gazing into each other's eyes, and then… beginning to kiss. I don't know how to explain it, but it was the sweetest, purest thing I'd ever done with a girl. We eventually laid down and made out for several minutes until Julie stopped us. "This is so silly. I don't know why or how our clothes have stayed on." She peeled off her top, got up, unbuttoned her jeans, and dove under the covers. Me? I just sat there. Finally, after a lengthy lull, Julie said under the covers: "What's the holdup, Rossorito?"

"I guess I'm waiting for an invitation," I said, without irony or sarcasm.

"Well, consider **this** *your invitation," she said before a pillow smacked my head.*

And that's how I really got to know Julie; Julie with the sparkling sapphire-blue eyes.

I thought there might be more to the story, so I played the song again, but no more movement came from Ross's hand. I switched off Crosby, Stills, and Nash's greatest hit and Stephen Stills' best composition "Suite: Judy Blue Eyes," and decided to gaze at Ross's gorgeous gray eyes. But, there was a problem. Somehow, they were now closed. "Ross, you all right?" I yelled, forgetting for a moment I could be overheard by somebody.

He answered me for the very first time, but his response wasn't in spoken words or the nod of his head, but with a small grin. Granted, it wasn't all that broad or wide of a grin, but a legitimate smile nonetheless. I realized Ross McInerney probably isn't in a coma any longer.

Chapter Twenty-Three

Sometime around midnight, a truck horn awoke us. After laying down again, Julie and I looked deeply into each other's eyes before smiling and making love for the second time. We held each other until sunrise and then… we had an amazing third act. And all I heard in my mind's ear were the Beatles' iconic singing of "Love, love, love!"

After showering and dressing together as though we'd been doing so for years, we called Al & Stu's room and agreed to meet at Denny's for breakfast. After filling up on Grand Slams and three pitchers of Kona Coast coffee, we hit the road. Julie and I resumed learning about each other's past and began acknowledging none too obscurely that a future together, both musically and romantically, might have arrived a bit sooner than either of us had expected.

As we lay there that morning, with the sparse skyline of Las Vegas punctuating the beige, slightly pink desert distance, I experienced a full rush of adrenaline, thanks to the images I conjured of an exciting future consisting of Glitter Gulch, our new band Propinquity, and the girl who might make me forget Salome and Delilah.

Waiting for us in the Hacienda lobby was Al & Julie's dad. Appearing to be about 52 or 53, Pops - a thin, gangly man sporting shoulder-length receding red hair and a matching beard - spoke not in a voice as much as a growl-like laugh. "Hi there. You must be

Ross. Glad you're joining the band. My kids have nothing but good to say about you. I'm Victor Garbarino but all folks call me Pops."

We shook hands and sat together on a couch while the other three got us checked in. Pops tried clearing his throat but was only slightly successful. "I understand you & Julie will be roomies, and the boys are sharing the other suite?"

I nodded before rubbing my hands on my jeans. Not wanting to appear rude by not answering, I forced myself to say, "Yeah, that's what I heard, too. I hope that's okay with you..."

Pops chuckled. "Hell, what matter should it make what I think?" Leaning toward me, he half-whispered: "These kids have been doing their own thing since their mother left, so why should Al or Julie stop now?" He cleared his throat. "For the record, I'm glad you two are together. I mean, Julie needs someone and, frankly, old Stu just didn't seem to cut the mustard."

I managed to nod again before exhaling and feeling nothing but relief. Despite how well Julie and I were getting along, I realized Pops still could've been a blockade. Instead, he stayed in the background and did his own thing, which more and more folks were doing back then.

*
**

That night, we rehearsed four hours non-stop in the hotel lounge. Except for the random waitress checking to see if we needed anything, we five remained alone. Acting on the assumption the others all wanted me to lead, I did just that. No one, including Pops, objected. Laughing to myself, I thought: I must be the only eighteen-year-old musician in America to lead a band in which he's the youngest member.

A short, small elderly man - speaking in an accent I assumed was Italian and holding a yellow cloth tape - measured me for a tuxedo he said would be ready tomorrow, two hours before our debut. As we rehearsed different segments of our three sets, Julie handed me notes of what to say on stage while introducing songs and transitioning from one segment to the next.

When we'd finished the blues set, I asked the others, "Can we sit for a few minutes and just talk? I want to know how each of you thinks we're doing and what we may need to do to improve the act." So, we sat in a large booth in the back near the bar and began chatting.

Stu the drummer, who showed off his broad, muscular shoulders by wearing tank tops, brushed back his curly brown shoulder-length hair. "Well, so far I think we're playing well, Man. I like the vibe between us all. And, we're organized, disciplined, and clicking along on both rails. Knock on wood." He then made a fist and tapped his head a couple times.

After we laughed, Al looked around at the rest of us and smiled. "I don't have any comments, except to say we're one lean, mean music machine. Let's just keep on truckin'."

Julie said, "Thanks, Al." Looking at her dad and raising an eyebrow, she said: "Pops?"

Taking a swig from his tumbler of twelve-year Scotch whiskey, he said: "All I can add to Al and Stu's comments is this one word – ditto!"

"Well," Julie began, "I guess that leaves me. Pops, Stu, Al, and Ross: You all are doing great. And the only thing I'd like to add to the act is some original numbers. I've gotten a few down on paper and have a few more needing some final touches. So, maybe we can start practicing some originals after we get settled in?" When she turned in my direction, I knew she wanted a response. I just wasn't sure what it should be, so I faked it.

"An original here and there wouldn't hurt a bit, but we have to make sure we don't overdo it. And, I'd like to see what you and anyone else has written. Who knows? Someone in the record business might see us one night, dig our material, and sign us to a recording contract." Looking around, I asked: "Anyone else have any more comments? Suggestions? No? Okay, cool. Let's keep having these confabs and, please, let me know if there's anything I can ever do to help and support any or all of you. And now... how about a complete minute of propinquity?"

As we sat in silence, I felt comforted by the realization we had already gelled into a tight, happy unit. "Okay, meeting adjourned. Let's all relax and have a good night's sleep and meet back here tomorrow at four-thirty for our sound check."

Al and Stu, looking at each another, then us, said: "Same bat time, same bat channel!"

After the others dispersed, Julie and I took our drinks to the pool and enjoyed the warm desert night beside the city's second largest swimming pool. An hour or so later, we retired to our room and caught up on our sleep.

I switched off Elvis Presley's "Viva Las Vegas" and wondered how Propinquity's run at the Hacienda might play out.

Chapter Twenty-Four

The band's month-long engagement at the Hacienda went great. Full houses almost every night and management seemed pleased with the bar receipts, reportedly up 30% from the previous band's run. I loved the Hacienda because it catered to a friendlier, more family-oriented crowd than the other hotels served. I didn't see any of the shady characters I'd heard inhabited many of the casinos both on The Strip and Downtown. However, even though we'd done quite well, management thought we might benefit from spending some time away, where we could 'pay our dues.' The owner, Judy Bayley, had three other hotels, all in California - Fresno, Indio, and Bakersfield. Stan Shorter, the chain's GM, decided we needed to perform a month at each of the other resorts before returning to Nevada and having perhaps a permanent residency on The Strip. I remember him telling us: "I really like you kids... and Pops, of course... but you need to get a little more seasoned before we commit to having you here on a permanent basis."

So, that's what we did. We took our act to the hinterlands, beginning with Indio, close to home. I figured I could check in on Mom every so often, to make sure she was doing all right. After all, I was her only kid and she had no one else except Rich, her boss and boyfriend.

In case you don't know where Indio is, it's south of Highway 10 between Palm Desert and Coachella, a couple hours northeast of

San Diego. Once again, we shared rooms. They weren't suites like in Vegas, but nice motel-type rooms. It reportedly got hot in the summer, but we played there in January, so it was nice weather-wise. However, it was Indio - a forsaken whistle-stop on the way to somewhere nicer, cleaner, and more interesting. The crowds were smaller and drank more, especially on the weekends. I don't have much to say about Indio, except we used our time there to tighten up musically. Our vocals, especially our harmonies, became considerably stronger than they'd been in Vegas.

And right when we thought we couldn't get any better, we moved five and a half hours north to Fresno. I know Fresno isn't a wonderland, but it was good grooming for us. So, when we moved on to Bakersfield, we felt on the brink of something promising and successful. In addition to adding a couple Buck Owens and Merle Haggard tunes, we began playing more originals and received great responses to every one of them. Some of the regulars even begged us for cassette copies, just to show how much the folks there dug our music.

At the end of March, Mrs. Bayley requested we return to the big Hacienda, so we packed up, headed back, settled in, and began playing to large crowds. Everything was going great; until the owner died suddenly. To make matters worse, we started hearing rumors that all four Haciendas would be sold to a group, which didn't sound promising for us at all.

A memorial for Mrs. Bayley was slated for the fourth Friday after our return. Management asked us to play, so we worked up a short set for the occasion. Since Mrs. B loved the classics and rock, we played her favorite "The Way You Look Tonight," two Rodgers and Hammerstein tunes, a couple Elvis numbers, and finished with her most loved gospel tune, "Peace in the Valley."

The service was held in the large showroom and attended mostly by present and former employees. Julie and the rest recognized virtually all the attendees, except for the half-dozen men clad in sharkskin suits who didn't mix with anyone at the reception following the memorial service. It was a sad but touching event that left many of us employees with a sense of unease about the hotel and casino chain's future.

Our second run at the 'Big Hacienda' went well, with crowds packing the lounge every night. Many customers returned multiple times, so we knew we'd built a following. And with requests for our originals coming more frequently, we thought we were truly on our way.

Among our regulars were dancers. We had a dozen or so couples who frequented the lounge at least once a week to dance. The band loved to see them because they created extra excitement and fun, which added to the vibe we strove for. One couple, however, stood out among the rest. Abe and Roberta were our biggest, most loyal fans.

They liked to sit at a table up front, next to the left wall when you entered, so they were on the band's immediate right. Their two chairs and table were mostly for holding drinks, her purse, and his blazer since they danced every number and sat only during breaks, to catch their breath. Roberta, about thirty, wore her wavy brown hair half way down her slender back. Standing five feet ten, she projected a striking presence. Slender and lithe, she was an excellent dancer and reminded me of a ballerina. Abe, on the other hand, was her counterpoint. Shorter by three inches, his receding hair line and paunch gave him a middle-aged look. Very deft on the floor and always in command of leading his partner, Abe was another dancer who could draw the crowd's attention and admiration.

Maybe five months into our second stay at the Hacienda, on a Thursday night, the couple performed a fast, fancy, old-timey dance step (the Bop?) when six guys in swanky suits entered and took the table just behind theirs. They sat and faced the dance floor, occasionally making comments to one another, but generally just watching the dancers. A waiter named Marty took their orders and receded to the bar in back. As the song ended and a slower one began, the couple shifted to a waltz. One member of the swanky suited ones, a squat, powerfully built guy in his forties sporting a head of slick black hair, approached Abe and tapped his right shoulder. Abe didn't react, but continued dancing with Roberta. After three seconds or so, the interloper clamped his left hand on Abe's left shoulder, causing the couple to stop dancing. The man said something, to which Abe responded by turning to face him.

The interloper grabbed Abe's upper arm, twisted it behind his back, and pushed him aside. Raising his hands toward Roberta, he said something like a command, and she began to waltz with him. Abe shook his head in disbelief and approached the man from behind, tapping him on the shoulder in the same manner as the black-haired man had done moments before. Instead of the man turning in response to the tap, two of his colleagues approached Abe from behind. Each grabbed one of his arms and rushed him to their table where they deposited him in the chair vacated by their leader. Abe tried raising up, but both guys pushed him down efficiently, forcefully. They seemed experienced, perhaps expert at these and other maneuvers.

When the song ended, Roberta turned to leave the floor, but the man grasped her by the upper arm and spun her back. Pulling her to him, there was no room between them as they danced to the next number. I remember looking around the room as I played my bass, wondering why the bouncers were nowhere in sight. Seeing my bandmates doing the same, I knew we had a problem. Some movements from the newcomers' table grabbed my attention. Abe tried standing again, but the man to his right stood and delivered a left jab to his jaw, knocking him out. Two of the others lifted Abe by his underarms and dragged him out. Since Roberta's back was turned, she hadn't seen any of it. Her new partner kept her back facing that area throughout the song. When it ended, she glanced around and, not seeing Al, flashed a look of horror.

Onstage, all five of us were consumed by the unfolding drama. Not knowing what else to do, I raised and dropped my right arm, signaling the band to stop. The powerful-looking man turned and strode toward us, allowing Roberta to run out of the lounge to find Abe.

"What the hell are you doing?" the man hissed, after climbing onto the stage and stepping within six inches of my face.

"We cannot continue to play with all this commotion going on," I replied, sweeping my arm to indicate the area where the struggle had taken place.

"You'll continue playing... or else."

Not knowing what else to say, I asked: "Are you threatening me, Mister?"

"No, Honey. I'm not threatening you; I'm promising you."

"And who do you think you are to order us around?"

"I'm your new boss, giving you a simple career choice - play or get fired."

He spun around and left the stage as if he owned it, grabbed Roberta's purse from her table, and led the remaining two guys out of the lounge. We kicked into our next song, one by The Doors, and pretended nothing was wrong or unusual.

I clicked off the player, leaving "L.A. Woman" by The Doors in mid-song.

Chapter Twenty-Five

After our last set ended at 1:30 am, a short, weaselly man with slick hair and a pencil thin mustache strode up the center aisle and stopped directly below me. I didn't want to acknowledge him, but figured I should. Before I could speak, he began scratching one of his pock-marked cheeks with what looked like a business card. "Yes? May I help you?" Without a word he handed me the card upside-down, pivoted, and left through the same door he'd entered.

Printed in large letters was: "NEED TO SEE YOU NOW." I drew a breath, got Julie's attention, and showed her the card. We had a moment when we stared at each other & non-verbally communicated. After I took her hand, we proceeded to the GM's office and knocked on the half-open door. "Come in," snarled a voice behind it. Entering, we saw the man from before seated behind Mrs. Bayley's gold desk. His posture was slouched because his feet were crossed and resting on the edge of the desk. "Sit," he said, so we did.

Taking a sip from a tumbler half-filled with a clear liquid and ice, he set the glass down. "What did you see tonight?"

"I beg your pardon?" I asked, a lump in my throat already formed.

"What did you see tonight?"

"Uh, I don't know to what you're referring," I said with a

break in the middle.

"You didn't see nothing."

I was going to ask if that was a question or a command but thought better of it. "No, sir. I – we – didn't see... nothing."

"Exactly. You may go."

We got up and were halfway to the door when Mr. Big stopped us. "No more hard rock."

I couldn't help myself. "Excuse me?"

"More Sinatra, more Dino, and more Dinah. No more of that heavy shit."

"Uh, yes. Sir."

"Yes, what?"

"No more heavy rock... and more classic music, like Sinatra, Dino, and Dinah Shore."

"Almost right."

"Sir?"

"Take out 'like.' More of those three and less of everyone else. Got it?"

"Got it... sir."

"Good. Close the door after you."

A moment after I closed it, I heard him laugh. And, that was my first meeting with the man whose name appeared on the simple white business card, Carmen Belucci. I still have it.

⁂

So, we kept playing at the Hacienda, even though all four hotels were sold to a group led by Mr. Glick, investigated by the gaming commission for organized crime and racketeering.

We did change our act to accommodate Belucci's 'requests.' We still played rock and roll, but none of the harder stuff (The Who, Allman Brothers, and non-ballad Rolling Stones). After inserting several songs each night by Old Blue Eyes, Dean Martin, and Dinah Shore, we had no more discussions about song selection. Once in a blue moon, though, we would receive a request printed on the back of one of his cards in the middle of a performance, usually asking for a Sinatra or Wayne Newton tune. And, we always accommodated his requests, even when it meant learning the newly-requested song between sets.

As to Abe and Roberta, our biggest followers - We never saw them again, but we did see a sudden change in the Hacienda's personnel, especially in the casino and lounge. The maids, bell boys, and concierges continued, but every bartender, most of the cocktail waitresses, and all the dealers & pit bosses changed. Most were reportedly family or otherwise connected with "the Glickers" (as we referred to them behind their backs).

Propinquity's line-up, however, never varied. No one ever called in sick and we kept attracting packed crowds. A couple times, for a week each, we filled in for the headliner in the main room when they'd been sick, and packed the place every performance. I will say we always got paid right and on time. Belucci must've never had a problem with us or our act because if he had, we would've heard about it pronto. Believe me.

As for Julie and me, we fell deeper in love. I bought a 2-carat diamond engagement ring and presented it to her on bended knee during our final set on Christmas Eve 1972... and she accepted. We scheduled our wedding for June at the Wee Kirk of the Heather Chapel because Julie had told me she always wanted to be a June bride.

Al and Stu continued rooming together while Pops seemed to do great living by himself in a bungalow on the grounds. We were all happy, and why not? We were doing what we loved most and getting paid fabulously to do it. What could go wrong?

Chapter Twenty-Six

After Ross grinned, I wondered what else he might do. So, I tried this and that, but this and that didn't work. I even got a brainstorm: What would happen if I Morse-coded on his arm? Would Ross know what I was saying? Well, yes and no. My tapping his arm worked only some of the time, but I discovered if I Morse-coded a song title, he'd respond as though listening to it. So, I tapped out the title of a Beatles' song that produced the following chapter. (I'm either getting smarter or less afraid to try new things. Either way, I give all the credit to Ross Gray Eyes.) Here's the next part of his story:

After an interesting '72, we fully embraced 1973. Everything was going our way. Crowds packed our shows every night. Bar receipts doubled and waitress & bartender tips skyrocketed. Famous, influential people from show business and other big shots attended our shows more and more, packing every performance. So much, in fact, that management started taking reservations and split our weekend nights into two shows. After two sets, the lounge would be cleared and then admit the overflow crowd that had been waiting to see our act during the previous set. There was even talk of charging admission beyond the two-drink minimum. Then, on New Year's Eve, we heard that A & R men from RCA, Decca, and Capitol Records were all in the house.

When things couldn't get any better, I received a letter from my mother in late January informing me she and Rich (now her fiancé) had booked a room at the Hacienda for Valentine's Day weekend. Although they hadn't set a date for the wedding, she hinted they just might 'tie the knot' during their stay.

Although Mom hadn't met Julie in the flesh, they got acquainted over the phone and began corresponding through letters. They got along famously and even mentioned having each other in their weddings. My rise in the music business couldn't hold a candle to the joy filling my life in the form of this beautiful, kind, wonderfully gifted woman. You could call our meeting and romance a case of Kismet. And, all at once, I was in Heaven, Nirvana, and - yes - Cloud Nine.

⁂

Valentine's Weekend arrived. Valentine's Day wouldn't be until Wednesday, so when Mom and Rich showed up at our early Saturday night show, it was a reminder to purchase my big surprise for Julie. Calling a nearby florist, I ordered a dozen of her favorite flowers (long-stemmed yellow roses) delivered to our suite on Wednesday. My mother and Rich had decided to wed on V-Day also. "We'd like you both to stand up with Rich and me at the chapel," she said.

"That's perfect, Mom. Wednesday's our day off."

"Rich rented himself and you, white tuxedos," she whispered, a few steps outside our suite. "I'm taking Julie to get her dress Monday. Won't it be great, Son?"

Beaming her biggest smile ever, I couldn't help but match her enthusiasm. I cupped my mouth and whispered my big secret to Mom. She hugged me even harder and maintained that smile. "Oh, Son. I'm so happy for you!"

That weekend and the first half of the week flew by. Wednesday night suddenly was upon us. When Julie and I returned from our weekly afternoon rehearsal, I popped the surprise on her. "You WHAT?" she screamed, jumping into my arms. After we kissed with her cradled in my arms, I set her down on the bed. "You mean, I'm going to be Mrs. McInerney tonight?"

Smiling like Felix the Cat, all I could think of to say was, "Yup." I opened the little velvet box I'd tucked away in my coat pocket and showed her our wedding bands.

"Wow, Honey. That's the widest wedding band I've ever seen."

"Well, I want everyone to know that you're officially mine. Even from across the Hacienda lounge, every guy will know that the beautiful, sexy blonde singer belongs to me." Slipping on both our rings, we kissed until Rich rapped on our door, signaling time to go. Life had become nearly unbearable with all this joy and bliss. I'd never felt so naturally high in my life. I remember asking myself, "Will this bubble last forever?"

⁂

The Love Chapel was a small stucco chapel on The Strip a couple miles from the Hacienda. I called the chaplain, Reverend

Noble Knoblock, on Monday to let him know the four of us wanted a double ceremony. When I asked if that was possible, he answered in a distinct Midwestern drawl, "Oh, that'll be just fine. We've performed double, triple, even quadruple weddings before. Just about any ceremony you can concoct or imagine, we've had it here at the Love Chapel. Just come a few minutes early and we'll fix you folks up properly."

Arriving at eight-forty, it was dark out. Of course, The Strip was lit up, but this was the early 1970's, before Las Vegas experienced a huge growth spurt. So, it wasn't lit up like it would be today. We guys put on our white tux coats, escorted our brides into the chapel office, and met the reverend. After filling out the paperwork with Velma his wife, we entered the chapel. The minister had us stand on the altar with him while Velma played the piano.

When the playing stopped, he beamed at us all before leading the double ceremony. The whole thing couldn't have lasted more than ten minutes, but it was nonetheless warm and heartfelt. I felt uplifted by the entire experience, especially during our vows when I gazed into Julie's eyes. At that point, I felt like I'd levitated a full foot off the floor.

After we finished, Mrs. Knoblock gave each of the women a corsage to wear afterward. Julie chose to wear hers on her wrist. Rich and I were then each given a Mylar balloon with "Just Got Hitched at the Love Chapel" emblazoned across it. Pretty tacky, right? I know, but it was the only real souvenir we had of the occasion. So, we men shook hands with Reverend Knoblock while

Mom and Julie hugged Velma. And that was it.

As we walked out, Julie grabbed ahold of our balloon's string. "Let me carry that thing for you, Hon. You can't drive around town with that bouncing around your head." We proceeded down the driveway to where our car was parked on The Strip. As I climbed in behind the wheel, I heard Julie say "Oops!" I guessed she'd lost her grip on the balloon and it began to slip out of her grip. I heard staccato steps as she chased it into the roadway before a loud crash sounded.

A van like the band's, slammed into Julie at a high speed. The explosion was followed by the loud rumble of the van running over something. I looked up and saw the white vehicle race off, leaving behind a clump of lavender, which of course was Julie.

My mother and the medical center's psychologist later told me that I ran to Julie, right in the middle of the road and laid down next to her. I reportedly kept hugging her while continuing to wail and yell. She might've been pronounced dead at the hospital, but her spirit left her body right there on the pavement. I remained in such shock they didn't discharge me from Psychiatric Care until Saturday morning. The funeral was held at the hotel on Monday, attended by over eight hundred hotel employees and fans of Propinquity. I can't tell you a thing about the service, but I still can picture every detail of Julie's face & dress the night of her hideous death. It was, without a doubt, the lowest point in my life; and I still haven't recovered from her death. Life seemed over for me. That time span felt to me like the proverbial 'point of no return.'

This is the first time the song on the player didn't seem to have relevance to the story Ross told, but maybe it'll make sense someday. Perhaps he'll tell me why the death of his dear Julie had anything to do with the Beatles' hit "Get Back." Maybe it was his way of exhorting his dear wife to return to Heaven, where someday in the future they will hopefully reunite.

Chapter Twenty-Seven

The new Hacienda management attended the funeral and offered their condolences on the loss of our bandmate and my wife. They donated enough flowers to fill the large showroom and gave us two weeks off to rebound, rest up, and somehow get over the tragedy. But, none of us could continue without her. I wasn't the only one reminded of Julie by every song in our act. Julie's father, brother, and former boyfriend also couldn't separate the music we played from our dear, sweet, lovely Julie. So, we disbanded and went our separate ways. Pops stayed in Vegas, but the rest of us headed home separately.

My mother and Rich, now married, bought a house on the other side of San Bernardino. I returned to the one-bedroom house where I'd lived with Mom after high school. Since I'd earned quite a bit during our stint with the Hacienda chain, I didn't have to worry about rent. I paid the landlord for an entire year, mainly because I wanted to be left alone and not bothered every month to write a check. Yes, everything I needed to do, but couldn't was just too... daunting.

For the next year, I did nothing but sit in my place with the curtains drawn. On good days I made it out of bed and laid on the couch. On bad days I stayed under the covers. What did I do all that time? I thought about Julie mainly, but I also cried, wailed, yelled, and pounded on inanimate objects. I also sat & talked to her for hours on end. After a few weeks of that, we began carrying on two-way conversations. She'd appear with a stoic expression on her angelic face and talk to me in the most somber tone imaginable - no smile, no teasing, and no humor. Of course, the scenes playing in my head weren't real, but my own morose manifestations of Julie.

The only person I saw for an entire year was my mother, who came over every Saturday, gathered up all my dirty laundry, and returned a couple hours later with everything clean. She'd cook a couple big meals & put what I didn't eat in the fridge for me to have the rest of that week.

While Mom cooked, she talked about life. How life is not only tough, but a gift we should always cherish. She told me I was the greatest gift she'd ever received; and that even though she'd grown to love Rich, I was the 'true love' of her life. She must've known I blamed myself for Julie's death because her recurring message to me was – most of life's major events happen beyond our reach, beyond our control, and beyond our influence. She was a huge believer in fate, Kismet, predestination. Mom was no follower of any particular code or creed, but over the years she'd sculpted a philosophical outlook that went like this: "We are all vessels of life that must protect not only our own lives, but those of others; sometimes, however, we're utterly unable to help ourselves or anyone else. Chance is a hugely underestimated factor in the universe that we can neither influence nor predict. But, what we do have control over, more than anything, is our attitude about what happens to us. We can't truly judge an event because we can't see at that moment what repercussions will spring from it. We need, more than anything, to let go and have faith that everything will work out, regardless of our present circumstances."

At first, when Mom gave me these talks, I rejected them. But after only a few weeks, I began looking forward to them. I even started recording them on cassette. And, for the rest of the week, when I needed a lift of spirit, I'd switch on my recorder and listen to Mom ('Mother Mary,' as I secretly called her) giving her words of comfort and solace.

Although I found myself in the throes of the deepest depression, at least one good result to come from it was my songwriting. I'd never been serious about it before, but now it wasn't about writing songs, but expressing my emotions & thoughts. Not wallowing in grief, mind you, but expressing the loss of my better half. So, every day I sat with my guitar and plucked its strings while imagining Julie - her smile, loveliness, sweetness, and humor. Every day I wrote at least one song and sometimes two. I continued with this regimen a solid year, accumulating scores of songs, mostly about Julie and us, which sat in stacks on my living room floor.

One day, as I put the final touches on yet another song about Julie, I heard a knock on my front door. Peering out the bathroom window, I got a good look at the person standing on my porch. And when she turned to yell something to a second person in a car at the curb, I recognized the girl on my porch as someone from my past.

Standing on the tile floor barefoot while only wearing boxers, I deliberated whether to answer the door and let the past in... or not.

I don't know why, but I decided I should seize the opportunity to speak with someone who'd left my life years before without any closure. So, I grabbed my bathrobe hanging on a hook on my bedroom door and wrapped myself in it.

When I swept the door open, all I said was, "Yes?"

Looking up at me with blue eyes, the long-haired blonde replied, "Oh, you are *home."*

"Yes, I am. Well... what do you need, Delilah?"

Smiling, she said, "Well, a cigarette and beer for starters."

Opening the door wider, I waved her in. "Tobacco I got, but no beer."

"Well, that'll have to do, I guess." She swept past me and sat at the kitchen table. Not thinking to check out the car parked in front, I shut the door and went for my pack.

"Is your mom home?"

Feeling both giddy and devilish, I replied, "Yeah, she should be. Why?"

Taking a Marlboro from my hand, she answered, "Just wondered. I always liked Mary."

"I'll give her your regards. So, what brings you here...... after all this time?"

Between puffs, she said, "Not much. Just wondered if you still lived here."

"Oh" is all I said. I lit up my own Marlboro and sat down,

tightening my robe.

Looking around, she said, "You keep this place dark."

"Yep."

"Are you sure you don't have a beer lying around?"

I stood. "No, but I've got some of my mother's brandy if you want."

"She won't mind?"

"No. She hasn't touched it for over a year." I grabbed the pint of E & J from a cupboard above the stove, got a glass, and set them in front of her. "Help yourself."

She laughed. "You don't have to ask me a second time." After knocking back a hefty swallow, she asked, "So, Ross my dear, what have you been up to?"

"Oh," I smiled back, "so, you do remember my name after all these years."

"Yeah, you're... how can I describe you? Semi-memorable. Yeah, semi-memorable." She sat up. "So? I guess I have to ask again: What've you been doing the past couple, three years?"

"Not much. You?"

"You wouldn't believe me if I told you."

"Go ahead. Try me."

She looked me in the eye. "Oh, I'd LOVE to try you... again." She threw her head back and laughed before taking a second shot of brandy. "Well, if you aren't going to tell Dee what you've been up to, I guess she'll tell you about her fascinating career."

I don't think she noticed how disinterested I must've looked but she continued regardless. Maybe the cheap brandy was already affecting her.

"Well," she began, looking around the place a second time. "I work in the schools."

"You?" I asked with plenty of emphasis. "You and schools don't go together very well."

"Yeah, I know. But, I'm back in high school... as a student."

"Say what?"

She laughed again. "Yeah, it's my career; not as a student, but an undercover officer."

"You're a narc?"

"Yep. A dyed-in-the-wool, bona fide, card-carrying narc. What do you think about that?"

"Well... the more I think about it, the more it makes sense." (After all, Delilah hated school and loved drugs, so she'd fit in perfectly with a certain caliber of student.)

She regaled me with stories of her time as an agent. How she got recruited after high school. How she teamed up with a female working partner. How the two of them did so well together and how they'd become close friends.

"I'd love for you to meet her."

"Gee, I don't know, Dee. You're lucky I let you in."

Without laughing this time, she replied, "Let's not waste your good mood. She's right outside, in the van. I'll get her." And before I could say anything, Dee was out the door. Seconds later, she bounced back through the door, leading another, much taller blonde by the hand.

"Ross McInerney, meet my partner Pearl Johnson."

I remember standing there with not only my mouth wide open, but my robe, too. Agape, I think it's called. Eventually, the other female said, "Dee, he knows me by a different name."

I finally found my voice. "Salome... Where in the—I mean, where have you been?"

She looked at me with the most compassion I'd ever seen in someone's eyes. "Ross! I can't tell you how much I've missed you." Walking up to me, she placed her hands on my cheeks and kissed me right on the lips. "Oh, how I've missed the feel of your lips."

After his index finger had stopped awhile, I switched off the Beatles' "Let It Be" and gazed at Ross's sad gray eyes. I soon couldn't see him, so I wiped my eyes on his blanket. I started to wonder what a toll all this storytelling must've had on him and whether I'd ever hear him tell some of his story with his own mouth.

Chapter Twenty-Eight

After catching my breath and throwing back a couple shots of the E & J, my mind-reeling began to slow a bit after seeing the first love of my life, Salome Stephens. My first question for her was, "What IS your real name anyway?"

As she prepared to answer, I took inventory. She appeared barely a day older than the night we'd met seven long years before. Her hair was cut in a neat bob and she wore a white sweater that complemented her nearly-platinum locks. As far as I could tell, Salome hadn't gained a pound and still possessed the body of a fashion model. After only a moment, I realized I was still in love. "Dear, dear Ross. I'll be glad to tell you my name, but you must promise not to tell anyone. It would blow my entire cover if you did." She leaned forward, cupped her hands around my ear, and whispered, "It's Sally, Sally Fontaine."

My first thought: I wondered why she hadn't just said her name out loud as I figured Delilah knew her actual identity. Secondly, I wanted to be alone with her and ask the four questions I'd saved for seven years: Why had she disappeared & abandoned me in San Francisco? Why hadn't she entrusted me with her situation as an undercover cop? How much older was she than I? And my final concern: How could we get rid of Delilah, so we could spend some real time together?

Coinciding with my last thought, Salome turned to Delilah.

"Dee, be a dear and take the van back to the station. I'll be here with my friend for more than a bit. Thanks, Hon."

Although the expression on Dee's face spoke volumes, the Reader's Digest version said: "I can't believe you're ditching me. Ross used to be my boyfriend, you know!" The age-old adage of a picture being worth a thousand words certainly proved true in her case. I saw instantly who the leader in their relationship was; and the realization thrilled me to no end.

No sooner had the door slammed than Salome began her story. "My first job as a narc was at Roosevelt High, when I was totally wet behind the ears. What a rookie I was! I had no clue what I was doing and let myself get distracted way too much."

After a lull of several seconds, I piped up. "Distracted by what?"

Giving me her soul-piercing look, she said, "You." Which is all I needed to hear to validate our relationship. Or, was it all I needed? Was she trying to con me? After all, a narc's stock & trade is deception. I remember thinking, 'I'll have to listen, wait for the truth, and see.'

"Go on." I still couldn't bring myself to call her Sally. Salome was as much a 'Sally' as I was a McCartney.

"My boss saw right away I wasn't prepared for that first assignment. And, my first partner proved right away to be a bust, so I was inside TRHS without any backup."

"What did you do?"

"My boss decided we needed a face-to-face meeting, but instead of him coming down all the way to see me, I had to find a way to see him."

A thunderbolt hit. "Whoa! Hold on. Your boss was in San Francisco?"

Salome took a poke at me. "Hey, you weren't supposed to figure me out so quickly. I'm supposed to be a 'woman of great mystery.'"

"Yeah, well, maybe you're a 'woman of great mystery' to a helpless fourteen-year-old boy who had a total crush on you, but not to grown men. So, who was your boss?"

"Well, I can't tell you exactly..."

"Can I guess?"

"Okay, you get three guesses, but the first two don't count."

"That's okay – I'll guess his identity on the first try."

Naturally, the only guess I could take was the hippie we stayed with who'd picked us up hitch-hiking. More amazing than this revelation – that Rusty was a dope-smoking, commune-running hipster – was that I couldn't care less about any of that - not her career; not our shared past; nothing. All that mattered was us - now. And, I hoped she felt the same way.

For the first time since we'd met, Salome displayed sheepishness. For someone who lived a double life she seemed quite transparent. I decided to head her off at the pass, so I jumped in as an attempt to quell the awkwardness that had sprung up &

squelched the vibe between us. "I don't have many questions, believe it or not, but the first one I do have is: what do I call you?"

The patches of rose on her cheeks darkened. "You have the chance to ask me any question under the sun, Ross, and you start with what to call me? Maybe this won't be nearly as difficult as I thought it would be. Call me 'Salome.' After all, Salome is my real name."

"But what about 'Sally Fontaine'? I thought ***that*** *was your real name."*

Scooting next to me on the sofa, she placed her hands on my face and whispered, "Ross, is your mother here? Delilah said she might be."

I laughed. "No, Mom doesn't live here... anymore. I was just messing with Dee."

When her face returned to normal, she smiled. "Good, so I can divulge my identity without worrying about anyone else knowing. Unless, of course, that thing is running." She pointed to my tape recorder.

"No, it's strictly for my mother's talks. She stops by weekly to dispense me wisdom, which I try to capture on that. So, in case I need to know someday – what ***is*** *your real name?"*

"Salome Fontaine. The name on my birth certificate is Sally Salome Fontaine, but I've always gone by Salome - except at work - where my name changes on a regular basis. When I started in law enforcement, I didn't think it mattered if I used my middle name, but

I learned soon enough – after meeting with Rusty – that I shouldn't use any part of it. Any information out there about me might not only compromise my safety but jeopardize my coworkers and the success of a given operation. Once an agent's cover is blown, everything else is compromised. Anyway... what I really want to do -- "She took my hands in hers and gave me another soul-piercing look. (I sure hoped it wasn't an act.) "What I want to do, Ross... and I don't care how long it takes... is to not only catch up with you but to reestablish trust between us. Will you let me into your life and allow me to rebuild that trust?"

I took my hands away and rubbed them together numerous times. After a deep breath, I said, "I know this sounds foolish, but I won't let you rebuild the trust that existed between us."

She dropped her gaze and, after inhaling deeply, said in a whisper: "I understand. I am so sorry I lost your trust. I don't know what else to say, Ross."

I smiled. "Good! Because you don't have to do anything at all to reestablish the trust between us. It never was disestablished. I trust you as much today as I did when we hitched to San Francisco and spent all that time together."

Judging by the look on her face, I could've easily knocked her over with a feather. "Are you serious?" she asked, maintaining a whisper.

"As a heart attack. Come here." I pulled her to me and we kissed for the second time that day and held each other for the first time in seven years. And, you know what's strange? It seemed like

it'd been only seven minutes since the last time. I can't explain this phenomenon of familiarity between us other than to say I was finally home... again.

Since I'd placed both headphones over Ross's ears, I'd forgotten the song's title. So, I tried another experiment: I tapped out on his arm, "What song were you just listening to, Ross?"

And, to my shock, he tapped back, "'Good Vibrations' by the incomparable Brian Wilson and the Beach Boys." And right when I thought he'd finished, he tapped some more. "By the way, I've been wanting to ask you something."

"Yes?" I tapped.

"What's your name?"

Even though I was thunderstruck, I shook it off. "Pammy. Call me Pammy."

"I'm glad to know you, Pammy."

It took me the longest time to reply. It must've been two minutes before I stopped crying and another minute before I wiped the tears off my face and hands. "Ross, you will never know how glad I am to know you, too," I promised without tapping. Then, the tears started to flow. So, after I wiped my face, I did what I'd wanted to do since I first laid eyes on him - I hugged him.

Chapter Twenty-Nine

Like I've mentioned before, I've been learning some new words. It's as if my brain's making up for all the lost time in school when I learned nothing. But, now? Boy, I'm learning double-, maybe even triple-time! I now read anything I can lay my hands on, including the dictionary. My vocabulary has grown *exponentially*. So, my newest word is one that really troubles me - *conundrum*. I looked it up, and the first definition best described the situation I found myself in: "A difficult, confusing problem."

Yes, that's what I certainly have now – a dang conundrum. The situation with Ross, of course, is what I'm talking about. After all, here's a man with no identity and no known past or background who hasn't received any health care for years and has been forgotten or given up by the people in his life. And, suddenly - without reason - he starts responding to just one person, someone with no expertise whatsoever in any branch of medicine. And that one person has no right to be touching him, much less giving him care in the form of 'music therapy.'

So, even though you've probably guessed my *conundrum* already, I'll explain anyway. I've discovered - through playing music for him - not only Ross's identity, but some vitally important information about him, too: his background, his family, his hometown, even his darkest, most private secrets. Hey, I know more about the man lying in that bed than almost anyone else on earth.

(Almost; and no, I haven't forgotten the two women who love him so very much – his wife and mother.)

You're probably thinking: "So what, Pammy? Just tell someone at your hospital." Well, it isn't that simple. I mean, let's forget about me for a second and the fact I could lose my job and face criminal charges for what I've done (or, more accurately, what I *haven't* done). More than anything, I worry about Ross. I mean, what if I had told someone here about this whole amazing situation? What if I'd informed Dr. Speckman about what was going on? First, she'd probably have me admitted for being psycho or delusional. And second, I'm sure she'd tell the hospital board and state of Georgia about me not telling her or anyone else about Ross's mental status and that I've known he could communicate awhile now. Holy moly. See what I mean about being caught in a big old *conundrum*?

So, what I decided right then to do was...... nothing. At least, not yet. I wanted, at this point, to learn more about Ross and maybe hear from him directly what'd be best for him. I mean, what could another week or two hurt? It certainly couldn't harm him like the head trauma and coma he's been in for the past two & a half years. Even a blind man could see he was improving, thanks to this therapy I stumbled across. In fact, me waiting until I've heard his whole story might end up being the best thing I could ever do for him. *Consequently*, I decided to play all the songs on Ross's playlist. Here comes his next chapter.

Salome and I reentered each other's life in August, when she'd been preparing for the new school year. The FBI, her employer for seven years, decided to place her once again at Theodore Roosevelt High School, my alma mater. The Bureau suspected a huge drug trafficking network included my old school. A powerful Mexican drug cartel had invaded southern California, with deep connections in San Bernardino.

The day we reunited, Sal told me about it. In fact, for three days and nights, she told me virtually everything about her career, her past, and anything else I wished to know. "Full disclosure," she said. "I won't hold anything back, Ross, because I owe you at least that. So, if there's anything - anything - you want to ask me, I'll give you the most complete answer I can."

During those three days off work, she spent every minute with me. On the first night she called Delilah and asked her to bring a bunch of her clothes over. When Dee arrived, Salome answered the door, spoke to her for just a moment, received the clothes, and bade her goodbye without inviting her in, which was fine with me. I was, after all, not used to talking with anyone besides my mother once a week, so two visitors at once would've been too much; and Salome probably sensed that. She said: "I want you all to myself. I'm not sharing you with anybody; not Delilah, not your mother, not anyone."

But, before you jump to the conclusion we had ourselves a three-day orgy, let me set you straight. We not only didn't have nonstop sex, we had no sex. At all. I was in no condition to dive headlong into another relationship after losing my wife. However, I did want to ease my way in, to become acquainted with Salome in every other way before we got intimate. After all, when I'd last seen her I was a mere fraction of the person I'd become seven years later. Plus, my bride and soulmate-for-life had died next to me less than a year before, so I had a lot to recover from.

You might wonder what we did for three solid days and nights. After catching each other up on our past seven years, I showed Sal some of the lyrics I'd written and played her some melodies I'd been tinkering with. Then, I got inspired; inspired to complete my songs and play them for my long-lost love. Although some were about Julie, most were not. I wrote two about my mother, a few about Salome (including our trip to The City), and one about my dad.

I spent the first full day going through my stacks of lyrics, reading the most promising to Salome, and then setting them to music. She helped me by listening and commenting now and then. Sal's the perfect audience because she strictly sits and listens. However, she claims to do more than that. "I drink in your songs, Ross. I sip, taste, savor, and swallow before digesting each song fully. I can't explain it any other way, Hon. I drink in your whole performance: your movements, your guitar playing, your words, and... your singing. And, you want to know something super cool? I always thoroughly enjoy you because you're a gifted storyteller and musician who can transport me wherever you like."

Wow, I thought. Where, in the world, have you been all these years? Of course, as soon as I had that thought, guilt overcame me. But then the reasonable side of me realized if Salome had been in my life for the past seven years, I wouldn't have met Julie; we wouldn't have had our relationship and - to a lesser extent - I wouldn't have a chance today to play professionally. Also, that moment of reflective guilt was worthwhile because I wrote a song titled "Guilty Love."

On that first day, I completed ten songs. I know it's hard to believe, but I became so inspired by Salome being there and listening that I couldn't help but create & produce. Besides, the heavy lifting – writing lyrics and choosing melodies – had already been done.

The next morning after breakfast, Salome recorded me playing those ten tunes on my tape recorder. Although it took much of the day, it wasn't at all a hassle. Some songs required many takes before I was satisfied enough to not erase them, while others took only a try or two. It's funny - the best of the batch were the ones that only took a single take. These were the songs that seemed already formed, as though already existing somewhere in the ionosphere before settling into my brain, after which I simply played them out on my six-string. Perhaps great works of art are never actually created by one artist but pre-exist before entering the author's consciousness.

On the third day, we rested. Well... sort of. Salome suggested we have a picnic. It'd be the first time in a year I'd ventured out of the house. I was shocked my Mustang started on the first try. (My mom later confessed she'd turned the engine over every Saturday during her visits and sometimes took my car instead of hers to the laundromat.)

"Let's go to Glen Helen Park," she suggested. When I said I'd never been, she described it as "a huge park at the base of El Cajon Pass with panoramic views of the San Gabriel and San Bernardino Mountains and hundreds of trees. It's one of my all-time favorite spots."

We packed my car with a picnic basket, two blankets, and my guitar and made the short trip to the park. The weather was so remarkable that even San Bernardino glowed, bereft of its usual dinginess and smog. We chatted and laughed all the way to Glen Helen before Salome said, "I know just the place to set up camp. You'll love it, Ross." I followed her directions to an outcropping of Douglas firs sitting on a knoll overlooking the entire valley. Perfect.

Soon after we laid out our spread, an old bus pulled up and let out fifty or more children apparently on a church youth group trip. Although well-behaved, they were typical kids reveling in getting out of the bus and into the outdoors. Consequently, they were lively. And loud. There was a nearby shelter where the adults prepared their collective lunch, while most of the kids played near our little spot. Although I've always enjoyed kids, this large of a group didn't prove conducive for a quiet, romantic picnic. However, we laughed about the chaotic scene and ate Sal's barbequed chicken and potato salad along with some Oreo cookies and soda pop.

Shortly after we finished eating, Salome asked me to play my songs, so I did. After I'd finished the sixth tune, the noise level of the kids hadn't subsided, so we packed up and left. On the way back, Sal touched my arm and broke the silence. "Ross, I have to say something."

"What's that, Hon?"

She laughed. "Your music is amazing. It is literally begging to be heard." She then squeezed my arm and planted a big kiss on my cheek.

We spent the rest of the day lounging & watching game shows, competing during 'Concentration' and 'Jeopardy.' 'Match Game' with Gene Rayburn and his cast of crazies cracked us up quite a bit. Overall, it was a laid-back day spent snuggling and kissing.

⁂

September arrived along with the new school year, so I didn't see Salome much, except for weekends. She explained she needed to lay low on school days, so we chatted on the phone every night and spent considerable time sharing how each of our days went. Before we knew it, summer left and October arrived, which was fine with me. I've always loved autumn and that year we had a cool fall, so there was lots of foliage to see and enjoy.

One weeknight, out of the blue, Salome called. "Be ready in ten minutes. I'm taking you out to dinner." So, since I presumed we'd be fine dining, I threw on a white shirt, sport coat, and my least worn pair of Levi's.

When Sal appeared in a crop top and ripped jeans, I had to laugh. "I thought we were going somewhere special, Sal."

Smiling brightly, she pecked me on the cheek. "We are. Lock your door and follow me." Guess where we wound up? Glen Ellen Regional Park. Salome had again packed a picnic basket, this time with pasta, salad, a bottle of Sonoma County's best wine, and two blankets.

Riding in her '63 Falcon Sprint convertible, we returned to the spot where we had our first picnic. This time it was not only quiet, there wasn't a soul in sight. Since it was an hour before dusk, we had enough light to eat our pasta, sip wine, and enjoy each other.

An hour later, with a couple glasses in us and the pull of romance tugging away, we made love for the first time. Our two blankets sandwiching us harked me back to seven years earlier when we'd lain between our zipped-up sleeping bags and slept so peacefully.

I won't describe any of it, but let's just say it was the most heavenly experience I've ever had, and that evening will always occupy one of the most special places in my heart.

Hey, Gang. I had become so relaxed by the time this story ended that I was woozy, as if I'd been intoxicated by their love & lust for one another. I switched off Van Morrison's "Moondance" and continued to savor the memory as though it were my own.

Chapter Thirty

I don't know how else to explain or describe it, but our special 'dance' beneath the full October moon stirred us both for several weeks afterward.

During this time, a great deal happened. I fully emerged from my longtime funk and began creating like I never had before. Every morning I rose from bed with a spring in my legs and a purpose in my mind - to create meaningful music. I decided to no longer write for money or an audience, but for myself and for Sal. When I'd finish polishing a song, I'd record it on a sophisticated reel-to-reel machine Salome bought me for my birthday. "Ross, you're a serious music maker now, so you need this serious music-making machine." And since I only saw her during the week at night, my days were devoted to writing, reflecting, reading, and exercising. Jogging had swept the nation, thanks to folks like Jim Fixx, and I was swept up with virtually everyone else. After just three weeks, I found myself running three miles every day. I soon became a "lean, mean songwriting machine," according to my beautiful muse & audience.

One weekday afternoon in mid-January, Salome showed up. I couldn't help but instantly notice her odd facial expression and awkward body posture. After pacing in my tiny living room for a time, she plopped next to me on the couch and clasped my hands. Looking me squarely in both eyes, she said: "I've got a confession to make; actually, two confessions."

I thought: Oh no, I'm about to get 'The Talk.'

Her sheepish nervousness mitigated her loveliness. There was an unmistakable, but indefinable something about her that deflated her beauty somehow. I just wanted her to tell me whatever was bothering her, so she could return to her normal state of calm and collectedness. "Lately I've been doing something behind your back, and I need to get it off my chest."

My mind reeled, and I had to literally catch my breath. Then, it was her turn to gulp air as she told me what was troubling her so much. "I know you haven't seen me during the day lately and you probably thought I was at work, but I wasn't. In fact, I'm no longer an FBI agent. I gave my notice a month ago, so I haven't worked since before Christmas."

"Okay. Well, I guess we'll deal with that, but I sense you have more to tell me."

She laughed irregularly. "Boy, do you know me! Okay, here's the rest of my confession: I took something valuable of yours and shared it with people you don't know."

My mind really reeled now. What could she be talking about? I didn't remember anything missing. I asked myself what I had that was valuable enough for her to share with someone else. Unless it was she, she was talking about, but she wouldn't refer to herself as the "something valuable of yours" that she "shared with people" I don't know.

"Now you really have me thinking. Should I start worrying?"

Boy, did I feel weak... and vulnerable.

I was about to blurt out a demand to tell me what it was, when she said, "I took that something of yours, gave it to someone for a couple days, and they still have it."

"What the heck are you talking about? I not only can't stand you keeping secrets from me, but not telling me sooner is unacceptable, Sweetie."

When she laughed again, I started feeling myself getting more peeved. "I hope you don't get mad, Ross, but I... I shared one of your tapes with a record company; well, three different record companies, and you know what? They liked it - a lot. All three labels didn't just like it, they loved it. ALL OF IT!"

"Okay... run that by me one more time, but this time - slower and make sure to include all the details." My hands were chafing away again at each other.

She said she'd knocked on lots of doors in L.A. for two long weeks and managed to get meetings with Capitol, Reprise, and Atlantic Records - and all three wanted to sign me. "So, Ross Honey, you're sitting right in the old cat-bird seat. You can choose whichever label you want, unless – of course – you want your music kept secret. But, what you've got, Honey, is a major bidding war for YOUR songs; for YOUR music; for YOU! So, what do YOU think?"

"I think... you're either the most delusional chick on Earth or the greatest woman ever."

I sat there speechless while Salome described the two weeks she'd spent visiting every record label, minor or major, in Los Angeles and shilling my work. She played a tape of me picking my acoustic and singing my lyrics to a bunch of record executives without having to rely on any traditional salesmanship. I wondered, however, how big a role she'd played in getting these execs – all red-blooded men – to accede to her wish of having me signed to their respective labels. After all, Salome Stephens was one stunningly beautiful girl who could sell iceboxes to Eskimos - provided the Eskimos in question were men.

When she'd finished, she wrapped her slender, toned arms around me and hugged me, hard. I sat there dumbstruck. Finally, she balled her hand into a fist and poked more than punched me. "Well, Mr. Speechless – what do you think?"

"I- I'm blown away - pure and simple. I've never considered shopping my music around, much less getting any of it recorded; and, by a major label? Wow. Those are the three biggest in the business, especially for rock & roll. Come on, Baby. Fess up. You are kidding; right?"

She giggled. "Sure. Uh huh. That's exactly what I'm doing – kidding you. I said to myself, 'Why wait till April Fool's Day? Why not start early and conjure up a crazy story to get Ross's hopes up?' Silly boy. This is real, and it is happening, Ross - unless, for whatever reason, you don't want it to happen."

I roused myself. "Okay, I'm down for whatever happens, but..."

"But what?"

"I want to rearrange my songs some and I'll need some real backing, by a real band. I need at least a bass player, drummer, keyboardist, and female singer. And I know just where to get the first three, but the singer might be tough to get... unless, of course, you agree to join us."

Her eyes became as large as teacups. "Us? Who is us, Ross?"

"My old band."

"You can't be serious about me being a singer..."

"Listen, I've heard you sing along to my songs and it's occurred to me you'd be perfect not only as a backup singer, but a lead vocalist, too. You're a soprano and have great tone. You'll be great." Without hesitation, she said she'd be honored to "pick up Julie's torch" and run with it. I was stunned by both her humility and genuine desire to help me.

So, all I had to do was contact Al and Stu, convince them to join Salome and me in this new project, and do a little recording before we meet the labels. After all, my music wasn't 'singer-songwriter folk material.' It was undoubtedly good old, straight-ahead rock and roll.

Luckily, everyone in the band had traded phone numbers in Vegas before going our separate ways. I called Al first, who seemed in a fog, but rallied and soon sounded encouraged by my call. "Yeah, let's do this for my sister... and your wife, Ross." I was genuinely moved by that additional phrase, partly because he wanted to dedicate our work to Julie and partly because he placed my status in his family on equal footing with his. He left me with, "Hey, you're every bit family as if you'd been born into it." I told him that meant a great deal; and when I got off the phone, I took some time to pull myself together. Julie, I realized again, hadn't only been a beacon shining into our individual lives, but the very light that had guided our efforts as an act.

As it turned out, I didn't need to call Stu because he now lived with Al, who promised to share with him my plans to resuscitate the band and include them both. We agreed we needed a new name, and I suggested we choose one that would honor Julie and her many contributions. Al told me he'd think about a name too, and was "totally stoked" about our new project. We set our first rehearsal for Monday at Vince's, and Al said he'd call his uncle to reserve the back room. Except for fine-tuning a few of my new songs, we were set.

⁂

I spent the next few days on one seemingly simple topic - what to name the band. Without Julie, we couldn't continue using Propinquity. However, her memory did need to be preserved, so I got out my yellow legal pad and started brainstorming. Although I jotted down enough to fill up four sheets front and back, I only recall a few of those monikers: The Propinquities, Julie's Jewels, The Jewels, Jewel's Touchstones, and The Sounders.

Obsessed with finding the perfect name, I spent virtually every waking minute for four days racking my brain. As a result, I compiled 426 names, which I whittled down to a short list of 'finalists' and decided to present them when we'd meet Monday night. Sadly, not a single name can I say with confidence represented this band. "I guess my talent lies more in composing music than naming this group," I told myself Sunday night before falling asleep.

⁂

Salome and I, arriving at Vince's just before seven-thirty, were let in by Al. I introduced Sal to Al and we shared a joke about their names rhyming. We went back to the rehearsal space where amplifiers, a drum kit, and various instruments awaited. Stu rose from his stool and gave both Salome and me a hug. He and Al seemed upbeat; in fact, chipper.

"Hey, let's go back to Vince's office and chew the fat," Al suggested, so we did. When we got settled on the couch and chairs, I flashed back to when Julie and I first met here less than three years before. I know I wasn't the only one remembering Julie because all of us sat quietly for some time, but not exactly 'in propinquity.' Instead, a palpable awkwardness pervaded the scene. I tried launching a discussion of a possible name, but it was no use. All we could think of was Julie. We agreed on one thing, though. If we did name the band after her, we'd be constantly reminded of her and her absence – especially while performing on stage.

"Plus," Stu pointed out, "we don't want our newest member to feel like she must compete with Julie's legacy. That would be crazy."

Salome's smile said it all. As much as she respected Julie's memory, it would be nothing but a millstone around her neck to hear her predecessor's name night in, night out. Once I showed the band the charts of my newest songs, it was apparent our material would be way different than the originals Julie had composed eighteen months before.

Al - slapping his thighs like a judge gavels 'court adjourned' – directed more than suggested: "Why don't we just rehearse and jam for a while? Our name will emerge, eventually. After all, wasn't it Shakespeare who asked, "What's in a name?"

"A rose by any other name would smell as sweet," all four of us said before busting into a round of laughter. We then jumped up and rehearsed all the new songs until midnight. Exhausted, but feeling content with our progress, we collapsed in Vince's office. After I presented the finalist list of names, there was a lull eventually broken by Stu. "I remember Julie once saying that songs can be touchstones to life experiences. Ross, you've got songs here that are obviously about not only Julie, but Salome, yourself, your parents, and life in general. So, how about a phrase that conveys that whole concept of songs as touchstones?"

Some of the newest nominees were "Jewel's Touchstones," "Salome's Jewel Touchstones," and even "Salami Jewel." And then one suggestion made by who-knows-who struck the target on its bullseye - "The Talismans of Sound." We all liked it so much that it became not just the name of our new band, but the title of our first album as well.

Not only do we forget who came up with the name, none of us cared. It was as if Julie herself had whispered the phrase into our ears before we unanimously declared it the victor.

We were now a new band with a new name, a new identity, and... a new beginning.

All along Ross & I had been listening to a Jimmy Cliff tune most people know as a 70's soul classic covered by Johnny Nash, "I Can See Clearly Now." This song always lifts me out of my doldrums, so I can only imagine what it must've done for Ross and his bandmates. And, I recognized the name "The Talismans of Sound." They had been hugely successful just three years before.

Chapter Thirty-One

The strangest thing happened again with Ross. His face had this odd, lingering smile; like Mona Lisa's *visage* in Da Vinci's famous painting. Not a big, bright smile, mind you, but a low-key, mysterious grin conveying a sentiment I'd never experienced before - joy. Pure, simple joy. Instead of snatching the headphones off him to hear which song was making him so happy, I started *transcribing* what he had to say with his right index finger.

Simply put, our band was in the penultimate groove. Somehow, we'd captured lightning in a bottle and refused to stop playing until this magic would cease or leave our band to join someone else's. Even after stopping for the night, our mysterious momentum didn't end. In only four days we produced twenty-two recordings of original songs. None of us could explain it, but we knew we were riding a horse named The Talismans of Sound that just might finish first.

We were so buoyed by this creative tidal wave that we weren't in the least bit nervous when we called on the big record labels; well, not until they started talking terms, clauses, and contracts. We looked at each other searchingly, shrugged, and decided to phone the first three talent agents in the Hollywood Yellow Pages.

Salome suggested we interview each of them an hour apart at Norm's Coffee Shop on Hollywood Boulevard. The first one, scheduled at noon, was a middle-aged woman standing five feet tall while wearing three-inch heels. Her graying blonde hair in ringlets, I figured her hairdo must've been inspired by the child film star Shirley Temple. Or perhaps, she had the same look at age four but instead of dropping it as Mrs. Temple Black had in the Thirties, had fully embraced it as her look for life. Miss Melba Flowers showed up twenty minutes late, smoking a Benson & Hedges 100 from an ivory-colored plastic holder held in her left hand while gripping three leashes with her right, attached to three white poodles, which she handed over to her assistant Pepito on the sidewalk before making her grand entrance.

Looking at me between staccato blinks and frequent glances out the window at Pepito and the 'three girls,' she began: "Well, Honey, I can certainly represent you and your little combo. And, I want you to know I won't let the fact you will be my very first rock band deter me from doing my absolute best for all you kids." Evidently, the majority of acts she represented fell under the banner of stage performers – tap and exotic dancers, magicians, fire-swallowers, jugglers, and former Burlesque and Vaudeville comics, to name only some. She provided me a list of the artists 'in her stable' but I didn't recognize a single name from the fifty-some acts. I thanked Miss Flowers for her time, paid for her 45-cent cup of tea, and told her we'd contact her soon about our decision. "Okay, but don't wait too long. I have new acts joining me daily."

After making her equally grand exit, she reunited with Pepito and their troika of fluffy white clouds of female doggies out on the sidewalk. (I hate the term 'bitches' so much I refuse to use it even when it's appropriate and apt – as it is here.) After all the high-heeled clicking & clacking, doggie barks & yips, and non-stop chattering receded into the urban distance, we did our best to not bust out laughing, but…… it was no use. Plus, we didn't just giggle, we freakin' howled; which - of course - caused us to howl even harder. We continued unabated, except for a short interlude when all of us tried slamming the brakes on our locomotive of laughter. When Ms. Melba Flowers reentered to retrieve her cigarette holder from our table, we four tried in our own unique ways to stop laughing. Stu - always the drummer - beat upon our table; Salome, holding her nose, sounded like a teapot almost ready to blow; Al tried holding his breath, but lost much of it when he spat out a mouthful of coffee; and me – I snorted like what I imagined a randy boar sounded like in search of a sow to satisfy his randiness.

"I'd be lost without this," she said, holding up the ivory item. Unfazed by our boorish behavior, she flashed her best 'Little Miss America Beauty & Talent Competition' smile, waved her holder as a gesture of thanks with her left hand while using her stubby, bejeweled right to message a non-verbal 'good-bye, but never farewell'.

When it seemed our train engine of laughter was about to gather its full head of steam and propel us into being booted out by Norm's management, a voice stopped us. "So, you're the band needing professional help… I meant 'representation.' My apologies, of course." I tracked the voice to a bald, bullet-headed man with

Buddy Holly glasses seated at the counter. He'd likely sat there throughout our previous interview, but we hadn't noticed. Dolled up in a white linen suit, he was the first man I'd ever seen to not just wear a pink dress shirt with matching socks, but a turquoise ascot to complete the ensemble. "Greetings. Allow me to introduce myself. Although my SAG card reads, 'Mr. Bernard Breeze, Esquire,' I prefer my clients call me 'Bernie.'"

I stood and invited him to join us while Salome tidied the spot left by Melba Flowers.

Although I fully intended to introduce everyone, Bernie did the honors for me. Sort of. After deftly plopping his coffee cup on the table and spreading his thin, angular arms across the white Masonite finish with red sparkles - thus laying claim to twice his rightful portion - he launched into naming each of us. "Okay," he began, pointing at Stu, "you must be the drummer. I'm calling you Bash because I'll bet that's your style of keeping the beat. Bash, bash, bash." Without waiting for validation of his split-second assessment, Bernie moved to Al. "Alright, this fellow's the brains of this outfit. I can tell by your overall vibe that you - my friend - are a deep thinker, so I shall hereby dub you with the Queen's blessing 'The Professor.'" Turning to beautiful Salome, he brightened. "Ah, yes, there she is – in all her beatific, goddess-like glory – the face of this ensemble. I hereby gift you, my lovely, with the name of Lady... Lady Lovely, the regal beauty so beautiful we forget Joan of Ark's face, which was once said to be impossible." After reaching over and kissing the back of Sal's hand, he added, "It is my great pleasure to make acquaintance with you, dear Lady Lovely." And then, he turned to me. Pausing long enough to look me up and down not once or twice, but thrice, he seemed to consult a data base inside his head before declaring: "And you are, undoubtedly, the pilot of this music machine. You are the creative force behind everything this group will accomplish. You, sir, I dub Maestro. My friend, you are the conductor, teacher, mentor, and the head of this body that will soon be known to the world as 'The Talismans of Sound.'"

If left to our devices, we all would've sat in silence for who-knows-how-long and stared at this oddly attired, uber-confident, nonstop-talking force (or freak) of nature. But, luckily or not, this strange, new fellow did not allow that to happen. "Moving on," he started, "I've taken the liberty of bringing along my dossier, consisting of my three-page resume and an equally long list of clients. Also, a contract of services that the four of you can peruse when I'm finished with convincing you why it is that I, Bernard Breeze (aka Bernie the Breeze), should be entrusted with the entirety of this musical entity's personal management and financial oversight."

For an hour and a half after Bernie began with his pretentious, but effective prefatory remarks, he maintained sole possession of the floor. He explained and re-explained his resume, litany of clients, and the service agreement. Time flew, but only as fast as Bernard Breeze wanted it to. Yes, the man known as 'The Breeze' could control the flight of birds with his hot air. The old joke I'd applied to Salome - selling iceboxes to Eskimos - came to my mind more than once during his colorful, powerful presentation. And before any of us realized the time for our third appointment had come and gone, we found ourselves signing the contract Mr. Breeze pushed in front of each of us.

Moments later, he jumped up, shook the hands of us three guys, kissed the back of both of Salome's hands, collected all the paperwork, and said with a sly smile, "Well, folks, it's been great getting to know you all. I'd stay longer, but I must shift into high gear if my newest act wants to sign a big, juicy recording contract."

After handing each of us his business card, The Breeze wafted out of Norm's and flew off to parts of Hollyweird unknown. And, no, we never did see or meet our third appointment.

Shortly after Ross stopped tapping, I checked his tape and saw Pink Floyd's "Money" printed on it. He certainly had my attention now. I couldn't wait to find out how Bernie Breeze worked out for the band and – more importantly – for Ross.

Chapter Thirty-Two

The next day at noon our new manager & agent called. After schmoozing for less than a minute, Bernie got down to "brass tacks." "Listen, Maestro. I got meetings with all three labels, so I have lots to do to prepare. We'll rap soon, my brother. Give my love to Lady, Bash, and The Professor." Click went the phone before my brain had fully engaged enough to respond or react. This was my first time dealing with an agent, so I had no clue how they operated or – better yet – how they were supposed to operate. All I knew was that everything was moving terribly fast.

Two days later, on Friday, I received a second call from The Bern. "Maestro, I've got two bits of news for you. Which would you like first – the good news or... the other good news?"

I had to play along. "I guess I'd like to hear the other good news first."

"Good. Your band is now a label mate of the Fab Four's, the one and only Beatles."

"Y-you mean w-we're with Apple Records?"

After his pause... "No, Maestro. You're on Capitol, home of the iconic round building."

"Oh okay, cool. And what's the 'good news'?"

"I have gifts for you guys and gal. Let's all meet at Norm's for dinner tomorrow night at seven – my treat, again."

"Well, alright; I guess."

"You what?"

"I said 'I guess,' Bernie."

The tone of his voice turned so quickly it took me a couple moments to absorb the change, but it became sharper, harsher, even angry. "Look, young man. There is NO guesswork involved here. You did want a bigtime recording contract for yourself and your band, correct?"

"Well…… yes. You'd be correct."

"Then what's the beef?"

"None. I have no beef."

"Muy bien, amigo. You had me there for un minuto. Okay, we're bueno then? I will see you all manana, a los siete, Norm's Coffee Shop. Comprende? Bueno. Felicidades, Maestro!"

*A click sounded, and I caught myself staring at my receiver with mouth agape, again. I literally did not know whether to sh*t or go blind, so I lowered myself onto a kitchen chair and took a series of breaths to calm myself down so that, hopefully, neither feces nor blindness would result. And eventually, after my head started to clear, I stood and placed the phone back on its cradle. The shock began to lessen some, but it did persist for several hours, long after I passed on both sets of good news to my three fellow Talismans.*

⁂

The next night, after Salome and I picked up Stu & Al, we

rode in my Mustang to Norm's. Bernie - wearing a maxed-out black and white plaid suit with a pink shirt - waved from the booth farthest from the door. Expecting to see a packet of paperwork at each of our settings, instead were white envelopes with perhaps greeting cards inside. Breeze, smiling broadly and looking not unlike the cat who ate the goldfish, gave a grand wave to indicate we should all take a seat.

"Well, Gang," he began, "tonight is a very special night, a night for celebration. Congratulations on your first recording contract. Capitol Records is thrilled to have The Talismans of Sound as their newest and brightest recording stars, and I couldn't be any prouder of you if you had all landed on the moon." We listened to Bernie for the next half hour, during which he ordered the steak & shrimp special for us all. After the waitress left, our new agent and business partner reached under the table and extracted a bottle of uncorked Dom Perignon, which we passed around, filling our water glasses. We first said a joint toast to the band, then to Capitol Records, and finally to success for all of us. The entire scene was surreal. Here we were... in the heart of heavenly Hollywood, seated in a leatherette booth drinking 100-dollar champagne from alkaline-spotted water glasses while watching and hearing a gaudily clad, effeminate, middle-aged man in a porkpie hat holding court. (Lewis Carroll himself would have doubtlessly approved.)

When the scene could not get one iota stranger, Bernie directed us to open our envelopes, which contained identical Hallmark-brand greeting cards. "ConGRADulations!" was the intentionally, perhaps cleverly misspelled inscription on the front cover featuring a graduate's gown and mortarboard. Bursts of fireworks decorated the corners, and inside the wording went thusly: "We are so proud of you, Graduate, as you step out onto the Road to Success. Congradulations are in order - for a job well done!" Taped to the card was a folded piece of paper, a personal check from Bernard Breeze for two hundred and fifty dollars, which he said was the "advance for our first album." "Get yourself something special. Maybe some new duds for our recording date, which is bright and early Monday morning at the big round building."

⁂

The next few days were beyond hectic, with twelve- to fourteen-hour rehearsals at Vince's store. We all shared a new urgency and desire to not waste even a single moment. Breaks to grab something to eat were held to a bare minimum. And even then, all conversation revolved around the music – our arrangements, tempo, the proper key, four-part harmonies, and anything else any of us had a concern about. Bernie checked with me daily by phone, but he never once made the drive up to San Bernardino to observe a rehearsal.

We all did buy new duds, as Bernie suggested. However, we had no interest in matching our outfits. Each of us had his or her own style, but Salome stood out the most, for darned sure. In fact, we three guys each gave Sal a hundred from our allotments to spend on dresses, vests, high heels, makeup, and whatever else she needed or desired. She was touched by the gesture, but especially grateful for our spontaneous generosity. None of us discussed it ahead of time, but individually took her aside and laid the same amount of cash on her. Before we took off Monday morning for Hollywood, Salome gave a semi-prepared speech punctuated by tears of gratitude.

⁂

Our first session began at nine a.m. and was scheduled to last till four-thirty. The producer, a colorless man in a tweed coat with elbow patches and a loosened bow tie named Fred, stood over us as we sat in Studio 2B and explained the ABC's of recording. We listened as though receiving last-minute instructions from our pilot before parachuting for our first-ever jump from twenty-thousand feet up in the air. I could sense our collective anxiety, but it was a good anxiety – reminiscent of how I felt before the math tests in school I always aced. Bernie Breeze, surprisingly, sat in the rear and didn't utter a word during Fred's talk. I don't know to this day if he was a seasoned veteran of recording or had no clue about any of it, but I do know one thing - he was as quiet as a church mouse.

After giving us a few minutes to set up and tune our instruments, Fred said: "This will be Cut # 1, take one, fellas; er, I mean 'lady and fellas.'" He turned pink, apologized to Salome, and repeated, "Cut one, take one." We jumped into a scorching rocker titled "Love at First Bite," a send-up of a first kiss between a boy and a more mature girl. It was, of course, based on my first chapter with Salome, which began at that dance where we first met.

Within seconds of finishing, I told Fred over the mic that I wanted to launch right into our next number, a ballad titled "First

Love." It, too, reminisced about my first relationship with Salome and featured her on keyboards and me on electric guitar.

Since each of my bandmates had a set list in front of them, they weren't surprised when I informed Fred we'd immediately play a third song, "She Was My World," chronicling the arc of my relationship with Julie – our meeting, dating, wedding, and the sudden, cruelly random end to her life and our loving relationship.

After concluding "World," I told Fred we'd need a moment, but he was shocked it took only five seconds, long enough for me to move to piano and Salome to take the lead vocal mic. "Don't you want a real break?" an awestruck Fred asked when Sal and I were ready to resume; to which I responded by telling him studio time was big money. "Okay, you all are organized & disciplined. Carry on... please!" So, we kicked off "Lonely Even in a Crowd," a composition of Julie's written during her last stint at the Hacienda before auditioning me with the band.

Fred insisted we stop and listen to all four song playbacks. What came out of the speakers blew away not only Fred, but everyone there. He shook his head throughout all four playbacks before leaving the booth to speak with someone. Returning a bit fatigued from his out-of-studio interlude, he slumped into one of the collapsible chairs used mostly by musicians and shook his head again before saying: "I don't know what to say, except to beg you all to continue whatever the heck it is you're doing. Every one of you came prepared and knows exactly what to do and how to do it wonderfully. You know your parts and play them as though it's your fifteenth or twentieth take. So, all I can say is one word to describe your performance, 'Unbelievable.'"

Since none of us had participated in a professional recording session, we had no clue how to respond. We probably looked like four bumpkins from San Berdoo who didn't know better than to overly prepare, which……… is exactly who we were.

After continuing his praise for several minutes, he said, "Now, normally, this would be an amazing output for an all-day, 7 1/2-hour session, but it's only nine-thirty and way too early even for lunch, so… let's see what else you've got and – if you're willing – just try and keep it going. I sure don't want to slow you down with any more of my prattling." Holding up his right hand, he curled it into a circle. "After all, I have exactly this number of suggestions to make so far." We four bandmates giggled a bit nervously before agreeing to his proposal.

With just five songs left on our 'set list,' we played them in order. "Undercover Lover" told the tale of a teenaged boy dating a girl narc in high school. A mid-tempo rocker replete with jokes and puns, it featured a lively exchange between Salome and me. "Fame Found (Amidst the Neon)" retold the saga of our second run at the Hacienda, which ended in Julie's tragic death. However, I chose not to include any lyric about her passing as I felt we already had plenty of songs with tragic themes. After all, this was our debut album and we didn't want to brand or cast ourselves as some maudlin, morose band.

After recording six cuts, we hadn't required a single second take. "Amazing," Fred continued chanting as we continued. Our final three songs didn't disappoint either. "Leading Lady," about Julie paving the way for our band, took up the seventh spot while "Long-Lost Dad" - about my father's vagabond musical ways - followed. Then, at 10:15, we launched into "San Berdoo Rescue," my true story of being rescued by Propinquity in San Bernardino to pursue success among the glitter and gold of Las Vegas. Slightly reminiscent of Creedence Clearwater's "Lodi," "Rescue" seemed the perfect coda to our first album. However, as fate would dictate, our album wasn't going to be completed as quickly as we'd ignorantly thought.

This time, I placed both phones on Ross's ears, so when he stopped tapping I had to check the tape's inscriptions to see what song had been playing throughout this latest chapter. "Dream On" by Aerosmith provided the soundtrack for his greatest achievement so far.

Chapter Thirty-Three

Since Ross and his new band seemed to be on quite a roll, I didn't have the heart to change the song. I did notice something significant when I replayed the song the following day. For the first time in this entire process there was something noticeably different about Ross - his color or skin tone. No longer did he have the pallor of a comatose patient but an actual blush on his cheeks. Even without any medical background, I knew this had to be a positive sign. So, I went ahead, played this for him, and here's the true story he told:

When the band huddled during our maiden session, I said to them: "Look, we've got all this studio time booked, but we're basically done with our first album. Anyone got any ideas?" I looked at each of the other three but received nothing but blank stares. "Good!" I exclaimed, to which they all busted up. I told them what I had in mind, and they all agreed to the plan. "Take ten, but don't get lost in this honkin' huge building, okay?" They laughed but stayed in place.

When I told Fred my game plan, he exclaimed, "You're kidding, right? That is so... unprecedented!" He held his head for a moment. "Okay, well, if it doesn't work out today or soon, it can always set in a can somewhere in our warehouse, I guess. As I like to say, 'Nothing ventured, nothing gained.' I'll tell the engineers and then we'll be ready for you."

What I'd proposed to the band and then to Fred, was we go ahead and record another nine songs, which could - potentially - comprise sides three & four of what might be a double album. Since I hadn't anticipated this happening, I had to sit for a few minutes at my pretend drawing board and put together a second set of original songs we already knew. Granted, this second set might be a bit rougher than the first, but we'd already practiced, revised, and re-rehearsed it at Vince's, so it wasn't like these songs were strange to any of us.

Here's what I came up with: The tenth cut would be "Bright Lights, Glitter City" about life in Las Vegas - told in a fairy tale narrative style. Next came "Your Smile Sears My Soul," another 'lost-love' song about Julie, followed by a companion piece titled "After Love's Death: A Blues Movement for Piano and Solo Voice." Rounding out the third side was "Mother Mary Comes to Me" about my mother's counsel, which – of course – we had to change to something not sounding like the Beatles lyric from "Let it Be." "Dear Abby has Nothing on Her" was the title I scribbled down on my 'drawing table.'

The fourth and final side began with "A Hole Inside Me Only You Can Fill," followed by "Surmounting the Void," a song of redemption after a great loss. I sat there identifying the songs to fill sides C & D but hadn't thought - until then - how to group them. I recalled how Julie and I met that first night at Vince's and how I'd floated the name Propinquity by her and then Al and Stu; and how this second band was a newer, revised, and perhaps improved version of that unit. So, I took one eighteen-minute song and chopped it into bite-sized, radio-friendly durations. I ended up naming cut # 16 about first meeting Julie, "Propinquity: Suite One;" cut # 17 became "Propinquity: Suite Two," about the band's interlude of collective silent satisfaction after rehearsing the first time; and "Propinquity: A Finale" about the present band, which now included my first actual love, Salome.

We reconvened and played the second set straight through, start to finish, completing nine songs in forty minutes & twelve seconds. Shortly after completing the "Propinquity" finale, Fred sat with us and told us we'd done "remarkably" on all eighteen cuts and he had no reason to replay or re-cut any of them. He did leave open the possibility of some 'final touches' in the control room after the session but even doubted that would happen. "I want you all to take a super-long lunch break, like three hours. I need to go upstairs and convene with management regarding this project. Let's all meet back at 2:30."

Fred shook everyone's hand, including Bernie's, before leaving the studio. Breeze exhaled loudly. "Well, Gang, I don't know what this producer's going to do, but it sounds like he's very happy, thrilled even, about our progress, so let's go to lunch. My treat." Naturally, he took us to the Norm's on Hollywood Boulevard. None of us minded because the place was already familiar, and we knew nothing about dining out - except for the Haciendas' coffee shops. And since Norm's was located "in the heart of Hollywood," we four musicians were all under the impression we'd see some big-time show-biz celebrities. I ask you: Were we naïve or what?

⁂

After piling into my Mustang, we followed Bernie's Plymouth Valiant to Norm's, where we feasted on the lunch special: chicken-fried steak & mashed potatoes, peas, cherry compote for dessert, and coffee or tea (all for the outrageously low price of $2.99). After leaving the diner, we checked out the stars embedded on the sidewalks on both sides of the street.

Bernie practically took us by the hand and showed us where many of the old-time stars of Vaudeville and the silver screen were honored with their own four-tile square 'monument.' You name it and he recognized them, either directly or by reputation. He especially knew the dancers and musical film stars; and not just their names. He regaled us with anecdotes about most of them. One I still remember went like this: "Bobby (not his real name) could dance like the wind, even better than Fred Astaire, but what both defined and ruined Bobby's career was his prolific love life. That boy was Hollywood's number-one skirt chaser, bar none. Name any starlet in the Thirties, Forties, or Fifties and Bobby KNEW her... you know, in the biblical sense." So then, of course, we took turns guessing if Bobby had 'known' this or that actress, dancer, or singer; and, in most cases, Bernie answered in the affirmative. "Yes, kids, he was the most prolific lover of women this town ever saw, including the great Rudolph Valentino, whose reputation was manufactured. You see, old Rudy was as fruity as your average orchard. Yes, it's all true, kids."

Before we knew it, it was time to return to Capitol's cylindrical tower.

Fred entered the studio shortly after. Without mincing words, he dropped a bombshell. "Lady and gentlemen, I have some rather... odd news to break. If you could all please take a seat, I will try to explain." After settling into chairs and the communal sofa, he continued. "In all my years of producing records, I've never had to say what I'm about to tell you folks now. Your album not only does not require a single dub or change, but "The Talismans of Sound" will be released in the shortest time I've ever seen – six weeks – in an altered format."

Bernie stood, tore off his Panama hat, and blurted, "But you just said there'd be NO alterations, sir. I, for one, think that an 'altered format' as you call it would be an outrage!"

Although I had the greatest urge to grab Bernie's coat and pull him back down to the chair next to me, I demurred. Why? Because I was just as perplexed as he. However, I could tell there was a big "but" at the end of Fred's sentence that hadn't been addressed yet, so I half-barked, "Bernie!" before telling Fred, "Proceed, sir. You were saying?"

Fred laughed sheepishly. Directly addressing The Breeze instead of me, he concurred that it certainly was outrageous what was happening; that he'd never witnessed such an unusual decision by Capitol Records (or any other label, for that matter) and he completely understood our mystification. "But," he said, finally delivering the punchline, "let me be clear. The alteration of which I speak is that management has decided to release your record……" Looking each of us over for precisely two seconds, he completed his sentence with, "as a double album."

Not only were we floored, Bernie was at an utter loss. So much, he lost consciousness. Luckily, he slumped onto my lap, both shortening & cushioning his fall. Although Breeze was only out for sixty seconds, it stands as the record for BB's longest silence in our presence.

Chapter Thirty-Four

Six weeks passed so quickly none of us knew when "The Talismans of Sound" would release, but Bernie had already distributed copies of the double album to each of us two weeks beforehand. Although the cover art hadn't been finalized, we sat as a group and listened to all four sides of the record. Everyone was thrilled with it, but none more than Salome, who told me later alone: "Sweetie, I can't believe how good a job we all did, but most of the kudos go to you. Let's face it, Baby, the whole project resulted from your vision, talent, and genius."

I will never forget those words. Of all the compliments I've ever received, her statement stands at the very top. Not only did Salome love the album as a listener, but as a participant in the process she knew exactly how much perspiration and inspiration went into the entire project. And though the recording was a team effort, I'd written ninety-eight percent of the lyrics and composed every note of the music.

So, our normal, relatively simple lives continued unabated until the fateful balmy day when Salome and I, cruising down Hollywood Boulevard in the '66 Mustang, heard something different on the radio. We were just a block from Hollywood & Vine when a song familiar to the both of us came on KMET 94.7. "Love at First Bite" burst forth from my dashboard speaker, telling the story of Salome's and my first kiss. My foot stomped on the brake and we made a complete stop in the middle of the block. "What the heck?" Sal yelled. It took me a bit to come to my senses, after which I pulled the car over to the curb.

"Our first single, Baby! Can you believe it?" I screamed. I pulled her to me and we kissed passionately. "We have to celebrate, Salome!"

My beautiful lady threw back her blonde head and let loose her wildest laugh. "Well, I don't know what you've got in mind to celebrate because that was the greatest kiss I've ever had. How can you top that?" I answered by promising to do precisely that. Our ride to San Berdoo took forever, but when we made it back to our place, we celebrated a few more times.

⁂

I was so enthralled by these latest developments I found myself in my own cocoon of consciousness. No, I hadn't taken leave of my senses, but I believe my senses had taken leave of me; at least, for the time being. To the point, Ross's face had changed since I'd last looked at it. I was hiding his Sound-About, so I could take a potty break when I noticed the change. His lovely gray eyes had gone into hiding behind his eyelids, which shocked me. At first, I thought his heart might've stopped, so I placed one hand on his chest and the other on his neck to get a pulse. And slowly, I could sense a faint, but steady beat. "Whew," I thought, "that was scary." I was afraid what might occur if I manually opened the poor man's eyelids, so I left them the heck alone.

After I returned and resumed playing music for him, here's

what Ross tapped on my arm:

The entire band was over the moon about having our first single play over the air. Every Top-40 AM radio station in Los Angeles (including the most popular, KHJ and KRLA) and the three heavyweights in FM rock (KMET, KLOS, and KROQ) had "Love at First Bite" on what the industry calls 'tight rotation.' So, if you wanted to hear our song, all you had to do was flip between those 5 stations and you'd get your fill. "First Bite" climbed the charts for three weeks until reaching #2 on the two big AM stations. Suddenly, we were a known entity in the most important record-buying market in America. Disc jockeys uttered the phrase "The Talismans of Sound" continually. In fact, Bernie called to tell us the hottest DJ in L.A., Sammy the Swashbuckler from the wildly popular pirate radio station XPIR, planned on playing our double album - totaling ninety minutes - on his show the following week, and called to ask if we would appear as guests on his show.

Since it was the first request from any station for an interview with us, we accepted. In fact, we leapt at the offer even before we heard the details, the most noteworthy being that the station was an illegal FM outlet in international waters started by a renegade, possibly 'looney toons' DJ known as Sammy the Swashbuckler (or "Sammy Swash," as he called himself on the show). Of course, The Breeze was ecstatic. He'd been tuning in to Sammy's show every late night for the past month. "This dude is off the charts crazy, but he's also pulling down the highest ratings in L.A. history. He might be wacky, but who cares? Just one spot on his show could catapult your star to the zenith of the constellation we call Fame."

So, after rehearsing one night in San Berdoo, we got a call from The Breeze's assistant. "You're about to receive an invite to appear on Sammy's show, but you'll need to call 555-6969 and Sam the Swash will rap with you directly." So, I did. Picking up on the second ring, a resonant, fortyish voice intoned: "Pirate radio, Captain Kook, aka Sammy the Swash at your service. Argghhhh! Who might this be?" Enunciated in a British pirate accent, Sam sounded crazed, but a controlled crazed.

"Sam, this is Ross from The Talismans of Sound."

"Arrgghhh, Matey. Shiver me timbers. What say you pay us a visit on deck Friday night? You, your band of brothers, and the beauty with a capital B should all show up at the Long Beach marina, find the Shady Sailor, and shove off at midnight sharp. Don't be late, Mate. Argghhh!"

A woman named Raven came on the line to confirm everything. We'd take the Shady Sailor to somewhere out in the Pacific before transferring to another craft, where we'd interview with Sam between cuts from our album. She didn't ask us to call again, but ended with: "We're all set, Matey. Sam and I will see you early Saturday morn. Wear good shoes."

On Friday night the four of us rode together to Long Beach in my 'Stang' and visited The Pike, a doddering amusement park on the rickety, splintered pier constructed sometime around the turn of the century. Dinner consisted of whatever each of us bought on the boardwalk at the ancient concession stands: corn dogs, corn on the cob, Pepper Bellies (cut-open bags of Frito corn chips with a scoop of chili and onions heaped over them), cotton candy, fresh squeezed lemonade, and so on. Bernie begged out, so it was just the four of us – Al, Stu, Salome, and I.

At ten to midnight we made our way to the marina and spied the Shady Sailor moored to the end berth. In keeping with the decrepit Pike & pier, the Shady Sailor could've been the photo subject for 'rickety' in Webster's dictionary. Painted decades ago with beige and forest green, she now sported dirty brown and a hue I call 'road-apple green.' As the four of us trudged toward her, a green light from the pilot house switched on. However, when no other sign of life appeared, we did the only thing we could under the circumstances – we waited. Consulting our watches constantly, the only sound among our quartet was the chattering of Salome's teeth, so I peeled off my sweatshirt and covered her shoulders.

Since there was no way for us to board, we waited... and waited... and... waited, until a wolf whistle split the silence. Turning around, I spied three men – all with flowing long hair and lengthy beards – clomping toward us in cowboy boots, which sounded more impressive than usual because of the wooden beams & boards under those six boots. The leader – a tall, muscular lumberjack-looking man somewhere in his thirties – guffawed. "Well, well, well – look who's in their places with bright, shiny faces. You must be the Scalliwags of Noise."

The man possessed such swagger I didn't dare correct him,

but I did laugh. Looking past us as though we'd turned invisible, he lifted his blackened fingers to his mouth and let loose a second whistle. "Hey!" he yelled. A moment later, a short Mexican man emerged from the boat's hold, waving broadly. Lifting and then dropping the wooden-framed metal gang plank in place, the little guy smiled and told us in broken English to board the Shady Lady.

No introductions or small talk followed. Instead, we were specifically instructed where to sit on the benches covered with frayed plastic. The 'Boss Man,' standing above us, said: "I'll be back" before climbing the ladder to the deck. The engine soon started and we felt the boat begin to move, first slowly then forcefully. The sound and smell of diesel oil was almost too much for us, restricting our talk and breathing. Time stood still while we waited with hands covering our noses for something to happen. That something was instead a who - Big Boss Man.

Standing above us again, he announced, "Two rules – no talking and no looking. Everyone gets these." He handed his assistants red and blue bandannas, which were then tied around our heads – one covering our eyes and the other our mouths. It happened so fast none of us could protest or try stopping them. Luckily, Salome sat directly to my left, so we continued holding hands. Although speech and sight were no longer possible, we squeezed each other's hands and communicated our concern, shock, and reassurance.

As I sat on the tattered, lurching bench, I couldn't help but worry. My mind raced with possibilities, not least of which was we were being kidnapped and might never set foot on terra firma again. The timing of this evening couldn't have been worse since newspaper heiress Patty Hearst had recently been nabbed by a band of revolutionaries and forced to subsist in a closet for several weeks under the direction of an outfit calling itself the Symbionese Liberation Army. And, I suspected this band of ruffians could be an offshoot of an organization like that. After all, they might not even be directly affiliated with Sammy the Swashbuckler. And worse still was the possibility they were in fact a part of his organization, fronted by a man past the point of psychic return. Throughout my review of a dozen other possibilities, I squeezed Sal's hand every so often and she reciprocated, until the strangest thing started happening. I sensed she no longer was simply tightening and releasing her grip on my hand but messaging me. I can't explain it, but I began sensing her transmitting me statements by some code. And that's when my Boy Scout training kicked in. I took about thirty seconds to go over the alphabet before I resumed deciphering her hand squeezes. And, you know what? My instincts were correct. Salome repeated the same three-word phrase three times, which easily translated as "I love you."

I responded in kind, but because I was afraid of scaring us both any more, I asked no questions. All I could think to message was, "I'm glad we can still communicate, Sal," to which she squeezed "Yes, Honey – me, too."

A moment later, the boat slowed before swerving right, then left. We appeared to stop, but the waves continued tossing us back and forth, up and down. Soon, I heard clomping bootsteps descending the ladder. It was Big Boss Man again.

After instructing his aides to uncover our eyes, he addressed us. "Okay, folks. Here's the deal: We're at the station, but that doesn't mean you have free rein to do what you want. I must impress on you all the importance of following my and any staff member's directions, so I need you each to nod your head to show you can hear and understand me. Let's start with the lady, then her man, then Frick and then Frack." He continued, "Here are the rules: No screaming for help. No attempting to flee, which would be stupid because unless you have Navy Seal skills, you will surely drown. Understand?" He looked each of us in the eye and saw we all did.

Whenever I could, I stole glimpses of Al and Stu. The former was as white as the average ghost while the latter appeared as he always did - to be awaiting the next song so he could resume bashing away on a collection of skins and cymbals. Quite a contrast in terms of states of mind, right? I needn't look at Salome to know she was full of spirit and tenacity - understandable given her extensive experience as an undercover cop.

The Big Boss Man nodded to his men to uncover our mouths, whereupon we all exhaled audibly. If it wasn't such a frightening scene, I would've laughed my butt off. We were each led by the hand by a different crew member to the bow of the vessel, where we waited until the plank was lowered by the little Latin, whom we hadn't seen since boarding back at the marina. We marched single file onto a much larger craft, a white yacht perhaps a hundred feet long.

Once aboard, I was separated from the others and led down a ladder to a brightly lit, spacious area resembling a living room. Electronic equipment - two turntables and six cassette tape machines - took up most of a kidney-shaped desk, on the other side of which sat a blond man about forty years of age. Clean-shaven but sporting shaggy, shoulder-length hair was the slim man with the unmistakably bright voice of a career disc jockey. Instead of addressing me, he directed his comments to an unseen entity. "Ladies and gentlemen, boys and girls, do we have a very special treat in store for you this starlit evening! Yes, I'm referring to tonight's special guest – the newest voice joining the club we call 'the pantheon of rock and roll': a multitalented musician, songwriter, and lyricist par excellence... rock and roll's newest find and southern California's very own wunderkind – the one, the only... Ross McInerney, front man for the band making the biggest splash (the effect of a crashing wave sounded, thanks to the push of a button) in album-oriented FM radio since the Eagles. Yes, friends, I refer to the fabulously talented upstart band, The Talismans of Sound, whose eponymous debut double album has risen to the number-two spot on the national charts and all the way to the pinnacle, the acme, the apex - if you will - of Pirate Radio's mast head. Let's give a healthy, hearty pirate welcome to tonight's guest, the uniquely talented Master Ross McInerney, Esquire!"

After another button push, a medley of Buccaneer "arghs" filled the airwaves and the interior of the seaworthy craft. A gleaming smile emanated as Sam finally directed his brilliant blue eyes onto mine. With a barely perceptible wink, Sammy the Swashbuckler addressed me: "Arggh indeed, Matey, and welcome aboard our humble schooner anchored somewhere in international waters, but within radio reach of the slice of America we proudly hail 'the Gold Coast of southern California.'"

I must've been in a trance because it took a very loud squawk from a recording of a parrot yelling, "Wake up, Matey! Wake up! It's time to speak..." to pry me from my reverie.

Bolting upright, I found some words to speak. "Oh, yes. Hi... or should I say, 'good evening'? Thank you for having me on your show, Mister Swashbuckler."

A maniacal laugh sounded, but not from any sound effect. Sammy cackled five whole seconds before announcing, "Yes, folks, you heard right. We have again managed to stun another of our hostages, er, guests. I must admit – we have a mesmerizing effect on most landlubbers." More chaotic, cacophonous effects ensued over the speaker columns before Sam promised an in-depth conversation with me when XPIR would return two minutes hence.

While several fifteen- & thirty-second spots played for various sponsors – Henry's Camera, record store giants Licorice Pizza and Wherehouse Records, and a new department store chain called Mervyn's – Sam introduced himself, shook my hand, and offered me an array of beverages and snacks, which I refused. "Well, if you change your mind, let me know. I'm going to leave this ice-cold beer right here for you to reach if the urge overtakes you.

So, please, sit back, relax, and enjoy yourself. We'll talk about your songs, starting with the first cut and proceed through all eighteen songs from the album. And, congrats on a brilliant first effort, by the way. I was blown away by the depth of your involvement, and I enjoyed the band's playing."

Which reminded me to wonder about Salome, Al, and Stu, but mainly Sal. Sammy must've intuited my concern. "I know you're wondering about your bandmates ... and your lady, so let's put you at ease. They're all doing well and in good spirits, according to my crack staff. Raven will usher them in before too long. Don't you worry. Sit back and enjoy. After all, friend, it's not every day you get to discuss your first album to the largest radio audience in the greater Los Angeles area, which is second largest in the good ol' USA. Alrighty then, here goes..."

My attention diverted to the in-house promo for the station bouncing off the walls. A conglomeration of sound effects, statements, and music spewed from the speakers chained to the walls; speakers with a German brand name I could see began with a K – Kripsch? Klipsch?

"Welcome back, Maties. It is I, your loveable, loyal Captain Kook - Sammy the Swashbuckler - but you may call me Sammy Swash. Arghh-right, kiddies, as promised & advertised non-stop for the past 48 hours, we have onboard our funky frigate tonight the fastest rising star in the galaxy of rock and roll. That's right, friends & fiends, we're graced with a visit tonight from Ross McInerney. Welcome aboard, Ross. Before we remove your gag & blindfold,

let's begin by listening to and then rapping about the first cut of your band's self-titled "The Talismans of Sound" album, which happens to be your first hit single, the vampire-esque 'Love at First Bite.' Open wide, Mates, and take a huge mouthful of 'Love at First Bite.' Enjoy every morsel, ort, and tidbit of this sumptuous aural delight..."

Serving as his own engineer, Sam cued 'Love at First Bite.' What's strange is that after starting the record, the man remained seated in his swivel chair and fell into a nap – but snapped right back to attention as soon as the last note disappeared. "Alright, my friend. May I call you Ross?" To which I nodded and said "yes."

"Okay, Ross. Now, could you please regale our beloved navy of first mates & scurvy privates with the tale of how you came to compose this instant classic?"

This time, not stymied by a frozen brain, I gave a comprehensive account of how the song originated, complete with a citation of the circumstances of how Salome & I first met.

Sam smiled and gave me a double thumbs-up before introducing the second song: "Up next on our sea-swept top deck is the aptly titled 'First Love.' Enjoy this gem of a Valentine, my sweet, but salty dogs." Since this song was so closely linked to the first, we dispensed with all discussion, except for me explaining it described Sal's and my first week together.

We proceeded to listen to and discuss the entire first side before Sam promised Salome's appearance after the next station break. Raven appeared suddenly, followed closely by Sal, who didn't look the least disoriented or dismayed. I figured her training and experience as an officer of the law had equipped her for such a trying situation as being kidnapped, handcuffed, blindfolded, and transported by a sea vessel.

Sam brightened when she sat between us. "Well, well, well! Allow me to kiss your delicate, lovely hand, Miss Salome." She smiled, allowing him to grasp her left hand and kiss it gently. "Welcome, Salome-"

"McInerney," she intoned in a sultry, emphatic way.

Sam blinked twice. "McInerney, but of course! So, you are the lone lady in the group…"

"Well, it depends, Captain."

"Meaning?"

"Well, Sham, I'm the only female in the band, but I don't know how much of a lady I am, especially in… well, tight situations, you might say." I noticed her slighting our host with 'Sham' but it didn't seem to register or annoy him. I couldn't help but laugh at her comments and marvel at how feisty she could be when the right situation and opportunity arose.

"I see. Well, you look very ladylike and luscious to these swashbuckling eyes. So, this next shanty was written about you and your former career as a… a--"

"Narcotics agent, Spammy."

This time the barb did land as he winced before recovering. "Friends and fiends, next up is 'Undercover Lover,' the first cut on the second side of this best-selling double album titled 'The Talismans of Sound'; a song written for & about our second guest, the scintillating Miss Salome, Salome ..."

"McInerney; MISSUS McInerney... matey!"

As I grasped Salome's hand and squeezed it as a statement of caution, Sammy's Adam's apple bounced twice before addressing the mic: "'Undercover Lover,' friends. Ahoy, ahoy. Enjoy, enjoy."

As soon as the cut began, Sam snapped his fingers at Raven, busy at Sam's console doing something with her back turned. He ordered coffees for the three of us. "And plenty of sugar and cream." Raven disappeared out the same portal from which she'd come just moments before. Sam again closed his eyes and returned to napping.

When 'Undercover' ended, Sam didn't engage us at all, but told his listeners, "And now, four back-to-back cuts from 'The Talismans of Sound,'" before shutting his eyes again.

Since Raven wouldn't return for a while, Sal and I spoke non-verbally, finishing with a lingering, open-mouthed kiss that lifted my spirits along with... my spirits. Whatever concerns I had had about our safety were now long forgotten.

As the final notes of "San Berdoo Rescue" receded, the three of us began sipping our French roast coffee. The caffeine must've jolted Sam because he reverted to hyperactive mode, engaging me to discuss the preceding four cuts. Then, he announced the rest of the band would join us after the break, at which time we'd discuss sides three and four.

Checking Ross's Sound-About, I jotted the titles of the Talismans' "Undercover Lover" and Procol Harum's "A Salty Dog."

"Wow," I told myself, "Ross is quite a DJ himself." The *narrative* of his story, supported by a soundtrack he'd *presumably* assembled, had succeeded in truly blowing my mind.

Chapter Thirty-Five

After a full station break, Stu and Al appeared, each led by one of Sam's henchmen / pirates. Folding chairs were placed in front of us, so we sat facing each other in a circle. Both men seemed not only dazed but confused - as though emerging from solitary confinement. I was about to cheer them up or make them laugh when Sam beat me to it.

"Ah, yes! We can now get down to the real nitty-gritty, Mates, now that The Talismans of Sound rhythm section is with us. Hey kids, give a big Pirate Radio welcome to Stu the drummer and Al, The Talismans' bass player. Welcome aboard our sacred schooner, gents. Make yourselves comfy, settle in, have a libation or more, and tell us all about your band's exploits."

Not only did a pregnant pause follow, but neither musician looked in the direction of his interviewer. Being my first-ever interview, I had no idea what to do or say, so I too sat there as silent as a statue. Ten seconds seemed to tick by until the not-so-resourceful Sam the Swash attempted a recovery. "Hey, folks, I know what let's do; let's give ol' Stu and Al a moment to get their sea legs, drink in the salty night air, and settle in properly. Until then, how about we play the first cut on the third side titled 'Bright Lights, Glitter City'? And upon our return, we'll rap with the entire roster of The Talismans of Sound. Cheers to all my fellow buccaneers. Argh!"

Instead of introducing himself to Al and Stu or tending to whatever needs they might have, Sam summoned Raven and commenced a long, whispered conversation. It appeared Sam was trying to persuade his assistant to do something, but she continued shaking her head "no" until Sam gave her a slight shove toward us, after which he got up and left the studio.

Brightening, Raven smiled and asked if there was anything she could do for us, to which Stu replied: "Yeah, you can get us the hell off this crate, and pronto, Sister!"

Raven crouched next to him and whispered loud enough for me to hear: "I can't promise you'll be leaving pronto, but when the interview's over, we'll gladly return you to the mainland."

Al replied, "You're holding us here against our will. There are international laws against kidnapping, you know."

She then said these words to keep us in our seats: "I can offer you any kind of adult beverage you wish – imported beer, French wine, Stoli, Tanqueray. Just name it and I'll bring it. And... I don't just mean beverages either, boys."

So, after they provided the four of us our poisons of choice (Salome - a wine spritzer; me - a Dos Equis; and Stu and Al - Tanqueray & tonics), things began loosening up quite a bit. The band no longer had trouble participating in discussions of the album, especially sides three and four, which played before and after. Sammy began to smile, laugh, rub his hands together, and manipulate his console, dispensing all kinds of sound effects from old cartoons, TV shows, and Three Stooges clips.

When the first strains of "Propinquity: Suite One" began, the tone turned mellower, more introspective, and what I'd label 'fireside comfortable.' The DJ's manic sounds receded, and our host reflected on the three-suite mini symphony. After the finale played out, Sam looked me in the eye for just the second time: "Ross, what was your inspiration for 'Propinquity'?"

"Simple," I replied. "My inspiration was Julie - our beloved, departed bandmate."

After Sam pressed me to elaborate, my mind flashed back on my beloved Julie, her songwriting, and the love we shared. And, just like that, guess who was blubbering like a baby. Al stood, draped an arm around my shoulders, and hugged me. Somehow, he kept it together long enough to talk about his sister and how she'd always been a gifted composer and musician. "Even when we were little kids, she could knock out some Gene Autry or Hank Williams on her plastic Woolworths ukulele. That girl always brought it, no matter the instrument, audience, or occasion. And, with all due respect to Ross - our undisputed, fearless leader of both Propinquity and The Talismans of Sound - Julie's creative, musical vision is what inspired not just 'The Propinquity Suites,' but this entire album. Without Julie's influence, none of this would've been possible: not this album, not this band, not any of this." What made me look up were the large, round drops plopping onto my shoulder. And, guess what? Everything he said was dead-on right. And if I hadn't had so much snot clogging my nose and tears running and dripping here and everywhere, I would've wholeheartedly supported and seconded

Al's comments.

The show, much like the vessel upon which we sat, rolled on. Finally, after Salome slumbered in the crook of my shoulder and Stu & Al snored in harmony across the way, it was time to call it a night. Sam thanked me and us for appearing on his show before instructing his listeners: "Before I close tonight's show, I want to encourage, implore, and beg every one of you fellow pirates listening to run out this weekend to Licorice Pizza, Wherehouse Records, Sears & Roebuck, or wherever else landlubbers purchase fine rock and roll music and pick up this amazing, instant classic album that will be extolled and exalted for not just years, but decades to come. The album, again, is called 'The Talismans of Sound,' and I have had the distinct honor of visiting with the band The Talismans of Sound, led by Ross McInerney, aboard our sailing vessel this evening. Good night, mateys and lassies. This is your old Captain Kook - Sammy the Swashbuckler - signing off and wishing you smooth sailing, a straight course through whatever narrows lie ahead, and a cool, strong breeze at your back until you reach your destination or destiny, whichever comes last. Bon voyage, farewell, ship ahoy, and to all a good night, mateys. Oye! Oye! – here cometh one more farewell in the form of a big, fat, juicy 'Arggghhhh!'"

And that - as they say - was that; our first radio interview was now officially in the books. We had no clue what kind of an impression we'd made, but were all beyond thrilled to disembark the yacht and then the Shady Lady - to be deposited safely on good old, stationary Terra Firma.

⁂

Salome and I awoke in our Long Beach hotel room to the amplified non-stop jangle of a phone. It was Bernie. "Oh, I'm so glad I caught you before you checked out. Guess what? I've got both good and good news. Which would you like to hear first?"

I only heard Bernie's voice because Salome had shoved the receiver into my ear. Although his screaming was gleeful, I couldn't bear it. So, I had no choice but to roll away. Sal laughed and then grabbed the phone & listened to his two bits of news.

After she hung up, Salome hugged and kissed me. "Well, Mr. McInerney, I guess you're quite the sensation not only in the City of Angels, but throughout southern California – all the way from Santa Barbara to Tijuana. Bernie said the overnight Arbitron ratings for Sam the Swash "went through the roof," especially the first hour when just you and Sammy talked. Oh -and not only that - but Capitol is absolutely thrilled and delighted about our sales; so much so that they're wanting – no, demanding! – another album from us already. Can you believe it?"

I don't know if it was all the Dos Equis I'd drunk just hours before or that I hadn't slept more than an hour & a half, but my head ached and pounded like it never had before. All I could manage was a whispered "Can we please go back to sleep?"

"I'd love to, but Bernie's sending a limo to pick us up in half an hour to take us to lunch with some Capitol suits at the Biltmore Hotel. The Biltmore! Can you believe it, Baby?"

"No, I can't. You shower first, Sweetie, so I can catch a few more winks."

I felt Sal's silky naked body embrace & caress me from behind before she promised to make our shower together "unforgettable." And, before I could consult my aching, pounding head, I rose to experience 'the unforgettable.'

⁂

Al and Stu, also hungover & sleep-deprived, filled up the back seat. So, the chauffeur dropped the jump seat for Salome and me. The fog of sleep stifled all communication throughout our jaunt to Hollywood, even though Stu helped himself to a Tanqueray & tonic from the bar inside the Seville. When we rolled up to the Biltmore Hotel's covered entry, I was both awake and aware. Bernie Breeze, wearing a pink & white seersucker suit and a Panama hat Truman Capote would've died for, flashed a toothy grin and shook our hands. "Well, I don't think it's premature to say you kids hit the Mother Lode. Congratulations are in order. I couldn't be prouder of all of you."

Having never witnessed the posh-beyond-words Biltmore interior, the four of us continually elbowed and poked each other as the ornate ceilings, rows of noble Etruscan columns, and glossy, white-veined marble floors marveled us in all their glory. It was as though the Clampetts of "Beverly Hillbillies" notoriety had visited Buckingham Palace on a surprise visit to see Queen Elizabeth. We were all so stunned by the beauty of the reception area and hallway to the dining room, it took several moments for us to recover. When the maître d - outfitted with white gloves, patent leather shoes, and an immaculately pressed uniform - led us up a circular set of stairs to a balcony table above the expansive, ornate dining room, we each acted as though we'd been punched in our solar plexus, depriving us of oxygen.

The big round table covered by the whitest, brightest table cloth imaginable had eight gold velvet arm chairs placed precisely around it. After the maître d seated Salome with great aplomb & finesse, we guys kept standing, expecting the same service. After that awkward moment passed, menus the size of guitars landed in our hands. Our waiter approached and - after greeting us in a foreign accent & introducing himself as Moshe - told us he'd be personally taking care of us before he launched into a ten-minute presentation of the special dishes the chef had prepared. After taking drink orders, he said our lunch companions would join us shortly.

The whole scene changed when Fred appeared. His unassuming, gentle presence was exactly what we needed. The man, without the least bit of pretense, put us at ease. "Listen, guys. Some Capitol big wigs will be here soon, but I don't want them to bug you… at all. So, please remember, they're only here for good reasons. Second, they don't have a clue *about what any of us do. They know nothing about music and couldn't care less about learning anything about it either. Third, their only interest is in making money, which you've already done so very, very well for them. And finally, these suit-wearing big wigs put their pants on each morning one leg at a time, just like you and me and everyone else. Dig, lady and gents?"*

I don't know which got us laughing most – Fred's frankness, his overall goofy, loveable vibe, or that he'd just said, "Dig?" to us, but we did – laugh, that is. All five of us. Fred was like a fresh ocean breeze in a smog-infested city populated by stuffed-shirt execs & phony celebrities. By the time the two appeared, we were in the middle of our third, er- fourth or fifth, drink – so, whatever tension had previously inhabited any of us took the lead of the late, great Elvis Presley and had 'left the building.'

The bottom line of our big lunch meeting was that Capitol Records loved us so much they wanted us to dive right back into the studio and record our second album ASAP. After we completed it, they'd "sit on it" a few months. In the meantime, our first LP would continue to sell like hot cakes while we toured the country opening for Jethro Tull.

The five of us, including Bernie, sat there for a moment - staring at the two execs as though statues, ghosts, or any other entity besides real people delivering what could only possibly be the greatest of news. They told us "no band other than Chicago ever released a double album for their first record"; and, we'd hopefully be recording another double album as our follow-up; that is, if "Mr. McInerney" was "up to the task" of composing enough material to fill out two 33 rpm discs known as 'long-playing records' or LPs.

I was so dumbstruck by the news of touring and doing another album that at first, I thought they were randomly bringing my father into the conversation. Because, after all, I'd never been called 'Mr. McInerney' before. Not that it swelled my head, either. In fact, I was humbled by the usually specious-to-me title. To "properly seal the deal," the big wigs ordered not one or two, but three bottles of Dom Perignon champagne to celebrate.

The song playing this time was Bachman-Turner's "Taking Care of Business."

Chapter Thirty-Six

Right when I thought life could not get any better, it did. After our lunch with Capitol Records, Bernie told us he had two properties he wanted Salome and me to see.

"What do you mean 'see,' Bernie?"

He explained two homes had become available and were such good deals he didn't think we should pass them up. So, thanks to the power of Dom Perignon bubbly, old-fashioned adrenaline, and dumbstruck youth powering Sal and me, we rode in woozy-headed, cloud-sitting silence in the Rolls Royce limo Bernie evidently hired for this purpose. Both residences in question I'd assumed were ranch houses with picket fences somewhere in the San Fernando Valley. And? I could not have been more wrong...but in a good way. We'd soon be luxuriating in the fabulous Hollywood Hills instead of Pacoima, Reseda, or Arleta.

The first property was an adobe castle, complete with three turret towers and red roof tiles shimmering in the sun. I half-expected to see a battalion of King Arthur's guards in full armor wielding lances adjacent to a wide, deep moat, but I did spy a drawbridge in the driveway, on the other side of the electronic fence. "Wow" was the single syllable uttered simultaneously by Sal and me. A three-story structure with a fully operational elevator inside the middle turret, Bernie dubbed the property "The Hollywood Palace." Only the iconic Sleeping Beauty Castle in Disneyland is more whimsical. However, even on this hot day, the insides of the walls glistened with moisture, so I imagined we'd freeze in autumn and winter. We agreed, begrudgingly, it was a showplace, but nowhere Salome and I wanted to hang our hats.

After returning to the Rolls, Bernie directed the chauffeur to take us "further on up the hill." Wending our way up the most twisted road I'd ever seen, we reached a large golden gate with 'Valhalla' written in the fanciest cursive lettering imaginable. And then, at the driver's touch, the sides of the wrought iron gate split between the 'h' and second 'a.' The driveway - composed of painted gold cobblestones - twisted and climbed until we reached a plateau stretching fifty yards or more. Halfway across, our car halted, and we gazed upward at a mid-century modern home of gold trim and panels of smoked-glass instead of conventional windows.

Bernie led us by the hand to the front entry, dominated by a pair of nine-foot high golden doors. "Watch and listen!" he proclaimed before pushing the doorbell. The loveliest tone of carillon bells resounded, welcoming us to Valhalla.

I couldn't place the composer of the familiar interlude. "Mozart?" I asked.

"Bach," Bernie answered.

The double doors swept open. A tuxedo-clad gentleman Bernie introduced as "Smedley, our head butler," led us inside to the grandest foyer I've seen - in film or TV. All the furnishings were made of leather, glass, chrome, or all three. "This is the parlor," Smedley announced.

He then led us through the five-bedroom, six-bath two-story overlooking the glittering gold of Hollywood below. "Wow" was the word Sal and I used exclusively during our tour. Words cannot possibly describe this beautiful home justly, but I must say I'd never seen such a sweeping, awe-inspiring structure as this gold and black beauty.

The master suite, located on the second floor, was the jewel in Valhalla's crown. Measuring sixteen hundred square feet, it featured not one, but three skylights, the largest of which perched directly above the king-sized bed. "You can star gaze to your heart's content almost every night of the year," Bernie whispered as I gazed up through the rectangular window that must've been twenty feet long by fifteen feet wide. As Smedley disappeared through what I assumed was the door to the master bath, I pointed to the bed and asked Bernie, "May we?"

"Please do."

Sal and I looked at each other and laughed. Grabbing hands, we stood with our backs to the foot of the bed. I asked, "Ready?"

"As I'll ever be."

"Let's count it down, Sal." We both said, "Three, two, one!" and fell back onto the bed together, gently bouncing just once. We lay side by side and took in the incredible hue of azure above. Somehow, the yellowish-brown bank of haze and gunk that was the usual air space above L.A. wasn't in evidence. We continued laying there a couple minutes before the piece d resistance materialized. The most brilliant white bird you can possibly imagine flew by. Not

just once or twice, but seven times. Neither of us uttered a syllable as the spectacle progressed. And after the seventh pass, I sat up and said to no one in particular, "We'll take it."

⁂

"Hey, Bernie baby. When can we move in?"

He smiled, swept his Panama chapeau off his graying head, bowed, and answered, "Today, if you like."

"Today?"

"Today."

"Just like that?"

"Just like that."

"And, what about the other place?"

He smiled. "I think it's already taken. You know the party. Two single, young men who just recently struck gold in the music business."

The Breeze, of course, meant Al and Stu.

And that is how we - all four Talismans - moved to Hollyweird.

For the first time since we'd begun our musical journey, I knew which song provided the soundtrack for this latest chapter in Ross's life – the Eagles' "Hotel California."

⁂

The next few weeks are now a big blur, but I recall the biggest developments. The band and I took only three days to record our second album, "The Return of The Talismans." (We agreed to drop "of Sound" from the album's title.) I remember Fred saying when we'd finished: "Gee, you guys are losing your touch. It took you three whole days this time to record two entire discs." He told us we'd already established a reputation as the most efficient band not only in rock, but in all genres of music. I heard it's rare for a band to handle all the instruments without any guest artists or session players to help, but that meant little to me since I was a veritable rookie at recording. All I knew was things were moving at warp speed, which was cool with me.

With our upcoming gig - opening for Jethro Tull on their national tour - set to begin in a month, we had some time on our hands when we weren't rehearsing. The four of us hung out every day and discovered Hollywood, the Los Angeles Basin, and the beaches of California. Although we didn't see much of Bernie, he dropped by occasionally, mainly to lavish us with gifts. Each of us received a brand-new car. Stu got a candy-apple red Shelby GT Ford Mustang; Al accepted a silver Aston Martin like James Bond drove in the movies; Salome got a pink Corvette; and I received an Alfa Romeo Spider Veloce 2000.

As a kid I never had much interest in cars. Girls and music had always topped my list, but now I added automobiles to my short roster of things that excited me. This quick Italian two-seat convertible roadster that could handle any-and-all roads became my newest passion. Although Bernie had intuited which car each of us would like, he really nailed it with my 'gift.' For 1975, this sleek ragtop convertible version of the car that won that year's World Sports Car Championship was the perfect choice for a guy who loved a good adrenaline rush to top off his day and help dissipate the pressures of show business from his consciousness.

So, for the entire month leading up to our tour, Salome and I jumped into "Alfie" and saw the sights of southern California – Pacific Coast Highway, the Mojave Desert, San Gabriel Mountains, Angeles National Forest, the canyons, San Diego, Santa Barbara, and more.

The Boys (Al and Stu) usually followed wherever we chose to go. Between the four of us, we logged 20,000 miles that month. We even took two trips to San Bernardino to see friends and family. My mother, although usually disdainful of anything relating to the music business, showed how proud she was of me by the looks of admiration she flashed on our visits to see her.

I wanted to lavish my mom with gifts, but I didn't have a good supply of cash. However, if I mentioned a need or want to Bernie Breeze, he usually took care of it for me. We didn't think anything weird about him controlling the purse strings, because he'd told us that's "what a good manager does for his clients. There are too many snakes in the Hollywood grass who'd love nothing more than to separate you from your hard-earned money." So, I wasn't too bummed I didn't buy my dear mom a brand-new car to replace the Mustang I'd returned to her. Instead, Bernie had the exterior repainted and the engine rebuilt. When I delivered it to her, she gave me a big hug and told me I was "the best son a mother could ever have."

⁂

When our tour began on October 1, 1975, all four of us had a bad case of nerves, partly because we hadn't yet played a gig as The Talismans of Sound and partly because Jethro Tull was the most popular band in America. Having released their "Minstrel in the Valley" album three weeks before, they planned on interspersing songs from it with tunes from their previous seven albums, including "Stand Up," "Benefit," "Aqualung," "Thick as a Brick," "A Passion Play," and "War Child." Each of their previous six albums had been awarded "Gold Records" in the U.S. while the last three attained either number one or two. And here we were, a band from San Berdoo, hoping to be remembered by legions of Tull fans after our concerts ended.

The first stop was San Francisco. To be accurate, the address of our first venue - the oddly named "Cow Palace" - was 2600 Geneva Avenue, Daly City, California, printed on a ticket I must've picked off the floor and still have. And adding even more hype and unnecessary pressure on the band, Breeze informed us it was the site of the first concert the Beatles played in America. I checked – and they opened their first North American concert tour there on August 19, 1964. And, if that wasn't enough to raise the bar for us, the Fab Four also played two shows there the next year, on August 31, 1965. So, I told myself: Let me get this straight: Our little, unknown band is not only opening for the biggest band in rock & roll for our first public performance, but the site happens to be the venue for the Beatles' first American concert? Instead of these realities building up my confidence, I began thinking I was in over my head both emotionally and musically. If I didn't already have an awful case of nerves, I did when mounting the storied stage for a sound check an hour before we'd play our first note in public together.

"Just forget about all that, Maestro," Bernie told me as we stood center stage in that massive barn of a building, looking out at 16,500 seats, all of which would fill in minutes. Somehow, I couldn't breathe and began feeling a thousand needles pricking my face, arms, legs, and the back of my neck. Luckily, Stu caught me from behind in mid-fall. "Get him some water. Quick!" Bernie stage-whispered to no one in particular.

Sitting on a crate drinking cool water from a Dixie cup, I felt Salome fanning me with a couple programs. I looked up & saw her smile, which was all I needed. Life was good again, and I knew I'd survive the night somehow. And with the love of my life just feet away during our performance, I knew we'd rock this arena surrounded by legions of houses that inspired the lyric "little boxes made of ticky tacky, little boxes on the hillside" written over a decade ago.

I don't recall anything about that first show, except for the sensation of flying high above the mass of humanity. Evidently, a stage hand who'd witnessed my fainting took it on himself to aim two of the five-foot-tall fans in my direction. He placed them just behind the curtains on either side, so a constant wave of cool air buffeted me as I stood center stage performing the most personal songs I'd ever written that were already familiar to the throng staring up at us and singing along. Time seemed to stand still for me that night, so when stadium management rebuked me for playing twelve minutes beyond our allotted time - all I managed was what Salome described as my "little boy's giggle."

If our set annoyed or offended the headliner in any way, we never heard about it. In fact, Jethro Tull's front man Ian Anderson sought me out in the green room after their second set and congratulated us on our music. In his rich British accent, he told me: "Your music is a rarity in today's scene – it's uniquely personal and yet universal somehow. Your first album is a precious collection of incredible tone poems and suites, the likes of which any band would be most proud. Cheers, mate." Long as I live, I'll never forget the man's kind words.

A song describing the suburban sprawl of Daly City, California in 1962, "Little Boxes" by Malvina Reynolds, played throughout Ross's story of The Talismans' debut.

Chapter Thirty-Seven

With that first concert tucked safely under our belt, you'd think we'd be overly confident or cocky. After all, Ian Anderson wasn't the only one impressed by our Cow Palace gig. Several major newspapers and magazines covering the kickoff to Tull's tour sat up and took notice. After just one album & a concert, the kudos, good reviews, and interview requests began rolling in.

However, we were one frightened little band, for which I take responsibility. Why? I was so overawed by the touring process – flying first class, staying at the finest hotels, interviewed by print and TV reporters, eating catered food before & after every show, and playing to multitudes of enthusiastic, adoring fans every night – I couldn't help but go inward. Oh, I partook of the various perks of touring, but I didn't revel in them. Some voice told me not to get carried away with the hoopla; to not take all the attention and acclaim to heart. "It's not who you are," the Voice said. "Remain at all times focused on who you are and don't let your head be turned by the fame, glory, tinsel, or adoration. Remember, this is all transitory and could end tomorrow."

Thus, the four of us hunkered down and pressed on, as though playing dive clubs and smoky lounges, just as three of us had done a couple years while comprising Propinquity. And though we played some big cities on the tour (Seattle, Los Angeles, Denver, Phoenix, Detroit, Chicago, and The Big Apple) in some huge arenas and stadiums (The Fabulous Forum, Joe Louis Arena, Wrigley Field, and Madison Square Garden), I reminded us all we were living in a bubble that could and probably would burst at any time.

The only thing I insisted Bernie do was shield us from the press corps when possible. Consequently, he granted interviews, but only one per day; and then the contact had to be with the entire band and never just me. I made sure he understood I didn't want to set myself up as the big leader or genius behind the Talismans of Sound. So, when our album shot all the way to number one in the U.S. and every music magazine in the country - including Rolling Stone - clamored to do feature articles on us, I insisted every interview include us all. When Jan Wenner made a personal call to Bernie mid-tour requesting a cover photo shoot by his ace photographer Annie Leibowitz of only me, I politely & firmly demurred. As a result, Wenner and Breeze argued back and forth a week until the founder-publisher relented, allowing the whole band to appear on the cover of his legendary magazine. And the piece's title? "The Humblest Band in Rock."

Now, don't get the idea the trappings of success – money, glory, fame – had no effect on us, because they did. They just didn't overwhelm us like they had every other fast rising star in the 20 years preceding our tour, including Elvis Presley, The Beatles, and The Rolling Stones.

The next thing you might wonder about is The Boys, Al and Stu. Were they overrun by women – groupies, hangers-on, etc. – all too eager to attach themselves to each or both? After all, this was

1975 and every band seemingly had a retinue of groupies always a few feet away. Well, Salome and I soon realized while driving all over the Southland that Al and Stu were more than just friends and bandmates; they were lovers. Evidently, during Propinquity's two-year run at the various Haciendas, when the two roomed together, they fell in love. Not only did they never mention it to Julie or myself, they resisted displaying any affection around Salome or me either. Both men had been models of decorum. Neither showed any proclivity for partying, carousing, or debauchery, which thrilled Sal and me because we never worried about their location, status, or state of mind. Except for an occasional bottle of champagne, they rarely partook of any mind-altering substances.

Our days - despite all the crowds, notoriety, and hubbub - were routine. In six weeks of trans-American travel playing our music, we adhered to a simple schedule: Wake before noon, eat breakfast, relax in our hotel before catching a limo to the venue, do a sound check, have our second meal of the day, play our set, hang out together backstage during Tull's two sets, get interviewed by the media, and finish the night by heading to our hotel or catching a flight to the next city. Since we rarely had days off and didn't play consecutive shows in the same town more than two, three times, the tour ended without us realizing it.

In that six-week span, we didn't trash any hotel rooms, have any knock-down, drag-out fights, get chased by crowds of screaming teens, or live out any other rock and roll cliché. Our bottom line the entire tour was playing our music as well as we could for our audiences, all of which were Tull's fans. We managed to not only avoid any bad press or ill will on the tour, we met a ton of people in the business and cemented all kinds of contacts and connections. Most of all, we relished every chance to perform this new music and give the crowds exactly what they paid good money to hear – professionally played rock and roll that closely resembled our album.

Our '75 national tour terminated after a sold-out show on Veterans Day at Madison Square Garden in the heart of Manhattan. It was time to say goodbye to the amazingly talented Tull for whom we'd opened all those shows, fly back to Hollywood, and chart the next steps in our musical journey.

⁂

"I can't believe it, Baby," I whispered in Salome's ear as I tried my best to wake her. "The pilot said it's 78 and sunny in L.A."

Stretching her well-toned body like a cat, she smiled without opening her eyes. "That was quite a dream I had, Ross. You were in it, too. I found out I was pregnant during a doctor's visit and he asked whether I wanted a boy or girl. I thought & thought, before telling him I wanted both. So, it ended with us having twins – a boy and a girl!" She giggled, opened her eyes, and kissed me more passionately than ever. "What do you think about that, Hon?"

Without hesitation, I replied: "That would be perfect, Salome; just perfect."

Kissing me again, she said, "That's what I hoped you'd say.

After all, Babe, we have a lot of bedrooms to fill in Valhalla."

"Whoa," I began. "All in due time, but until then let's enjoy each other."

"Of course, Hon. We'll have plenty of time to make our babies, but we do need to keep making music while the iron is hot."

"Exactly," I said, as I contemplated the direction our band might take on our next album.

⁂

"The Talismans of Sound" not only climbed to the top of Billboard Magazine's American Best-Selling Albums chart during Christmas 1975, but hung on until another album came along to knock it out of the top spot in February. Our second record "The Return of the Talismans" released on January 26, took off like a NASA rocket and almost broke the record for the fastest album to reach number one in only two weeks.

With eighteen songs recorded, we made it another double album. The A side began with "Love at Second Bite," a tribute to Salome and sequel to our first hit ("Love at First Bite"). "Boomerang of Love" - a song about losing my first love, but eventually getting her back - occupied the B side of "Love at Second Bite," our first single from this record. Both songs landed in the Top Ten and held down the top two spots for four weeks. Our third cut, "Lie-Lie Land," is about LA and the traps a musician can fall into in Hollywood, which all begin with a lie. Cut # 4, "Kidnapped," is a veiled tale of our first night with Sammy the Swashbuckler; and closing out the first side is "The Breeze That Blew Us Away," a tribute to our agent.

I received lots of press for writing such "transparent songs," but discovered it to be the easiest, most forthright way to write lyrics. The second side followed in that vein. "Ma, Let Me Watch Sullivan in Peace," about the Beatles' first appearance on Sullivan and my mother's aversion to the Fab Four, was the first cut followed by "Music is a Love/Hate Thing," which examined the effects music has had in my life (taking my father from us and, later, my obsession both as musician and composer). "Professor Fred, Roll Tape," about our record producer Fred Sebastian, came next, followed by a tune about the end of the war, "Good Night, Vietnam." Closing out B-side was "Big House on the Hill," about Valhalla - our new home on a knoll.

Before you assume my songs dealt exclusively with me, I'll show I used a range of subjects in writing lyrics. I found a good formula is to swing the pendulum between the personal and public. Side three opens with "Patty Paige's Pup," about my first remembered song ("How Much is that Doggie in the Window?"). Second was the autobiographical "Is That Me Up on The Stage?" followed by the topical "Good Bye, Mister Nixon." After writing again about my love life, "The Girl is Ultimately Mine," to close Side C, we opened D by paying homage to my earliest musical influences "Brother Ray, Uncle Louis, and Mister Durante." Continuing that vein, I included "Why Do the Great Ones Die So Young?" - about the three rock luminaries who perished during my senior year in high school: Jimi Hendrix, Janis Joplin, and Jim Morrison. Next, was "Hollyweird," another parody of Tinsel Town, which precedes the album-closer about our prior band, "Propinquity Revisited."

While rebounding from our first tour, Salome and I settled into our new home. Although already furnished nicely, my talented lady utilized her decorating skills to full effect - either buying tapestries, craft items, and rugs or deciding to create some herself. She even got me 'hooked' on rug-making. I was trying to cut back on tobacco, so I'd pick up a rug hook and continue whatever pattern she started. It worked well as I cut my consumption to half a pack.

I also spent time fooling around with the portable recorder Sal gifted me, writing new material and putting it on tape. Usually it was just me and my acoustic, but sometimes Salome backed me. Most were romantic songs, while the rest are best described as 'itty bitty ditties,' what Sal & I dubbed them. We wiled away the time by ourselves, with occasional visits from The Boys, who otherwise kept occupied with decorating their place and becoming increasingly domestic. Or, "home bodies," as Al called them. You can see we weren't your typical rock band mired in decadence and debauchery.

However, a few reporters who had different notions of us began sniffing around. We locked the gate, but that only attracted more 'paparazzi,' a term I'd learned lately. Bernie called one day about a business issue when I told him regardless of day or night, rain or shine, a spate of photogs gathered at the bottom of our hill with telescopic lenses, watching our every move.

Right before our second tour commenced - with us headlining - Bernie became deluged with media requests for interviews, bio pieces, and photo essays. The Breeze, becoming savvy and shrewd, told every magazine, newspaper, and television outlet we'd be selecting only the three top-bidders to have any direct contact with the band. This caused a brouhaha throughout the entertainment industry. After all, no artist had ever charged media to interview or photograph them before. It was counter to how everything had always been done. Neither The Beatles nor Elvis nor The Stones had ever insisted on such an arrangement. Consequently, an uproar ensued not only in Hollywood, New York, and London, but everywhere else on the planet. "Sixty Minutes," "20/20," and "NBC Nightly News" ran headline stories on their networks - CBS, ABC, and NBC respectively - about The Talismans refusing to meet any media for free.

As a result, a bidding war ensued - besieging Bernie with offers to photograph, interview, and film us, by not only national, but international media as well. Finally, the top three bidders (two national magazines and a foreign publication) were selected, resulting in the band receiving three cover stories in the same month. So, take that - Bruce Springsteen. It took us only two albums (instead of The Boss's three) to land on the covers of not 'just Time and Newsweek' simultaneously, as Springsteen had, but the most distinguished British music publication in print – Melody Maker. After receiving courier-delivered copies of the three publications, I had two responses: 1. The guys at our gate would multiply; and 2. We were doing darned well for a little band from the purported 'armpit of California,' San Bernardino. I know I never expected this sudden windfall of publicity and fame landing on the four of us.

I wasn't too surprised by the song title – David Bowie's "Fame," but then I was beginning to not be as surprised by things Ross McInerney did. After all, I was getting to know the man well; maybe even very well.

Chapter Thirty-Eight

Our tour began the spring of 1976 and extended past the bicentennial celebration on July 4th. Most of the fifty dates' venues were large indoor arenas or outdoor stadiums - the Los Angeles Coliseum, San Francisco's Kezar Stadium, Chicago's Wrigley Field, Washington DC's RFK Stadium, etc. Almost every date on the "Return of the Talismans Tour" had sold out, with scalpers selling ducats for several times the original four-, five-, and six-dollar prices. Stadium security was wound as tight as twine in a baseball, and the demand for interviews skyrocketed. Everywhere we went we saw billboards promoting our albums and concerts. The biggest radio personalities around vied to land us on their shows. Our popularity was second only to The Stones & Dylan. "The world is your oyster!" Bernie said before shows, not far from the truth.

Leading into the tour, there was discussion between the band and Capitol over which material should be in our shows. The record people wanted a streamlined set list consisting of the top eight songs from each of our albums, but we four felt we should perform our entire catalog of thirty-six songs, which would take exactly three hours to play, not counting applause time between numbers. I told Bernie, "Our two albums aren't just collections of songs, but tapestries that tell stories. With even a song or two left out, an incomplete narrative will result. We need to tell our whole story, and our fans deserve to hear it all, too." After a few conferences -

comprised mainly of The Suits' head shaking and angst - they allowed us to play exactly what we'd intended to perform all along – our entire catalog in original sequence.

When word got out we'd be performing both our double albums in their entirety, the response was overwhelming. Fans, promoters, journalists, and the rest of the media galaxy roared with approval. Instead of staging a slick hits-heavy set, we played all eight sides of our two double albums in strict, sequential order. Consequently, Rolling Stone Magazine, Creem, and Hit Parade featured stories about the tour, heralding us respectively as "unflinching purveyors of theme-oriented, double-album productions," "the band that fought back against the recording industry," and "THE # 1 rock act in giving their fans what they want." (The capital letters in that last quote were theirs.) Of course, all this buzz resulted in ratcheting not just fan interest, but scalper prices and a subsequent demand for beefed-up security.

Because our shows would span four and a half hours, including a half-hour break, the promoters insisted there be no opening act. That way, they wouldn't have to pay a second band, light and cool the arenas an extra hour or pay parking and concession staff for overtime. We four couldn't care less about an opening act, so there wasn't the least argument from us. Every patron would be there to only see us, so we figured - hey - if there had been a preliminary act, they would've likely been treated coolly by the amped-up, sometimes surly sold-out crowds.

There was, however, one costly addition to our concert that I insisted upon – a light show. Bernie, hopelessly mired in the Thirties & Forties, knew nothing about them, but the big wigs at Capitol did; and so, they bitched and moaned about it big-time to Bernie. "Light shows are a thing of the past. They're so passé & unhip your fans will boo them off if they use one."

When the Breeze passed the Suits' message on to us, I stood my ground. "Hey, we don't need their approval, Bern. They're not paying for it anyway, so why are they bothering to form opinions about it? Get us the best light show around, and we'll show them who's out of touch."

We Talismans gave Bernie pictures of us, our old band Propinquity, and anything else we thought related to us or our two albums. The result was a scrapbook of our lives, including excerpts from the Beatles' TV appearances on The Ed Sullivan Show and the film clip of Patty Paige singing "How Much is that Doggie in the Window?" And that's just a taste of what went into the light show. I wanted it to be twice as big and artistic as the first one I saw back in my freshman year, which had blown my socks off right before Salome blew my entire being. Since we didn't see it until the first show in San Francisco, we were as surprised as the audience. The enormous screen behind us displayed every image in magnified form, so it was difficult for us to watch, but we saw most of it eventually, especially during sound checks. What I mostly recall were pics of Julie and Salome, which gave me both exhilaration and pause. Exhilaration, because I loved both women and enjoyed seeing their faces. And pause, because I will always mourn Julie's death –

so long as I live.

The tour's three months zipped by. Hotel rooms, sound checks, all-night diners, and charter plane rides are the most prominent memories, besides the shows themselves. Without exception, our concerts were smash successes. The crowds clapped, stomped, and roared after every song, every night. And because our shows followed the order of the four discs, fans always knew which song was next and gladly sang along with us. As we ventured deeper into the tour, the audiences accompanied us more and more. We began including segments where we'd let them sing instead of us, and they responded with unbridled glee and passion every time. And speaking of time, the only part of our days that flew by was the time we played on stage. It seemed for four hours, six or seven nights a week, we lived our lives perfectly, expressing the truth inside us that insisted on breaking out of our hearts and consciences. We were - simply and sincerely - doing what we do best without a care or worry in the world. How (we used to ask ourselves and each other) could life get any better than this?

When we played our last show, at the Los Angeles Memorial Coliseum, the Times reported our tour shattered longstanding records for both attendance and revenue. Becoming rich was not on any of our minds but keeping our musical success rolling, was.

Jackson Browne's "The Load-Out," about the ups & downs of touring provided the soundtrack for Ross and The Talismans of Sound's time on the road. After replaying it five times, Ross's finger finally stopped. So, I immediately played the next song on his tape.

Chapter Thirty-Nine

Returning from the tour to settle back into our respective routines was nothing but blissful... for a while. The four of us continued decorating our homes and puttered around them almost daily. And almost every night Salome and I jumped into Alfie, my Alfa Romeo Spider, and coasted down the hill for dinner at various cafés, drive-ins, and bistros. Bernie issued each of us an American Express card for eating out. "Just don't go nuts with it, because there is a limit. Oh, and make sure you talk business for at least a minute, so we can claim them as expenses on taxes." So, we all did exactly that.

One evening, as the two of us sat at a candlelit table in the back of an Italian ristorante on Melrose about to enjoy a bottle of Chianti, Salome said, "I've got some news, but I'm not sure how you're going to react. I don't know if the timing is good, Ross."

"What is it, Baby? You know you can tell me anything, right?"

"Well... yeah, but I also know we need to record our next album and tour again."

I wiped my brow on my sleeve. "So, is it good news or bad, Sal?"

"Well... it's mostly good news, with just some bad to go with the good."

"Okay, then lay the bad news on me first."

"Let me start by saying I shouldn't be drinking any Chianti... for the next nine months."

I remember taking Salome's head in my hands and bringing it to my forehead. I began to stroke her face with the back of my hand. "You mean, you're going to be a mommy?"

"Yes, Baby. And you know how our first two records are double albums?"

"Yes..."

"My first delivery will also be a double event."

"What?! You mean... your crazy dream is coming true?"

"Yep, so far. One boy and one girl."

I don't remember anything after that because I passed out. And so, instead of me taking care of my dear, sweet pregnant wife, Salome had to revive me and apply a bag of ice to the back of my head where it hit the marble floor.

A song I'd never heard or heard of was labeled, "Twenty Tiny Fingers, Twenty Tiny Toes" by the Stargazers. 'Boy,' I thought, 'this is unexpected. Ross has two children. Or, does he? I don't want to ply him with questions and stress him out, so I'll wait to find out for sure.'

⁂

News of our double pregnancy changed things. Sal became sicker than a dog, so her doc ordered bed rest for the next eight months. Second, Bernie started pressuring us to record a third LP. Since the first two had been received so well, he was convinced our third would be even more successful financially, the only criterion to which he gave credence.

Our manager had become a taskmaster when it came to demanding more music from us – or "product" as he called it. "Time is of the essence, Maestro. We must strike while the iron's hot. The average longevity of a music artist's career is extremely short; three, maybe four years if he or she's lucky. Who knows? Our days in the limelight might prove to be very short indeed." You would think he'd be happy with our success and willing to pause a moment to smell the roses and enjoy the journey, but – then again – he was the 'bean counter,' the accountant, and the watcher of the bottom line. I didn't resent his prodding, but assumed it was just standard operating procedure for agents - to motivate their clients to create more and more successful music and thus make more and more money for everyone.

I looked through my catalog of unrecorded songs and realized I'd already picked the cream of my crop for the first two albums, so I started trying to write, but it wasn't easy. And - with Salome bedridden - I attended to her every need around the clock. My lady needed help with everything - getting to the bathroom, bathing, dressing; you name it and she required assistance with it. Because Sal was so nauseous, I never knew if a meal would stay down; and many didn't. In fact, for the first five weeks, nothing stayed down. As a result, I had to wear not only my nurse's hat, but carry a janitor's mop around too.

We continued this way for about a month, until one day Sal suggested: "Why don't we have Delilah come help us with chores?"

"You mean, I'm not keeping up with everything to your liking, Hon?" I half-joked.

"Sweetie, you're doing amazingly, but you need to think about your career, getting the next album done, and having time for yourself. Dee can relieve you when you need to go in the studio or run chores, but right now you don't seem to have a single moment to yourself."

"Well, since you put it that way, it does make sense. Okay, if you're up to calling Dee, it will probably be better if she hears from you directly."

"Okay. I'll see if she's interested. She can use our second master suite rent-free. I'm not sure if she's still working, but it can't hurt to ask."

⁂

During this time, I wrangled Bernie into installing a 16-track studio in Valhalla. The space we used had originally been a walk-in closet in the center of the ground floor and lent itself perfectly to soundproofing. Right away, I dubbed it my inner sanctum, and that's what Sal called it, too. She'd ask, "Are you going to your inner sanctum today for some peace and quiet – or maybe just peace?" She never resented my working on music, but encouraged me often to write, compose, and record. "It's what you're born to do and you're happiest when you create."

"You know what's funny, Salome?" I asked. "I think we people get a glimpse of what it's like to be God when we create. After all, he's the creator of everything and made us in his image. So, when we create, we're closer to his nature than at any other time." Although I struggled with the God thing and wasn't sure who he really was, I considered him the source of all creativity.

So, during this stressful season of Sal being sick and me wanting to make everyone happy by creating new music, I retreated to my 16-track inner sanctum, where I spent much of the time chronicling what I was undergoing personally, relationally, and professionally. I decided to record everything I did in my 'laboratory' – whether it be jamming on various instruments to laying down tracks to ad-libbing lyrics I needed that day. All of it, I figured, could be viewed as me documenting my life for someone to possibly see and hear someday. And when I'd finished, I stashed those tapes separately from the band's because I felt mine were too private, too personal, and probably unfit for anyone to buy. I had no way of knowing either way because only I knew of their existence, so feedback hadn't been possible lately.

One day, Delilah buzzed the gate, and I answered the intercom. She said she'd decided to accept Sal's offer to be her caregiver for the duration of the pregnancy and then the first months after the twins' arrival. If you're wondering why Salome didn't have any family help her, it's because she'd never known her biological family but had been a foster kid moving from one placement to the next from infancy till her sixteenth birthday. When we first met, Sal had been on her own for two years. No siblings, cousins, grandparents, or parents – that she knew about. The closest thing to a family unit had been her colleagues in the Youth Narcotics Division; and the closest she had to a sibling was Delilah. So, this could be an arrangement that might give Salome a sense of well-being while surrounded by family, provided it's possible for a person to be 'surrounded' by two people. In other words, Dee and I comprised her entire family.

Delilah settled into one of the spare bedrooms, one with its own bathroom. Since she'd quit the force shortly after Salome had, this arrangement seemed to fit the bill for her in terms of food, shelter, and extra cash to live on. I was relieved she'd be taking some of the load off me, so I could focus at least part of my time on producing new music.

I stayed mostly to myself because the truce between Dee and me seemed tenuous and off balance. Delilah spent most of her waking hours attending to Salome, which mainly consisted of the two chattering, discussing, and gossiping; about what, I had no clue. However, I knew they passed the days talking in hushed tones, either in our bedroom or out in the back yard. They took all their meals together without me because I'd grab something on the run, to maintain my nearly non-stop writing and recording schedule.

Stu, Al, and I began meeting at Capitol to rehearse some of the material I'd recently composed. The guys seemed in excellent spirits, excited even, about the prospect of our third album. With

Salome sidelined, we mostly worked out the instrumental arrangements for our new tunes. It sounded okay, I guess, but it just wasn't the same without Sal. Her keyboard and singing skills were sorely missed. Everything we did seemed incomplete and lacking the extra dollop of sweetness Salome always brought to the mix. So, after only four sessions, we decided to take a powder and await the return of Princess Salome of Zebedee.

Two weeks after our last rehearsal, I was in the home studio strumming my six-string and singing a tune I'd written the day before. Like the songs we'd been working on at Capitol, it sounded incomplete. As I prepared to I quit for the day, I heard Delilah knock on the door.

"Hey, what's up, Dee?"

"Not much. What're you up to?"

"Trying to figure out how this album's going to sound when Sal rejoins us."

"Yeah, that must be a real drag to not have her singing with you guys."

"Exactly. It's almost impossible to put together music intended for multiple instruments and voices with just this guitar and my voice."

"Well… do you mind letting me hear what you have so far?"

After I invited her to sit & listen, Delilah remained standing and closed her eyes. I started playing this dreamy song I'd tentatively titled "You & I Fit Together Like a Puzzle;" as you may have guessed, it was a love song about Sal and me. I played it through start to finish by myself.

After I finished, Delilah kept standing with both eyes shut. As I tried to summon courage to ask her opinion, she beat me to the punch. "Play it again, Ross. Please." So, I did. And, as I got past the bridge and began the chorus, Delilah's voice came in behind me. Honestly, I was surprised because I didn't expect her to join in; and her singing was better than I had imagined. Though her speaking voice was nasal and bland, her singing voice tone was a lovely, lively soprano - a perfect counterpart to mine. When we finished, I asked if she'd mind singing along with me a second time. "Whatever you like. I have nothing else going on. Sal's napping."

I set up the reel-to-reel and we did two takes. Somehow, they sounded equally impressive. "Wow, I'm pleasantly surprised, Dee, to hear you singing so well." She smiled sweetly, looked at her sandals, and blushed. Since the moment was awkward, I busied myself with some settings on the console that I didn't really need to make. I ended up just moving all the levers back to where they'd been. When I finished threading a new tape, I looked around and realized she'd left.

***

After Delilah had been with us three weeks, Mom visited us in our new digs. She decided to drive down and stay a night or two. "I've been neglecting my son, daughter-in-law, and soon-to-be grandson and granddaughter!" And, sure enough, just her presence put us all in much better spirits. In fact, Salome began feeling better;

so much so she and Delilah joined the rest of the band and Mom at a Capitol rehearsal. We were cutting a demo of "You & I Fit Together" when Sal grew white as a ghost and stopped singing. None of our home remedies worked on her, so we stopped trying and Mom took her home to rest. Dee stayed behind to watch.

As we played the song again, Delilah began singing as wonderfully as she had back home. Al, playing bass next to her, took notice. "Hey, why don't we get this girl a mic? She's good; darned good." So, Fred got her a hot mic along with a stool. She thanked us for our kind words about her singing, sat, and awaited the song's intro. I asked her to back me through the whole tune, and guess what? The result was a big improvement of the way she'd sung the chorus part back home, which is saying something. Dee nailed the vocal and we guys played so well Fred told us we had "a perfect take."

After huddling, we selected four more songs to possibly record. I handed Delilah some sheet music after she said she knew how to read, which surprised me as much as discovering the professional quality of her voice. After running through all four without rolling tape, Fred said the crew and sound board were both set. When we finished the last one, he shook his head. "Your band's perfect record of needing no redubs or second takes is still intact. I couldn't improve any of those four if I had the rest of the week to sit and analyze them."

It was strange, but Delilah gelled with us nearly as well as Julie and Salome. She was a perfect interim replacement for Salome;

and since the two were great friends, there shouldn't be any resentment or envy about her standing in. I was so thrilled with the session I bounded out of the studio, wanting nothing more than to get home and tell Salome how well it had gone.

The two songs I'd been playing were David Bowie's "Under Pressure" and Crosby, Stills, and Nash's "Our House." I began realizing how much wider my musical horizons had spread since meeting Ross, because I liked both tunes very much, despite their diversity.

Chapter Forty

Although our record sales and concert receipts reached stratospheric heights, we four Talismans were nowhere close to rolling in the dough. Listen, don't get me wrong – we lived comfortably, but nowhere close to the 'neighborhood of comfort' we'd expected, considering how great the albums and tours had done. We'd just crossed the metaphorical tracks and begun entering the proverbial nice side of town. We acknowledged our lives had improved the past two years, but when we looked at the numbers, it seemed we should see more in our bank accounts.

Our first two albums had scaled the Top 100 in Billboard, landing at #2 and #1 respectively. Millions of LPs sold; millions of singles sold; our second concert tour virtually sold out. So, where was all the money left over after everyone else - the studio, Uncle Sam, and Uncle Bernie – had gotten their takes? I'd started wondering about that more and more lately. The four of us received modest checks every month to cover expenses, sure, with a few bucks left over to spend or deposit in our bank accounts. But! Here's the combination to unlock the safe that is this mystery. Since none of us had previous experience in the business, we wouldn't know normal if it bit us on both butt cheeks with its sharpened canine chompers. But, considering how wildly successful our tour had been the year before, we weren't raking in the dough like we thought we would. So, I did the only thing I could think to address this troubling issue: I made an appointment to see Bernie at his new office on Sunset. Arriving before noon on a Wednesday, I was first taken back by the parking lot, which had 'valet-only parking.' So, being a Roman while in Rome, I permitted some stranger in a turquoise tux jacket to take my beloved Alfie and park him somewhere out of my sight, after handing me a little orange ticket I'm supposed to hold onto as though my life depended on it. I entered the building from a rear door and was immediately asked by a uniformed man what my business was. "To see Bernie Breeze." He had me follow him down a hallway to the front foyer, where a receptionist seated behind a bunker greeted me.

"May I assist you, Sir?" she asked.

"I'm here to see Bernie Breeze."

"I see. Do you have an appointment?"

"Yes, at noon."

"Mister MacErrNinny?"

"Close enough."

"Please have a seat in our lounge, Mr. MacGenery. Mr. Breeze will be with you shortly."

"Over there?" I asked, pointing to an anteroom with several stuffed leather chairs and a glass and chrome table bearing magazines. Getting no response, I thanked her anyway and sat.

After opening the current Billboard and seeing our albums still occupying spots in the Top Twenty, I set the trade publication down and focused on the walls. Framed photos of various Vaudeville and Burlesque acts decorated the light gray walls around me. There were eight huge movie-poster-sized photos hung spaced apart as far as possible on all four walls. Between two of them on a non-door wall was a much smaller photograph, 8 ½ by 11 inches. Despite its humble size, I recognized its four subjects. To verify their identities, I got twice as close. Yep, there we were - our faces reduced to thumb-sized images – Al, Stu, Salome, and I. "Well, at least we made the cut," I murmured. Hunching over the 8 by 11 1/2 photo, I recognized the inside cover shot from our first album - the only picture not featuring a personal note to Bernie. "Huh," I said, before I felt a presence behind me.

A thin man in old-fashioned black frames tried smiling as he said, "Mr. Mac-Er-Ninny?"

"Not quite, but closer. Please, call me Ross."

"My name is Arvin Minaretto. I am Bernard Breeze's administrative assistant."

I maneuvered around furniture and stuck my hand out expecting a handshake, but Arvin had already pivoted and begun walking toward the foyer. "Let's walk together," he said over his shoulder without a trace of irony as he led me up two flights of stairs to the second floor. "Follow, please," he instructed after we reached the tiled hallway. "Mr. Breeze is expecting you," he announced while leading me another seventy or eighty feet to a massive double door of mahogany wood and mirrored glass. "After you," he said as he held the door for me.

Almost falling when the floor ended and two steps took its place, I recovered enough to look up and see Bernie seated behind the largest desk ever. Larger even than the massive bunker of a counter out in the lobby the receptionist used as her desk. Yep, that large.

Looking up as though he hadn't expected me, Bernie said without smiling: "Welcome, Maestro. Pull up a chair." Half expecting his assistant to do that for me, I noticed Arvin had already seated himself behind the fortress-like desk structure on the other side of Bernie. Looking around, I saw two round tables with six chairs around each. Dragging one of the high-backed chairs over to his desk, I sucked in a breath and sat. Bernie - continuing to sift through his sheaf of legal-looking papers - asked if I wanted anything to drink.

"No, I'm fine, Chief."

"Okay, Maestro. What would you like to discuss?"

"Well," I began, pulling a single sheet of paper from my back pocket. "I had just a few questions, mainly about financial matters."

"Alright. May I see them?"

"Well, I sort of wanted to ask you..." Without finishing my sentence, I came to a full stop and felt the considerable weight of awkwardness dominating and pervading the gigantic space. I watched myself hand the list to Arvin, who'd appeared at my side without warning. After unfolding the paper and handing it with a flourish to Bernie, Arvin pivoted and returned to his chair twelve feet

away. It took every shred of self-control to not bust out laughing, given the fact I sat only three feet from Bernie Breeze. No reason for him to demand my personal notes, unfold them, and ceremoniously present them to another man **who works for me**. *Now, that is what I understand to be a great illustration of officiousness.*

Without speaking, he consulted my list. Finally setting it down, he looked up and asked, "What exactly do you need, Maestro?"

I didn't know to laugh or wait for him to, but when his stern expression remained, I said: "I need to know why we're not being paid accordingly."

No longer looking at me, Bernie asked, "According to what or whom?"

Fighting the urge to laugh a second time in my hireling's face, I proceeded. "According to the millions of records we've already sold, and all the tickets to our sold-out concerts."

"Okay," he started, "we can discuss that. I have no problem discussing your fiduciary concerns. But first, I must explain to you there are many costs involved in managing not only you, but the entire band. Costs I don't like to worry you folks about. Expenditures for paying all kinds of bills and salaries in addition to remunerating the four of you monthly as we'd agreed."

I shifted in my seat. "What I need is a print-out of all royalties and concert receipts."

"Okay," he said, which seemed his standby word, but not

necessarily having anything to do with compliance. "Capitol has given me – us – a monthly accounting of all record sales for The Talismans of Sound. I can furnish you with that but let me tell you upfront the band's royalty rate is at one percent of net sales, which is standard for a new band."

After more shifting, I said, "Two things: One - we should renegotiate our royalty rate with Capitol, pronto; and two, our concert gates should comprise most of our revenue, right?"

It was Breeze's turn to shift around. "Uh, yes… to an extent. But, you see, it's not a simple matter of transferring all our gate receipts into our private bank accounts."

This time I couldn't keep from laughing. "Bernie, look. I'm smart enough to know it doesn't work that way, but what I need to see is how much net profit from record sales and concert receipts we have. And how about my copyright royalties from writing all our songs?"

Swiveling, he barked: "Arvin! I need the Capitol Records revenue schedule. Pronto."

"Yes, sir," he said, snapping to attention and exiting the cavernous office.

After Arvin had closed the nine-foot-tall door, I turned back to Bernie. "Wow, Bern. You've really got that kid hopping. Where'd you find him?"

"Now I've got some numbered points for you, Maestro: One, I've known Mr. Minaretto for many years; and, two, it's none of

your business where I 'found' him."

I blinked a few times to relax the tension in my upper face. It's a technique that only works occasionally for me. It's my version of Thomas Jefferson's famous advice, which I like to call "Let Me Count to Ten Before I Beat the Unholy Crap out of You." After all, my business paid the rent on this mausoleum pretending to be an office building. So, instead of me telling him it most certainly is my business where he got an employee of mine, I didn't. I had bigger fish to fry. "Bernie, I don't recall signing any agreements on copyrighting my material. I know that most rock and pop artists today even have their own publishing companies."

"Okay, here we go," Bernie said, sounding relieved that Arvin had returned. After receiving an inch-thick stack of white papers from his assistant, he said, "Thank you, Arvin. That will be all for now." They then exchanged looks before the minaret backed out of the office, appearing to execute some type of deferential gesture only seen in a royal court.

Taking three different colored highlighters, Bernie spent twenty-five minutes marking up his packet of papers without speaking, leaving me with nothing to do but fidget and think. Finally, as though his markers might've run out of ink, he ceased his coloring, straightened the pile, and managed a smile. Handing me an inch-thick stack, he said, "Here's a summary of the Capitol Records account for the first two albums." It was marked up by the three pens; bands of green, yellow, and pink flowed horizontally across every page. He explained what each color stood for, but I didn't bother to listen. I was simply too pissed to do anything but try to keep my act together. "And here are the concert gate receipts, complete with expenditures, taxes, and other fees & levies." I gripped the thinner, but still weighty pile and rose from my seat.

Without shaking his hand or saying a word, I stood and walked out of the huge office my music was paying for, ignored Arvin at his desk adjacent to the outer door, and nearly sprinted out of the building. When I arrived at the valet booth, I realized I hadn't had my ticket validated. "Damn it! Just bring my car." When the short man in the faux tux jacket brought up Alfie, I jumped in and took off without paying. I didn't even have the two bucks for parking, to show how little money I had. But, I now had information regarding this whole situation, provided I could understand it, which could result in me never having to worry about having enough cash again.

⁂

Not knowing where else to go, I drove to Los Angeles' main library downtown. Without any money to spend on a parking structure space, I found a spot on a side street whose meter still had an hour's worth left. I grabbed my paperwork, marched around the corner, climbed too many stairs, and entered. Finding an unoccupied table, I began the process of deciphering what Bernie had furnished me. Equipped with only a # 2 pencil, I did my own notating – underlining discrepancies, circling numbers, and trying to make sense of everything. "This'll take months," I guessed, after poring over the Capitol packet for two hours. I knew I had my work cut out for me, so I headed back to Valhalla hoping I could do just that when I got home. And, to show how luck or God had smiled on me that day, I acknowledged the fact I hadn't gotten a parking ticket, which I couldn't have afforded to pay anyway.

As I drove through the electronic gate, my gut sensed something wrong. And when I didn't see Salome's pink Corvette parked in back, I knew things weren't good. Entering from the rear door, I yelled "Salome! You here? Delilah, are ***you*** *here?" a few times, but with no response. I went to our suite and noticed Sal's toiletries, robe, and her favorite shoes gone. I visited Dee's room and saw all her belongings were gone. "This can't be good," I reconfirmed as I entered the kitchen and spotted a page of loose-leaf notebook paper stuck with Scotch Tape on the oven's hood. I recognized Delilah's handwriting (sweeping loops with plenty of outsized curlicues). Since I've read it so many times since, I committed it to memory. Here's what Dee wrote apparently on Salome's behalf:*

Dear Ross,

Honey, I had to get out of here. I started feeling so terrible it began to freak me out. I don't want to scare you, but I'm afraid of losing these babies. So, Delilah's taking me where I can get extra-good care for the rest of this pregnancy. I haven't told you, but I've gotten so sick I might harm our babies by retching too much or too hard. I can't keep anything down and have been dizzy and ditzy for the past couple weeks. You've been so busy with your music, Ross, and I've been so out of it when you were around I couldn't tell you what's been going on. Either Dee or I will call to update you on how I'm doing and where we'll be. Love you to pieces, Salome

PS – I was too dizzy to write this myself. Please forgive me. And, Ross? DON'T WORRY.

I was - to say the least - at a total loss. My wife, lover, and mother of my two soon-to-be bouncing babies was gone. And at that moment, I realized Salome had not just been my biggest supporter, she'd been my support system. And the realization struck me like a thunderbolt. Sal had supported me from the moment I met her in my freshman year. And, as soon as she reentered my life, she loved and supported me without condition. No one, including my mother, had ever done that. However, because my mental processing had stopped, I froze from taking any immediate action. I had no clue, no direction, and no way to find her. So, I did something I hadn't done in years – I meditated. Remaining seated on the hardwood floor, I shut my eyes and began hearing my mantra. My mind went blank for who-knows-how-long and I just... let go.

When I awoke, I was sprawled on the floor. But instead of being stiff or sore, I felt reenergized, regenerated, rejuvenated. I grabbed our six-inch-thick phonebook and began dialing everyone I could, to see if they had any idea where Sal might be. Not a single person, including my bandmates and Mom, had seen her nor did they have any advice on how I should find her. So, I flipped to the 'Hospitals' section of the Yellow Pages and began calling one after another in hopes Sal had been admitted there. After reaching every hospital in the book and my fingers beginning to blister, I was still at a loss.

"Money" by Pink Floyd played countless times before Ross finished tapping.

Chapter Forty-One

Man, oh man. I felt like I'd lost all chance of finding Salome. Plus, I didn't know if she was alive, healthy, and in her right mind. And the twins? I couldn't think of them too much or I'd be inundated with grief. So, instead of uselessly looking for prospects not on my radar, I decided to double back and do something against my instincts - I called Al again. He made it easy by suggesting I drop by his and Stu's place to talk. So, I did. After I pushed the intercom button and greeted Al, he buzzed me in and the gates opened slowly, but grandly. When I arrived at their door, both Al and Stu shook my hand. "Come in, Ross. We were just sitting out back," Stu motioned for me to join them in mid-party. Following them through the house and out the slider, we sat under the umbrella at one of three tables by the sky-blue pool.

After Stu poured me a glass of lemonade, I told them about my strange meeting with Bernie, leaving out nothing. "So, I'm thinking Breeze is taking us to the cleaners," I concluded. They looked at each other before Al said, "I know you're frustrated, Ross, but we think Bernie is on the up-and-up and really has our best interests at heart."

"That may be, but he's treating us like children."

"Meaning?"

"Meaning, he doles money out to us monthly and has final

say whether we get more money for something we need. He's acting like our mother and father, for crying out loud. It's like we're all twelve years old and are forced to rely on the 'generosity' of Mr. Breeze."

Al said, "You know, Stu and I talked about this and we think he's holding onto the purse strings with a firm grip because he doesn't want us to blow through our cash and be broke."

I drained my glass. "Yeah, but what he's not taking into consideration is that we're adults. Plus, I don't think I'm getting anywhere near what I deserve for writing all those tunes. And most important, we haven't been able to deposit anything into our savings accounts. I mean, come on. We can't live indefinitely on each month's check, plus my family is about to double in eight months." It got quiet after that, so it seemed there was nothing more I could do or say to convince them that maybe we shouldn't be trusting Bernie with all our finances after all. So, I changed the subject. "It's hard to think straight right now with Salome gone and me having no clue where she is." Before I knew it, I was blubbering like a baby. Both guys patted me on the shoulder and tried their best to console me, but it wasn't any use. When I sensed I was about to lose it altogether, I excused myself and ran out of their house, down their driveway, through their gate, and down the street. I didn't just run home, I ran a whole three miles both ways, to make sure all that pent-up angst had left my system. If I could just identify which system that was, I might have an easier time keeping it in optimum running order.

I decided it was time to call the LAPD. I told the desk sergeant about Sal disappearing and me wishing to file a missing person's report. I summarized the whole situation, including the letter she and Delilah had left. Sarge then concluded, "You don't have grounds to declare her missing. The letter explained she needs time to focus on her pregnancy and she'll keep you updated. I tell you what: call us in a week and if she's still gone, we'll file a report for you."

I felt my anger rising. "Are you serious? A week? She might be dead by then. This is ridiculous. Let me speak to your supervisor, Sergeant." I heard the phone drop before a long silence ensued. After holding at least two minutes without any music, I heard the line go dead.

⁂

A week passed with no word about Salome. For seven days, I called every person, facility, and agency I could think of, and each night I wrote and recorded music. Music has always been the best way for me to express my feelings, especially my anger and fear. Most of the anger concerned not only my own financial situation, but the entire band's, too. After all, we had no information and zero control over our income, so I called Bernie's office. Arvin Minaretto answered, but wouldn't patch it through. When I asked why, he replied, "I'm following orders, Mr. McInerney." After four or five more robotic responses, I knew I'd get nowhere unless I saw Bernie face to face. I drove there at two-thirty and had enough cash this time to have my car parked by a valet - in case I'd forget to get my ticket validated.

Walking past the receptionist without 'checking in' - I knew she'd insist I sit in the lobby - I arrived at Minaretto's desk. Looking up from a file labeled "Talismans of Sound," he flinched when he saw me standing over him. "I need to see Bernie. Where is he?" When Arvin didn't answer, I barged through the tall double doors and found Breeze behind his fortress masquerading as a desk. "Bernie, we need to get to the bottom of our finances."

Looking horrified, he gulped. Pushing a button, he said, "Security: in my office now!"

"Bernie, that won't be necessary," I began. "I just need to know what's up with the band's profits. And, I'm not leaving here till I get some real answers."

"Maestro," he said sighing, "you can't just barge into- "

I sprinted around his U-shaped desk, so he would have nothing to hide behind. "First of all, I can barge into your office any time I feel like it. Why? Because I PAY YOUR SALARY! If I want to barge in here at midnight, I will. And secondly, my name is NOT Maestro. Comprende?"

He gave this smirky, iffy half nod, but that wasn't confirmation enough for me. "No, I want to hear you say with your own mouth WHAT MY REAL NAME IS. Say it, Bernie."

A commotion starting outside and continuing into Bernie's office involved three uniformed guards wielding Billy clubs and canisters. "Ross, you need to leave this office now."

Appealing to Bernie, I asked: "You won't even give me the courtesy of an answer? I have every right to-- "

Before I could finish, a guard on each side grabbed an arm and forced my hands behind me. The third rental cop must've sneaked behind me because I felt cold steel enclosing both my wrists. Never having been cuffed before, I now knew how it felt and I didn't like it, so I struggled and fought the three thugs as best I could, but it was futile. Before I could up my resistance, all three bum-rushed me. Turning to Bernie, I yelled: "You cheat, I will get you. Don't worry, Dude. I will be back, and you will talk until I tell you to shut the hell up, you sissified piece of crap!"

I half-expected the LAPD to arrive, but the lead guard explained if I promised to not return without an appointment, they'd let me go and not press charges. Obviously, they had me over a barrel. So, I agreed – with reluctance.

***

Having never felt this frustrated before, I had no clue what to do. However, I did conclude that drowning my sorrows was probably the best way to go, so I frequented not one, but three bars in Hollywood – and got bounced from all of them. I don't remember much of what happened after the third bar, but I do recall glimpses of a blurry scene at the gates of Valhalla. I stumbled out of Alfie and tried unlocking our gate for the longest time. Finally, even in my advanced state of inebriation, I realized the lock had been changed. "Bernie, you evil, greedy, no-count bastard!" I yelled. Exhausted and needing to lie down, I devised a plan to get in. Driving around the corner to my neighbors behind me, who'd been out of town a month, I pulled up their driveway and parked Alfie out of sight. Which wasn't hard to do since the house, like mine, stood on its own knoll. Plus, it was a wooded estate that provided me a measure of invisibility. Reclining my seat as much as I could, I shut my eyes and tried to achieve calm.

Awaking to a pitch-black, moonless night, Alfie's dashboard clock read four-thirty, so approaching Valhalla from behind, I scaled the wall and landed in my backyard. Crouching to avoid the low-lying branches of my citrus trees, I managed to bang my head several times. Each time, I plopped down and tried to rest and clear my mind. It took me so long that I realize now I must've completed more than one circle through our orchard, and maybe three or four. At last, I felt the mesh of screen on my bedroom window and realized that sleeping in my own bed was now possible. Luckily, I had my Swiss Army knife, so I popped out the screen. I reasoned I'd have to bust the glass to get in, so I picked up a log from the woodpile and used it as a battering ram. Instead of hearing broken glass, my ears were assaulted with the loudest screech ever. It struck me that someone, at Bernie's request, had set the burglar alarm. I decided I might as well complete the job, so I climbed through and headed for my studio. Grabbing my master tapes and the Sound-About Salome bought me for Christmas, I stuffed them into my canvas bag, stumbled to my room, and threw several shirts and a pair of jeans into the duffel. After climbing back out, I figured I'd make faster time crawling back to Alfie instead of crouching and walking. I must've been sobering up because it worked. Jumping into my two-seat roadster, I coasted down the driveway before popping Alfie's clutch and turning left, away from Valhalla. Police sirens began harmonizing with my house alarm. I am fairly sure the racket-on-steroids awoke every canine for many miles around, but I was free - at least for the time being - from the 'long arm of the law.'

Jumping on Interstate 10, Alfie took me to the one place I could seek refuge, San Berdoo. Unfortunately, neither my mother nor Rich was home. Pulling a road map out of my glove, I spied the one highway in America as iconic as Dorothy's Yellow Brick Road – Route 66. Heading east as the sun began to rise ahead, I knew I was in for adventure.

Another Nat King Cole tune played on Ross's tape, "Get Your Kicks on Route 66."

Chapter Forty-Two

Riding the licorice ribbon by myself all the way to Flagstaff, Arizona, I pulled into a Flying A station and within seconds fell asleep inside Alfie. I had several vivid dreams in a row, concluding with being inside an oil barrel about to fall over the Niagara Falls, when someone or something began pounding on the side of my barrel. I yelled for the pounder to stop so I could make it over the falls without any glitches, but when he or she wouldn't cease pounding, I had no choice but to open my eyes and confront them. Through my side window a patch of blue hovered above a pair of patched-up Levi's. Continuing to bang on my car was a man about my age with a beard, straggly hair, and knee-high moccasins. Ten feet or so away sat a pair of backpacks – one on the other. A cardboard sign bearing "CHI" in bold print leaned against the packs.

Mainly to get the guy to stop pounding on my car, I lowered my window, but just a crack. "Yes?" was all I could think to say.

The guy brightened when he saw my face. "Hey man, could you help a brother? My friend and I are heading to Chicago and could really use a lift."

I really had to think before taking on this kind of commitment. Plus, I'd never picked up a hitch hiker before, much less two. And I knew nothing about the social norms while hitching rides until...... I remembered my trip with Salome to San Fran all those years ago when we had so much trouble catching a ride. "Well, I'm not sure where I'm going to finally end up."

He laughed. "Isn't that true of us all? My cohort and I are good and make groovy company, man. You'll see. And one of us will sit in back with our packs."

It was my turn to chuckle because I felt like he was trying to sell me a puppy or give away a kitten. In fact, the guy did resemble a puppy, a beagle puppy. Truth be told, he looked a lot like my one pet in childhood, my pup Point. He had an amiable, forlorn vibe about him that proved irresistible, so – after further review – I conceded: "Okay, climb in. Where's your friend?"

"She'll be here in a sec. She had to fix her makeup." Then, a splash of yellow reminiscent of corn silk glinted in the early afternoon sun - a mane of long, full golden hair bounced along atop the tall, angular woman jogging our way. After she flashed her smile, I knew I couldn't back out. She was, in a single word……… gorgeous.

'Goldilocks' and 'Beagle Boy' snatched up their backpacks and managed to shove them into my trunk without any trouble. Without hesitation, he climbed into the shotgun seat beside me. Blondie settled into the back and flashed a second beaming smile. "He's Gabriel and I'm Vesta. But folks prefer to call me 'Vesta.'" The most endearing giggle danced out of her mouth and I felt a sudden connection with this vagabond with a capital 'V.' Because she planted herself in the middle, I kept eye contact with her throughout our conversation.

Gabriel fell dead asleep seconds after being introduced. I can't quote you anything Vesta and I said, but because of my complete immersion in meeting and talking with her it was impossible to focus on anything or anybody else. Let me first describe the type of fascination I had for Vesta, so you won't think I'd suddenly fallen out of love with my wife and mother of my future children. No, I hadn't transformed into an adulterer or coveter of other women. The love of my life will always be Salome, without doubt. But, the most fascinating aspect of Vesta's persona had to do with her character. If she'd been a man with the same brand of integrity, she would've been my best friend, from here to eternity. I say that to prove I can find someone of either gender to love with all my heart. Furthermore, I felt this way about Vesta without being disloyal to Sal in any way. Again, Salome was the love of my life. Call me a romantic if you must, but also consider calling me a lover of people. Pure and simple.

Two hours out of Flagstaff, Vesta had already learned of the major people and events populating my life's landscape up to that moment. She learned of my upbringing, my father's musical career, and my marriages. Somehow, I didn't tell her of my professional music career or the struggles I'd been having. She might've sensed something awry, but I can't say for sure.

We drove until Albuquerque, where we decided to eat at a roadside diner called Clara Jo's. As we emerged from Alfie, Gabriel told us he'd decided to stay outside. Instead of eating, he wanted to walk around town and meet us back at the car after we finished dinner and became "properly acquainted." Before I could insist he join us, he'd split.

As we reached Clara Jo's front door, it opened. Seated on a bench in the vestibule was a bald man wearing Buddy Holly glasses, a white shirt, black tie, and a badge that read: "I'm Mel. How can I serve you?" At first, I thought he was the manager seating us, but when he ignored us, we approached a lectern piled with menus. A dark-haired girl, clad in a blue waitress dress asked, "Two? Follow me, please." Seating us in a high-backed booth in a corner where sunlight streamed through the windows, she promised to return and take our orders. Since I had little cash, I surveyed the children's menu. Because I hadn't eaten for 24 hours, I felt a ravenous hunger rising after seeing pictures of food on their bill of fare.

Without looking up from her menu, Vesta said, "Order anything." I was dumbfounded. However, the yelps emanating from my stomach's depths drowned out the protests in my mind. My eyes swerved to the bottom section of the front page where the Lumberjack Special announced an all-you-can-eat breakfast feast of flapjacks, eggs, bacon, ham, and biscuits & gravy for the princely sum of $7.99.

"Really? Anything I want?" I stammered.

Still scanning her menu, Vesta asserted: "Anything you want, including the Lumberjack Special." How she knew that was the order I so desperately wanted is anyone's guess, but I took it as a sign; a harbinger that my circumstances might be improving. When the waitress returned, Vesta insisted I order. When our server looked at my companion, she said: "Just hot water."

And then, our conversation began. I can't quote what either of us said nor do I recall the topics discussed, but I felt electrified by the entire exchange. I had this distinct sensation of being lifted... in every way. All my worries seemed to have been swallowed up by the river of light flowing through the large picture windows around us in our corner booth.

Somewhere in the middle of our talk fest, our server collected the various plates recently holding my bacon, hashed browns, ham steak, biscuits & gravy, two tall stacks of buckwheat hotcakes, and a wedge of cinnamon-apple pie. Every plate had been wiped clean. Although I had not a single sense memory of any of those dishes, I felt not full, but …… satisfied.

Minutes or maybe hours later, our waitress asked, "Can I get anything else for you?"

I answered, "Just our check, please," even though I couldn't have paid for most of it.

"Oh, that's been taken care of."

"Taken care of? By whom?" I managed to ask without stuttering.

"Some man."

"Could you describe him?"

"Easy. He was bald and wore a white shirt, big black glass frames, and a badge."

"Mel," I said to myself.

When I pulled my wallet out and tried to pay the tip, our waitress said, "Oh, that's not necessary either. Your friend took care of that, too."

All I could do was smile, resume my talk with Vesta, and bask in the glow of the warmth and light flooding this humble, yet lively roadside eatery.

⁂

As Vesta and I approached Alfie, the car appeared uninhabited. But after we both climbed in, whom did I spy in my rear-view mirror but Gabriel? Sitting where Vesta had earlier. As we pulled out of the lot, I told him about the stranger paying our bill. "Huh," he said, without a trace of interest, as he lay down and fell asleep instantly.

⁂

After Albuquerque, we proceeded on 66, stopping in Amarillo, Texas; Tulsa, Oklahoma; and Springfield, Missouri. Each time, only Vesta and I ate because Gabe split to "take a walk around town;" and at each stop our bill was taken care of by some man with a name tag and big glasses. If I hadn't been so transported by the non-stop conversation with Vesta, I would've totally freaked out and demanded we call the cops on our stalker.

Another phenomenon occurred. For the first trip of my life, I felt sad about approaching my destination. We were nearing Belleville, Illinois, where Gabe said they'd leave me and continue to

Chicago. That morning I'd decided to head for Atlanta, Georgia, but without a clue why. Once there, I thought I might contact the Allman Brothers Band office in Macon to see if I could meet Gregg, Dickey Betts, Jaimoe, and Butch. Who knows? Maybe they'd take me on as a second guitarist, even though no one could replace their leader, founder, and lead guitarist Duane Allman, who perished four years earlier in a motorcycle accident.

When I verbalized this plan, neither Vesta nor Gabriel laughed. In fact, Vesta offered to accompany me on the final leg, another five hundred miles south. Which was THE best news I could've gotten at that point. I thought, 'Wow, another day or two in the presence of this amazing being and then, who knows if I will ever see her again?'.

So, when we let Gabe off at the junction of U.S. Route 66 and Illinois State Highway 159, we said goodbye. As I climbed back behind the wheel, I thought I heard them say to each other: "See you soon." As I pulled off the shoulder and power-shifted Alfie, I looked in his rear-view mirror to give Gabriel a final wave but dropped my hand when I saw he was nowhere around.

⁂

So, Vesta and I took our epic conversation on the road. The main bummer, of course, was that this jaunt of ours would end soon; too soon for my liking. Our non-stop dialogue about everything and nothing zipped along, juxtaposed with the historic Mother Road and the scenery spreading out around us, sometimes all the way to the vanishing point. (By the way, the movie that blew me away like no other counter-culture film during the genre's peak from 1965-'75 had the title "The Vanishing Point."

We had our moments of nearly crashing Alfie into all sorts of hazards and obstacles along the way, including hay bales blocking the entire lane of this two-lane blacktop, wandering farm animals of the goat, sheep, and cow variety besides flocks of vultures feasting on road kill provided by highways I-64, US-41, US-60, and I-65. However, amidst all the close calls, curving roads, swerving, ducking, and dodging, I happened to be having the time of my entire life.

Are you wondering why I continue discussing the fantastic repartee between Vesta and me? The simple answer is Life; meaning I had never been so alive or so vibrant and it was the first time a conversation with anyone I'd ever met - in San Berdoo, Vegas, show business, on the road during a tour, or wherever I've been - contained every element and aspect of life. In this time span, we'd laughed, cried, cackled, giggled, and cackled & wept again. It seemed as if tomorrow didn't exist and we would be sharing this day forever. If there's any possibility that the concept of soulmates exists, then Vesta and I were that. I don't care how corny, sentimental, or ridiculous it sounds, that girl and I were two halves of a whole, a pair of adjacent interlocking pieces of a puzzle, and two sides of the same proverbial coin. Although all three expressions are clichés, it doesn't keep them from being accurate.

As we sped, sputtered, and crawled across the wide strip of pavement, V and I forged a connection two humans have rarely (if ever) achieved. It was beyond finishing the other's sentences or other low-grade compatibility phenomena. Sure, I felt a great affinity with her, but it was more than that. In a nutshell, I felt like I'd become a better person since making this friendship. Moreover, the 'weight of the world' and my many troubles took a back seat to what was happening inside me. I'll put it this way - if I had to label this experience, I'd call it my 'awakening.' I felt, for the first time, a spirit had awakened & embraced me while restoring all that had been broken, confused, or lost in my existence. It's a rare state of peace I don't understand and probably never will, but I figured after some reflection it must be the comfort one experiences when relieved of the chore of steering the wheel of one's life and navigating around its manifold obstacles.

Boy, talk about being blown away. I'd been unprepared for this latest installment of Ross's life, but it sounds as if his life's greatest highlight occurred shortly before the crash that put him in this coma - preventing him from enjoying and savoring this precious interlude with Vesta and keeping him from living out his life the way I thought he richly deserved.

What struck me most was learning of the intimate bond Ross had formed with someone else; and, even more painful for me, another woman. I know it sounds silly, but this discovery hit me so hard I had to leave Ross's motel room and get enough air to breathe again.

Standing out there on that slab of concrete, I reflected on the parts of Ross's life I knew about so far. I looked skyward at the moonless night and marveled at the number and brightness of stars constituting the Milky Way. The breathtaking image of millions of light years arranged for my viewing put everything I'd 'heard' into a context I could now maybe begin to understand. The vastness of the galaxy reminded me of how insignificant one life seems compared with the entirety of a cosmos. However, despite the humbling nature of seeing something so huge as the Milky Way and realizing it's only a snippet of the entire universe, I experienced a sense of comfort myself realizing that all of this – our earth, all the planets, suns, moons, comets, et cetera – must've all happened for some reason and some purpose nobler than making a pretty scene.

Because of the universe's vastness and the importance of all I'd seen and known in my lifetime, I decided to give myself a little 'Come to Pammy Talking-to,' which went like this: "Listen, Miss Wertzhog, you mustn't be petty and allow yourself to envy another woman you've never met who brought a few moments of happiness and joy to the person you care most about."

So, I have to say the break I spent out on that patio was just the respite or time-out I needed to push my own life's reset button. And, after my Pammy Pow-wow concluded, I went back inside to jot whatever story or message Ross might tap out next.

As we drew closer to my destination, I became distracted from the edifying exchange of thoughts, words, and encouragement Vesta and I had been sharing. An unease began asserting itself, like someone tugging your sleeve while you try focusing on something else more important. As we merged onto I-75 toward Atlanta, I spotted a mileage sign and stiffened. "Only a hundred miles," I said softly. Not knowing whether to rejoice or weep, I sensed a crossroads in my journey looming ahead, perhaps awaiting my arrival. An unfamiliar voice inside said three times in a row, "Many miles to go before we sleep." And, all I could think of was that poet we studied in school who'd read his poetry at President Kennedy's inauguration in January 1961 when I was in the second grade. The venerable white-haired, frail, hunched-over scholar and farmer once wrote a poem about a horse and cart in the snow featuring a similar phrase. Who knows? Maybe it was Robert Frost's ghost himself trying to tell me that this was not the end of the journey. And then, a whole different work of his took center stage, "The Road Not Taken."

Somewhere along Marietta Highway, around fifteen miles out, I felt the weight of the past three sleepless nights begin to lower over and eventually around me, enveloping my body as though a cloak of chain mail had been laid across my shoulders and neck. Its weight pinned my chin to my chest just long enough for me to let loose of Alfie's leash, causing him to veer wildly off course. After busting through some newly painted white cross-hatch fencing, all I remember is sitting in a field 150 yards from the road. By myself. Looking around, I saw only one trace of Vesta's existence. Her book, which she'd read now and then, lay open on the spot she sat only a moment or so before. Leaning over, I read the verse highlighted in blue in a book called Hebrews, chapter 13 and verse 2): "Do not neglect to show hospitality to strangers, for by so doing, some have entertained angels without knowing it."

The last thought I had was, "What a message, sent by an angel other than Gabriel."

I jumped up, grabbed his Sound-About, and checked the cassette's label. The cut playing was one I'd never heard before, one titled "Everything Goes Black." Hmmm.

Chapter Forty – Three

Dr. Speckman, feeling guilty for not checking on John Doe the last two months, decided to make amends. One Sunday evening after midnight, she paid him a visit, and the first thing she noticed was change. "My god. Is this the same John Doe I put on the back burner?" She read Ross's chart over twice before deciding it had to be him. "This time his eyes are closed, but he looks better… somehow." Since it was Pammy Lee's night off, she was nowhere around. The doctor continued looking Ross over, including pulling back his top sheet and blanket. "If I didn't know better, I'd say he's gained weight. How is that possible?" She lowered into the chair by his bed and studied what she could of him. "Well, there's no rational explanation for it. Weird." After adding a couple notes to his chart, she also wrote a reminder to herself to check on him in three days, on Wednesday. She decided if he looked the same or better, she'd request a resumption of therapy. "I'll let him rest now and check him Wednesday."

Seconds after she left the room, Ross's eyelids moved. Not enough to reveal his gray orbs beneath, but both lids did move. The motion could be from rapid eye movement caused by dreaming, or he could be on the verge of reopening them for the first time in a thousand days.

⁂

I missed Ross so much on my day off I doubled my time with

him Monday night. Of course, the man looked gorgeous as ever, but with one exception. It looked like he was frowning or… what's that word? *Furrowing*; yeah, furrowing his brow. I noticed the dent between his full, manly eyebrows had become deeper than when I last saw him. And since the facility seemed even quieter than usual, I clamped both headphones onto his lovely ears and returned to the business of transcription.

After my incredible three-day, non-stop, soul-baring journey with Vesta ended by Alfie crashing through that fence, everything went black, eventually. Coal-mine black. No light of any kind and no images, forms, or colors… nothing. Life, as I'd always known it, was over. And ever since – who knows how long – I've been shut away from everything, including life and death.

Is this what purgatory is supposed to be – a nether land consisting of nothing? Do I just continue for eternity in this state? And then, I don't know how long after the crash, something started happening. My lifelong best friend - Music - reunited with me. Why? I had no idea but – boy – was I glad it had. Regardless of whether Music was sent by my guardian angel or some crazy miracle delivered her to me, but it's comforting beyond words to have Music, the most important element of my existence, back. (Yes, the most important part of my life is my family, but music is the air I breathe to not just survive, but to thrive throughout its span. And, speaking of life, what about our babies? Are they still babies? Did they survive their births and, if so, how old would they be now? And finally, most importantly, in what condition would I find Salome?

The joy Pammy Lee brought into my life by reintroducing music might now be blotted out by the awareness that the love of my life and my hopefully alive twins are unaccounted for. And, replacing the exquisite reverie brought by music was a weight so intense it obliterated everything else. So, I still wonder: Is this state in which I find myself, death… or just more purgatory?

When Ross' index finger stopped after a couple minutes, I was taken back. Surely, the song I'd played for him wasn't over. So, I pulled the headphones off his head and listened for a song. And guess what I heard that was too unbelievable to believe, much less accept? Nothing. Ross's Sound-About was not running. I had somehow, in my haste to get on with the rest of his story, forgotten to push "play." So, for the first time, Ross had been messaging me without the aid of any music. It didn't dawn on me then that his 'acapella' story was a big deal, but its import later hit me like the *proverbial* ton of bricks.

⁂

Since my shift was over and day shift had begun, I put Ross's Sound-About back in the top drawer of his night stand and planted a good-night kiss on his forehead.

For the next couple days my mind preoccupied itself with questions; questions about Ross no one I knew would know, including Ross himself. Questions such as: Where was Alfie, his Alfa Romeo? Where were his other possessions from the journey, including his ID? And perhaps the most compelling question of all: Why had only one possession – his trusty Sound-About – made it to the hospital? These and other questions poked and prodded my mind non-stop for forty-eight hours, depriving me of rest or sleep.

When I started my shift Wednesday evening everything went as usual. I cleaned my route - mainly rooms and restrooms - in my same normal order, but when time came for my first break, something was different. Ross's room was vacant. Not only was he nowhere to be seen, his bed had disappeared, too. I felt devastated and freaked out, as if I'd lost my best friend because… I had. Lowering myself into the chair I'd always used when 'speaking' with Ross, I just sat there, not knowing what else to do.

After who-knows-how-long, I looked around and saw one piece of furniture was there – his night stand. "Well," I thought, "if that's still here, maybe his Sound-About is, too." I stared at the two-drawer cabinet for another lengthy moment before prodding myself to see if the contraption was still there. I tiptoed to where the stand had been shoved into a corner and stood over it, wondering what I'd find if I opened it. I imagined two likely scenarios: 1. The Sound-About would be there and in the same condition I'd left it the morning before; or 2. The drawer would be empty. I spent two minutes processing through both possibilities and preparing myself for either. When I consulted my watch and saw my break should've ended ten minutes a go, I jumped into action. Before pulling the top drawer open, I inhaled and held my breath. Somehow, some way, his player was still there. (Whew.) I picked it up, inspected it, and decided no one had messed with it. Looking around, there wasn't anything I could use to carry it in, so I wore it.

Now that his player was back in my hands, the big question remained: Where was Ross?

Chapter Forty – Four

The conference room adjacent to the hospital administrator's office was almost empty, except for Alpharetta Convalescent CEO Larry Doster and Dr. Regina Speckman. On top of the large conference table sat a file folder between them. "So," Doster said with a dismissive wave of the hand, "if you can't produce a good reason to reinstate John Doe to full neurological care, I'll rule he remain in 'maintenance mode.' His vitals are fine, but nothing else indicates an iota of appropriate brain function and activity."

Regina straightened, arching her back to release some stiffness. "Although I can't 'produce a good reason' why we should resume intensive care, I can tell you Mr. Doe's color and overall mien have improved since I last provided care."

Doster chuckled. "So, John Doe's 'color and overall mien have improved'? How do you know that? Can you prove he's improved at all? Did you happen to photograph him during your past two visits, so we can compare them with one another?"

"Well… no, I didn't photograph the patient. That's not standard procedure, Larry, but I do know Mr. Doe's appearance has noticeably improved over the past eighty days."

"Eighty days! That's how long it's been - almost three months. Which precisely proves my point. It has been such a long time you can't possibly remember what his mien and color were.

Doctor, I need quantifiable proof, not your opinion about his color. And, as for his so-called *mien*, the man's in a coma, so there is no mien possible other than that of a pale, lifeless, expressionless...... mien." On each of the enunciations of "mien," Doster emphasized the single syllable with a tone approaching mockery. He reached for Ross's file, tucked it under his arm, and frowned. "I won't approve your request to resume treatment, so you'll need to transport him back ASAP. We have bigger fish to fry than a comatose John Doe with no improvement whatsoever in two years-plus at Alpharetta Memorial and now almost three months here. We have *all* done our best, including you, so we need to simply cut our losses and move on."

⁂

It had been an entire day since I last saw Ross *or* his bed and four days since I'd last slept when I reported for work that night. While entering, I knew something was *awry*; awfully awry. Instead of seeing only one staff member other than me, I saw two dozen or more. They were mostly in pairs, but some individual nurses and aides clad in scrubs also appeared to search the facility for something. Since I'd never seen activity like this before, this was a definite first. However, because I didn't know any of the others, I pretended to ignore all the drama. I proceeded to Ross's room, where I saw two strange things: 1. Ross's bed, but no Ross lying in it; and 2. A pair of 8 ½ by 11' posters, one at the head and the other at the foot, featuring a picture of Ross Man with his eyes closed and a caption stating, "MISSING: PATIENT 'JOHN DOE.' If you have any information, see Mr. Doster in Administration IMMEDIATELY!"

I nearly fainted. A billion questions streamed through my sleep-deprived head, but the first three were these *verbatim*: Why was Ross's bed back in his room again, but he wasn't? Did that lady psychologist know all about his situation? Or better yet, was *she* the one who had him? And, most important of all: Would I see ever Ross McInerney again?

I got so dizzy I ran for the nearest toilet (Ross's), where I relieved myself of the vomit that had bubbled up. I then lay down, rolled onto my side, and pressed the right side of my face onto the cool, white tile floor. Eventually - after having pressed each side of my face twice on the frigid, soothing tile for a count of one hundred - I thought I'd try & stand up. So, I did. After tidying up both the toilet and myself, I marched out to the front lobby, wrote a note to my supervisor explaining I'd taken ill, and tried to get myself home.

Since I'd yet to take a day off from work for any reason, I was ignorant of the protocol for calling in sick. I racked my brain, but finally decided that writing a note to Custodial Services would have to suffice to explain and excuse my sudden absence. Since I didn't know his name, I addressed it to "Custodial Services Mgr., Alpharetta Convalescent Hospital."

I drove myself home and made it to bed somehow before having another relapse.

⁂

After sleeping twelve hours, I was good to go and decided to reread what I'd transcribed having to do with Ross crashing his beloved Alfa Romeo, Alfie. As soon as I'd finished reading my notes a second time, I jumped in my faded green 1974 Datsun B-210 and scoped out the scene of the crash, somewhere out on Marietta Highway. Hopefully, I wouldn't have too much trouble finding it. In rereading my notes, I turned to my entry of Ross describing the stretch of road right before he lost control of Alfie and crashed.

So, believe it or not, within minutes I found myself ringing the doorbell of a ranch house next to a large wheat field on the left side of Marietta Highway if you're heading south to Alpharetta. So, there I was… standing on the concrete front porch of a yellow-shingled farmhouse with gingerbread trim, which I figured had to be the scene of Ross's crash. The door, after five minutes, swung open. Stopping short of the doorway in his white-sock feet, the man's protruding, watermelon-shaped belly wrapped in a 'wife-beater' undershirt broke the plane of the door's threshold. Below the untucked tank top were a pair of navy-blue sweatpants, the type folks used to wear only to gym class or to wash their car. And above the tee was the sleepiest face I'd ever laid eyes on. The bags under his eyes were doubly droopy, to coin an *alliterative* phrase. His full head of wavy, wiry dark-brown hair seemed to have a mind of its own, stretching out in every direction. The man had obviously not slept long enough to be rested and capable of having a conversation. Nonetheless, I brightened and said in as perky a way as I could manage, "Hi! I think you might be able to help me, sir. I'm looking for my friend's automobile. I believe it crashed through that fence over yonder a couple years ago, but my friend couldn't stick around to see to his car's care. He incurred a serious head injury but made it to the highway, where someone stopped and called for help."

Without answering or looking anywhere close to my direction, the man raised his head and half yelled, "Honey, you got a visitor!"

The man disappeared, leaving the door open. Thudding on the carpet were approaching footsteps, I figured, of either a child or tiny adult. When I saw her, I knew it was the latter, probably Sleepy's wife. Looking half as fatigued but more chipper stood the shortest adult I'd ever seen, (except for circus midgets or Munchkins.) I'm not good at estimating height but put it this way: I've heard through the years I'm just under five feet in height. And to show how short this woman was, I stood a head taller and literally looked down at her. For such a short person, she had a huge head of curly, frizzy hair. Her face looked drawn and careworn, like a woman who'd known more than her share of defeat or tragedy.

"Yes?" she asked softly.

"Hi, ma'am. I've come here to get my friend's car, which he crashed through your fence two and a half years ago." I pointed toward the highway with both hands. "I'm sure you remember that."

Looking straight ahead, the woman stared through my chest. And right when I'd concluded she couldn't speak, she did. Though her eyes continued focusing on my upper body, she brightened. "Why, yes. I remember when that happened. I sure do."

I struggled to think of what to say. "Oh…… I hoped you would. It's not every day a car comes crashing through someone's property like that."

Then, an unexpected thing happened - the lady smiled. She didn't just grin, but gave a full-fledged, genuinely sweet smile that should be featured on a toothpaste commercial. "No, I imagine you're right, miss. It's not every day a car does that." She took two steps toward me and closed the door behind her. "It's over there." It was her turn to point, but with only one hand. Before leading me to the rear of the property, she turned, raised her right hand, and introduced herself as Bertie Triplett. She reassured me she was pleased I'd shown up on her property out of the blue to deal with something that happened almost thirty months before. I looked at her hand for a moment and smiled.

"I'm Pammy Wertzhog," I announced, replacing the usual "W" beginning with a strong "V" sound. And although I'd never pronounced it that way before, it sounded right. I resolved then to pronounce my name that way from now on. (In fact, I liked the sound of it so much I had to restrain myself from saying it a second time.)

Bertie and I walked around the yellowest house I've laid eyes on, before stepping onto a carpet of the lushest lawn imaginable. So lush, in fact, it would win, hands-down, any comparison with any Kentucky racetrack infield. After curling around to the left, we arrived at a low-slung, tin-roofed wooden she'd painted a bright white identical to the cross-thatched fence running by the highway.

The structure she referenced as a 'garage' was no taller than six feet, but neither of us had to fret about hitting our heads. Bertie tugged on a steel latch with no lock and pulled it open. Tugging again on the door, her efforts revealed a stunning sight. Stunning for more than one reason. Not only was it surprising to stand before Ross's Alfie, but the condition in which this rare convertible had been maintained inside the little shed was twice as stunning.

Alfie looked like an auto you might see on a fancy car magazine's cover in 1975, as though he'd just rolled off Alfa Romeo's assembly line somewhere in Italy. And though the walls surrounding us were short, hand-painted white, and austere, I felt as though I stood inside an elite automobile museum in New York City, London, or Rome.

Instead of jumping up and down like I did as a child whenever I thought magic happened, I turned my back on Mrs. Triplett and said to the back wall: "Well, thank you for taking such great care of our little baby."

As a long silence ensued, I felt the flow of sweat oozing from every pore. Then, Bertie Triplett whispered, "I'd like to talk to you, but I can't if you don't turn around and face me."

I didn't realize then how ironic it was for someone who hadn't once looked me in the eye once, to suddenly insist I not only face her, but look her smack in the eye. After I turned and faced her, Bertie resumed her focus on my chest and it dawned on me that she was either on the verge of a huge decision or gathering courage to tell me something big.

To my surprise, she did both. “Before I give you this --,” she nodded at her right hand, which clutched something I couldn’t see, “I must ask you a question.” Since I had no idea where this was going, I had no words with which to respond. Luckily for me, the proverbial ball rested in her court. After another pause, she asked me slowly, deliberately: “What I need to know, Miss Pammy, is…… what took you so long?” Clueless on how to answer, I remained stiff as a board with my mouth clamped shut. “I never thought you’d wait more than two years to return, but you promised you would and today… today you’ve kept your promise.”

So, here’s the more bizarre of the two things she proceeded to tell me: She recognized me as the woman with Ross on the day Alfie crashed through their fence. She said I asked her to keep the car until I returned to claim it. I then supposedly walked off her ranch with Ross holding my hand. Okay…… hmmm. (How much more mind-blowing can this get?)

“So, we cleaned it up real nice for you and put it in this shed. My hubby, ever since, has checked on it every day. He’s done everything he could to maintain it: changed the oil, washed and waxed it, and even tuned it up just yesterday. I hope you don’t mind… and he started it up every few days, to make sure it ran fine. But, he didn’t drive it nowhere. Oh, and he gassed her up, too.” She tilted her head and nodded twice toward the north. “We got a pump over yonder for our own use. It came in real handy, so we wouldn’t have to take it on the road to gas it up without your permission.” Bertie unclenched her hand, revealing a pair of keys bearing the words “Alfa Romeo” on a steel chain.

“This larger one is for starting it and the smaller one is what Hubby calls a ‘valley key.’ He told me some man called a valley can use this while the bigger one stays with its owner. The valley key can’t open the trunk or the glove department.”

I felt myself nodding to her description of both keys, even though I had no clue what she was saying. I didn’t want to do anything to lose this woman’s trust or in any way screw this unbelievable situation up, so I said as little as possible.

After I accepted her invitation to sit in Alfie’s driver’s seat and start him up, I looked around the interior. The first thing to catch my eye was a hardback Bible opened to Hebrews, just as Ross had described. I leaned over without touching it and read the verse about showing kindness to strangers because someday you might be talking to an angel without knowing it. I kept the car running but unchained the bigger key. Unlocking what Bertie called the “glove *department,*” I saw a black leather wallet setting on top of a stack of maps. Inside I found Ross’ California driver’s license with his handsome face smiling at me and pictures of two women I figured must be Salome and Julie, both pretty and blonde. In the trunk a small pile of men’s clothes sat a box of Scotch reel-to-reel tapes labeled “My Songs.” After dropping the bigger key into my bra, I shut the trunk and returned to the driver’s seat. Looking up at Bertie & locking eyes with her for the first time, I asked: “Can I ask a big favor? You don’t have to do it though.”

“Yes, Miss Pammy. You may ask a favor. I can’t promise

I'll do it, but I can at least hear it and think it over." That's when I made my proposal. After which, Bertie stared at me and frowned. She then lifted both of her drawn-on eyebrows and asked, "Let me get this straight. You want to take this car and put the one you drove up in, in this shed?"

"Yes, Miss Bertie. For all you and your husband Mr. Triplett have done to help us… I want you to have my Datsun. I've got the proper Georgia registration I can sign over to you now, but would you mind doing me one more favor? Could you please not drive or take her out until I call and let you know it's okay? I don't have need for two cars now that we have the Alfa Romeo, but I do need to take care of my insurance before you can drive it legally. Is that fair?"

Bertie's wide smile revealed two crooked incisors that – had they been more parallel, would've looked even more like fangs. "Honey, you don't have to do that. We took care of your little sports car because… it was the right thing to do." Only after I insisted she and her husband accept my car, did she relent. It took just a few minutes for the two of us to pull Alfie out of the shed, replace him with Dotty Datsun, hug each other, and exchange phone numbers.

Since it was a beautiful, sunny day I decided to lower the top, which I did without trouble. As I drove Alfie down the long gravel drive and approached the cross-hatched white fence, I braked momentarily, so I could raise my hand high and give Bertie a wave. After beeping Alfie's horn, we headed to my house in town. My only question for the Man Upstairs was: *Exactly how many angels were involved in this miracle?* As I pondered whether there were two

(Vesta and Mrs. Triplett) or one, a voice said, “Don’t bother counting.”

The funny thing is, that voice didn’t scare me. In the least. In fact, it seemed like the most natural thing in the world. Who really knows for sure what it was? I don’t. After all, it’s not a voice I’d heard before. I won’t even rule out it’s the same voice Ross hears when he composes.

Chapter Forty – Five

My home had once been Ma's, a tiny house in the oldest part of town, surrounded by other old, humble homes. To be more precise, she sits next to a tract built as a government project (PWA? WAP? WPA? – yeah, that's it: WPA) back in the Thirties as part of Mr. Roosevelt's New Deal. So, you can imagine she wasn't much, but… she was all I had. The paint of this pinkish-orangish classic began fading sometime before that, probably during the Coolidge Administration. Nevertheless, she was mine. My best friend until the day I met Ross had always been Rose'. Not Rose like the flower, but Rose' like the wine. With an accent mark, her name is pronounced "Row-zay." So, my little Rose' was where I was when I wasn't working. She was my… *sanctum sanctorum*. I think *sanctum* means sanctuary, and *sanctorum* means sacred. So, what I'm saying is, Rose' was my best & only friend. I could disappear inside her and forget everything about the outside world. I had no phone or other way with which to communicate, but so what? Having those things would have taken away from my Rose,' but she deserved ALL my attention when I was home. Which is why I also didn't own pets. By the way, here are my reasons for *not* having pets. One: Pets poop; Two: Pets poop AND pee; and my most important *dictum*: No pets pooping AND peeing on my friend, whose full name is 'Rose' Residence.'

Miss Rose,' created in 1888 by a gentleman named Sven

Nordstrom, was built for Sven's family. Mr. N moved to the area while Alpharetta had been a wide spot on the road. He was a first-generation Swede who came to America in the 1870's. Although not a contractor or builder by trade, old Sven really knew how to work those long Swedish hands of his. Instead of being a masseur, he used his strong and nimble Swedish hands to design, carve, shape, smooth, and polish woods - any kind of wood he could get his hands on. It didn't even matter what material he might have in supply because the man could improvise in the most resourceful of ways.

And, since Sven and Ingrid his wife hadn't stopped producing babies until having number seven, this brood of nine somehow squeezed into their two-bedroom, eight hundred square foot house. Because of time and space, I can't tell you about all the things Sven built inside Rose' to accommodate nine people, but he was simply … a genius. And, his genius is a major reason why Rose' is such a special lady. Unfortunately, Ma never recognized her greatness, but mocked her, ignored her, and even beat her instead. In other words, Ma treated Rose' the same way she'd treated her only child; but time and Ma's only *progeny,* Pammy Lee, built Rose' up again. I hope someone will build me up, but for the first time.

⁂

I had quite a night after climbing into bed. The chance of bagging eight hours of sleep disappeared when I realized this night might be the last I'd spend at 38315 Maureen Street. As a result, I lay there all night, watching the movie of my life. And long about three, I changed the channel on my inner TV to ways my future would turn out - provided I play my cards right.

⁂

When I arrived at the hospital for what I thought might be my last shift ever, I saw things still weren't right: Staff running around like chickens with their proverbial heads cut off and folks engaging in all kinds of weird activities that weren't weird when I realized their purpose. Many engaged in a hunt, scouring various areas to find whatever the lost item of value was.

I joked to myself as I headed to my area. *So, who'll be the one 'gone missing' tonight? If this continues, this place will soon be out of business.* Guess what? I soon realized not only was Ross missing from his bed, but for the second night in a row. I figured that sometime after I saw the missing patient posters on his bed the night before, Ross had been returned to his bed. Question: Brought back from where? Answer: From wherever he'd spent the early part of the evening. And, I had no idea if it was that mean Dr. Speckman or the CEO Mr. Doster, but one of them must've ordered Ross placed under their care. (Or… would 'placed under lock and key' be a more apt, accurate description?)

So, now I officially freaked out. If no one knows where Ross is, where could he be? It's not like the man could move on his own. I looked around at all the 'scavenger hunters' and decided to join them in their efforts. After a while, I took it upon myself to search the restrooms. After checking all four and not finding Ross, I began feeling depressed. (Yes, I did enter and check both the men's restrooms. This was, after all, a life-or-death search; so why take the chance of bypassing a place I'd normally not be permitted to enter?) I then realized not only the futility of my search to find Ross, but how flawed my premise was that I could free him from this now heavily supervised institution.

After my search proved fruitless, I figured there was nowhere else to check but outside, so I searched the unlit areas, consisting of trees and shrubs, but saw no one. To show how small the facility is, I searched its grounds three times in ten minutes before heading to work.

As I walked through the parking lot near my building, I turned a corner by the entrance and heard, "Pssst!" Not wanting to be jumped out there in the dark or to put myself in some other vulnerable situation, I ignored the hiss and kept walking. A couple steps before reaching a side door, I felt a tap on my shoulder. Afraid of being punched in the face, I backed away and turned before resting against the wall by the door. A tall shadowy figure, like those in horror movies, stepped into the semi-lit walkway. Against all the sense and logic screaming for me to run away, I took a couple small steps toward the now more-visible man. I looked up, homed in on his face, and tried several times to form words with my mouth, but it was no use. It was like my *recurring* nightmare where I can't - for the life of me - yell, talk, or make a peep of any kind.

After a long lull all I said was, "Hey, Good Looking." I never heard his response because a whirling spiral of light struck my head, then the rest of me. I have no idea how long I was out, but when my eyes opened, this much was certain - I locked eyes with

Ross McInerney. Finally.

You might want to know how I recognized him out of his usual context. Simple. It *had* to be him; *had* to be. After all, who else on earth has gorgeous gray eyes with just the right amount of bright blue flecks running through them? And, who else wouldn't run away?

"Ross McInerney! It warms the cockles of my heart to see you up and around. All I want to know are two things: How did you get out? And, are you up for a road trip?"

He stood there clad in clothes he'd worn when he arrived. I could tell he wanted to communicate in the worst way and maybe even say something, but since he hadn't spoken for twenty-eight months, how could I expect him to now? Or, maybe he was so out of practice he had to mentally go through a bunch of steps before he could speak, and then hope like heck he would be understood by a human being, who would also hopefully help him in his time of need.

Instead of speaking, Ross motioned with his right hand. I moved closer and guess what happened? He balled his hand into a fist and stiffened his whole arm before raising it toward me. His fist was now four inches from my chest. With his left hand he motioned me to copy him by tightening my arm and pointing at him, so I did. He dropped his arm, focused his eyes on my left forearm, and placed his right hand on top of mine. And, with his right index finger he began tapping. I said each letter out loud as he tapped them out. h-e-y-g-o-o-d-l-o-o-k-i-n-g. I wondered if what he was trying to say was *"they good looking."* You see, Ross' fingers had fumbled a couple seconds before seeming to start by tapping out the 'h.' I had no idea how to proceed without knowing for certain what he'd just then tried to tell me. So, I drew in a breath, looked up, and realized how much taller he was than I. Then, I had this idea to tap on his arm instead of talking to him in the conventional way. Perhaps he'd be more comfortable and less shy using the Morse code. So, I signaled him: "Hi. Could you repeat what you just tapped out?"

He smiled down at me and tapped on my extended arm. *"Hey, Good Looking. Do I call you Pammy... or something else?"*

I giggled and whispered, "Pammy - or even something else - is fine and dandy."

(That is, if that *something else* sounds as great as 'Hey, Good Looking.')

When Ross bent over, a rattle sounded and continued a minute or more. At the end of his outburst, I had an epiphany about the noise. It wasn't a cough, but the most thrilling thing he could have attempted. Instead of a plain old cough, Ross had let out the rarest of human sounds - a deep-down laugh coated with a thick layer of rust. If barrels could laugh, this would likely be the sound or noise they'd generate. It might best be described as a 'resonant rumble.'

Then, he smiled. After a moment, Ross gave what must've been a short laugh before tapping my arm again, which he now supported with his left hand. *"Hi, Pammy. I sure am glad to see you. Where's Alfie?"*

And that, my friends, was the beginning of our first actual two-way conversation, even though he hadn't spoken a word. I told myself, "One miraculous step at a time is fine with me. I hope, Lord willing, to hear his precious voice sometime in the not-too-distant future."

I whispered over my shoulder, "Follow me," as I headed for the parking lot. Although I couldn't hear him, I sensed his presence. Then, as I stepped onto an embankment I use as a shortcut to my car each morning after work, I realized Ross might have trouble climbing it. So, I turned around, and dang if we didn't collide, my face slamming into his chest.

After we both stepped back and before I could say a joke about Ross having the boniest chest ever, he reached for my arm & tapped *"Stop,"* so I did. *"You know what we forgot?"* he messaged. As I began to rack my brain for what we could've possibly forgotten or neglected to bring, he laugh-coughed and repeated his question: *"Do you know what we forgot, Pammy?"* Before I could answer, he reached toward me with both arms, smiled brightly, and hugged me as firmly as I've ever been hugged. If there wasn't an army hunting the hospital's compound, I would've enjoyed that hug to no end. In fact, I would've insisted that hug *never* end. But, we had places to go, people to see, and things to do, so hugs would just have to wait for the future.

When we reached the car without mishap, I thanked God. And after I deposited Ross into the passenger seat and revved up Alfie's feisty engine, we were off.

⁂

On behalf of her boss, Larry Doster's secretary dialed the Fulton County Sheriff's Department. After a young desk sergeant named Cooke came on the line, she transferred the call to Doster, who tried filing a missing person's report on John Doe. But since Mr. Doe hadn't an actual name, fingerprints, dental charts, or a photograph to go by, it would be extremely difficult - if not impossible - to find him. The conversation, though cordial, ended when Larry realized it was a fool's errand to reclaim his patient, much less try. Nonetheless, as he hung up, one other possibility occurred to him. Regina Speckman might be able to describe John Doe to a crime artist, whose rendering could be broadcast statewide and perhaps nationally, with the chance - unlikely as it may be – that someone watching the evening news might see the sketch and recognize Doster's first-ever escapee in his long tenure as the hospital CEO. Because the state of Georgia would be watching this situation closely, Larry did something he hadn't done since childhood - he prayed. Not for Ross to be found, but for Larry's reputation to not be tarnished by these fast-moving developments that could develop into a PR catastrophe of tsunami magnitude.

⁂

As we headed northwest toward Route 66, we sped along semi-rural Marietta Highway. As I turned to my right to check on Ross's status, his eyes told me everything. They were as bugged as any I'd ever seen, except for maybe in some crazy cartoon, of course. I tracked his gaze and knew exactly to what he was responding. Pulling over to the shoulder, I saw the white cross-hatched fence glimmering in the morning light. As I leaned forward to unstrap my seat belt, Ross's left arm sprang out in front of me. Shaking his head and pointing first at himself, then at the ranch to the side of us, he signaled he'd prefer we both stay in the car. And, I was good with that. After ten seconds, he motioned for me to start up Alfie, I did, and we took off.

⁂

Two and a half hours later, we stopped in Clarksville, Tennessee for a pit stop and perhaps our first meal together. During the ride, we tried communicating inside Alfie - despite his top being down and his radio up all the way - as best we could. Granted, Ross didn't have to be heard because he continued messaging me on my forearm, but me? I was feeling all kinds of inner conflicts, so it became rather *daunting* to both drive and listen by internalizing all his tapping on my right arm. Meanwhile, I had to maintain at least a little eye contact with my passenger while also responding by yelling above the music blaring away on Alfie's dashboard. And, on top of all that, I can't describe how much trouble it was to not succumb to this crush of mine that was off-the-charts infatuation. Frankly, this crush affected me ten times more than any other I'd had up to this point. My entire being seemed to melt and meld with the rich cream leather interior of Ross's Alfie.

You could say it's a miracle no fatalities occurred on that stretch of highway. And, on top of all the sensory challenges I'd been contending with, I had all kinds of trouble preventing us from leaving the asphalt and crashing through another freshly painted white cross-hatch fence.

So - with all that confusion and uncertainty swirling and twirling around our open sports car with a name - I was having a world-class emotional overload. After all, here was the only man I'd ever had in my life, including classmates, neighbors, and so-called family. And, the man was not only alive, but awake with both eyes not just open, but wide open and using a form of communication *only he and I* had in common. Yes, for the very first time, little old me felt exclusive and special. Life couldn't have been better, although Ross wasn't speaking just yet.

We talked, talked, and talked some more in our *inimitable* way, which included both my normal speech and tapping on the other person's body. So, because of all the earlier-mentioned challenges, difficulties, and so on, I have no recall of what we discussed, but I do know one thing for sure: Ross McInerney had become the center of my world. No, honestly, I'm lying. 'The center of my universe' would be the more accurate *predicate adjectival* phrase.

We stopped in Clarksville, Tennessee to pee and eat. We found a good place to do both – the Taco Bell next to the highway. I decided to drive through, mainly so Ross wouldn't stick out but could retain his privacy. As we rolled up to the menu board, I told him, "The menu's coming up on the left." I said that because he'd been keeping his eyes closed. I read aloud most of the options, after which Ross tapped out that he wanted two crispy beef tacos.

"That's *all?*" I semi-demanded, and he confirmed all he wanted was just the two tacos. Then, he asked if he could have a *small* Dr. Pepper to go with those tacos. I got really tickled - not only by how little he'd ordered but how he humbly asked permission to have a small drink.

For myself, I ordered two combination burritos, a cheese quesadilla, and an extra-large diet Coke. I'd have ordered more, but I didn't want Ross to judge me. (Remember, I'm a woman with 'hog' in her name who likes to pig out, so it's understandable I wouldn't desire to be perceived as a pig, especially by the person I care most about, right?)

After receiving our order, I parked Alfie, put his roof up, and suggested we eat at one of the picnic-like tables Taco Bell had on their patio. After vacating the restrooms, I claimed the least conspicuous table. Once Ross and I unwrapped his two tacos and I'd started munching on my quesadilla, we tried having one of our unique confabs. Eating finger foods doesn't work well with intermittent messaging with index fingers, so we didn't converse much. But - when we did - we discussed music and *only* music. This thread began when I told Ross I mainly liked country & western, but also enjoyed such classic crooners as Old Blue Eyes, Dino, and Perry Como. I then turned to face him.

"How about you, Ross? What music do you like?"

He tapped on my hand, *"Rock, pop, soul, blues, folk, but no country, except for Johnny Cash, Waylon Jennings, the late Patsy Cline, George Jones, and the late, great Hank Williams."*

You know what's crazy? Even though his tastes were different than mine, I still got excited listening to him share what he liked. And by excited, I mean… in a sensual way. I basically now thought this guy – fresh from a two-year-long coma – could do no wrong, despite him coming from a different background, possessing much more intelligence than I could ever hope to have, and being totally out of my league. Isn't that strange? Talk about weird, right?

I did stop in my tracks though when I realized I'd loved every song I'd heard so far on Ross's Sound-About. "Would you like to listen to your player while we ride?"

"Really? You'll let me do that?"

"Silly boy," I teased, "of course you can listen to your own headphones in your own car." Changing the subject slightly, I asked: "Can I ask you a question, Ross?"

"Sure, Pammy. What's that?"

"Do you mind if I listen with you?"

"You mean share my headphones?"

"Well, not exactly. You do know you have a second pair under your seat, right?"

"Oh, yeah. I forgot I had those with me."

Since the Sony Sound-About had two headphone jacks, we could listen together while riding inside our open Alfie. But, what I thought was super cool happened right after we got going again. Ross resumed not only playing his playlist but tapping my arm. And, not only do I love the touch of this man's hand, but he was choosing to confide *in me... and* *no one else*. I mean, talk about a girl feeling special. This must be how everyone else feels when someone lets them know they matter so much that they're privy to intimate topics and important secrets. The only word that begins to describe how these things made me feel was 'wow.' Just 'wow.'

What was super cool about this specific message was it wasn't Ross just retelling his past. Instead, he'd begun narrating the present - the here and now. And, a major character in this story was *me;* little old, (formerly) friendless me - Pammy Lee Wertzhog. But, this time was different. Ross messaged about the time we were sharing right then as we embarked on our *odyssey* together. Amazing. And here, to the best of my memory, is what he described.

Flying along the highways and byways of America with my new friend Pammy in good old Alfie is such an improvement over what I'd endured for more than two years – absolute nothingness. I'd believed for what seemed like the longest time short of eternity that I'd been in Purgatory and clueless about when, if ever, it would end. And throughout that awful period, I thought it might continue until the end of time, and then beyond to eternity. See, Pammy Lee, I thought I was being punished for something – a mistake, a sin, maybe even a crime. I wondered why else I had to lie on my back with nothing but blackness behind my eyelids. So, I made two transitions – the first was from thinking I was dead to waiting for death and then, after that phase, believing I was caught in some spell that would isolate me from the rest of humanity.

And then, you began visiting me and brought my favorite

thing in life - music. You literally brought me back to life, and I don't think I will **ever** *forget that. You aren't just a friend, you're an angel. A guardian angel, perhaps mine. At least, that's my take. What do you think?*

For the second time in minutes, the only word I could conjure up to describe the circumstances in which I found myself wasn't a legitimate word, but a sound; one summing up my response better than any word in my ever-growing *lexicon;* one starting and ending with 'w' with an 'o' sandwiched in between.

Chapter Forty-Six

Since I found I couldn't keep my head above Alfie's steering wheel one more mile, we stopped in Springfield, Missouri for the night. But, please don't ask what time we arrived or how many miles we'd logged since Alpharetta because I not only wouldn't know, I wouldn't care.

You might ask or exclaim, "You don't care?!"

And I'd tell you that throughout our journey I couldn't have answered *any* questions about *any* topic under the sun, including our time of arrival, the number of miles from here to there, or anything else. "And why not?" you might ask. I'd tell you with all the conviction in my soul that nothing could possibly compete with Ross for my attention. The fact is, this man from a faraway place had a vastly different background and wanted desperately to reconnect with his family after being in a comatose state for twenty-eight months.

So, I must admit something here. As head-over-heels as I was with this gorgeous man, I could no longer partake of the luxury of dreaming about a romantic relationship with him. "No," I lectured myself, "Ross McInerney is *married with two children and a wife* who has no doubt been searching for him all these twenty-eight months he's been missing from home. You have no business, Pammy Lee, enjoying the company of a happily married man like Ross." And you know which habit was first on my list to quit, related to Ross? I made a sacred vow to never write the name 'Pammy McInerney' again.

"Not even just to see how lovely 'Pammy McInerney' looks in cursive?" I inquired.

"Never," I demanded. But then, after more thought, I altered my policy… a bit. "Well, I can't say 'never' because there might be a time when I actually - against all odds - could become Mrs. Ross McInerney. If that ever becomes the case, Pammy-Lamby, it *would* be legal and therefore allowable to scrawl the title Mrs. before your new name."

"But," I concluded, "unless that happens, I'm breaking one of the commandments (the one about coveting thy neighbor's wife) every time I dream of Ross being my Prince Charming." (And that's not right. If I can't have Ross the right way, I don't want him at all.)

So, we sped westward in Alfie, stopping at motels in Amarillo, Texas; Albuquerque, New Mexico; and Flagstaff, Arizona. We were able to sleep separately since I always requested a room with two beds. And, we continued conversing in our weird way, with me speaking to Ross and him answering with his right index finger. The only major difference was he didn't want to wear those headphones and listen to his music while he 'spoke' to me.

I know this may sound weird, but I really think his way of communicating with me was much more in-depth and intimate than if he'd spoken orally. It felt to me like I was inside Ross's mind, directly behind his eyeballs, and maybe even somewhat close to his soul.

Check out for yourself what he told me during our first night together:

As I said early on, Pammy, my world has always revolved around music, but don't get me wrong. I have twice been deeply in love with and completely committed to a woman. And both times the woman in question was inextricably linked with the music in my life, which I refuse to call my own or even 'our' music. Why not? Because, I don't believe anyone can honestly consider the music they composed as being strictly or exclusively their own. For instance, I had so much help in writing every one of 'my' songs. I figured people like Julia, Al, Stu, Salome, Fred, and anyone else in the mix when I wrote a song should get some of the song credit. Well, anyone but Bernie Breeze, who never once had a hand in the creative process of making any of this music. He was strictly the money man, so it's beyond ironic that Bernie has control over the fruits of my labor as a composer and our collective work as The Talismans of Sound.

And then there's the portion of credit that must go to my inner voice, over which I also cannot claim any ownership. Call it my muse, inner voice, or eternal being, but that voice I hear during the process of songwriting I simply call 'The Voice.' I don't know about other composers who 'create' a song, symphony, or jingle, but I believe music is a product of collaboration. The lowest number of voices involved in any of the music I've composed over the years has been two. So, if we're talking about, say, a ballad I wrote alone and accompanied myself on, there would still be two voices. One's mine and the second is The Voice's. After all, how could I write a good song by listening only to my own voice? It's not possible. If this Voice didn't exist, mine wouldn't and couldn't exist either. Although I'm not a religious man, I have no doubt this other Voice wields way more power than simply writing music. The Voice's parameters may be limitless, for all I know, but I do know I cannot author, pen, or compose a song without another voice.

⁂

Each night of our trek we stopped at a motel and checked in before eating dinner somewhere nearby. And, regardless of the offerings on each menu, Ross always ordered the same two items: a grilled cheddar cheese sandwich and a green salad with Italian dressing. The first of two surprising aspects of his ordering lunch or dinner was that every café, restaurant, pizza joint, or bistro without exception delivered on both items, regardless of whether they existed on their menu or not. And the second, more shocking aspect was that Ross ordered the food himself. That's right - with his own mouth. In fact, each of the few times Ross spoke to anyone other than me during our trip, he did surprisingly well. What's curious to me is that his voice seemed to grow stronger each time he used it. That's amazing considering he hadn't uttered a word in the previous twenty-eight months. However, he still – up to and after this point – spoke to me only once using his voice. Not since those fleeting moments we spent getting ourselves in Alfie, starting him up, and launching this odyssey-like voyage had he spoken to me.

And, did you just now notice something even funnier and

more curious about that last sentence I wrote? I used the phrase "launching this odyssey-like voyage." Just months ago, I would've written "startin' this here trip" instead of "launching this odyssey-like voyage." What a difference even a short amount of time can make. Or, closer to the point, what a difference the past twenty-four hours made in both our lives. And then I started wondering what the next twenty-four hours might bring; and the 24 hours after that; and then the twenty-four following that; and so on and so forth for the rest of Ross's & my lives. What on Earth will happen tomorrow and the day after that and so on and so on *ad infinitum*? (Yes, since I met Ross not only has my vocabulary increased, but so has my usage of the supposedly dead language of Latin. I know there must be some link between speaking to a man once thought dead and speaking a language once considered dead as well.) I truly think mankind is too hasty in pronouncing people and things dead. Latin & Ross Man are Exhibits A & B, for sure.

⁂

I know, Pammy. I set myself up for all kinds of abuse from you about "hearing voices" when I write songs. So, this Voice of which I speak has narrated my life since I first remember. Years before I began learning to play bass, guitar, and piano, I heard it. I heard it not only when I was alone, but as I grew older I allowed myself to hear The Voice while in the company of others. I could be doing anything – walking to school, doing my homework, brushing my teeth, or eating – when I'd hear That Voice. And, I never told anyone about it. No one – not my mother, nor Delilah, Julie, nor

Salome; I have told a grand total of ***no one*** *about this personal narrator... until I told you. And why didn't I entrust anyone with this quirk of mine? Perhaps because I'd lived all my childhood as an only child, mostly with a single parent who worked two and sometimes three jobs to make our ends meet. I remember sitting on the hardwood floor of one of our first apartments at age three and, while playing with a few wooden blocks, I first heard the Voice. I can't describe its sound, but I know it wasn't mine or anyone else's. I can't tell you if it sounds like a man's, boy's, woman's, or girl's voice. And even though it's crystal clear inside my head, I can't unequivocally state whether it speaks English or any language, for that matter. Well... that's all I'll share tonight. It's been a long day's journey and if we hope to reach Amarillo tomorrow, we better both get plenty of shut-eye. Good night, Pammy. Sleep tight and don't let the bed bugs bite. (Smile.)*

Well, well … did you hear all that - including Ross's use of "we" and "both"? And he didn't just wish me good night, but told me to "sleep tight" and "don't let the bed bugs bite"? That was the moment I became reasonably sure the love, affection, and dedication I'd spent on Ross just might be reciprocal. Perhaps my love for Ross McInerney will not go…… *unrequited.*

⁂

Ross and I…… ***we***... continued our trip west, but at a leisurely pace. I'd never driven more than twenty miles in a row before and I wasn't skilled in navigating freeways, highways, or even simple two-lane blacktops like Route 66. Plus, I was in no hurry to reach our destination. In fact, I didn't want the trip to end, ever. I not only enjoyed driving the adorable, cute Alfie, but even sweeter were the pleasures of sitting next to his owner and receiving taps from his finger on my arm on a continuing basis. Here's what Ross Man had to say about our ride together.

Riding in Alfie again was sheer joy, but feeling the wind streaming through my hair was the frosting on this cake. Somewhere around the middle of our journey, life began promising positive things again: adventure, great potential for good, and maybe some dreams becoming realities, not only for me but for those few people whom I love.

Instead of feeling trapped inside a tight, black box with only one tiny hole to permit a speck of light to reach my eyes, I'm back in the world again. No more laying in a state best compared with being trapped inside a closed coffin. No more being stuck with only my own thoughts and no one else's. No more laying in a paralytic position for thousands of hours without any forseeable end. No longer am I stuck in Purgatory, wondering which direction my spirit will head next – toward Heaven or… the Other Place. However, I do believe I'm heading toward Heaven now, on good ole Route 66. How can I believe that, you ask? Well, I've already spent years unplugged from life, which was my own private place of uninterrupted, non-stop suffering. I'd been unplugged for two years, four months, one week, and four days. Unplugged from Salome, our children, my mother, bandmates, and the rest of humanity. Unplugged from the present and the future, too. And - maybe worst of all - unplugged from Music itself.

Pammy, while I tap this message on your arm, I continue to remain disconnected from Salome and the twins. And I'm not only disconnected from other people, but everything else in the world, with one exception. And that exception is... you......... Pammy Lee Wertzhog. I know nothing about you, but I've already reserved a special place in my heart only you can occupy.

You see, without you entering my life, I would've no doubt spent or wasted the rest of my existence in a Podunk convalescent facility somewhere in Georgia. And speaking of your home state or, more specifically, your state's official fruit... you, Pammy Wertzhog, are a Peach. So, now you'll see how a Georgia Peach fares out West in the Golden State. All my money is on you. I'm sure you'll do just fine. Or, as they still say in the South: mighty fine. You'll do mighty fine.

For the first time since birth, I'd lost use of my voice.

Chapter Forty – Seven

After spending our last night in Flagstaff, we got an early start, making it to Bullhead City by noon. After devouring some down-home cooking at a Southern café on Highway 75, Ross made this announcement aloud while we approached Alfie: "We need to take a detour. I have somewhere special I need to show you. And since this will be a surprise, I must be the one who drives us there. That way the mystery will be prolonged, and the element of suspense will be enhanced." Since it's his car and… well, since it's his car, I couldn't think of a reason to deny him; but then, I can't think of a reason to deny Ross for any reason under the sun.

Yes, I'll admit I'm in love with Ross McInerney - completely, undeniably, unquestionably, and *irrevocably* in love with him. So, I wondered where he and I might be heading – both geographically and otherwise.

I know I go on and on about the mysteries involved in making music, but it's a topic that fascinates me to no end. No one seems to know how it's done. There's no correct formula for composing and no proper process for writing lyrics to complement the music. If anyone tells you he or she has a tried-and-true method for writing good music, they're lying. If a method for writing good music existed, everyone would be good at it. And, as I mentioned before, if you don't have the Voice in you, you don't have squat. At the end of the day, it's all about The Voice.

Back to musical composition, I give major credit to the women in my life for much of my inspiration: my mother, my wives Salome and Julie, and - yes - even Delilah the Deserter. Each woman inspired, provoked, or in some other way caused me to write lyrics or compose music. And although my mother detests most of the music in this world, she was my first 'muse.' Or better yet – Muse, with a capital M. (Yes, Pammy; there's another word I insist on capitalizing every time I use it in writing this story, so you might consider following suit.)

⁂

As we passed Boulder City and began our descent into the Las Vegas basin, I wondered where we could be going. Will Ross skirt the town and take me to some dude ranch out in the middle of nowhere? Or, will he head straight for the most famous street on Earth, 'The Strip'?

It didn't take me long to realize we were heading for the latter. Yep, we were surely headed for the heart of Vegas. (I *would* say, 'heart and soul,' but everyone knows Sin City has no soul.)

As we crested the buttes and headed west toward the blazing, almost-setting sun, we saw a splinter - or even a woodchip - of civilization stretching out across the vast pink desert floor. According to Ross, Las Vegas was beginning to look and act like a city. "In just the five or so years I've been gone from here, it's really expanded. Well, shall we see how The Strip has fared?" Although Ross had been here semi-recently, he still was *overwrought* with anticipation, like a kid at Christmas more than eager to unwrap his presents. And since it was my first time in 'Lost Wages,' I told myself: "Pammy Dear, we need to learn a whole big bunch about this *infamous* place; just as we've also learned about the cycle of life, this world of chaos & hatred, music, and … last, but not least - the man sitting beside 'us,' every day since we first saw those gorgeous, gray-with-streaks-of-blue eyes of his - lifeless then or full of life and love now. No, how much I would learn in the future wasn't what I wondered about the most in life. Uh uh. That prize, friends, would be awarded to…… 'The Question to End All Questions': Would I continue learning about life while in the company of the man who made all this possible? That, my friends, is what Ma used to call "THE Sixty-Four Thousand Dollar Question." I never understood the reference but knew it had to mean *the* most important question. So, I sat on the edge of Alfie's seat and eagerly awaited what Ross planned for our Las Vegas experience.

Two miles from The Strip, Ross pulled into the first paved lot I'd seen all day. "Let's have dinner here. I'd take you somewhere nicer, Pammy, but we need to kill some time first."

Twenty-One Coins was a roadside restaurant featuring a small casino with two Blackjack tables, an ancient roulette wheel, and three banks of nickel slot machines. Red was the dominant color; so dominant I can't say whether there was a second color in their scheme. The short, harried woman clutching two huge menus led us to a booth in the corner, a spot from which we could watch the goings-on in the place. Underneath the glass on each of the table tops were twenty-one coins, all foreign, from countries such as

Belgium, France, Great Britain, and Spain in addition to my favorite – Australia's gigantic penny with a large kangaroo on it.

The wine-red, velvet-like drapes and wall paper impressed me, so I told Ross. He grinned. "It's okay, but when it comes to fancy, you haven't begun to see anything yet." And, as it turned out, truer words have never been spoken. We wiled away our time looking around, chatting with our server (a middle-aged gal named Nell), and then small talk before, during, and after our meal. I tried to catch Ross up with current events, but he seemed more interested in me and the other diners around us than any of the recent happenings in America or around the world; which was totally fine, since I don't even try to keep up with recent news or current events.

After checking my cash situation, I figured we could make it to California on what I had if we didn't eat at more than one fancy restaurant the rest of our trip.

When Ross deemed it dark enough outside, he said: "Let's see how Vegas is tonight."

As we made our way to Alfie, I noticed a canopy of white stretching out above us in the recently darkened sky. "What's that - a meteor shower?"

"Seriously? You've never seen the Milky Way before? Yep, there she is in all her glory."

As I looked up, Ross said: "That's the sight I've missed most these past few years." I was so overwhelmed by the majesty of the Milky Way that I continued crooking my neck, so I could continue taking in this amazing tapestry of light. As I did, I heard sniffles, then Ross blowing his nose. "Of course, if I could see Salome, I'd trade in all my Milky Ways for that."

I didn't know what to do or say but was so touched by Ross's love and devotion for his wife that I found myself wanting to give him a big hug, so I did.

It wasn't romantic, sexy, or anything like that, but a genuine gesture of my sympathy and affection for the man. I patted him on a shoulder and said, "I pray you two get back together." I don't know what got into me, but do I know this: I wanted nothing more in life than for Ross McInerney to have a much happier, more fulfilling second half of life than his first.

We wound our way into town and onto The Strip, which was – of course – all *aglitter*. Although the sun had set an hour before, The Strip (officially Las Vegas Boulevard) projected such intense light it seemed daytime had returned. The lights cast a glow onto everything around it, including the roadway. "I'm so glad you lowered the top," I declared as I continued looking up. "The light bill for this street alone must equal the rest of the city," I exclaimed as I craned my neck to spy the towers of light stretching for the desert sky.

As we passed the largest hotels – The Desert Inn, Riviera, Sahara, Flamingo Hilton, Frontier, Tropicana, Showboat, and the space needle-inspired Landmark Hotel – I became limp and speechless. Why? Because flashes of color sprang out at us cat-like with facsimiles of the following: muscular cacti, courteous cowpokes, and perky cowgirls vying with the flowers, clowns, dollar signs, heads of Washington & Lincoln, busty showgirls, and toga-clad Roman statesmen - which dominated (or obliterated) the long, straight stretch of roadway with various messages, images, and artwork. Signs the size of aircraft carriers informed us the Desert Inn presented Rich Little, impersonator extraordinaire; the Riviera boasted of the floor shows "Crazy Girls" and "La Cage" nightly; the Sahara *sequestered* comedian Red Foxx and the "Ain't Misbehavin'" floor show in separate venues; and LV's oldest and first hotel & casino, The El Rancho, offered not only $1.49 breakfasts, but steak & lobster specials galore and something called "the loosest slots in town;" Keno; and – of course – a 'daily buffet.' "Wow" was all I could say to the bursts of silver, gold, white, and red light.

Ross took us up & down The Strip twice, so we got a good sample of what Las Vegas had to offer. I can't describe the mixture of various emotions I was having, but let's just say Pammy Lee Wertzog was struck by both inspiration and depression during our two junkets. Depressed and feeling empty due to the glamour and ostentation, I was also impressed by those two elements. It was as though I'd time-traveled back to the Middle Ages.

"The Emperor's New Clothes."

"What's that, Pammy?"

"This town reminds me of that story we read as kids - 'The Emperor's New Clothes.'"

"How so?"

"Well, there's all this danged hoopla, hype, hoity-toity-ness… And for *what*? Cheap food, cheap drinks, cheap slots, loose slots, loose sluts in big hats, and - the piece d' resistance – the chance to get rich fast …… (or poor, even faster). The expectations are so high, like when the emperor was told how splendid he looked in his new duds, only to be let down by the reality that there had literally been nothing on him all along. All these lights, signs, and statues reminded me of that pathetic old emperor from that fable. You know… all the illusion, delusion, and confusion. I mean, what a charade!"

For the first time since we'd left the restaurant, Ross looked me in the eye. "Wow, Pammy. You have depth to you. I mean, you're not blown away by all this glitter and gold? Hallelujah. In that case, I'll show you somewhere way less phony and way more down to Earth. In fact, I once considered the place we're heading toward as my second home."

Even though Ross had told me all kinds of stuff about his past, including the time he spent here with his first wife Julie and the band, I had no clue what he was talking about. And, not because there was some big mystery I knew nothing about. Rather, it was because the 3 G's - glitter, gold, and gab - had stuffed my brain, leaving hardly any room for more than a thought or two to wedge itself in. Physically, I was in Sin City, but mentally & emotionally, I sat atop my old friend Cloud Nine. It had never crossed my mind before that riding in a luxury sports car with the top down could feel like riding on a fluffy cotton-ball of a cloud, but it did. It really did.

Right then, Ross swerved right, around a corner, and speed-shifted Alfie into fourth. When I looked over at him, I saw a picture identical to the one I had had in my head a while back when I'd played "Who's Gray Eyes & Where's He From?" This time, though, I witnessed with my own eyes the wind sifting through the same man's thick head of jet-black hair while wearing an 'I Must Be in Hog Heaven' expression on his chiseled face. Then, when those gray eyes locked with mine for the second time that night, I no longer could remember any of our previous conversation. We turned left twice, and then everything changed. No longer did colorful glitter and piercing light surround us. Instead, only a blanket of dark desert lay ahead. And way, way off to our left I could make out The Strip. In front of us were two things - a black strip of unlined road and the profile of desert sagebrush forming Mother Nature's low skyline on both sides of the road. In fact, it was so peaceful out there in the dark after the hustle and bustle of The Strip that I whispered a wish…… that this spell of peace & quiet would last forever. I raised myself up as far as my seat belt would allow to face the blurring fresh night air streaming in from the east.

And sadly & way too soon, Alfie slowed and cleared the up-sloping entrance to a smallish, almost blacked-out area I gradually identified as a parking lot composed of asphalt. After Ross cut Alfie's lights, the three of us coasted a hundred yards till he flipped his lights back on, just a couple feet short of a structure of… who knows how many stories high. Since we found ourselves nestled up to the back wall, there were no ground-level windows and only a trace of light shimmering from a neon sign above the door labeled

"Employees Only." A short, grim guard shone his industrial-sized flashlight in my eyes, and while I struggled to recover from my blindness, the gent shifted his beam to Ross. And then, something strange happened. The man yelled, "Hey, young fella! How the heck are you? Welcome back, Ross Man!" And just like that, we arrived at the first casino I'd ever set foot in. Ross - on the other hand - had returned back to not only the site of his highest highs, but the place where his first wife Julie rested *in perpetuity.* (May she rest in peace.)

Chapter Forty – Eight

After the lone guard on duty emerged from beneath the neon sign, he unlocked what looked like the employee entrance. As he held it open for us to pass through, we entered the Las Vegas Hacienda Hotel & Casino. And then, the freakiest thing happened. Ross scared the bejeezus out of me by speaking not only audibly, but confidently and boisterously loud. “Thanks, Jerry. I’ll take it from here. I remember this place like the back of my hand. Ha ha. Oh, and Jerry? Listen, if I don’t see you again before my friend and I leave, please give my love to Janet and the girls. Joni’s your older girl and Jenna’s the baby, right?”

Brightening to the level of light on The Strip, Jerry smiled & grunted something sounding like “right.” Ross interpreted the man’s unlocking the door as permission that would allow him, an employee from several years ago, free reign around a casino holding millions of dollars of someone’s money. And, all this permission was granted without question from the resort’s gatekeeper. I must be honest - that moment so puffed me up with pride for having this new friend of mine. Never had anyone affected me like that, but the moment had - at long last - arrived. We then walked together down the longest hallway I’d ever walked down. It had to be the length of a danged football field, for corn’s sake. So, while Ross and I sashayed side by side down a long, white-tiled hall, a vision in my mind played out. I know you won’t believe me, but I visualized my new friend and I walking 'down the aisle' together in a cathedral with open-beam ceilings and masterpieces of stained glass standing in the arched windows for all to be inspired. No, I'm not proud of what was projected on the screen inside my head, but at the time it seemed perfectly fine. You see, both of us had 'alternate versions' of reality we'd been living in.

"Hey, let's get a drink in the lounge," Ross tapped.

I wanted to slow his pace by grabbing his sleeve, but I couldn't take the chance of harming him in any way. So, I did all I could to keep up with those long legs of his. We took a quick right down a wide hallway and followed the red & gold runway leading to double oaken doors at least ten feet tall, which opened to the dark interior of what must be a tavern or club of some kind. Sure enough, it turned out to be the first alcohol-serving establishment I'd set foot in during my thirty-year stay on earth. The only way for me to keep up with Ross in the dark was to grab ahold of him and hold on. After a bit, we arrived at a massive wooden structure I gradually, but slowly identified as a bar. Once Ross saw enough in the almost pitch black, he hoisted me onto one of the high stools and ordered two Tom Collins. (Up till then, the only cocktail names I'd heard were considered 'virgin' - without booze - Shirley Temples and Roy Rogers.)

Though almost empty, the joint had a few tables with two or three patrons and a couple on each end of the bar. Since Ross and I sat in the exact middle, no one else was near, except an occasional bartender passing by with drinks every few minutes. What I found strange, though, was Ross's behavior while sitting there. If no one else was around, he'd speak, but when someone walked by, Ross tapped out his words on my arm; which I liked because it helped me feel closer, more intimate with the man. Then, he messaged: "This is how I'll communicate with you, Pammy… when the situation warrants."

Instead of speaking, I tapped: "You're the boss." He got a big kick out of that and laughed so *vigorously* he coughed till I fetched him a glass of water from a passing waiter.

His coughing caught the attention of a passerby toting an instrument case. "Hey, Bud. You okay?" the older, bald man asked. Despite nodding his head 'yes,' Ross turned pink, then beet red as the coughs continued exploding from his mouth. Then, he emphatically shook his head 'no' and pointed to his throat. Before I knew it, the man dropped his case, spun Ross around, and gave him what I knew was called 'the Heimlich maneuver.' And, guess what flew out of poor Ross's mouth for a whole four feet? One of those Maraschino cherries. Ross had begun chomping away on the cherries from our Tom Collins at the same time when I'd tapped out the message "You're the boss" on his arm. So, my comment caused him to swallow the fruit whole until they caught in his windpipe.

Naturally, all this commotion caused a stir in the Hacienda lounge. A whole bunch of people streamed in to see what the ruckus was. And, before I knew it, a crowd of fifty patrons surrounded us. And right when I thought this scene couldn't get weirder, it did. The old gent who'd dropped his case and saved Ross's life dropped his jaw. "Hey, I know you! You're none other than my old bandmate and son-in-law Ross McInerney!"

As Ross opened his mouth wide to show his disbelief, something even stranger happened: Someone in the crowd yelled "Ross Man" and then others began repeating the phrase. How weird, I thought, before it hit me like a ton of bricks: "Ross Man" was one of the many nicknames his first wife Julie thought up and called him on stage. Know why I remember that? Because - as I told you when I started telling this story - names, nicknames, and name-calling have always played huge roles in my life - first as a little girl and now as a grown woman.

Then - after dialing back to the present from my name-dominated past - I witnessed a progression of the growing crowd's behavior. Calls of "Ross Man" turned into a chant circulating the entire room. And then, the guy with the case set it down again and waved his arms for everyone to be quiet so he could speak and be heard. Although I didn't know whether he wanted to be heard by just Ross or everyone in the room, I sensed my answer was *forthcoming*. "Okay, okay. Settle down enough for me to ask Ross a question and hear his response." Turning to his former bandmate, he asked: "Ross, would you like to jam with me and the band?"

Ross straightened and glanced at my arm as if he considered tapping it instead of using normal speech. He then whispered in my ear, "What do you think, Pammy?"

If I hadn't been leaning on that solid oak bar, you could've knocked me over with a feather, causing me to fall off my 'throne' and break my gall-darned 'crown.' Yes, sitting next to a regal man these last few days caused me to feel a sensation I can only describe as 'royal.' And… guess whose voice I heard in my mind's ear at this moment? Who else but my departed, not-exactly 'dear' Ma yelling her favorite dig: "Oh, you're royal alright; a royal PAIN IN THE ASS – that's exactly what you are, Hammy over Miami. A royal pain in the old ass."

And I started thinking of her for a while, wondering what she might've thought about Ross… Maybe what changes / improvements would she have --?

Suddenly, I cracked up enough to beat the band because I realized the 'new me' couldn't care any freaking less what Ma thought of anything or *anybody*, including Ross and me. (The last three words make a great phrase, don't you think? "*Ross and me.*")

It was …… *an epiphany.*

So, the next thing that happened was this speech Ross gave to a group, which now had swollen enough pack the Hacienda's Padron Pub. I believe I captured what he said *verbatim*.

"I don't know what to say that's appropriate, but some of you might remember me from the last time I was here." (Everyone in the room but Ross and I laughed; and many repeated "*might remember*" as a gentle mocking before the crowd proceeded to laugh a little harder.) Finally, Ross raised both hands. "As many of you know, I played here with my band and my dear, departed wife Julie in the lounge for quite some time." Ross started to choke up and didn't resume speaking until the lump in his throat gave way. "So, we happen to be passing through town, and thought I'd stop by and see all my old friends again and…" I had no idea what he'd say next, but if I had, it certainly wouldn't have been the words I heard coming from his mouth. "I met this wonderful person, who's someone I already consider a great friend. Everyone, please give my friend Pammy Wertzhog a proper Hacienda howdy." And the wackiest thing happened: An entire crowd yelled at once, "Howdy, Pammy Wertzhog!"

There are two pieces of information about me you might find interesting relating to this warm, unexpected welcome from all those sweet people, so I will reveal them now. Number 1: No more than one person at a time had ever addressed me before, much less with a name even close to mine; and 2: Everyone said my name correctly, on the first try. Yes, everyone had pronounced my name perfectly. And try guessing the absolute best thing about their welcome. Not a single "Hammy" or "Wart Hog" could be heard in the bunch. Life indeed began to seem wonderful. And all because of just one person. I'd give you three guesses, but you only need one.

So, after the chorus of "howdy" died down, the guy with the big, black instrument case said: "I'd like to invite you all to see my old friend Ross McInerney as he sits in with our band in… fifteen minutes." A cheer exploded all around, including the three bartenders behind us. Evidently, 'Ross Man' was great for the Hacienda's bar business. And, as soon as the din died down, the crowd race-walked to the lounge's showroom to stake out their seats. By the time Ross and I had completed the short walk next door, the entire room had filled. (Of course, I couldn't have been prouder.) And, for me - Yours Truly - to place a big, red (non-Maraschino) cherry on top of this delicious hot-fudge sundae, I would finally get to hear not only Ross's singing, but the songs he'd written & the instruments he played. Life was now perfect and couldn't get any better. Am I right or…… am I right?

The teeniest table appeared a moment after the snap of a finger along with four chairs placed for Ross in the corner of the large room, farthest from the stage. The old guy set his case on the stage before following Ross to where I now sat. "Pammy, meet my dear friend and former bandmate – "

"Don't you mean *future* bandmate, Ross?" The old man flashed a mouthful of false teeth before extending his freckled, tanned hand for me to shake. "Hi, Pammy. I'm Pops. Welcome to Lost Wages." He threw back his head and guffawed as though he'd just invented that pun.

Ross bid me goodbye for the moment and headed to the stage with Julie's dad. With Pops doing most of the talking, the men worked out their first set together in a long time. (Or, what folks back home in Georgia call 'a coon's age' - as in 'raccoon.')

⁂

Ross, after leaning over a set list on stage and conferring with Pops for fifteen minutes, didn't straighten up right away, but took his time returning his spine to its default position. He thought: *Luckily, I haven't fallen tonight or done anything else to embarrass myself or my friend Pammy.* The back spasm he now began experiencing was the first overt effect of laying prostrate in a hospital bed for two and a half years. Shooting pains from his sacrum succeeded in straightening Ross' spinal column to where it had been before the 'accident.' Otherwise, he wouldn't have been upright enough to play keyboard, piano, bass, etc.

Pops tapped the microphone before reciting "test, test" three times and then nodded at the back of the house to the sound man. When he glanced across the stage and saw Ross's ready signal, a grin spread across his tanned, bearded face. Clearing his throat, he again faced the mic. "Good evening, ladies and gents; welcome to the Hacienda Hotel and Casino. Tonight, we have not only my talented band of kick-butt-& take-no-prisoners bandmates, but a very, *very* special guest, too. The gentleman you see at the controls of that Hammond B-3 organ over there is none other than the driving force behind the bands Propinquity and, of course, the super successful Talismans of Sound… Please give it up bigtime for Mr. Ross McInerney!" The crowd burst into applause and whistles before the chant "Ross Man, Ross Man" kicked in again.

Pops held up his arms again to quiet the crowd. "Just so you know, we'll be playing tunes from what is known as The Great American Songbook tonight, so please don't expect or request any songs of Ross's." The band then kicked into the memorable chestnut "That Old Black Magic" to start a set of nothing but the classics of American jazz and popular music.

The set began a little slowly, with the crowd content to sit and watch Ross & the band play the first three songs. Pammy, on the other hand, sat as mesmerized as she'd ever been about anything. She couldn't keep her blue, tear-filled eyes off Ross, who seemed unfazed by the scenes both onstage and in the audience a few feet below. A few couples began dancing, but because the lounge was so packed, they had to dance where they stood or risk knocking into someone else or, worse yet, that someone else's drink. Consequently, they each danced a bit like they were wedged inside a telephone booth and forced to step in place. The dance floor wasn't available since eighteen tiny tables identical to Pammy's had been set up to accommodate the large crowd. At two of those tables sat a group of well-dressed men in suits with their even better dressed dates. The men watched the band, especially Ross, intently. Only between numbers did they cease their vigil and converse. One - a short man with a boxer's build and cufflinks that glittered more even than the pomade in his slicked-back head of thick black hair - was clearly in charge. The other men nodded their heads animatedly and smiled whenever he spoke, while the women sat still as statues still, except when spoken to by a man.

Pops' band, Dow Jones & the Above Averages, featured Pops on various horns; a longhaired drummer named Russ, who remained unengaged throughout the hour; a bearded, rail-thin bassist named Ernie who appeared downright catatonic; a 20-year-old lead guitarist everyone called Buzz, whose auburn red hair reached his waist; and Ross, who took turns at the organ, piano, guitar, and flute. Without a single vocal, the band's set consisted of only instrumentals, but the crowd hadn't seemed to mind. In fact, when Dave Brubeck's legendary "Take Five" ended, everyone in the house stood to whistle, clap, *and* cheer… yes, *all three.*

⁂

During the break, the other musicians remained onstage, except Ross, who - heading on a beeline for me - grabbed my hand and tapped it. "Follow me… please." So, I did. Since he moved so fast, it took every single bit or *iota* of my will to keep up with him. I had no idea which route we took, but we wound up again in the totally dark parking lot next to Alfie.

"Do you mind driving?" he asked. I nodded 'no'. "Good. Let's split." When he tugged me by the hand, I dug my heels in.

"Whoa, Cowboy! What about your gig?"

He stood there with the blankest stare. (Yes, as blank as when he'd been in the coma.)

It fell to Yours Truly, of course, to keep the dialog rolling. "We can't just leave now – in the middle of your comeback performance, with nowhere at all to stay the night tonight." Ross frowned. "You're right. I'll talk to Pops and see if we can stay with him tonight."

Instead of debating him on where we'd lay our heads, I said, "Do what you can, Ross."

We walked together (but not hand in hand this time) back to the lounge. As we approached Pops in front of the stage, the short, powerful man in the audience wearing the fancy suit stepped into our path. Smiling for no more than a second, he said: "Good evening, Mr. McInerney. Welcome back to the Hacienda." Extending his right hand for Ross to shake, Ross raised his own arm in a "Stop right there" gesture, with his palm playing the role of Stop Sign.

"Mr. Belucci, I would like you to meet my new agent, Pammy Lee Wertzhog. Pammy, this is the general manager for Hacienda Hotel Group, Mr. Carmine J. Belucci."

After we shook, Mr. B invited us to his office for a drink and any refreshments we may like. *Wow*, I thought, *he's really being nice to Ross. I wonder if Carmine has gotten nicer?*

Sitting on his desk's edge, Belucci began: "Let me get right down to brass tacks, Ross. The Hacienda wants you to return… but not to our lounge. You became a big fish after your residency here. I know your albums were - what do you call records that shoot right to the top of the charts? Bullets. Yeah, your first albums were number-ones… with bullets. So, Ross, I'd like to book you into our main room as soon as possible. And, I'll pay you fifty percent of the gate each night. I'll even leave it up to you, as to how many shows you do. Period. You're the boss."

Without looking up, Ross tapped on my arm "Take charge," so I looked him in the eye and lifted an eyebrow for confirmation. After he tapped, "go for it," I did. As I took in a breath, I managed to smile the same way Belucci had earlier – fast and big. I decided the best thing for me to do was listen, so I began by asking the man a question: "What else do you have in mind for my client besides a 50/50 split and a lengthy extended engagement so you can make tons?"

Smiling at me, Mr. Big said: "Ross Man! We got a hot one here. Where'd you get *her*?"

Since Ross's head was still down, I realized he wanted me to field all of CB's questions, so I did - by bouncing the ball back into Mr. Carmine's half of the court. "What's the showroom capacity, Carmine? Oh! and, we also will require a 50/50 split on the bar."

"To your first question, the capacity is six hundred. And to that second question, we don't normally tie bar receipts to a performer's take."

Time for me to smile again. "Well, first off, that wasn't a question of mine, but a stipulation of *ours*. We are seeking, not *asking* fifty percent of all bar receipts, including all food purchases. And secondly, Ross McInerney is no 'normal' performer. Why, you are seeing for yourself, tonight, how much excitement and bar sales my client generated just by showing up unannounced and jamming with your little lounge band only capable of half-filling your lounge; and that's on a good night. Mr. Belucci, do you remember how you had all those employees bring in *eighteen* extra tiny tables because my client attracted them? Oh, and I also noticed those *ten cases* of assorted booze hustled in at the same moment you approached my client to work for you, for pay. Tonight's performance is gratis, free, no charge, Mr. B, but just realize that if you wish to procure my client's services anytime in the future, you will need to reciprocate by acceding to whatever favors he asks."

Instead of smiling, Belucci mad-dogged me, but I would not - for the life of me - back down. Mustering up my best impression of a bulldog face, I sucked my breath in through my nostrils and held that breath till the little guy spoke. When he saw I wasn't about to back down from his stare-down, he turned to Ross and tried reasoning with him. "Listen, Ross Man, you and I have quite a successful past; am I right? So, listen, my friend - why don't just you & I hammer out an agreement that both of us like? I'm sure you will like what I'm prepared to offer you, sir."

Standing up, Ross said, "It's your choice, Boss: Either deal with Pam or we're done."

Big Boss Man (BBM) jumped up from his swivel chair and did everything to stall Ross and me from leaving. He tried by first asking Ross and then me a question, which resulted in strikes one and two. The man was on the verge of facing a third pitch and possibly striking out, when - thanks to Belucci's fast and fancy footwork around various office furniture - he reached the door first. Grabbing hold of the brass knob with his hammy fists, he assumed the pose of a man clinging to the dearest thing in his life, his livelihood as a big-shot casino and resort owner. Or, to retreat to baseball *allegorical metaphors*, it was like Yogi Berra blocking home plate at Yankee Stadium the last out of the seventh & last game of the World Series to win it all. Instead, reality was that this cockroach of a man was trying to turn the tables, so he began by turning his own back at us as though just realizing we'd entered the room. And then, he pulled off not one, but two slick tricks. The first trick was to beam his fiercest, friendliest used-car salesman's smile; and the second was he 'busted a move' opposite to the one I would've choreographed for him. Instead of a sneer stamped on the little Sicilian's clean-shaven, sweat-dripping bulb of a face, there was a sudden shift of weight in the knee of his pivot leg - telegraphed by the rustle of polyester blend. A move intended as a grandiose sign of humble deference instead became a *figurative* white flag of surrender so large it wiped all our faces while Mr. Big Boss Man waved it back & forth, back & forth, ad infinitum. (Note: I'd never use the phrase *ad nauseum* here.)

The almost imperceptible dance move Belucci cut right then was a dip. Just a wee little dip, mind you, but the only kind a straight male adult could hope to pull off in mixed company without receiving a chorus of chortles and guffaws. This choreographed move, in the less-is-more tradition, could've escaped a more casual observer's gaze, but to Ross and me, it was - without a doubt - a dip. (When I realized we had a case of 'A dip doing a dip,' I almost busted my gut.) And then, as if to blow both our minds a second consecutive time, this tough, grizzled kingpin of a gangster adopted a tone of *solicitude*. He even bordered on sounding beggarly when inviting Ross & me to stay longer; or, as he worded it, to hear him out. So, being fair-minded professionals, we did exactly that.

Chapter Forty – Nine

After Mister Big led us back to his desk, he made a sweeping gesture to signal us to sit in the pair of ladder-back chairs facing up at it. Pulling out a black walkie-talkie and lowering his head, CB spoke in a whisper, perhaps ordering drinks and food for us from Room Service, but without consulting us on what we might wish to consume. And, to make matters worse, I began wondering what kind of a man would order for others, especially someone like Ross who surely had a delicate stomach after fasting against his will for thirty months.

As I continued *ruminating* on this subject in this manner awhile, two women in blue uniform smocks took our orders separately, with the tall one waiting on Ross and the short one on me. But, after receiving a wink from Mister Big as a message to make it quick, they collided in their race for the door. Both apologized to the other at light speed, curtsied, and left. Wow.

"So," Belucci began, "how's about we start over? Shall we?"

We looked at one another, nodded, and I'm the one who spoke. "Yes, that's agreeable for my client, Sir. Since I have been closely monitoring his health for quite some time now, I've asked Mr. McInerney to remain with the two of us while we discuss and hopefully finalize an agreement between both parties. That way, we can kill two birds with the one proverbial stone by consulting Mr. McInerney about his wishes at any time throughout this process while also monitoring his health. Is that agreeable to you, Sir?"

The short, powerful man in the white tight-fitting, long-sleeved shirt relit his ugly Cuban cigar and stared at the end of it several moments, as though admiring it as an art expert would 'The Mona Lisa.' Eventually, he tilted his head back and blew a thick stream of grayish brown smoke at the acoustic tile ceiling. As we watched the bank of it collide with the tile and disperse, an idea smacked me right on my forehead with the force of a heel from my own hand. Ripping a yellow sheet from the pad in front of me, I wrote down ten items, each a condition of what I thought was best in Ross's best interests. When I'd finished, I was about to hand it to 'my client,' but instead he lifted his hand to block my move. His mute message spoke loud and clear, though it would've struck anyone else as strange or ambiguous. I totally understood the message Ross transmitted to me non-verbally: He had total confidence in me and wanted – no, demanded – I do whatever I thought best for this and any other situation he'd want help with. He told me wordlessly that he, Ross Robert Padraig McInerney, had complete and utter trust that I, Pammy Lee Wertzhog, would not only negotiate on his behalf with my best effort, but without me requiring any further input from him. He was, in effect, handing me 'the keys to the kingdom.' And, you know what? Regardless of the duties I may be performing for Ross or the title or office I might occupy in his future, for the time being I felt as though I belonged in the inner circle of this man's people in his life; and, I felt fully *ensconced*. Not only is it my newest word, but it describes to a tee how I felt at that moment - completely *ensconced* in the life of my new boss… or client. Yep, client is the word I'll try to use. Who knows? It might be the label Ross prefers I use. Hopefully, someday, I'll be able to refer to him as more than just my "client." But, what that role will end up being is anyone's guess, but… I certainly can think up one or two possibilities I've spent much time outlining; just in case I need to make a 'pitch' to him sometime.

I know this all must sound crazy or perhaps *I* sound crazy to you, but I swear on Ma's grave that everything I mentioned in the previous paragraph zipped through my brain just in the time it took for me to nod to Ross and then pivot to hand him the ten conditions I'd concocted out of the desert air to the Chief Executive Officer of the Las Vegas Hacienda Hotel, Mr. Carmine Jaco Belucci.

Here I was - Pammy Lee Wertzhog from Alpharetta, Georgia - negotiating a potentially very lucrative contract for us, and I wasn't in the least intimidated by any aspect of this situation. I looked Mr. B square in both of his black-coal eyes, smiled my sunshiniest Southern belle smile, and said: "We have a plan here that will result in success for both parties. If you agree, Sir, then please sign here." I then drew a line with my blue Bic pen and placed a large 'X' at the left end of the line. And then, the freakiest thing happened – the man leaned over my yellow handmade kiddy contract with the funny handwriting and signed it! And that, my friends, is the first time I ever felt confident, strong, and in control. But being all three of those supposedly great things is not the only signs of a strong woman - or an equally strong man, either. No, I can now assert that there's a fourth sign, one that looms high above the others.

Holding up the long, yellow sheet of lined paper, he said, "I'll have someone run copies. And, I'll keep the original… if that's okay with you."

The little voice inside spoke, causing me to change my response. "Oh, let's do this right, Boss. Let me scribble out the exact-same conditions and we'll just sign both. That way, both parties will have an original and can run cross-copies for each other as well. That way, there's no chance of confusion about who should get the original. Do you… *capisce*?"

Raising both eyebrows, Belucci looked me in the eye as he said: "Ross Man, you've got yourself quite an agent here. She not only has lots of moxie, she's a true beauty."

Turning to Ross, I saw the biggest smile yet on that handsome, chiseled, stubbly mug of his. Which reminded me, he needed a 'shave and a haircut' – but without the two bits. (It's a *venerable* reference, so don't feel bad if you're not old enough to get it.) Anyhow, I don't want to forget to tell what Ross Man said: "Oh, I'm quite aware of Miss Pamela's competence and compassion, which is why no one – ***no one*** – speaks for me, except for my agent & friend… Pammy Lee Wertzhog."

I guess Ross and Belucci shook hands right then to seal the deal, but I can't tell you for sure… in fact, I can't tell you at all. I don't recall much of anything about that meeting, but I do remember right before falling asleep late that night, I played back Ross's words about me with *exactitude.* I had never felt even half as proud as I did the first and second times I heard Ross say those words … about me.

Me. Sometimes, words - our own words - are all we have left at our disposal, so we should select them at least as carefully and wisely as we choose our clothes in the morning for a complicated day ahead; which might be why I took this agent job so seriously. If I do nothing else in Ross's life than to protect his music from being misused or misappropriated, I will die a woman happier than I ever thought possible before. But, at the end of this opera, when the fat lady in the weird get-up sings, what the whole shebang will all come down to is this: Any day spent in the presence of Ross McInerney is a good day, regardless of anything else – be they circumstances or any other entity about to hit the proverbial fan.

Chapter Fifty

The next day, at the literal crack of dawn, we left Vegas and headed for California. Without another car on the road in either direction and all the signage turned off, the desert stretching out ahead of us promised nothing but peace and quiet. "Well," Ross began with a smile, "if nothing works out in L.A., we still have a way to make dough in Sin City."

I fell into a giggle fit to beat not just the band, but any band. I mean… whooey! … was I laughing or what?! Oh, and you should've seen Ross. He kept looking back and forth, back and forth between me and the road. I wasn't afraid of us crashing because there wasn't danger of that. As I said, not a single vehicle had passed us on that highway. So, I didn't mind that Ross kept looking over at me. The look on his face was both delightful and… delighted. The same man I'd watched lying in bed for months on end without a movement or sign of life was now laughing, driving, and enjoying life while a desert breeze flowed through his lovely coal-black head of hair. His entire being, especially the mane on top his head, seemed more alive than anything or anyone around him. I recall thinking that all the time Ross had spent vegetating in some unconscious state back in Georgia conserved energy that was now flowing from the precious force of life inside him. It was as though The Voice had said to him: "You've been trapped in an extreme state for years, so now it's *your* turn to live it up!" After all, who knows what any of our futures will end up being?

This life all of us human beings have is like that: a happy day today, maybe tomorrow, and maybe even the day after that, but then – Ka-Boom! - a day full of despair on the day after any of those good old days. If we're lucky and play our cards right, though, more happiness than despair just might visit us. And then… maybe not. I wouldn't know first-hand because my life has always been mired in despair. But, now that I have my first true friend all my own, the seesaw of happiness is tilting in my direction for the first time.

Even though I had never been high on a substance of any kind before, in that moment I felt higher than a kite catching a thermal - a flowing stream of warm, bouncy, supportive air - while the weather remains good. Riding on this crest of joy, it felt as though my twenty-first birthday, the Fourth of July, and Christmas had been all bundled up together and gifted me as one single beyond-amazing day. And boy, how I wished that day would never end.

⁂

We were on a roll, enjoying the wind blowing through our hair and the music pouring out of Ross's Sound-About. (He had other tapes to listen to besides the one he had at the hospital. They were full of his unpublished songs, and all were lyrically and melodically brilliant. I already knew they would be classics someday in the not-too-distant future.)

Anyhow, we were having such a great time basking in the sun and warm air we blew right through Bullhead City, converged onto Route 66, and headed full-steam onward, toward the Golden State. California, here we come. And, not 'right back where we started from' either.

So, as we journeyed along, Ross began to speak more and tap less and less. I had mixed feelings about it but was thrilled he began showing signs of recuperation or rehabilitation or whatever fancy label Dr. Speckman would slap onto his case and call it good. (Don't get me started on that 'lady' and her self-centered ways. She dang near caused my Ross to die.)

He talked about all kinds of subjects, but none of them current – as is understandable. I mean, how could he know about anything going on in the world since the day Alfie crashed through that fence and Ross lost all his faculties? It was as though he'd fallen asleep for 28 months and then, awakening after all that time, realizes the world had continued doing its thing without him, and he might try to begin catching up with the rest of us who've remained coma-free. His situation reminded me of Rip Van Winkle, who'd also fallen asleep, for twenty or so years. It was fine and dandy with me that Ross wasn't 'up to date.' After all, ever since I'd been a little girl, I'd never gotten involved with or kept up to date with the world. Current events, even as a child, were not my thing and still aren't today. So, I was thrilled to talk about the weather, music, life, anything Ross wanted to discuss.

As though he'd been reading my mind all along, he said to me, "I have some bad, maybe awful news to break to you, Pammy Girl, if you don't mind."

Oh, boy. Did those words ("bad, maybe awful news to break to you") totally freak me out or what? What they did was render me clueless. I mean, what kind of recent news would possibly Ross know about that I didn't? And, is that even the kind of news he was referencing? Or, was it personal news about him – like maybe he felt the lump of a tumor this morning while toweling off in the shower? (God forbid *that* should ever happen.) I will tell you my brain – now happily out of semi-retirement – kicked into high gear and even began 'haulin' ass' - *conjecturing* all kinds of possible references the man could be making. But, after racking my brain, I decided just to smile and bat my eyelashes. (*Maybe,* I thought, *if I don't say anything or take a wild guess at what "bad, maybe awful news" means, Ross will tell me anyway.*) Yes, for the first time in my life, I was playing the 'dumb blonde,' although I am blonde, but… am I even half as dumb as Ma and all those kids at school used to say I was?

Sure enough, Ross started laughing to beat every band that ever was - falling out so much, in fact, I had to reach out, grab Alfie's wheel, and hold it firmly but gently; firm enough that if Ross lost his grip again, I could maybe steer us out of trouble. Which, of course, made him laugh harder. So, I did the only other thing I could: I yelled. "I give up. What's the awful news?"

After managing to stop laughing by taking a sip from his iced coffee, he said: "Well, if you really want to know… what the bad, awful bad news is… then, I guess I better… spill the beans… that is, if you really want me to do that, Pammy Lee …"

Well, hell's bells, I knew he was messing with me now; you know - pulling my leg or putting one over on me. So, I drew a big breath, smiled, and said: "No, I don't need to hear any bad news today; thank you very much. Keep it to yourself, Ross, if you really don't mind." Which got him going again. I must say, the man does possess quite a sense of humor. At the very least, I will *posit* that he can appreciate a funny situation when it presents itself.

"No," he began, after his third round of laughter, "I can't keep this news, awful as it is, to myself, so here it is. Here's the bad, awful bad news I need to break to you."

So, right at the word 'break' I punched the silly man in the arm and repeated my request to not hear his awful news. That did the trick because he blurted out, "The awful bad news is that this trip is almost over… and about to end." Silence ensued.

Ross started doing a lot of thinking since 'our escape' and realized he wasn't prepared to reach L.A. just yet. He was in no great hurry to thrust himself back into all the drama - especially in finding his wife, his two babies, his agent, and then fighting with said agent over the money Bernie had stolen from the band. Plus, he said he truly loved driving Alfie on the Mother Road and didn't want it to end without us staying one more night somewhere along the way. So, we pulled over, got out his U.S. map, and decided to keep on 66 and stop in Needles for the night, even though it was only 8:30 am and dusk was a whole twelve hours away.

"Okay," I laughed. "That's fine with me. I don't have any schedule to follow. I'm just here to support you, Ross Man." Which is when he smiled and squeezed my leg.

Oh Lord, I thought, *I'm fixin' to black out!* (And then I got struck with the sensation of bees buzzing in my head I get every time something or someone overwhelms me.) Things went from normal color to just black and white and then black… almost…. *Nope… false alarm. Whew, now that was close.*

You see, I almost passed out on the spot because Ross had extended his tapping hand, squeezed my thigh, and smiled at me – all in one *fell swoop*. No wonder, then, I almost swooped. Or swooned. Or… whatever it is women do when the man of their dreams does something like that to them. All I knew was that someone 'up there' must like me, because all my dreams (okay, fantasies) were starting to look like they might possibly come true.

So, we continued for another spell until Ross decided to pull this great big U-turn in the middle of Route 66 and drove us all the way back to Boulder City, where we decided to stop and have lunch. Why? Because we both had been having so much fun laughing, talking, joking, and maybe even flirting a little that we both didn't want the fun - or our road trip - to end.

We had no trouble finding the Denny's smack dab in the middle of beautiful downtown Boulder City. (I shouldn't use that expression because the town wasn't any worse than where I grew up. We just had more trees, which is the only difference between Boulder City, Arizona and Alpharetta, Georgia in the Eighties.)

We chose Denny's because we're both familiar with their food and hate any surprises when it comes to eating. (See how much we're alike? Kidding… maybe not.) The hostess put us in a corner booth way in the back. And since it was slow (according to Midge our waitress), no one had been seated in that corner of the restaurant. So, after a bit of time spent looking over menus, we lowered them together and - without blinking - asked the other: "What are you having?" Which amused both of us, naturally. Then, we turned to the other again and said: "No really. What *are* you having?" Which busted us both up for another spell. After we calmed down and put on our sober faces, we agreed through tapping that we'd say our choices at the count of three. So, after tapping 'one, two, three' we both yelled "The Grand Slam Breakfast," which caused us to lose it altogether. I ask you: Were Ross & I having a ball or what?

When Midge returned, pad in hand, to get our orders, it sounded like this could be the ten-millionth time she asked the question in her lifelong career of waiting on people she'd never seen before and would likely never see again. My made-up 'mind movie' about Midge perked me up. I realized, as though just hit by a proverbial ton of bricks, that there are worse lives than as a night janitor in a convalescent facility in Alpharetta, Georgia. Right? But - on the other hand - who knows? Maybe Midge owned the whole durned restaurant, too. I mean, you can never know someone's whole story right away, but comparing your life with another's is *futile.*

Since I felt perky and 'leader-like' I decided to order for the both of us. But, if you think I said something like, "Two Grand Slams, both with sausage and eggs over easy, please," you'd be greatly mistaken. Instead, I ordered my own Grand Slam in minute detail and with much *finesse*. You see, it felt so good for me to not only order food and sound like a *real lady* but appear like I'd been ordering food for *my man* for a few years at least, up to now. But, I didn't go overboard in playing this wife role and start 'taking on airs' or pretend like I was impatient for my food or any nonsense like that. No, even though it was an act, I meant every word & every gesture.

Then, I ordered for Ross. "He would like the Grand Slam Breakfast, with his eggs over easy, please; and sourdough toast, too, please; with his butter on the side; and - if you could be so kind - his hashed brown potatoes need to be extra-crispy like mine, please." And, so on and so on, with maybe eight or nine common instructions for our breakfasts and a couple differences thrown in, just to keep the boys in the kitchen on their tippy-toes. I turned to Ross and did my best impersonation of a loving wife asking her darling, loving husband the logical question wives have asked for *eons* when ordering for their men: "Will that be enough for you, Hon?"

Oh, and get this: After Ross replied he didn't "need anything else, thank you," he winked at me real sexy-like. (Or, it looked and seemed sexy to me.) And guess what? Ol' Midge didn't flinch a single inch in disbelief. No, sir. Instead of a cynical or snarky chuckle, the gal stuck her pen behind her ear, shoved her pad into her apron pocket, collected our menus, and said something I'll never forget so long as I live as she prepared to walk away from our table. "Thanks, Hon. I'll bring you and your love's breakfasts as soon as the kitchen staff get off their duffs and cook 'em."

She and Ross shared quite a laugh about her comments, but not me. No, I was busy memorizing the first half of her comments, especially the "I'll-get-you-and-your-love's-breakfasts" part. Either I had delivered one awesome Academy Award-winning performance playing 'the doting wife' or Midge was a perceptive woman who'd concluded Ross and I, based on our interactions, were – in fact – *loves* in the purest form of the word. And, I think someday I just might ask the old gal if she thought the two of us, Ross and I, were *in love*… or better yet, if she truly thought we were ***loves***. And so, I promised myself that - if or when I ever land in Boulder City, Arizona again - I'll ask Ol' Midge the Waitress that question. And from what little I gleaned about her during our short encounter, Midge wouldn't have a problem giving her opinion based on her intuition as to whether she'd been convinced that day Ross & I were in love. And, like everything else we hope is in our futures, we must all wait and see. Who knows? Maybe Midge is be my personal eight-ball, like the game many of us had as kids. You know, you ask a question of the thing and turn the thing upside-down to read an answer imprinted on a hexagonal plastic doohickey that swirls around in a sea of black inky liquid behind a round window. Lord, how I loved that silly 8-ball game. Why? Cause I got the answers I wanted. Well… sooner or later. What's the old saying? "Good things come to those who wait." I'm adopting that philosophy in life because the one commodity I have an abundance of now is time.

⁂

So, guess what Ross Man and I did all day long? We rode Alfie, with his top down, on Highway 95 between Boulder City, AZ and Needles, CA. Yep. When we arrived in Needles, Ross pulled a U-turn on the main drag and headed back for BC. And then right in front of Midge's Denny's, he maneuvered another 'U-ee' and took us back to Needles. And then, just for kicks, we completed one more Needles-to-Boulder City round trip, arriving in the California town about 4:30 pm. According to Ross, we'd logged 470 miles commuting between the two wide spots on Highway 95 - the entire time laughing, talking, and laughing some more; all the while our hairdos tossed back and forth in front of our smiling faces, pushed here and there by the bursts of warm wind blowing in and out of Alfie's interior. What's funny is that this potentially boring exercise of shuttling back and forth between two isolated desert towns five times in a row had all the earmarks of a traditional road trip. In fact, our trip met all the usual criteria: our destination, music, non-stop conversation, some interesting sights along the way, and a whole lot of fun. And, since we both knew exactly where we headed each time, the stress that goes with getting lost didn't exist. We had nothing at all to fret or concern ourselves about, except for the vague worry of what might await Ross back home in southern California.

⁂

After checking us into the Needles Motel 6, Ross said he had "some more bad news." "What is it this time?" I asked, fighting to keep any trace of frustration out of my voice.

Frowning, Ross muttered, "The desk clerk said there's not a

single decent place to eat here, so the bad news is… we need to fill up Alfie and drive him to dinner 92 miles away."

I fell backward onto my bed and let loose the laughs that had been stored in my belly for who-know-how-long … just like the wild woman I am. I can't tell you exactly why I found this bad news so funny, but I did. And, matter of fact, I still do.

"What's so funny?" he asked, in an almost-normal-sounding way. And, why would it be strange for Ross to already be normal-sounding? Ross's story, remember, *is* real. It's not like cartoons or The Three Stooges, Laurel & Hardy, or I Love Lucy. No sir-eee, Bob. But, before I try to draw a picture of exactly how Ross was, I will tell you how he'd been doing overall in his transition from Head Trauma Ward Patient a hundred hours ago to a speaking, listening, walking, rational, reasonable, and go-to-the-restroom-on-his-own-without-any-help type of man. Or, as folks like to call this type or variety of adult male - *a real man.* Yeah, I know. You're saying: "That's no big deal, Pammy Lee. Millions of men on Earth are just like that." To which I'd reply that - of all the men I've ever known - not even one was like Ross. Nowhere close.

So, believe me when I say Ross McInerney has not only attained to the *top one percent* of men alive on Earth today, but he's risen all the way up to the top three men or women to have walked this earth... in history. I mean, after counting Jesus and the woman who birthed him, who else has ever proven to be better than Ross? I understand that none of you can possibly answer that question, mainly because you haven't met the man in the flesh. So, even though I'm fixin' to finish explaining how Ross is such an amazing specimen of a human being and just being in his presence is beyond hanging out with anyone else in this great, big universe, I still must interject this *conjunctive qualifier* for Ross's condition - "but."

No, I don't mean Ross was in any danger of falling apart, reverting to a comatose state, or - God forbid - dying soon. No, it's none of these, but before I tell you the awful hidden truth about how Ross *really* was during this ride of ours, let me first remind you what I think of Mister Mac: There *is* no better man. However, (here comes the ' big but'), if I was forced to include, in real time, everything happening during the dialog you've been reading between Ross and me along with all three of the narrators' comments – three or four chapters of our story would be nothing but bodily noises and herky-jerky bodily movements, with just a word now and then from Ross Man or myself. And go ahead, take a wild guess as to who singlehandedly made 99 % of those noises and movements. Yep, even though my wonderful new friend was making fantastic progress in every way (including adapting to a totally different environment), his body had resumed the processes of waking up every day, opening his eyes every day, moving in a million different large and small ways every day, and – on top of all that – talking, walking, laughing, dressing, eating, reasoning, debating, and even singing while driving Alfie and giving the woman seated next to him his biggest, sexiest, most mysterious smile. In fact, I couldn't have conceived of a better dream for myself if I'd tried for three decades – which, by the way, I had.

So, on top of all the discussion about Ross being so amazing, there's more to the story than first meets the eye. Here comes the 'down side' of being in the presence of Ross Robert Padraig McInerney all those hours, days, and nights. To start, the *flatulence* was... awful. And, I don't mean the smell. In fact, I'm not sure his farts *had* any smell, though I can't say for sure. Also, most folks' gas stinks because they're all plugged up, but Ross couldn't be constipated after living for 28 months on sugar water. And since he hadn't had a chance to eat much meat or any Mexican food, his gas didn't smell. But, let's just say that the sound (too loud & way too long) and the frequency (24/7) could've been beyond annoying, except for the fact I was used to being around a huge amount of farting from working in hospitals, especially 'post-op' patients encouraged to let loose their flatulence.

So, all this talk about 'tooting' happened for two reasons: One, to show how Ross McInerney is NOT the perfect man I might be making him out to be; and, second, despite this disgusting, annoying *proclivity* of Ross Man's to pass gas, I still admired, loved, and respected him more than anyone I've ever known, met, read, or heard about – besides the pair I mentioned.

Chapter Fifty – One

Driving back and forth on Highway 95 between Boulder City, Nevada and Needles, California would probably be as boring for some of you as watching paint dry or some little snail crawling the length of a football field. However, I harbor no negative thoughts or feelings about 'Nine-Five,' as Pammy Lee & I dubbed the strip of asphalt connecting those towns. In fact, spending forty-eight hours of non-stop 'commuting' between the two burghs - except for a night's sleep in each town - was conducive for Pammy and me to have some genuine heart-to-heart talks. Wanting nothing more than to ride around in a racy sports convertible with the sun and breeze wafting through our hair and browning our skin, we independently conducted pep talks with our own hearts about moving on to southern California. After we each decided, yes, that would be the best plan to pursue, I realized I wasn't only sitting in the driver's seat of my beloved Alfie, I was piloting my own life for the first time in two and a half years and hopefully co-piloting the lives of Salome, both twins, and perhaps my newest friend, Pammy Lee Wertzhog.

⁂

The next dawn, after waking & making necessary visits to the restroom, we returned to our beds, sat, and talked. I think our beds were 'doubles,' but since I'd stayed exclusively at quality lodging throughout my performing career, I'd never slept on anything smaller than a queen-sized mattress. And though the idea of lounging on one's side while wearing pajamas sounds so laid-back that nothing could possibly be accomplished by either or the both of us, nothing could be further from the truth. Pam and I are both in chronological order – organizers first, planners second, and reorganizers third. Or, simpler still: Organize, rinse, repeat.

Discussing our problem-solving processes, we agreed to always acquire & organize the raw elements involved in any process ourselves. Then, we plan. Planning, by its nature, is akin to having a bunch of seemingly irregular puzzle pieces in your possession and eventually joining them all together into one large picture. We planners think we can see the end of a matter - any matter - before we begin the first step known as the beginning. And then, we start to not only see our plans come to fruition, we find ways of improving this plan we foolishly thought of as ingenious and perfect, but now consider merely 'in development' or 'a work in progress.'

So, here's what we discussed in three hours of organizing, planning, and reorganizing our master plan for what we hoped would happen in California once we arrived and took care of a few situations, but Pammy Lee got super-excited, super-fast. "Hey, Hon, there are three questions we need to ask ourselves before we even consider taking our first step forward."

I must've frowned momentarily because she started explaining, "Every time I'm faced with a challenge in life, I use this simple strategy to plot or devise a plan to solve any problem. I compose three questions about the decision or project I'm about to face. So, with your approval, Ross, let's put our heads together and devise a set of plans to address whatever possible problems we might encounter somewhere or sometime soon."

And, that's what we did. In the true spirit of backward mapping, we began at the end. What is the most desirable result (or results)? I jumped in, describing and explaining the complex plan I had in my head, but I could tell Pam wasn't buying it. "Nope. Our 'master plan' needs to be simply stated, easy to remember, and practiced to a tee."

Well, before we could state, remember, and practice everything in our 'simple plan,' Pam jumped in with, "How about this? How about the two of us set three goals? What do you think those three goals (or wishes) should be?"

So, for a solid hour Pammy Lee and I discussed and brainstormed ideas, concepts, desires, and – of course – goals. Finally, we tried achieving closure to the whole process by naming our "new baby" project our 'Trident Mission.' Each prong of the trident was a problem needing a solution. Our three to solve were couched in questions. Question # 1: How can we - Pammy and I – succeed in reuniting me with my family? Q # 2: How can I finally reap the financial rewards due me for writing and composing all those songs and all three of our band's platinum albums? And then I looked at Pam and asked: "And Question # 3?"

She looked beyond confused. And even after I explained (I thought fairly) that at least one of the three questions should be based on her, Pam looked dumbfounded. So, I coaxed her to come up with a question that would be one of our three goals. Eventually, after considerable hemming and hawing, she smiled with a hint of intrigue and said, "Question # 3 will be the mystery goal. I won't share it with you until it's achieved." *After I came close to badgering her about Q # 3, she stood her ground and repeated:* "I won't share it with you until it's achieved."

After we showered, dressed, and ate the inn's 'continental breakfast' in the lobby, we packed Alfie with clothes and my trusty Sound-About and headed for The Golden State. More specifically, we headed for the hills of Hollywood (where the 'gold' is mere artifice, sparkling or glinting or whatever else fine gold is supposed to do in their money-hungry, always marketing contorted minds, but is - in fact - some other material painted, air-brushed, stamped, or in any other way counterfeiting what is held in most societies as THE most precious commodity on Earth, with the asterisked exception of diamonds). And, in keeping with our newly established, linear approach to reaching goals, we left Alfie's top up and drove straight as an arrow to the golden city on a hill overlooking the vast Pacific Ocean – the one and only Tinsel Town.*

Chapter Fifty – Two

Before I knew it, we'd reached L.A., the largest city I'd ever visited. (I'd been to Atlanta on several occasions, but the capital of Georgia was far smaller than the city that had recently been declared "Second Largest City in America!" (like that's supposed to be a good thing for a city to be – 'number 2' behind Numero Uno – The Big Apple). What struck me first about L.A. was its freeways, supposedly arranged into a 'system.' *Freeway System…* Ha! Ross & I could riff and rant on that phrase for hours, but, I *digress*. Everywhere the eye could see were four- to eight-lane roads curling, twisting, then uncurling, and flattening out. These freeways had *numerical designations* with a name attached as an after-thought. It seemed to me like every digit from 1 to 710 labeled every road, highway, or freeway in the Greater Los Angeles area.

All joking full of *hyperbole* aside, the next thing I noticed was that every one of these freeways named by number was in excellent shape. No potholes, no ruts, nor any other impediments to people driving or riding in all manner of vehicles gliding along the gray and black paths paving the way to a destination of their choice. And, all in a snap!

But then, alas, I discovered L.A.'s freeways weren't always accommodating or 'free-ways.' Uh, big no. When 'Rush Hour' arrived, whatever joy or fun the city had given was snatched back – like that. And, all in a snap! See, the entire Southland's roads, highways, paths, and freeways would – around four-thirty in the afternoon every weekday – become jammed with cars, vans, motorcycles, and eighteen-wheeler truck & trailer rigs. Before long, everything (and I mean *everything*) came to a full & complete stop; sometimes accompanied by tires screeching and brakes squealing. Or, worse, these caravans of metal beasts of burden would slow to the pace of a baby's crawl. And when that occurred, Los Angeles took on a whole different *persona*. Paradise transformed into whatever the opposite is. (I hate to use "Hell" because that would be too drastic and hateful of a label, but the word does come closer to describing the flip side of Paradise than any other term I might concoct on my own.)

So, anyway, back to Ross's story. We rode The Five, the backbone of L.A. freeways, and wound up eventually at a mansion perched on a hill behind a huge metal gate. "Is this Valhalla?" I asked, but I don't think Ross heard because he kept staring at the metal gate in front of Alfie.

⁂

*Driving all the way to Downtown LA in Alfie, I debated with myself (argued, really) about where I should drive first. But since 'we Rosses' could not agree, I asked a neutral source – Miss Pammy Lee. Her response began with, "You are asking **me**?" And, when I didn't answer with my own response, she continued.* "First off, you know what's so… ironic? Yeah, ironic. Do you know, Ross, what's so ironic about you asking **me** for advice?"

I had no idea what she could possibly be getting to, but I did see that whatever it was, it must've been an issue of importance to her. So naturally, I listened to what Pammy Lee had to say. "Until this moment happening right now, this very minute, Mr. Ross McInerney, no one – and I mean **no one** – has ever asked little ole me for advice… of any kind. Ma never did. No classmate ever did. In fact, no one else I've ever known, even at the hospital, has ever solicited my advice for any reason on any subject under kingdom come. Anyway, dear Ross, please don't be taken aback by my shock, but I must say that your asking me where we should 'drive next' is THE single greatest thing to have ever happened to me…. Well, with one exception, which was you and I meeting."

Then, it was my turn to be "in shock." Hearing PLW's description of never being asked advice in her life until that moment affected me two ways. Number one: I hadn't realized how tough this woman's life must've been, although I was quickly learning. And number two: I realized how much of life I myself had taken for granted since childhood. Up until this moment, I thought **my** *life had been difficult, but Pammy's statement about no one ever caring enough to ask her opinion or advice blew my mind beyond description. It sounded like, for whatever reasons, no one had ever treated her right, respected her, or given her compassion. And I had no idea why. Not even a clue.*

If you want to know the truth, this woman was the nicest, kindest, most caring person I ever met. And, she is also very easy on the eyes. All I can ask myself is: How on Earth could anyone treat such a wonderful, exceptional human being this way? And, of course, I have no response to my own question because there is no reasonable response to why anyone would ever mock, deride, or in any other way disrespect an amazing person like Pammy Lee Wertzhog.

After our conversation we agreed to head straight for Valhalla and see what kind of condition my house was in. Wending up my hilly street, I saw every home we passed before ours looked exactly like it had before I left on my 'adventure.' All that, however, changed. I pulled Alfie up to the gate and was so stunned I had to turn his engine off. See, even though Alfie's engine idle can best be described as a velvet hum, it still could've been a distraction that might've kept me from focusing on the scene in front of us. Although a gate was still there, everything was different. First off, it was an entirely different gate – a solid wall of metal resting on matching brown rollers instead of the hinges the last one had. Secondly, the name "Valhalla" was no longer visible – not on the wall nor the gate nor even on a small sign to simply identify the property for visitors, delivery personnel, etc. There was, however, a speaker nearby on a post, with a console consisting of a small speaker and a button.

I pulled myself out of Alfie and tested the new system by pushing the red plastic button. No more than three seconds later, a female voice answered.

"Yes, may I help you?" the senora asked with equal parts fatigue and professionalism.

She sounded nice, just overworked or beleaguered. I figured she could help. "Yes, I used to live here two and a half years ago and was wondering who lives here now..."

"Oh," she started. "I, I really can't give out any information like that, Senor -?"

"McInerney, but - please - call me Ross."

"Okay, Mister Ross. I will come down and talk with you in just a minute, okay?"

"That'd be great. I'm just looking for someone very important to me."

While I waited for the unnamed Latina, I stared at the intercom and steeled my nerves. I then looked up at the front door, which began opening. A solemn woman about forty-five dressed in a uniform of white blouse, shoes, and skirt emerged. She gave a wave, but then tried pulling it back. Too late! (Her entire movement was so herky-jerky I won't even try to describe it without insulting a percentage of people who can't control their arms well.)

As she made her way along the wooden deck and descended three flights of stairs, the lady kept her head down as though walking through a rainstorm. After finishing all those steps, she walked in my general direction, but with no sign of urgency. In fact, she seemed to slow as she approached. Finally, without looking at me at all, the lady said: "Mister Ross, I didn't introduce myself because... I thought you were a salesman or somebody else Mr. Breeze doesn't want me talking to. You know – salesmen, Jehovah's Witnesses, or anyone else who might come to the door who might be – how you say in English – 'a pest'? You understand, Mister Ross?"

I smiled and raised both hands in agreement. "Si, yo comprende, Senora -?"

"Dolores, Dolores Hidalgo. I'm the housekeeper for… for this residence."

I extended my hand over the six-foot fence for her to shake. Getting on her tiptoes, she reached my hand just enough to tap it. "Mister Ross, I'm sorry I'm so short."

We laughed, sharing the moment together. I was in no hurry to change subjects, but I knew Dolores could only stand by that gate talking to a stranger for so long before having to rush back to her duties & responsibilities and maybe admissions of impropriety according to a boss with an unnaturally high standard for his flunkies, er I meant, employees. So, as cool as I could, I asked in an off-handed, casual-as-hell way, "Oh, Mr. Bernie Breeze lives here now?"

She frowned awhile, as though searching for something safe to say. "Oh, no. Mr. Bernie does not live here, but he… rents it out, shall I say … to a………………… tenant."

I could tell by both her restraint and use of the word "tenant" that Dolores was a smart cookie who'd been prepped by Bernie Breeze to not give any information to "Mr. McInerney" or – as she prefers to call me – "Mr. Ross." But, since my sources of intel in the immediate area were next to nil, I thought I'd give it the ol' college try, as Pammy Lee likes to call it. "Dolores, I am looking for my wife, Mrs. Salome McInerney, and our twin children. Have you heard anything about any of them?"

"Mr. Ross, Mr. Breeze does not let me give out <u>*any*</u> *information to* <u>*anyone*</u> *who comes to this gate. I am so, so sorry." She ducked her head, pivoted, and rushed back up the flights of wooden stairs, across the porch, and through the front door.*

Looking back at Pammy Lee, all I could manage was a shrug. Discouraged, but not downtrodden, I said: "Let me show you a bit of 'Hollyweird' before we head out."

⁂

I'd never seen Ross as forlorn as he had been standing at that gate, but he did brighten after a bit and suggested we cruise through Hollywood (or Hollyweird, as he called it). But, truth be told, I didn't hardly look at any of the bright lights or strange folk on either the Sunset Strip or Hollywood Boulevard. I was too *preoccupied* trying to read Ross Man's mood or state of mind or some indication of how he was faring. It started to dawn on me that this man who'd been driving almost non-stop for the past two days had been in a comatose state just days ago. So, instead of being star-struck or glitter-gone by *Hollyweird*, I ignored it… pretty much.

Ross hunched over Alfie's wheel as we sped through the town's two most famous streets as though disgusted by the area. In addition to his mood and *demeanor* changing, he began mumbling. And then, continued mumbling for the next hour, non-stop. When I observed he no longer looked in my direction or touched my arm, I realized Ross must not be mumbling to me. So, since I had no right to eavesdrop on his private business, I tuned his sounds out (including the farts) and instead said a prayer that things would work out for him – and for the both of us.

Chapter Fifty – Three

Because of the high winds in the mountain passes, Ross pulled Alfie over to put his green top back on. Alfie's head was forest green with a cute window in back for the driver to see behind him or her. So, the three of us (yes, I'm counting Alfie) descended into a vast valley that featured no more than some box-like stucco houses surrounded by the Mojave Desert's assortment of mesquite, tamarisk, sagebrush and my favorite – the weird-looking, pointy treelike plant I mistook for a cactus. But, Ross did courteously set me straight: "Pam Honey, those are Joshua trees. Named after Joshua in the Bible. I heard the only other place on Earth that has Joshua trees is--" That's all I remember. In the middle of that sentence, everything went black.

I passed out fully. And since I'd never discussed with anyone the physical phenomenon of fainting, I hadn't the slightest idea what happens when someone is considered 'out," but I can tell you that in my case, my abilities to see, taste, touch, and smell went bye-bye, adios, and vamoose. However, somehow I'd retained my hearing. As a result, I heard every word out of Ross's lips, but I couldn't physically respond. At first, I was clueless as to why. I even asked myself whether I'd seconds before had a seizure or perhaps my first stroke.

Now, if you think I'm about to tell you I'd caught some dreaded disease or developed some life-threatening physical condition, you might be diagnosed as *certifiable* by the lady in the white coat, Dr. Speckman. No, the only reason I'd passed out was because I could neither endure nor contain the extreme joy I'd derived from something Ross said right then. And even though he'd uttered the phrase so casually and naturally, those two words had struck me with such force and compassion that I know I'll never, ever forget all the sensations I experienced while hearing them. The phrase that struck me so powerfully I'll treasure it for the rest of my life consisted of the words 'Pam' and 'Honey.' But what it made it so gall-darned special and noteworthy and all that is this. This man, this real, genuine American musician of a man put those two words together and said them directly to me. I know I wasn't dreaming because I dug my nails into my hand and realized it was all for real.

Pure, unadulterated joy burst inside me, filling & lifting my entire being. This pure strain of life's rarest, most powerful emotion grew so intense inside me, an explosion went off in my head. Yes, two English words strung together were more than enough to put me out, like a double knockout punch in a boxing match.

You might be telling yourselves, "That girl is out of her ever-lovin' mind." And, surprise! I was certainly 'out of my ever-lovin' mind' because I did lose all consciousness. (Or, rather...... had consciousness lost *me*? Well, whatever the case, I can state with ultimate confidence that I was out of my mind, but only just for a moment. And then, after one deep breath and the two words of internal encouragement I uttered to myself, I commenced the reopening of my eyes. And who looked intently at me from a crouching position at the very moment I opened them? Ross McInerney. THE Ross McInerney. I know for sure that most of you women (and some of you fellas) would have fainted, too. Or, as Ma used to call it – swooning. Or, "catchin' the vapors." Whatever vapors were. All I know is that no case of post-menopausal "vapors" back in the days of bonnets, hoop skirts, and parasols could ever hope in their wildest dreams to compete with the swooning I experienced the instant after I heard the man say, 'Honey.' And all because the only adult who'd ever treated me right also happened to be a man who looks like he does, thinks like he does, creates music like he does, and loves life like he does. Yep, true perfection in life starts and ends with love. And, it most assuredly does for Yours Truly. Not only is this story all about Ross Robert McInerney, it is also all about love.

How – you might ask – could this narrative be focused on two seemingly different entities? Simple. To me, the entire concept of human love and this human being I've come to know in Ross are one and the same. They are to me - little ol' Pammy Lee Wertzhog. So, getting back to the climactic end of our epic road trip……

After taking Pearblossom Highway and joining Hwy 138 at Four Points, we began heading east toward San Berdoo. And after seven or eight miles of hair and clothing fluttering inside Alfie's chassis, we saw a town perched on the edge of the Mojave Desert with the name Littlerock - consisting of orchards, plain and humble ranch houses, even plainer and humbler farm worker cabins, three junk stores, piles of sand, five or six roadside fruit stands, and a variety of dead desert animals on the road - all of it surrounded by the Mojave Desert's largest ingredient - sand. As far as my naked eye could see was sand, more sand, and – yes – more sand after that and more sand even after that, and so on, and so on for seemingly forever.

And, for the first time on our trip, Ross pulled Alfie over without asking. Wow. The nerve of that man to decide something regarding his own car without my permission! Who does he think he is – a real man? (Which, he is - not just in spades, but in dozens of decks of spades.)

⁂

So, Pammy Lee and I were having a great time talking, cutting up, and laughing when we came upon this little burgh by the name of Littlerock. At first, all I saw were semi-dilapidated, weather-worn stores strung along both sides of Highway 138 in ragged rows; each building set back a different distance than the ones on either side. However, on the right or south side of the road stood this large red and white barn sticking out from the rest. The only identification was in the form of a simple, hand-painted, venerable sign above its barn doors stating: "Harley Joe's."

I couldn't have told you why at the time, but I yanked little Alfie off that highway so fast that his smallish wheels screeched and squealed on the concrete drive leading to the prodigious building. I parked right in front and scoped the place out a bit before deciding whether to enter. Thanks to all the picture windows, I could see Harley Joe's was a country store featuring not only a sandwich shop, but a candy store, too. Since I wasn't at all hungry, I started searching for a reasonable excuse to venture inside. "I think I'll grab a cup of coffee, Pammy, if you don't mind. Would you like to join me?"

She looked at me funny. "Of course I would like to join you, Silly Boy." We passed through the front entrance – one of those Dutch half-doors Captain Kangaroo used to open and talk to Mister Green Jeans or us, his audience – and stepped inside. I gravitated to the candy section, located on the west side of the sprawling building at least twice the size of your average-sized cow barn. A bald man sporting wire-rim glasses & clad in a white long-sleeve shirt held by a pair of old-fashioned red, white, and blue garters with a red tie who resembled the town grocer Sam Drucker on the Sixties comedies "Petticoat Junction" and "Green Acres" greeted me with: "Hey, young fella. I haven't seen you in a coon's age. What can I get for you today?"

I looked at the man, sized him up, and asked: "You've seen me before?"

"Why, of course I've seen you before. If I hadn't, I wouldn't have told you so. You see, young feller, I never forget a face, not once in my eighty-two years."

Pointing at his collection of glass cases of confections of every shape, color, and size, he asked: "See anything you'd like to sample?"

"Why, yes. May I try your black licorice, please?"

Mr. Drucker smiled broadly. "Well, since you asked politely and included the magic word, I'll tell you what -"

"You'll let me sample ***two*** *of the licorice?"*

"Why, how did you know that's what I planned on saying? See? You ***have*** *been here before. It's been so long you just forgot our most important rule. Need any help remembering it?*

"Kindness," I said.

"Exactly, young man. Say, your name – starts with an R, right?"

"How did you know, Mister?

"Oh, I've been around the block more than once or twice; and since a Littlerock block is at least a mile around, you'd be amazed how far I've traveled and how much I've learned about things and have had the privilege of knowing a man like yourself."

As I turned to locate Pammy, I didn't have to look farther than a foot since she stood right beside me. "Would you like to sample some old-fashioned candy, Pammy?"

She smiled not just with her eyes this time, but with her mouth as well. "Sure, I would. Why, I've never turned down an offer of something sweet in my life." As I tried handing her one of my two braids of black licorice, she amended her "never" treatise with: "Well, Ross, there is a sweet I will never ever accept, and that one exception is black licorice." Her shoulders shook at the thought of her tasting one of my black treats.

The old man said, "Little lady, we have over a hundred

different confections for you to choose from today. Look around and please let me know what you'd like to sample."

Since Pammy said she needed to spend time freshening up in the women's lounge before selecting her 'double sample,' I said: "No worries. I'll just enjoy my black licorice and the store." I sat at one of the small tables on the periphery and continued sucking on my first of two licorice ropes while I concentrated on one question: How could I know the old man? I sat for I don't know how long, with my eyes closed and no movement except for the slight exertion of sucking on the rubbery candy. This one question revolved in my head, demanding to be answered: How did Harley Joe know me?

After returning to the candy shop, I discovered it wasn't only closed "until further notice," the old man was nowhere around. I planned to just look around until I found him, but after a good fifteen minutes, I abandoned my foolhardy process and discovered Plan B to be a quicker way to find 'Mister Drucker.' It took asking three different confused, shy, and scared-of-their-own-shadows teenagers, but I eventually learned the whereabouts of the 'old man.' He was reported to be in the employee lounge eating his lunch.

The lounge was nearby, so within seconds I saw Harley Joe by himself in the middle of a huge, otherwise vacant lounge, stooped over a ham-and-cheese on a Kaiser roll he'd built moments before. And even though he didn't appear in the least bit intimidating, I felt the weight of the world pressing down on my puny, mortal shoulders. The pressure I put on myself was that I hoped against hope I could solve a mystery haunting me nearly thirty years.

Before I approached and addressed him, I checked my watch. I mentally gave myself five minutes to gain all the information I needed. "Uh, hi" is how I opened, but it didn't elicit a response from Sam the Grocer. When I drew nearer, though, he stirred himself and smiled. Waving for me to sit with him, he tended to his hearing aids while I realized the gent was hard of hearing. So, since I'm not the least bit glib when it comes to small talk, I decided not to try being clever, but to just be me. "Hello again. I really hate to interrupt your lunch, but would you mind if I ask you just one question?"

Sitting up straight and giving me that famous sidelong Mr. Drucker look, the one Sam Drucker would give whenever either Uncle Joe on "Petticoat Junction" or Oliver on "Green Acres" said something to startle or irk him. He smiled and responded with a drawl: "Of course I mind you asking me one question during my lunch. Why, I'd be offended if you didn't ask me at least two and maybe as many as a hundred. Please, young man, sit down and take a load off. And, before we exchange names and pleasantries, I want to present you with the other sandwich I have here – my specialty, a turkey Reuben on rye along with this crunchy, crispy kosher dill pickle. By the way, I'll guess your name & then you try to guess mine. How does that sound?"

I managed a hoarse, hesitant "okay" and that was all the buy-in the codger required for conversation. Of course, I should really be placing quotation marks around the word conversation because it was more like the shyest interrogation conducted in history than an actual two-way conversation. I asked a total of eight but our 'conversation' lasted for ...... five and a half hours. And, it all began with the man saying, "You're Ross McInerney. Who am I?"

"I had no idea until now, but logic and reason tell me you must be Mr. Harley Joe- "

Clapping his hands and doing a little dance while remaining seated, he uttered between laughs: "Yes... I am he... Harley Joe Zimmerman - at your service, sir."

Sitting there trying to reintroduce moisture to my mouth, I realized how thirsty I'd become. And, so did Harley Joe. "What's your poison, young feller? You name it and we have it." Since I was incredibly thirsty, water seemed the only drink capable of slaking my thirst. Harley Joe brought me three different brands of natural water in glass bottles and I selected the closest. This was my first experience ever of drinking bottled water. It didn't taste any different from the water I'd previously drawn from a sink or garden hose, but it did the job. However, plain old water from the tap would've probably tasted just as good. But, since it is the thought that counts, I appreciated Harley's generosity of spirit and thanked him a couple times.

My first question for Harley Joe, of course: "How do you know me?"

He started by explaining he'd been involved with the store since founding it in the Thirties. He'd always prided himself on being a 'hands-on' type of proprietor. In fact, he'd worked every single day since the store opened, explaining that his fiftieth anniversary of owning and operating the business on that same site would arrive within the year. He told me again how he never forgets a face before explaining that my father frequented his store quite often, usually with me in tow. Now, this revelation of Dad taking me for a treat several times at Harley Joe's presented all kinds of possible questions, but Harley anticipated them and answered them as best he could, considering how long it had been since he last saw me.

"Yes sir, your father was quite a guy back then. He's a talented jazz man who plays a variety of instruments. I saw him a few times while he played in What's His Name's band. You know, the black fella who had all those hits in the old days. Anyway, Bob would bring you in, usually carrying you on his shoulders. He explained if he carried you up high like that, you could see what he could see and maybe even more. Bob said it was important to him that you experience this store and life in general the way he did; and he always brought you over to my candy section. And you always wanted the same thing for your sample – real licorice. I tried and tried to persuade you to sample something else, but you held fast to black licorice. And since your dad taught you good manners, I used to give you a second sample for saying 'please,' 'thank you,' and 'may I.' Ross, you should've seen your father's face when I'd reward your manners with a second strand of licorice. In fact, I have a photo of him and you somewhere around here after such an instance occurred. Your dad even signed it on the back for me."

"Why the back?"

"Because your dad used a Polaroid that would spit the picture out almost instantly. He didn't write on the front because he was afraid it would smear." After encouraging me to eat my sandwich & pickle, Harley excused himself a few moments. I ate in silence until he reappeared, clutching the picture he'd told me about. He said he'd snapped the shot, which consisted of Dad standing at the high glass counter filled with assortments of candy with a two-and-a-half-year-old version of me nestled in his lean, freckled, tattooed arms. What struck me most about the portrait were the happy, serene expressions on both our faces. Evident to me was that father and son not only loved each other but basked in a moment of intimate father-son love.

Harley handed me the four-inch square paper, which I flipped over and read its inscription on the white backing: "My son and I wish you and your entire 'staff family' all the best in the years and decades to come." And then, the best part of all. Underneath Dad's 'John Hancock' was another note: "My son Ross, future musician and decent human being."

Overcome with shock and other emotions, I sat to catch my breath. After a pause, I asked my second question: "When did you last see my father, Harley?"

Fully expecting the old man to wrestle with his memory and not come up with an answer that would lead me to him, he surprised. "Well, let's see... last week. And, he bought his usual."

"Which was?"

"Go ahead. Take three guesses, but the first two don't

count."

I really had no idea, except for one possible guess. "Was it black licorice?"

"Bingo!" he yelled before falling into laughter again. He then turned my laughter into tears. "Your dad would be so proud of you today, Ross." I can't say I have a clue why Harley Joe said that, but I accepted his kind comment with all the aplomb I could muster. It seemed when he looked into my eyes he saw something he knew Dad would approve or be proud of.

Our talk continued two solid hours until I interrupted it by looking for Pammy Lee, whom I found sitting inside Alfie. What she did that was so surprising was what she didn't do. Pam neither yelled nor fussed nor in any way demonstrated her upset, impatience, or angst by my abandoning her to search out and speak at great length with a total stranger. So, I told her what was going on and that I had six more questions for Harley Joe.

Without hesitation, she said: "Go back and finish your confab, regardless of how long it takes. There's nowhere I'd rather be nor anything I'd rather be doing than sitting with Alfie and waiting for you to finish important business." So, with Pam's blessing, I returned and continued my Q & A with a man who'd known my dad for as long as I'd lived and, more importantly, had seen him very recently.

Still seated at a table of four eight-foot-long tables connected end to end was Harley Joe. No trace of our lunch remained, so I deduced he'd cleaned up whatever mess we made and put away anything that might distract from our project. When I returned, he sat as straight as any eighty-year-old can and beamed a smile full of real teeth. "Welcome back, Ross. Did you find your wife? She's welcome to join us if you'd like."

I demurred, explaining Pam insisted on 'staying out of the way'. So, we continued.

To my third question, "How did my father look?" Mr. Zimmerman spent quite some time cobbling together an answer that still didn't provide any information of substance. I figured Harley was either shielding Dad or hadn't thought of a detail he could share. However, that didn't restrain him from expounding about broad generalities, all couched in the disclaimer, "After all, Ross, your dad must be close to sixty now." Luckily for me, the old boy had the gift of gab and wasn't afraid to use it. The downside, though, was that I had to wade through a steady stream of evasive responses, theatrical asides, and non-sequiturs.

My next query related to Dad's career. "Do you know if he's on the road; and, if so, where he'll be playing in the future?"

Harley looked me in the eye and declared as though being sworn in, in a court of law: "He's touring now, and I know where he'll be playing soon. But…" He grasped my shoulders and seemed more worried than curious when he asked, "Are you sure you want to see him?"

I felt my brow furrow and my face & chest heat up. "Of course. Why do you ask?"

"I sincerely do beg your pardon, Ross, but I'm asking on your behalf, not your father's. You're the person I'm concerned about most." As he spoke, he emphasized "you" and "your." Which caused me to wonder whether Harley Joe was hinting my father might be in a condition too difficult for me to accept. But then, that Voice inside me declared Dad's condition shouldn't be an issue. So, I found myself at an impasse - half of me wanting to do one thing and the other half desiring to do the opposite. And then, those two voices spoke with equally strident tones, both demanding I accept that voice's opinion about the bittersweet, mixed-bag situation in which I found myself at the center. But, all things being equal, I decided the family factor should trump all others. Just because Dad hadn't been in my life for thirty years didn't mean he shouldn't be in it and part of it now. My whole perspective on 'fate' or 'destiny' began to change at that moment. I realized everything might not be set in historical concrete as I'd always thought. Time, though, was of utmost importance since Dad did have to be nearly sixty now. As a lifelong musician who'd never put down a single root, perhaps he'd like to make up for lost time. Who knows? He might finally put down roots and stay in one place – near his presumed only son.

I arrived at a point I sensed should be our goodbye, for now. Harley Joe gave me a bone-cruncher of a handshake, which reminded me of all the times in my childhood when a man squeezed the heck out of my hand – I guess to model proper manly behavior. I've always hated to shake with someone who prided themselves on their firm shake, but I considered Harley Joe's a veritable tip of the hat to not only my father, but me as well.

Chapter Fifty – Four

When Ross emerged from Harley Joe's, I saw him deep in thought. I decided not to ask him even the most innocuous questions, such as "How'd it go?" or "Did you learn anything new?" Instead, I'd already secretly vowed to give Ross what we call back in Georgia 'a wide berth.' Why? Because, I could tell from feeling his vibes and observing his body language that Ross was deep in something – thought, emotion, or probably both.

So, when Ross approached Alfie and me outside, I pursed my lips until he needed me to say something, which was after he smiled at me, started Alfie up, and pulled back onto 138. His first comment after a 5 1/2-hour-long confab with Harley Joe was, "What a beautiful day we have, Pammy Lee. Who could ask for a better one?"

I couldn't have worded it better if I'd dug into my new *lexicon* or consulted Merriam-Webster. In the mcantime, our operative phrase was 'San Bernardino – here we come!' (Or, should it be, 'San Berdoo or bust?')

⁂

As we rode roller coaster # 138 East from Littlerock, past Pearblossom, by Phelan, and up through Wrightwood, we did so in silence. By silence, I mean there wasn't any talking, music, or distractors of any kind. As a result, I had an hour-long two-way conversation with my inner self, in which I delved into all the major issues of my existence – my wife Salome, our boy and girl (whatever their names were), music, money/finances, and whatever other subjects presented themselves. As I flipped through the pages of concerns and what-ifs regarding the future I'd stored in the notebook in my brain, I sensed nothing but calm. I can't explain it, but there existed a sublime serenity in my body, mind, and spirit that can neither be described nor explained with words. And, what's odd or weird about this hour-long meditation was I felt a closeness to the lady sitting next to me in Alfie. In my gut rested a sense of serenity and unity with another kindred soul, and although I don't know if Pam felt the same sensation, it resembled the sense I'd felt with Julia, my first wife. And that special brand of mutual acceptance and contentment I can only ascribe to one word – the same concept Julia, the Boys, and I embraced years ago – propinquity... pure and simple.

⁂

Ross, Alfie, and I arrived in "San Berdoo" sometime after nightfall. I can't tell you what time it was when we parked in front of the one-car garage at Ross's old house. After pulling into his driveway, he sat awhile - staring at the garage door whose cracks were not only widespread but embedded deeply in wood veneer. But, since Ross hadn't been there for two and a half years, some weather damage might be expected. Perhaps fifteen minutes of silence later, I decided to evaluate the situation. I patted Ross on the shoulder and asked, "What would you like – to spend the night inside Alfie or somewhere else?"

As though shaking himself awake, Ross's head of hair tossed in every direction for more than a few seconds. When it stopped, he turned to me slowly. "No, we can't stay here in Alfie all night. And, no, I can't think of anywhere else to go and stay the night, so… the bad news is we have only one place to spend the night, but the good is that each of us gets our own bedroom."

I must've looked as dumbfounded as I felt because Ross took one glimpse at me and laughed. (The nerve!) I thought, "Here we are, stuck with nowhere to lay our heads for the night, and this man is laughing his behind off. I mean, what's up with that?"

I must've thrown him quite a look because his gray eyes blinked several times before closing. Bending his head until his chin rested on his t-shirt, he resembled a nine-year-old who had to tell his teacher that his dog *had*, in fact, eaten his homework last night. I knew not what was going on, but I knew something was wrong. So, I asked.

Ross looked off in the distance before rebounding and flashing those sad, sexy gray saucers. Snapping his fingers with both hands, he displayed his award-winning smile for me. "Problem solved. I remember a way in."

"Uh, did you just say what I thought you said? You remember a way to… what - *break in*? You can't do that, Ross. Someone else lives here now."

After he climbed out, I stood on my seat and stage-whispered: "Where are you going?"

He smiled and, turning away, said: "Follow me and you'll know." So, I did.

We wound up in the small backyard, where a well-kept cactus garden welcomed us with not just the usual array of needles, but flowers and colors that caught me by surprise. I had no idea that not all cacti are green. Who knew they could be any possible shade of green, not to mention a variety of grays, browns, pinks, and yellows, to mention just a few? Ross stepped around several plants before picking up a faux plaster human skull in the rear of the garden and extracting a shiny object from its hinged mouth. He held it aloft, so I could see it was a key. "Mom and I hid an extra house key in this skull we bought at Disneyland back when I was ten. It's been in this spot since we moved here fifteen years ago." Striding the short distance to the back door, he tried the key and… it opened.

Stepping inside, we could tell by the heat and smell the place had been shut up for a while, but not terribly long. After Ross opened every window and switched on the swamp cooler, the bungalow began feeling more personal, homey, and … cozy. Although he'd been gone all this time, Ross's place remained his home. I saw his mother's touch here and there, but - overall - this sweet little house reflected Ross's personality and passion to a tee. Everywhere I looked, I saw *irrefutable* evidence of Ross's passion. Framed photos and drawings of various musicians took up most of the wall space. If you said the name of a musical artist of any consequence, his/her image leaned against one of his walls. Even I recognized them: Chuck Berry, Elvis Presley, the Beatles, Ray Charles, the Beach Boys, James Brown, Janis Joplin, Neil Young, Joni Mitchell, Van Morrison, and Ross's favorite - Bob Dylan. But, if you think that was more than a small fraction of them, you're sadly mistaken. This line-up comprised the thinnest sliver of the pie that is Ross's musician-picture collection. Others' likenesses occupying his beige walls included Mozart, Beethoven, Bach, Frank Sinatra, Dinah Washington, Ella Fitzgerald, Tony Bennett, Dean Martin, Jimmy Durante, and someone named Nina Simone (whose facial expression of despair kept me spellbound every time I looked at her image again).

Besides pictorial tributes to hundreds of musicians, other images depicted music in various media. Even his abstract paintings had musical overtones. And, what's funny is that after Ross described the subject of every abstract, all I could see was the person, instrument, or symbol he referenced. (Either Ross wasn't pulling my leg or I'm *that* gullible.)

Much of the furniture - the Masonite kitchen table and the chrome kitchen chairs along with the black-and-white Zenith TV set he described before - were as old as Ross, but I did see newer pieces here and there that brought the place a bit closer to the present. Still, Ross's humble abode was anchored in the Fifties, Sixties, Seventies… and early Eighties. It resembled a museum gallery dedicated to the development of musical genius Ross McInerney.

After I toured everywhere but the bedroom a second time, Ross asked me, "Would you like to see where you'll be sleeping?"

"Sure," I responded, trying not to sound too curious (or hopeful).

"Good." He held out his hand, which I took. "Follow me," he said quietly, so I did. It became difficult to walk because my equilibrium had left my body - due to shock, nervousness, or both. Ross then led me to the only bedroom, which surprised me because it contained two beds. (I'd forgotten he and his mother had shared this room, so of course there would not be one, but two beds.) Ross demonstrated another feature I hadn't anticipated – a curtain running the room's length that could be drawn when necessary. "I'm sure you'd like your privacy," he said gallantly. (My silent retort: "Not as much as I want to cuddle with you in the same bed.")

The bathroom, despite having only one sink, was surprisingly roomy and featured both a tub and a shower. So, like folks say, I was good to go.

Returning to the bedroom after freshening up, I saw the curtain was in full display and a small light next to my bed was on. Fairly sure Ross was already asleep, I climbed into bed and turned the little lamp off. After a couple minutes, I heard, "Good night, Pammy. Thanks." And right then, ooooh, I was overcome with the same dizziness I'd had before. And, boy, was I glad I was lying down because otherwise I would've surely fallen and broken my crown. Although I couldn't form the two-word response aloud, I silently bade Ross McInerney "good night" a hundred times or more until the veil of sleep descended upon me.

⁂

After waking & stirring around in bed because I had to pee so bad, I heard from behind the curtain: "Good morning, Pammy… or should I say, 'good afternoon?" (Oh my, it was almost one o'clock.) "Feel free to shower, use anything in the bathroom, and - after you dress - we'll have lunch somewhere on the way to Hollyweird." So, I followed his instructions.

A few blocks from Ross's place, he pulled Alfie into a driveway leading to a narrow commercial building featuring not one, but two drive-thru bays – one on each side. The only thing besides the skinny structure was a row of tall, elegant palm trees. And, when I received my 7-Up, the cup had the same type of palms decorating the area below the brim. Emblazoned across the rest of the cup was the phrase, "In and Out." Ross pulled into the space next to a block wall, where we tore the packaging from our cheeseburgers and began devouring the best burger ever. Mine had a funny name: "The Double-Double." Two juicy beef patties interspersed with two layers of the freshest cheese available. I was – simply put - in Heaven. I told myself: "See? California has a lot going for it. I could never find a burger like this back in Georgia." I guess I'd already begun to appreciate this new part of the country. (And, the fries weren't bad, either.)

While we ate, Ross roughed out an itinerary that would hopefully succeed in us finding Salome, the twins, and any & all information about Ross's legal situation.

Before Pammy awoke our first morning in San Bernardino, I

wrote a list of the things I needed to find out or get done. I scribbled them on the back of an envelope and stuffed it in the non-wallet back pocket of my Levi's for future reference. After enjoying In and Out, our first stop was Bernie Breeze's building. Instead of going through another possible hassle in the parking lot over me needing to pay to park in a lot my own labor paid for, I ruminated on all the ways Bernie had ripped our band and me off and then I fantasized about ways I could not only torture but kill my business agent. I got so absorbed in this train of thought, especially in reviewing various torture options, that I hadn't noticed the uniformed man planted in front of me. It was the same guy who'd thrown me out the last time. Without expression, he addressed me: "Ross McInerney, you are hereby served with a court injunction to not trespass on this property for any reason until further notice by an appropriate officer of the court of the County of Los Angeles."

"A court what?! You mean my agent has a restraining order ***against me?****"*

The man responded by handing me a plastic pen with which to sign a paper verifying I'd received the document. Document, my ass. The whole irony of this ridiculous charade is that I'd been paying for all this security, all these parking spaces, and who-knows-what-else. In a nutshell, I'd been paying big money to employ around-the-clock security guards whose main purpose was to keep me off the premises. Or, in straight-talk terms, I paid lots of filthy lucre to screw myself. And, though I could sense in my body Mr. Rage wanted to make a big entrance, I put him on 'standby' and acted calm instead. Somehow it worked, but then I began laughing.

'Laugh at the irony of it all,' I told myself. 'Laugh at the situational irony, the dramatic irony, the verbal irony, and every other possible form of irony that may be floating somewhere out there in space that would also bear my name.' And, that's what I did – I took time to pay my offering of laughter to every variety of... irony. In fact, I cracked up so long and so boisterously that I had to catch my breath three different times. But, I didn't give a hoot. Not one damned bit. Why not? Because it felt so flippin' good to laugh; to release all that energy that had been pent up inside me for way, way too long; and – most importantly – it felt so great to be alive again.

*I was in such great control of myself (except for the hysterical hyena hijinks) that no one insisted on escorting me off the property (**my** property, remember) lest I do something rash. No, I can proudly report nothing rash sprang forth from any part of me - not from my hands; not from my feet; and certainly not from my teeth & mouth. As much as I would've reveled in the kind of violent revenge that could've employed all three sets of those body parts, something in the meantime had changed; and that something was a person. You only get one guess who.*

Chapter Fifty – Five

The trip to see Bernie Breeze ended bizarrely before Ross could even meet with him. Instead, the muscular, mean-looking gentleman made him sign a paper before handing Ross an envelope containing a restraining order for him to stay off the premises of the complex where Breeze ran Ross's business. And, as we discovered later, a second piece of mail had transferred from the uniformed guard to Ross. At the time, though, he had no clue the second item was taped to the underside of the Manila envelope until after we made it to our next stop – Valhalla, the beautiful-beyond-words former home of Ross and Salome McInerney.

When Ross pulled up to the gate, he didn't get out. Instead, he flipped over the envelope in his lap and saw a smaller envelope taped to it. "What is this?" he wondered. After I suggested he open it to find out, he did. He unfolded some notice only half a sheet in length. Although the message took maybe five seconds to read, Ross stared at that paper long enough to read the "A" section of the Alpharetta phone book back home. With the most downcast expression I'd ever seen, he handed me the notice: "Bernard Breeze and Main Man Productions VS. Ross Robert Padraig McInerney, Los Angeles County Superior Court, on September 21, 1986." I joined Ross in staring at the small rectangle of crinkled white paper a spell. What stunned us was the "day to appear in court," just six days away. Six days. Yikes.

"Well," I said, "we've both got work to do." Ross nodded, which is all he could do. This poor man who'd pulled himself from a twenty-eight-month-long coma six days ago, was expected to fight a team of attorneys in a "superior court of law?" Whatever that is. (How can truth in one court be "superior" to the truth in others? Maybe truth isn't those courts' goal.)

If I were given that situation myself, not only would I have been stricken speechless, I would've lost consciousness. Which spurred me to think about something, which I knew I couldn't discuss with Ross; at least, not yet. And, considering the way things were going in so many different directions, who knows if we might ever get the chance?

⁂

We continued sitting near the only place in Hollywood not hostile to us and our interests - Ross and Salome's first real home together. Those last seven words reverberated in my mind afterward. Within a minute of Ross honking Alfie's horn, Dolores Hidalgo - Valhalla's housekeeper - emerged from a side door and came toward us. As she drew within ten feet but no farther - because of the wrought-iron fence separating us - she smiled. "Senor Ross, welcome back." Looking first in both directions, she whispered, "I can't talk long, but let me say this: Your lovely wife and beautiful children are fine. All three. They're just not… together."

After looking both ways again, Dolores stage-whispered: "If we get caught, I can't tell you what might happen to us. Here…" She held something metallic by her fingertips and allowed Ross to reach through the opening to receive it. When he held it on his open palm, I saw a brass double locket of two hearts melded together. He unlocked the first one with a press of his thumb and smiled. "There she is – my little Salo-manda… she must be the elder since she's in the left locket. Salome always places things in logical order." After clamping the first heart shut, he opened the second. Laughing, he shouted, "Oh my, there he is!"

I waited for Ross to say his son's name, but he didn't. So, I did what I always do when I need to know something – I asked. "Who are we looking at – Ross Junior?"

After lowering his head and shaking it, his face flushed pink, then red. "No," he began with a laugh, "I'm not sure what she named either kid, but I hope she named the girl after herself. Our preliminary agreement was if one of the twins was a girl we'd name her Sally Amanda." Of course, if she did, I'm prepared to give her one of two nicknames – either 'My Little Sal-Amanda' or 'Sallymander' – depending."

"Huh" was all I said. As you remember, I don't enjoy nicknames, given all the awful *monikers* people called me over the years. But then, the realization hit that it was my own background that bothered me instead of the two innocent cute nicknames Ross was choosing between. No, it won't matter if they call this girl Sally Amanda, Sal-Amanda, Sallymander, or Sally Field… because she will likely have a better chance than I had of becoming somebody.

Regardless, Ross didn't say much after Dolores handed over what is today his favorite possession. Instead of staring at his two hearts, Ross kept glancing up at the second-story windows, almost willing the curtains to part and reveal his beloved wife standing there with both boy and girl holding her hands. And maybe, just maybe they'd wave to Ross with their free hands to show just how much they missed him, but ……… that did not happen.

However, some weird stuff did happen right after we jumped in Alfie and waved good-bye to Dolores. Ross drove with a lot on his mind, so it didn't surprise me when he didn't see what I saw when we pulled away. Sitting sideways in my seat to maintain eye contact with Dolores as she and I continued waving, I saw two flashes of color upstairs. In the right-most window stood a woman behind a tiny girl while holding her shoulders. In the left-most window I saw a near-mirror image of the other – a little boy standing in front of another woman who had her hands resting on his shoulders. It took me a sec to figure out which woman was which.

⁂

Not until we'd transitioned from the 101 to the 10 toward San Bernardino did Ross say a word, but not because he was disturbed, worried, or anything like that. No, he looked concerned, perhaps deep in thought, but it was like he'd been analyzing this situation with the same facial expression an engineer studies a challenging problem just thrust in front of him. His *mien* communicated his focus & preoccupation, but in no way did he appear daunted or fearful.

But, he did mutter: "Salome… Sal-Amanda…The Boy…McInerneys all." After sitting there with him five minutes, I was about to ask Ross about these three most-loved people in his life, when he enunciated clearly: "Salome…Sal-Amanda…. The Boy… McInerneys all;" and then for another hour 'til we pulled into Ross Man's driveway bleary-eyed.

If you think we turned in and fell asleep shortly after returning home, you're mistaken. We compiled a long list of everything needing to be asked or done. We split up the *litany* and began preparing every way we could for the next couple days when we hoped to get everything in order before our big date… in Superior Court. You know I love the magic phrase in that last sentence: "our big date." You don't have to tell me I have a one-track mind; or, more accurately, a one-man mind. Ross Man was and is all I think about during both my waking & sleeping hours. You might think I'm 'obsessed' with him, but I'm not. What I am obsessed with is Ross's happiness. Long ago, back at the facility, I dedicated my life to helping this man regain his life.

⁂

The next morning, while Ross and I stood sipping coffee in his kitchen, the phone rang. I tiptoed toward the wall phone. Answering it, a strange voice asked, "What are you doing tonight, Beautiful?" I instantly knew who it was – three boys of junior high age who'd been dialing our number almost non-stop. Without gracing their call with a verbal response, I stuck out my tongue and gave them a 'raspberry,' which succeeded because I heard a click on the other end right before I stopped making the refreshing-for-me, obnoxious-for-others noise. Smiling, I realized that even though I previously thought I didn't have any life skills or street smarts, I now possessed at least one skill regarding a class of people who needed their comeuppance. Yep, Pammy Lee had acquired the ability to deal with bullies in a straightforward and effective way.

So, the effects of this experience of standing up for myself or someone else were many. First, I slipped into the best mood I've ever had. Second, I genuinely felt good about myself; maybe the best I've ever felt about me. No, change that; there's no 'maybe' about it. I felt great - freaking great! - about myself. And Ross? How did he feel about me being so up, happy, and vibrant? I have no idea because all he did was look like a wolf who hadn't eaten for weeks. And though he did the driving, I don't think he was conscious of much other than what needed to be done to help us complete our Trident Mission.

I won't bother telling you the details of our full day of going hither & thither to talk to him or her, or speaking into his or her message machine, but let it suffice to say Ross and I got a heck of a lot done. Not only was our defense for the first trial charted out, we'd completed all the paperwork to mount a countersuit against Mr. Breeze and Main Man Productions. We listed ourselves – "Ross Robert Padraig McInerney and Pammy Lee Wertzog" – as Ross's legal team.

⁂

So, the next morning (Friday) was almost déjà vu - Ross and I leaning against walls while facing one another and sipping coffee from our designated mugs when it happened again. When the wall phone went "br-iiiinnnngggg," I answered and heard the weirdest voice on the other end. "Arrrgghh, Lassie. Good tidings to ye! Is the Honorable Captain McInerney aboard?"

Oh, lord. It's one of those idiotic kids messing with the phone again. I wish I could just hang up on a kid, or anybody, but dang it. I really don't have the –

"Ships ahoy, Lass! Is the Captain on deck? Sammy the Swashbuckler at his service."

Sammy the Swashbuckler? Sam the Sham? It's the pirate DJ Ross talked with on the air while riding on his yacht out in the Pacific.

I waved at Ross to get his attention and mouthed "Sam Swashbuckler. Talk to him!"

Ever the agreeable gent, Ross smiled and nodded before I handed him the yellow receiver. "Hello. Is that you, Sammy?"

"Arrggh… Is it I, Captain? Aye, aye to your query, Sir."

"What can I do for you, Sam?"

"I'm going to drop the pirate act, Ross, if you don't mind."

Ross laughed, "Hey, whatever floats your boat, man."

It was Sam's turn to laugh. "Hey, listen. We haven't heard a peep from you for a long, long time, and there are all kinds of rumors & stories circulating about *you know* - you, the band, and why you haven't released an album or played any concerts for almost three years."

Between sips, Ross asked, “Is that a question, Sammy?”

“Not really, Mate.” (The phony British accent kicked in.) “I’ve just always fancied your music. So, what do ye say, Captain? Will ye board me ship once more and appear on me show?”

Ross said, “Hold on.” Covering the receiver, he whispered, “What do you think?”

Without wasting time or words, I said, “Do it, Ross Man.”

And I’ll never forget his verbal response so long as I live. Sounding like a child remembering an important truth, he responded with a rhetorical question: “Am I Ross Man?”

Then, the man almost knocked me over with what he did next. He grabbed my arms, slid his hands down to mine and held them, saying: “Pammy Lee Wertzhog, I love you. You’ve given me my life back!”

Although Ross’s second sentence contains the best compliment I’ve ever received by a country mile, it was the first sentence that darn near made me swoon right then and right there. And, the weirdest part: I’ve never been a “swooner,” unless Ross is part of the picture. R.R.P. McInerney, in my mind, makes everything possible.

Chapter Fifty – Six

Pammy advised me to write about my life since I 'woke up,' but I'll postpone 'til later any discussion of my condition, medical or otherwise, during my twenty-eight-month residency in the Comaville section of Alpharetta. However, Pam did ask me to 'explain, describe, or summarize' my time since I 'woke up.' So, I'll do my best, but I can't guarantee it will make complete sense.

First off, I know everything Pammy told you about my time at the facility where she worked, but that isn't the whole picture of what was & wasn't going on for twenty-eight months. I won't go into detail, but I will admit to being conscious some of the time.

Secondly, what I'd rather focus on is the time spent after my hospital stays. I swear, more happened during the week Pam sprang me loose than an average year for me up to that time. So, if you'd like a short walk in my shoes, here's what you need to know. My body and mind were on maximum overload every moment of the day or night. Check it out: Pretend you or someone dear to you falls asleep for a long time and misses everything that went on during that span. So, not only would you be clueless as to what's going on in the world, you wouldn't know what's happening with your wife & your own children, both of whom you haven't laid eyes on yet. You would be understandably clueless about your career, your former bandmates, the music business, and life in general. So, my mind and body were running on fumes when I got the call to appear on Sammy the Swashbuckler's show aboard his boat somewhere in international waters.

I won't spend much time describing my appearance on his show, but I'll set the scene. Since I couldn't reach any of my bandmates in that short of time, the only person I took with me was Pammy. We met part of Sammy's crew at the same boat in the same berth as the first time. Although we had to sit below again, it was different this time. It didn't feel like the virtual kidnapping it had been three or four years before. Again, we met at midnight, but – thankfully – blindfolds weren't wrapped about our heads. The whole 'veil of secrecy' thing had disappeared somewhere - perhaps into the dark, choppy waters of the Pacific Ocean below us.

Sammy was different this time around. Sure, he was older, but more obvious was the shift in his personality. He almost jumped from his chair when Pammy and I entered with our escorts. "Great to see you again after all this time, Ross Man. And who, may I ask, is this lovely lady?"

Pammy answered, "Pam Wertzhog - proud to represent Mr. McInerney as his agent."

"Excellent," Sam began. "Listen, Pam, if you're half as gifted at talent management as you are beautiful, you must be one amazing, world-class agent. Wow."

Despite Pammy's face growing pinker, she nonetheless suggested firmly where I sit, what Sam and I would discuss, and what we wouldn't discuss – under any circumstance – during my time behind the mic. Sammy nodded, agreeing with every condition

Pam set down. It amazed me that a rogue veteran of rock radio like Sammy the Swashbuckler would comply with all my new agent's conditions. And, to be honest, I felt for the first time I had someone on my team who not only commanded authority but would back me up – come hell or high water – when the time would come where that tenacity would not only be welcomed but required. Sammy and I respected Pam so much that we both had already accepted her leadership.

The interview, lasting two hours or half the time of my first appearance, was much more professionally conducted, organized, and satisfying for me and Sammy, too. We managed to stay on track because we stuck to the outline Pammy handed us before we went live. We discussed my first three albums along with the work I'd done since. Although I thought everything went smoothly and quickly, I didn't expect much of a public or industry response. After all, it was late at night and neither my fans nor Capitol Records had seen nor heard me in almost three years. Naturally, Sammy wanted me to account for my time 'off duty,' but I dodged his questions by following Pammy's plan to a tee.

The lone low point was when I let slip I'd be facing my agent Bernie Breeze in court the following week. I could tell by the shock on Pammy's face I should've avoided the topic, but the damage had been done and I knew I couldn't 'shove the toothpaste back in the tube' now. What could I do now that the truth was out in the open for everyone to know?

We returned to the marina safe & sound about two-forty a.m.

before checking in to a nearby hotel room Sammy's show paid for. When we awoke around noon and took advantage of room service, I began reading that morning's Los Angeles Times. Their resident rock critic, a nationally known scribe named Roderick Balaban, devoted his entire column to Guess Who? Balaban had evidently tuned into Sammy the Swashbuckler's show and heard me talking about my 'comeback' and impending court trial for the rights to my music. He lavished a generous amount of praise on my music and concluded with this stunner: "Regardless of the circumstances surrounding Ross McInerney's present situation, this reporter is overjoyed Ross Man's back in the fold, raring to record and perform his amazing music for a still-adoring audience starving for distinctive, transparent, personal-to-the-core rock & roll."

I would've read the article aloud to Pam, but I'd started sobbing. When she asked what was wrong, all I could manage was, "Nothing... at all!" before handing her the article. She read it carefully before smiling at me through her own tears. I must say, this moment ranks high on my list of positive experiences because it validated what I'd hoped. I'd been placed on earth to tell my story through music. And then, I had a profound epiphany – my time in an unconscious state all that while might've been the best thing to happen besides having Salome and the twins. Provided, of course, that all three are alive. I'm not entirely sure they were the boy and girl standing in different windows at Valhalla watching us leave. Besides not knowing if they were alive I was also caught up in what their names were – depending on what transpired in the time I'd been away from home. Only time will tell, I half reassured myself.

⁂

I'm sure you want to know about our big court date. The best way to describe it is to call the entire day a dream. Everything happening in that courtroom had the qualities of a dream – the slow-motion pace of the trial in front of the judge, a woman as rail-thin as she was old. Not only did she hunch over her 'bench,' but her shoulder-length, bang-less hairdo stayed in front of her face ninety-nine percent of the time, masking a long, angular face. Whenever my eyes settled on that poor thing with her hair cascading down a good foot and a half from her brow, I thought of the bizarre little guy from The Addams Family that creeped me out as a kid. 'Cousin It' was its name. (Never did figure out if It was a he or she, so maybe It was truly an *it*.)

The way the judge's hair stuck to her face made it look like a mask with no eye holes and reminded me of It so much that I couldn't 'un-see' the image of a foot-tall, covered-in-hair creature, no matter how hard I tried. That image seared itself into my vision field, resulting in me seeing a live version of the Cousin adorned in black judicial robes, speaking louder, slower, and more audibly than the incomprehensible Addams Family member. I worried about what I'd do if I suddenly busted out in raucous laughter. I'd learned during the legal process there is no worse infraction than laughing loudly while court is in session. So, I looked around until I spied a Kleenex box setting atop the bailiff's lectern. Even though the judge hadn't entered the courtroom yet to the usual pomp and circumstance, I still didn't want to cause any disturbance, even the accidental kind, so I remained still. But, I soon felt a series of contractions building in my sinuses and shooting downward to my abdomen, no doubt warning me of the contractions' imminent escape. So, I did everything in my power to avoid making a scene but had to wave at the bailiff & motion for him to fetch me the box of Kleenex. He responded with a nod and quickly handed me the blue cardboard box. I snatched a single tissue out of it just in time to have the paper cover only half my sneeze. Yes, I'm not proud to report that some of my spit and snot projected not only onto the furniture around me, but the sleeve of our court-appointed, lame-duck counsel Jim Johnston. Just to show how completely 'out to lunch' Johnston was, he didn't notice what had landed on his navy-blue blazer with the four faux gold coins on each cuff. And even after I wiped his left sleeve several times with a fresh wad of Kleenex, he didn't respond in the least. I couldn't tell whether he was willfully ignoring me, or worse, wasn't aware of my - or anyone else's - presence. In a way, it was a blessing we'd opted to argue Ross's case ourselves. A rock musician equipped with just a high school diploma and his new friend - a high-school dropout who'd never set foot in a court of law - comprised the legal team representing a musical artist whose recordings and radio royalties added up to several million dollars at 1986 value.

So, when our case was announced as "Bernard Breeze and Main Man Productions VS. Ross Robert Padraig McInerney," Ross and I looked to the prosecution's table for guidance as to what we should or shouldn't be doing. And, since Bernie and his troika of attorneys stood and faced the judge, the Honorable Betty (or Betsy)

McGiver (or MacGillivray), we also stood and faced our *distaff* jurist.

There was much said during our session before Her Honor – most of it by Bernie's attorneys – but everything was 'postponed to a date determined later.' After Betty-Betsy McGiver-MacGillivray gaveled the session adjourned, I kept standing in one place until someone tapped me on the shoulder. Once I 'came to,' the finger tapping resumed and repeated its pattern. I managed to decode the message: "Are you ready? We've got a defense to mount."

I looked up at Ross Man, gave a little wink, and tapped: "Am I ready? Heck, I was born ready. Let's go mount that sucker and break it rodeo-style." It's probably a good thing our courtroom had emptied because Ross began losing it. That boy cackled, roared, giggled, snorted, and even sneezed twice. I never saw anything like it. It got so loud and ran so long I got tickled and joined him in making all kinds of non-verbal noises and utterances myself.

Both of us were blessed not once, but twice. The first was the moment we shared of uproarious laughter and excitement; and the second? We were lucky our butts weren't tossed in jail for disturbing the peace or the legal process. (Which, by the way, the latter needed big time – disruption, that is. Things moved too smoothly and too effortlessly, so the little hairs at the base of my neck stood at rigid attention.) "Nothing good in life comes easy," Ma used to say. Even though she spouted that platitude several times a day, I realized now it was nevertheless true. So, if things went too easily in this case, there was someone somewhere greasing the wheels of justice.

Probably someone in a position of power who had some arrangement or 'understanding' with Bernard Breeze. Nobody informed me, nor did I read it anywhere, but I thought it to be true. See, I knew beyond reasonable a doubt there was something *fishy* going on in a courtroom not far from the ocean. And how did I know it 'fo sho' - as they say down South? Simple. I felt it in each of the little hairs at the base of my neck. I call that little clump of helpful hairs 'my intuition.'

The whole legal battle thing dragged & stretched on & on, so long I can't tell you how many months or weeks it was. At first, Ross and I holed up in our hotel and waited to hear from the 'superior court' when it would schedule our next session. After the first week, we learned we were on our own for housing. So, we did our darnedest to find somewhere in The Basin we could lay our heads at night. Otherwise, we'd be forced to sleep in 'San Berdoo' and commute every day to downtown L.A. Our invitation came from the unlikeliest of sources, and since it was our only offer, we accepted. When Ross broke me the news, all I said was: "I hope I can sleep without getting seasick." Our new home, at least for the time being, was aboard a luxurious yacht I figured would lean or list whenever I'd attempt to sleep. Yes, Sammy the Swashbuckler had not only come to bat for us but, frankly, slugged a grand-slam home run that flew like a missile out of the entire stadium. And, Sam did us a huge favor by dropping anchor much closer to L.A. than Long Beach. We dropped anchor twelve miles straight out from a place called Marina del Rey.

However, we stayed on board the Shady Lady in international waters every night for many weeks. Sammy set aside the largest bedroom for Ross, but my friend – being the perfect gentleman – insisted I sleep there. "But, where will *you* sleep?" I insisted. He just smiled, and I never did find out. Wherever it was, he made the best of it because he always seemed rested. I think he slept in the studio where Sammy interviewed us, but I can't say for sure.

The whole *smorgasbord* of experiences preparing for the case, our appearances in court, and dealing with all the fanfare circling the trial was surreal. If you saw our schedule, you'd know what I mean. By day, we researched, consulted, and strategized, spending at least twelve hours on the mainland sitting in libraries, the courthouse complex, and coffee shops (mainly Norm's); by night, I slept soundly while Ross stayed up to appear on Sammy's program. The DJ played Ross Man's music, discussed the trial with him as much as Ross allowed, and took lots of listener calls – all of them supportive and complimentary. In fact, because of the glut of calls to Sammy's show, the station had to hire two new operators to field them all. And even then, the lines jammed throughout Ross's appearances and for a couple hours afterward. Before I knew it, Ross's case had become a media *juggernaut* not only in SoCal but throughout the state and beyond – quickly increasing its fame (or infamy) around the U.S.

All the local outlets - TV channels KNXT, KNBC, KTLA, KABC, KHJ, KTTV, and KCOP; radio stations KHJ, KRLA,

KNXT, KLOS, KMET, and KROQ; the city's two daily newspapers, the Los Angeles Times and the Daily News; and scores of publications such as Rolling Stone, Creem, Time, and Newsweek – sent reporters to cover the trial. When these journalists weren't in the courtroom, they ventured around Tinsel Ville, scouring the town to investigate various side stories – including seeking interviews with Ross and myself. Because of our need to gather evidence and interview our prospective witnesses, we limited press access to one hour a day – from three to four p.m. – at Norm's Hollywood location. It started innocently when we grabbed a late lunch there one afternoon. When we entered the first time, the place was empty, but after word got out we'd be there more than not - it filled daily with reporters and fans.

After I approached Norm's manager and proposed how we both could benefit from all the media hoopla, he allowed us to set up at one of the larger tables from where we'd field questions. There was only one condition everyone entering Norm's had to follow – we had to buy more than just a cup of coffee. Consequently, what had been the *nadir* of Norm's daily business quickly became its busiest time. Bill the manager hired several more employees to staff their afternoon shift. Thanks to him enacting the 'more than a cup of coffee' rule, sales of apple pie ala mode and other dessert delights went through the roof. In fact, word on the street said Bill negotiated with a local, nearby bakery to bring in additional assorted goodies.

I guess word spread fast about us holding daily news conferences because of Ross's nightly appearances on Sammy the

Swash's program. I say 'guess' because I had no idea why so many folks started joining us for pie every afternoon at Norm's; not until Ross confessed he'd mentioned the cafe on the air the night before. And then, another unexpected phenomenon occurred – people flocked to Norm's before midnight to listen to Sammy & Ross Mac and eat a slice or two of pie. Of course, Norm's corporate management were ecstatic. Their formerly forgotten cafes now found themselves at the center of L.A. consciousness. No longer did Norm's evoke images of lonely diners wolfing down $2.99 steak & eggs specials. Now, it meant so much more. Tacky Norm's had become a hip hangout – somewhere music lovers could hang out 'after hours' listening to pirate radio while having pastry and/or pie.

After getting hip to what was transpiring over the air, I showed up once for Ross's nightly midnight spot. I managed to slip into the studio and hide behind a large monitor, so Ross and Sammy didn't detect my presence. What I heard and witnessed blew my mind. Ross hadn't been sitting for interviews with Sammy every evening, but instead performed a new, original song live. With only his trusty six-string acoustic guitar, Ross regaled the late-night PRPs (Pirate Radio Pirates) each appearance with a brand-new song he'd penned that day. "So, it's bakery fresh, Ross Man?" Sammy always asked. The connection between Ross's "bakery fresh" compositions and Norm's late-night pastry sales hadn't been lost on Sammy Swash, who labeled the new song each time as the "newest of Mac's Morsels – brought to you by the fine folks at Norm's Coffee Shops." As I sat stuck behind the large box, I wondered if Norm's would be the sole beneficiary of Ross's reemergence on the music scene.

⁂

By the time our court case finally began, Ross and I had put in a thousand hours of research; research on everything from labor practices to record company royalty policies to the record industry's remarkable success over the past decade, and anything else we suspected Bernie Breeze and our record label had never informed us about. Consequently, we probably looked as much like a certain critter as we felt we did. You all know about moles, right? Those disgusting little animals who live underground and can barely see? They're furrier, cuter versions of possums. So, between the hundreds of hours spent inside dark libraries doing our due diligence and the all-too-bright morning light rays glinting through Alfie's windshield that always tortured us on our trips downtown to Superior Court, we identified with those visually-impaired rodents by the time we arrived. When an army of reporters descended on us inside Alfie the first morning we knew we were in trouble. Let me put all this chaos into context by explaining it took an hour and a half to find a parking spot, enter the courthouse, visit the restroom, and find our courtroom.

The entire trial lasted two days. Most of the evidence we tried to introduce was deemed "inadmissible," meaning the judge decided she couldn't allow most of the information we shared with her to be considered in court. You'd think we would've responded to this development as a major loss, but we didn't. However, the case did take a toll on us. Maybe it was all the research we'd done over the last month because we were both glad that first trial was over, even though the verdict went against us. Our level of exhaustion and need for sleep both rated a 9.9 on a ten-point scale. If we'd been any more tired, we'd have been dead.

⁂

"So, how much time do you think you'll serve, Ross?" I asked, only partly joking.

"I won't be serving a single day."

I laughed. "Well, don't you sound cocky. By the way, where do we get our hands on $1.05 million? I don't think we'd qualify for any kind of loan to pay it off."

As soon as I finished saying that, I felt bad. No........... terrible. I mean, here we were, in the middle of a potentially life-ruining legal situation, and all I could think to do was be stupid and basically insult the man I respect more than any other. But, Ross didn't react negatively at all. In fact, he behaved as though he hadn't been offended by any of my remarks. Instead, he said: "Listen, kid. I don't know how it's going to be paid for, but I have such great trust in someone on my side that I am not stressing about it in the least."

"For real?" I asked, shocked. "Who is he?"

He looked puzzled. "What do you mean?"

"Who's this guy you trust so much? Or, is it God you're talking about?"

"No… and no."

I laughed. "Ross, what do you mean by 'no and no'?"

"Well, the first 'no' is because the person in question is not a man, and the second 'no' means I'm not referring to God...... provided God exists and cares about our case."

"So… that leaves someone from the other half of humanity."

"Right."

"So, who is 'she'?"

He took me by the hand and led me to the bathroom. "I'll show you. She's standing right there… beside me. See? That's the woman who'll help me sort this all out. And, you know why? Because I have all the trust in the world in her. That's why." Ross first indicated the mirror, but then pointed his Morse code finger directly at me.

My knees buckled, but Ross caught me before I fell. "Are you okay?" he asked.

"Yes and no."

"What do you mean?"

"Yes, I'm more than okay, but, no, I feel so excited that I'm light-headed."

Ross scooped me up and carried me to my bed, where he laid me down like I only weighed what a feather does. "Two things I must tell you: One, you need lots of rest. And, two, once you're rested, how about helping me figure out how to pay off the one million plus?"

Even though he asked me so casually you'd think he'd

requested a small favor, I knew a *prodigious* challenge lay ahead, which is exactly where I wanted to be – in position to help this wonderful man. While I laid there alone on that comfy bed, the biggest smile spread across my face and stayed there probably long after sleep kicked in. My body felt so light and relaxed I thought for a while that instead of reclining on a hotel bed I'd spent several hours atop a cloud. And that soft, accommodating cloud is one you might already know by name - Cloud Nine. I wished I could've stayed forever, but I knew we had plenty of work ahead of us.

While Ross and I waded up to our chins in a sea of research and prepared our counter-suit, a few things occurred behind our backs. There was a movement afoot to help Ross out financially. It wasn't recording industry folk or Capitol, but a groundswell of support from a large, activist-oriented faction of fans known as 'Ross's Hosses.'

Chapter Fifty – Seven

Even before the countersuit had been scheduled in Superior Court, Ross and I went over all the evidence with a fine-toothed comb. After getting beaten the first time, we learned how to better use information that could assist us in winning this second bout. We took a drubbing in the first trial, but it didn't mean we couldn't re-claim Ross's title belt in the return match.

The hangdog expression on Ross's face along with his hunched-over posture spoke volumes about the toll this post-coma period had on him physically, mentally, and emotionally. Here he was, a husband and father of two, who hadn't seen hide nor hair of his wife for three years and had yet to meet his two-year-old children. I began to fear this trial might do the man in altogether if I didn't protect him from at least some of the turmoil and confusion. So, I promised Ross I'd organize our case as plaintiffs this time by myself, insisting he take a break off from research and just enjoy life as a survivor. Well, the results were both interesting and unexpected.

While I sat hip-deep in documents, notes, and various other stacks of paper, I assumed Ross was relaxing and doing next to nothing - per my instructions. However, after checking around our room, lobby, and front desk, I realized he had to be somewhere else. When he arrived home that night, I discovered exactly what he'd been up – talking to the press. And, I don't mean interviews or articles in local newspapers or shoppers. No, I'm referring to the national media – all three television networks, syndicated radio shows, dozens of news and music magazines, and some prominent newspapers (including the Los Angeles Times, both San Francisco papers, the Chicago Sun Times, the London Times, and the New York Times). Interviews, articles, and even letters to the editor about Ross's legal battle with Bernie Breeze appeared that night & continued throughout the trial and beyond. Just to give you an idea how pervasive the media coverage of Ross was, I saw the man on all the local news programs, heard him on a dozen L.A. stations, and watched an entire segment of "Sixty Minutes" on him.

Can you guess where he set up shop every day after we'd finish our room-service breakfasts? Norm's, of course. The management opened their conference room in the back for Ross Man's daily contacts with the media, but the overflow filled up the rest of the café so much that they soon designated most of the restaurant for the media. If regular customers continued to frequent the place, they were given seats either at the counter or in the conference room. As a result, eighty percent of the eatery's square footage was dedicated to Ross McInerney and whatever media reps chose to do stories on him each day. A simple one-hour news conference no longer satisfied the investigative needs of all these news and entertainment outlets, so Ross spent twelve hours a day, seven days a week meeting reporters or TV hosts when he wasn't holding impromptu conferences with a whole corps of them. Consequently, word spread across America, Canada, and Europe about Ross's story. Despite the fact he'd been out of the public eye close to three years, his music continued to enjoy a great deal of popularity. So, with his return and the public's expectation of new music, Ross McInerney and The Talismans of Sound permeated every medium. Without three of them lifting a finger, their prospects were more than promising.

Because security became an issue, someone stepped forward and committed to provide both of us with suites at the world-famous Biltmore. Two bodyguards, Chip and Butch, stood between the doors of our suites when we were home and escorted us everywhere. Since they were identical twins, we never figured out who was Chip and who was Butch; but, it didn't matter. Both men – tall and strapping – wore identical gray suits with white shirts and red ties and never spoke unless spoken to first. Their large, jowly faces seemed stuck in identical expressions of stern blankness, so we never knew what mood they were in nor what they were thinking. "Just here to serve and protect" was their stock response when I asked about their jobs. So, even though "But-Chip" (my name for them) rivaled Buckingham Palace's Guards in terms of sternness & personality, one or the other was always present. The strangest thing was I knew nothing about either brother, not even where they slept. But, I've never felt as safe as when they guarded our rooms and persons. Who knows what might've happened if they hadn't been there to "serve and protect" us? I hate to think about it, so I won't anymore.

After the media blitz kicked into high gear, every big attorney in the country contacted us about arguing Ross's case in Superior Court. Even prominent defense attorneys such as Alan

Dershowitz and F. Lee Bailey contacted us, but Ross never took the bait. "You, Pammy Lee, are all I'll ever need." As you can imagine, that phrase resonated in my ears for weeks. Even now, I can't think about his *hyperbolic pronouncement* without blushing and feeling appreciated.

⁂

Mrs. Edith O'Brien, the Superior Court administrator, called our suite one morning in late October to schedule the civil case between us and Bernie. "We're looking at next year's docket, Ms. Wertzhog, for Mr. McInerney's arraignment."

After we discussed the plausibility of various dates in January and February, I expressed our desire to wrap up all proceedings by the end of 1985. "I don't think that's possible, Ms. Wertzhog, but if you'd kindly hold while I check into one other possibility, I'd appreciate it." Seven minutes later, Edith came back on the line. "Well, I've got good news and bad news for you." After I asked the obvious question, she said, "The good news is we can set the arraignment for this year. And, the bad news is that the only open date of any court is… two weeks from today." So, November 7, 1985 suddenly became our 'Big Day in Court'.

This time around, we had a male judge named Arguello who not only had a reputation for being fastidiously 'by the book,' but uttered a word only when all other options had been exhausted. Most of the time in court, he appeared to be asleep, but he squashed that misperception during our trial. We'd been told by folks in the DA's office that the quicker the trial, the less chance we had of winning.

So, on the morning of the third day in court, when both sides' attorneys gave their closing statements, my head started spinning. Dozens - maybe hundreds - of questions infiltrated my consciousness. Most were questions of myself – whether we emphasized certain points enough or too much. Had the jury followed the information I'd given them about Bernie stepping out of his professional role to steal not only from Ross, but the other Talismans as well? And then there was the jury. Most of them appeared to be unconscious. Since they rarely made eye contact with Ross or me whenever we addressed them, we knew we'd lost this second battle.

So, after Judge Arguello gave the jury its final instructions before deliberation could begin, I took deep breaths to try and calm my nerves and slow my vertigo. "We will now adjourn this court for the deliberation phase of this trial. Although the bailiff, court reporter, and I will remain available for questions and information throughout the jury's deliberation, the rest of our court staff may resume their other duties and plan on being available on a 'stand-by basis.' We will now sequester you, the jury, in the Jury Room, where you will begin deliberation after a short break. At noon, if you haven't reached a verdict by then, we will adjourn for lunch. And then at one-thirty, deliberation – if necessary – will resume until no later than five o'clock."

As Ross and I watched the seven men and five women noiselessly file through a designated door, a flock of butterflies in my tummy began to stir. Instead of accepting Ross's invitation to lunch, I told him I'd rather return to the Biltmore and await the jury's verdict there.

"Okay, suit yourself, Pam. Rest up and I'll bring you some takeout from Norm's."

So, I fell asleep and stayed asleep until evening (or so I thought). Have you ever fallen asleep too early in the day and when you awoke, it was dark out and you had no clue what time of day it was? Well, if you've been in that boat, you know the position I was in. And, I was afraid to look at the clock because it might already be the next day and I'd have no idea what happened during my sleep binge. Who knows? Maybe the jury already delivered their verdict. Then, I began picturing Ross all freaked out about losing a case for the second time in which he's been one-hundred percent innocent and a victim of someone's evil nature and greed.

When the phone in the room clanged, I awoke from the deepest sleep. *Who could that be?* I muttered as the hotel phone continued to jingle. *You'll never know, Pammy, if you don't pick up and find out.* So, feeling like a child who'd lost her parent in Times Square or somewhere else with a million people, I knew there was but thing I should do – pray. "Uh, hello," I whispered.

"Is this Pammy Wertzhog?"

"Why, yes, it is. Who's calling?"

"Before I tell you that, let me break you the news from the trial. Is that okay?"

"Yes, that would be fine. But Mr. McInerney, whose case

this is, is not here right now. But, I am his manager and agent and will be glad to help you."

"I know who you are, but it's obvious you have no idea who I am. Let me give you the news of the trial first."

"Okay, Sir."

"Well, Miss Wertzhog, I need to ask you a question."

"Yes, sir. Ask me anything you'd like – as long as it's reasonable."

"Alright, let me ask you: what do you want first – the good news or more good news?"

I was struck speechless, for two reasons. First, how could there be not one, but two sets of good news? And second, only one person shares the joke of "good news?" with me.

"Uh, well. This is very confusing… unless you happen to be Ross Robert McInerney."

The laughter on the other end was all I needed to hear to confirm who it was. After his bout of *guttural cacophony* subsided, Ross asked: "Well, which do you want first – the good news or the other good news?"

"Oh… how about the good news?"

"We don't have to worry about the 1.05 million."

"And, why not?"

"Well, two reasons – and they're both good."

"Okay, I'm waiting with bated breath, Ross."

After an interlude of more laughter spilled forth, Ross answered: "The presale of tickets for the concert has already exceeded one million and continues rising daily."

"What concert?"

"I guess we have more friends out there than we thought, Pammy. A benefit concert to help us pay off the court costs and judgment of the first case was scheduled initially for the Santa Monica Civic, but now it's moved up to the much larger and more lucrative Inglewood Forum."

"Wow. Well, someone still must produce a benefit concert. Who put up the money?"

"A certain celebrity, but I'm not at liberty to say yet. But, I will tell you this much, Pammy. Our anonymous benefactor lives on the largest ocean on Earth."

After I laughed myself breathless, I asked: "And, the other news?"

"Are you sitting down?"

"I am now. Fire away."

"The verdict is in on our countersuit."

"AND!?" I screamed.

"The judge ruled in our favor… to the tune of a familiar sum."

Which really got me chomping at the old bit. "ROSS! WHAT SUM?"

"Why, one million, five thousand American dollars, of course."

So, it turns out Bernie Breeze had broken every possible rule, regulation, and statute in his 'distribution' of royalty monies from not only all Talismans of Sound albums and singles, but from every publishing commission as well. I figured this verdict had to be earth-shattering.

"Wow" is all I could utter after sitting up in bed.

"We need to celebrate" is what I wanted to say, but I knew what was on Ross's mind. He wouldn't spend a minute celebrating until he got his family back, which I support, of course.

Chapter Fifty – Eight

Ross and I spent the rest of the evening discussing the results of our case and charting a course of how to proceed on everything else. Our all-nighter of coordinated planning & mutual commiseration somehow refreshed our spirits because we went through that day as though we'd slept soundlessly for nine hours. We decided Ross should continue to discuss his and the band's situation in whatever medium or venue he could find to tell his story, which would hopefully result in more tickets sold, more albums sold, and more new fans of Ross's created. After all, he reasoned, America is the perfect country for a comeback of a known person who's been cheated, especially monetarily. Plus, he continued, "Americans have always fought for two entities - justice and the underdog." I knew Ross's case was no exception. Bernard Breeze and his sleazy excuse for a talent agency had become representations of the following in no special order: the fat cat, the weasel, and the rat. They were nothing more than bullies who'd deceived, cheated, and outright stolen the creations of a genius and then feasted on their ill-gotten gains. That's all I need to say about Breeze and his ilk because I know that if they never face justice in this life, they most definitely will in the next.

We agreed my job for the time being should be finding the whereabouts of Salome and the twins. *A piece of cake*, I thought since I already knew their location.

⁂

Pammy Lee and I had been so slammed during both trials and in between researching this, that, and the other, that I'd begun to forget not only the world outside our bubble, but anything that didn't pertain to the goals we'd set for ourselves to protect my musical career from ruination and, more importantly, find my amazing wife and our two babies, infants, toddlers, or whatever they were at this stage. In my mind, they'd always been my babies and would remain so for however long our lives would be.

But, first things first, I told myself. I figured the simplest, best way to draw attention to our legal problems would be if I discussed them over the radio, on TV, in print, and by old-fashioned word of mouth. I'd already interviewed with Harry Reasoner from "Sixty Minutes," Irv Kupcinet and Larry King on their nationwide radio shows, and the legendary Paul Harvey. Each gave their blessings and support by not just having me on their programs but encouraging and advising me how to proceed with getting the word out about both the upcoming benefit concert and the search for my family. I explained on every show - in addition to the dozens of interviews with other reporters, columnists, and talk show hosts – that my wife Salome and our twins could not be found. I tried dancing around the question about the LAPD's support or lack thereof during the search for them, but it was little use. Since I wasn't a pro at fielding questions, I told more than one media gathering that only I had been searching for these three missing persons. And then the inevitable follow-up question would be: "If no one else is looking for them, how can they be considered missing?" All I could do was shrug and change the subject, which – of course – made me look like either a scumbag who'd done something terrible to his family or the certifiable idiot I used to think I was.

So, every morning after sharing room-service breakfast with Pammy Lee in our suite, I sauntered down to Norm's on Hollywood Boulevard and set up shop for multiple interviews with anybody and everybody. At first, I simply took all comers and didn't format our exchanges, but the repetitious questions soon beleaguered me so much I had to set down a short list of standards and possible topics. The whereabouts of my missing family was one subject I brought up every day because it was my prime concern – more so than my career. However, I refused to discuss my own whereabouts for the past two and a half years. Regardless of or perhaps because of my refusal, my time away from the music business became the paramount topic of interest with the media. New rumors, tales, and jokes sprang up every day about where I spent all those years & months between the day I left L.A. and the day I returned.

The subject of interest occupying a distant second in the minds of the journalists and fans was the whereabouts of my old bandmates Al and Stu. When asked about my effort to see them, I'd begin by saying I rang the doorbell at their gate several times with no response. And then the reporter or host in question would give me the weirdest look. I had to just sit there in silence until someone asked another awkward question. However, I persisted in answering their questions as sincerely and simply as I could, so it seems many of them weren't ready to demand the LAPD do an investigation on me. What's strange to Pammy and me is we'd been in L.A. two months without a single tidbit of news about either man. I rang their gate several times, but no one ever answered the intercom. I didn't know if their staff lived there or not. And, they knew even less about me than I did of them since I'd literally been missing for a long time. Two and a half years may not sound long, but in show business it's an eternity.

One positive development in my life was the concert being planned to generate funds for my court costs and monetary judgment while also hopefully recompensing me partially for all the lost revenue from my songs over the past seven or eight years. At first, the event was scheduled at the intimate Santa Monica Civic, so I didn't get my hopes up about it generating enough revenue to put even a dent in my sizeable debt. But, I began getting my hopes up about the concert helping in a major financial way when Sammy Swash told me over the air he hoped to get a larger venue, perhaps even the Long Beach Arena if ticket demand was there.

Another interesting development was the renewed interest in my music. All three albums had reappeared on the Billboard Top 100 list three years later in 1985. And since Bernie now no longer held claim to any of our royalties, a temporary trust for each of us band members had been established by the court until we could claim our money and invest our individual trusts wherever we wanted it. It's funny – three of the four members of the Talismans of Sound were either incommunicado or M.I.A., even though they all stood to finally receive some serious cash.

With every interview or appearance on TV, radio, and print, our albums grew in popularity and generated new discussions about our music. And, an unexpected development – a huge demand for my solo music – became an oft-discussed topic on radio and throughout the media. There was a tremendous demand for my new songs, even without a band. The critic from the L.A. Times spearheaded a movement advocating for artists who'd been ripped off. So, it was doubly cool when another landmark court decision involving artist royalties occurred. John Fogerty of Creedence Clearwater Revival fame won the right to not only play his own music, but recoup some of the royalties his manager & agent had cheated him, to put it accurately. So, 1985 was a bright year for artists who'd been taken to the cleaners by management.

The day after our trial ended victoriously, the suite's phone began ringing off the hook. And whenever a reporter, agent, talk-show representative, or magazine editor couldn't get through because our room's line was busy, the front desk took handwritten messages. At last count, we'd received over ONE THOUSAND telephone calls in addition to untold faxes, letters, and telegrams. Everyone wanted me, and no matter how inconvenient or unwanted their desire might be, most of them never took "no" for an answer. But! Of all the calls received and logged at the Beverly Hills Hotel front desk, at least one could be described as a positive one. Buster Romero, Capitol Records' Vice President of Research and Development, called one day while I rested in our suite. I listened politely while he made a generous offer. Unfortunately for both of us, I had to refuse for the simple reason the other three Talismans, without whom we had no act, were unavailable. I remember laying there on my cushy bed laughing out loud about the irony of everything that had transpired. Here I'd been completely unavailable while in a coma for all that time and when I finally did make it back home and wanted to seek out my wife and our two bandmates, none were available. As I continued laughing, the imagined faces of my two children, boy and girl, appeared. Behind them stood their mother and the other woman Pammy had described for me after our visit to Valhalla.

One thing that kept me going throughout this excruciating waiting period was my nightly appearance on Sammy the Swashbuckler's Pirate Radio Show. The experiences of being on his yacht, hanging out with him before, during, and after his show, and playing my new music on the air were what grounded me for at least that part of my time. It was the one time of the day or night when my wife and kids weren't at the bull's eye center of my focus on reality. During my childhood, I'd seen the icon of an Indian chief's profile appear on our TV's screen as a "test pattern" after stations went off the air, as early as midnight or as late as two in the morning. That stalwart chief's face had been framed in a bull's eye. And, projected onto the screen in my imagination was a bull's eye pattern with the faces and heads of my dear Salome & our children enclosed. I couldn't take my imagination's eye off them but soaked in all I could store so I'd subsist on it later when I'd need the benefit of all that energy even more.

A real bummer for me was worrying about my three loves continually. I became more anxious, hyper, uptight, which I dubbed "Stressed Out to the Max" or "SOM" – the code I used with Pammy when someone succeeded in driving me crazy, but I didn't want them to know. "SOM" was Pam's cue to do what she could about the person or situation causing me the stress. She'd take my hint and do whatever it took to alleviate whichever stress or hassle was getting to be too much. She admitted being "worried to death" that a sudden shock to my nervous system might set off a stroke, seizure, or – the worst thing besides death – another coma. "Ross, perform your music on the radio at night and write your new songs by day. Just leave the other stuff to me, Hon. You'll see." And so, that's what I did throughout the legal process.

Each night, at midnight, Sammy would introduce me and ask about that night's song, which I'd usually written & taught myself earlier that day. At first, I named the songs by the dates I composed them, but people got confused over which song was which, so I took Sammy's off-air advice and gave each composition a specific name relating to a lyric or two in the song, virtually every other musical artist has done since the dawn of time.

I'd sit there in a rickety chair each night with my six-string in my lap and sing into a round old-fashioned studio mic secured to the deck. I usually leaned forward a bit, but not so much my guitar strings would collide with the mic stand. However, on a couple of occasions I did use the rounded metal bar as a slide for my six-string, which caused much excitement from my new friend Sam the

Sham. (I only called him that off the air, by the way). He'd naturally sit there in silence throughout my playing, but he made all kinds of noise when I finished a song. Sam did everything under the sun (or, in this case, moon) to show his excitement & appreciation for my newest song. His responses always consisted of his own verbal and sound-effect sounds, including whistling, stomping, cymbal-striking, kazoos, and dozens of other possibilities. Sam also relied on his sound-effects machine, which spit out such auditory delights as clanging bells, cartoon effects, explosions, voices; you name it and he had the recording.

To illustrate, I'll do my best to reproduce what Sammy said and did after I finished "Satchmo and the Mop Tops," but it won't begin to capture the magic of that amazing moment. Here's a rough reproduction: "Whoa ho ho, Mates. (Sound of horse neighing and kicking up a storm in an arena or paddock somewhere in the cosmos.) Woe, woe is me… NOT! I mean to tell you (sound effects of Fred and Barney's feet propelling Fred's car through Bedrock) that this ROCK-AND-ROLL rock-solid performance by our guest Ross McInerney can only be aptly described by Mr. Flintstone's famous signature motto… Yabba, dabba, do!"

After a series of catcalls, recorded applause in many various forms, cartoon sound effects, and – of course – pirate cannon explosions, Sammy the Swashbuckler exclaimed at the apex of his voice: "If ye don't fancy that wondrous shanty, ladies and gents, ye don't fancy music itself!" The symphony of manufactured and human cacophony would die out and Sam would pose a single question about that song. I always tried to answer it fully, but succinctly. I neither wanted to leave Sam's listeners hanging about the song's message nor sound like some lecturer or salesman. As soon as I fielded the first query, I'd take my leave and ride the Pacific back to terra firma and my waiting bed.

⁂

I knew nothing about being a detective or private dick, except I'd once heard a good one stays on the trail until (s)he finds a scent and follows it to the person or creature she's trailing; and so, that's all I needed to know about 'detectiving.' Since Ross delegated me with starting the process of finding Salome and the twins, I took my job seriously. Very seriously. My first task was to jot down the names of everyone with whom he'd had any association before abruptly splitting L.A. two & a half years before. Surprisingly, it was a short list and by noon that first day I'd narrowed it down to seven leads: Salome, Delilah, Dolores the Valhalla housekeeper, Fred the producer at Capitol Records, Stu & Al, and – of course – Mr. Bernard Breeze. Since I knew the whereabouts of Fred and Bernie, I figured I'd start by looking for the other five and then proceed to the hottest trail. Or trails. Oh, and the second rule of all detectives (or 'gumshoes') I learned – he or she should never, ever assume anything. I'm sure you heard the old saying about 'assume;' that when we *assume,* it has the potential to make asses out of you and me. If you've never heard that gem of wisdom before, I'm sure you will again sometime. And, if you don't get the play on words or letters now, you will. Just be patient, like all good detectives. Hey! I now know *three* things about private eyeing! But, before you waste any time being proud of me, let's wait and see how this all turns out.

The first place I went on day one 'on the case' was Stu and Al's, down the hill from and on the same street as Valhalla. After Alf and I pulled up to their gate, I climbed out and pushed the intercom button on the beige stucco wall. Almost instantly, I heard "Yes?"

"Oh, hi. Yes, I – uh – I need to speak with Al and Stu, please."

"You're too late, young lady."

I leaned into the speaker and was about to say "late" with much more passion than the disembodied voice had, but the hairs at the base of my neck stopped me. Why? Because something wasn't right. I knew pressing the button a second time would prove futile. Why? Because the voice came from directly behind me. I turned and tried seeing who it was. Unfortunately, the SoCal sun was extra intense because the sheet of glare assaulting my eyes kept me from identifying her. Fortunately, the woman recognized me and identified herself as Dolores, the housekeeper from Valhalla, whom I assumed still worked for Bernie Breeze.

"If you're looking for Mister Stuart or Mister Allen, you're a little too late, Miss- "

"Wertzhog, but – please – call me either Pammy or Pammy Lee, Ms. Huerta."

Dolores and I spoke for a spell, but all that conversing didn't reveal much except that The Boys had moved to another house in the Basin. She didn't volunteer where. Perhaps if Ross were with me, she would've told him, especially if he pressed her. However, I learned more from watching that housekeeper's movements and facial expressions than anything she told me with her words. It was obvious she'd not only been sworn to secrecy about anything having to do with the present or former occupants of Bernie Breeze's properties, but she kept her responses as brief and vague as possible, which was fine with me. I knew a large part of being a professional detective was the phase of sorting through all the evidence and non-evidence first before beginning the process of piecing together the crime involved with the person they're seeking, who was usually missing. I did manage to learn The Boys had left the day before with most of their belongings and had already begun to settle in to their new home.

There were also a couple bits of *intel* I was able to glean from my visit to The Boys' old place that might help me. A mover specializing in transporting 'special cargo' had been hired to move some unspecified form of cargo the next morning around eight. And second, I learned The Boys weren't in the best of shape. I didn't know if it was one or both, but someone had been battling a medical problem. As to any info about Salome & the kids, Dolores wasn't forthcoming but messaged with her hands that both kids were healthy. Which was great news, but then ...... that was it. When I asked a couple follow-ups, the sweet lady laughed while shifting & stepping around in her white nurse's shoes until I began to take my leave.

"Maybe we'll meet again, Dolores?"

"Es posible, Senorita Wertzhog. Es posible."

And that, friends, was my first call of my first day on the job as a detective. It would be some time before I'd know if my entry into private eyeing had been *auspicious* or not, but it was time to plan my next step. I later thought, "It *could* be an auspicious one." I felt hopeful.

My next stop, after an hour of clothes shopping, was Valhalla. This time, I'd try an approach different from our previous attempts. Instead of driving up in Alfie, I ventured to the estate in a different fashion. After parking just around the corner, where Alfie couldn't be seen from Ross's, I checked my look in one of his outside mirrors. Practicing various looks I thought my 'character' should use, I gave myself a pep talk. "Now, Pammy Lee, this here's your big chance to finally help Ross with his… situation. So, don't blow this chance, but usc it to the best of your ability. Yes, God is up on His throne and all that, but you need to take some initiative here on Earth, too. So, I won't wish you luck, Hon, but I will start praying for you … now."

Adjusting my newly acquired dress until it didn't annoy me near as much, I tried on the cat's eye glasses for which I'd spent a quarter at the nearby Goodwill and then blotted my lipstick with a Kleenex like I'd seen in Claudette Colbert's movies. Reciting the twenty-third psalm as I click-clacked down the sidewalk for my first time in heels, I must've cut quite a figure for anyone looking out a window on that block. Any casual observer would say without doubt

I was seriously inebriated by all the unsure steps and demi-trips. After a hundred feet, I rounded the corner and looked up at the two-story wonder that is Valhalla. In much the same way as when I'd laid eyes on Elvis Presley's famous home, Graceland, I felt a chill and then goose bumps popped up on my bare arms even though it was ninety-five degrees out. However - and a big however this one is - the heat in the Hollywood Hills was 'as dry as a bone in the Mojave desert,' so all my perspiration wasn't from the heat, but the nervousness cloaking my head, shoulders, and feet. The latter I counted on to help me walk to wherever I needed to be, so I had to - at all costs - shed this handicap of a cloak. But then it got even worse.

I then realized if I wanted to become even more nervous, all I had to do was list the reasons I shouldn't be standing in front of a mansion owned by Ross's arch enemy and legal nemesis. Following the instruction of my inner voice, I drew a breath before approaching the intercom. Before I could reach it, the gate began to slide. Struck dumb by my good (bad?) fortune, all I could do was stand on the right side of the gate by the intercom and watch for what would happen next. When the long black metal gate on the matching metal track had rolled all the way open and stopped its squeaky-wheeled progress, I heard a mechanical door opening somewhere. Shortly thereafter, I saw a black Cadillac limousine creeping down the *precipitously* steep concrete driveway toward the just-opened gateway. Although I could see a driver in a black cap behind the wheel presumably guiding the creeping car, that was the extent of what I saw. The side & rear windows were black, so seeing who - if anyone - was inside wasn't possible. The vehicle took an entire minute to creep two hundred feet, just to show how slowly it moved. Creep… Creep… Creep… When the crawling Caddy reached the opening and slithered across the black metal track, I continued standing as stiffly as a stone and taking in the scene with all my senses. As the limo passed and began crossing the extension of the sidewalk, the black and chrome hunk of heavy metal halted. Sitting there for a spell, the driver shifted to 'park' and got out. A towering, serious man who could've been cast as either a really mean criminal or extremely stern policeman approached in his mirrored glasses. He also could've passed for General MacArthur's younger brother, and who knows? Maybe he was. This fella had the same kind of command and handsomeness to boot. And, speaking of boots, Driver Man wore black polished paratrooper boots that would've made any airman, pilot, or parachutist proud. Their heels made slight, crushing sounds as he crossed the cement drive to stand five feet from me.

"Ma'am" was all he said but, with that single-syllable word, the driver-stormtrooper conveyed a *veritable plethora* of messages. But before I could figure out which one he wanted to verbalize, he spoke again, but longer this time around. "What is your business here, Miss – "

"Wertzhog, Miss Wertzhog – at your service." I didn't feel offended when he didn't take my hand to shake. However, before he could ask me the 'what-business-brought-me-to-this-guarded-estate' question, I thought I'd make sure I had the *entirety* of his attention. So, instead of giving him some phony story that he and his passengers might see right through, I answered plainly: "I'm here for Ross." If that chauffeur's jaw hadn't been securely attached to the rest of his chiseled-in-stone face, it would've surely fallen to the cement and broken into a hundred smithereens. In fact, Chauffeur Man was so taken by my four-word statement he stood still, motionless, gawking in my direction for quite some time, even after a drop or two of slobber began sliding from his mouth and running down his clean-shaven, stone-stiff chin. Pulling a hanky out of my purse and waving it at him to recapture his attention, I smiled & asked: "May I?" I took his lack of a response for a "yes," so I did what any other Southern lady would've done in that very same situation – I wiped his chin free of all that spit.

He must've been humbled by my gesture because every iota of sternness in his being fell away right in front of me, landing invisibly where his jaw should've unhinged & shattered just moments before. A smile broke over his face, brightening the air and space between us. "Miss Wertzhog, ma-am, how may I assist you today? Ma'am."

I again took the simple route – the truth. "I want nothing more in this wide world than to reunite Mr. Ross McInerney with his family… Sir." Chauffeur Man, now promoted to human status, looked deeply into my eyes (and I into his). We then connected on a level I hadn't been or known before, though we'd known each other all our lives. Strange, right? But, 'good strange.' No, better than merely good strange, but I don't have time to label it now.

Anyway, whatever I did or didn't do seemed the right

method of getting this hunk of a man over on my side of this war. He held up his right gloved index finger as though asking me to 'stand by just one minute.' I nodded in agreement as he stepped to the limo and the window directly behind the driver's lowered slowly, electronically. Since Driver Man's torso blocked the person lowering the window, I couldn't – for the life of me – see who it was.

The exchange between Mr. Dreamy Driver and the person behind the window lasted maybe a couple minutes. After the glass finished its upward glide, DD turned and approached me in his handsome uniform and paratrooper boots. "The ladies would like to meet with *just you* tomorrow noon here at this address. Do you accept their invitation?" This new, brand-spanking development was so beyond what I'd expected or hoped for, I dared not ask a question or insist on including Ross. All I could think to do was reply "Of course," thank the man, shake his hand, and stand by stiffly again while the gate slid closed and the black & chrome limousine glided away at its signature crawl. So, since I'd already procured an appointment with The Ladies tomorrow, I gave myself the rest of the morning off from my very first case. "I just hope one of those ladies is the one I need to meet," I whispered to myself several times as I clicked and clacked without falling even once to meet my second-best friend awaiting me – AAR (Alfie Alfa Romeo). He must've been glad to see me when I rounded the corner because I think I spied the slightest of smiles beginning to spread across that cute little grille of his.

Although I had plenty more folks to interview and a couple

leads to chase down that afternoon, part of me insisted on returning to the suite, changing out of my fancy duds from Goodwill & Hollywood Thrift, and just relax. After returning to the suite, I propped up my feet on our desk and smoked a Sherman cigarette I'd bummed off a hippie outside the hotel, to celebrate my day's accomplishments. Mike Hammer would've approved; no doubt about it.

Chapter Fifty-Nine

When she returned early with a bunch of stories and some bits of news, Pammy Lee stunned me by announcing she had only one kind of tidings – and it was all good. Wow! "Well, I'll be gall-darned," I thought – to borrow my newest friend's strongest expression. But instead I thought of another, more powerful word of Pam's to depict more accurately my confusion at that moment; and the funny-sounding adjective I'm referencing would be the bizarre-sounding slang word "bumfuzzled." See, I was so completely taken aback by the absence of bad news that you could've selected me as the national poster boy for 'bumfuzzlement.'

"Ross, I've got only good news for you, Hon. No; hold up, Pammy," she self-corrected. "How does that saying we use go? Oh, yeah. Okay - here goes: 'Ross Man, which do you want to hear first – the good news or… the good news?'"

I laughed, hard; and you would've, too. Pammy looked and acted so darned cute as she tried announcing the news in a joke format while peeling off some clothes unfamiliar to me and recounting virtually everything that had happened in the five or six hours she'd been gone. What struck me more than anything was that her spirits had never been higher. I don't simply mean this was the highest I had ever seen her spirit-wise. No, no. To prove my point, I'll quote her as she wrestled the last of her dress over her head, revealing her white slip. Pammy claimed she had "never felt so ...

bubblicious" in her life and proceeded to convince me with every word, expression, and movement that this moment was, in her words: "the acme, the apex, the absolute highest point" of her existence. Little did I know this huge victory of hers - meeting The Ladies the next day - would not be so huge – when later compared with other breaking news.

⁂

I was so excited about meeting the two ladies, Salome and her friend Delilah, that I took Alfie to not only get washed, but detailed inside & out the morning before we met at Valhalla. After gassing him up, we visited Ross's old place. When we pulled up to the gate, it was wide open. Parked just inside was someone's (Salome's? Bernie's?) black and chrome Cadillac limousine with Mr. Chauffeur next to it, standing at erect attention. With a pointing gesture, he showed me where to park – next to him, but without blocking his Caddy Fleetwood Deluxe.

I assumed Mr. Dreamy Driver would chauffeur us a couple hundred feet to the house above, but when he opened one of the car's doors for me, I realized I wouldn't be his only passenger. Two women, both dressed in business suits, sat side by side in the back seat. My new, nameless friend the driver motioned for me to sit in the seat facing backward before saying, "I'll let you two ladies introduce yourselves, but I would be remiss if I didn't properly introduce Ms. Pamela Wertzhog to you. Pamela is visiting us today on behalf of Mr. Ross McInerney." He smiled broadly and said, "Please lower your window and give a holler, Ms. Wertzhog, if you need me. I will promise to remain within earshot." Dreamy Driver then shut the door gently and walked a short distance away, to evidently give us privacy – from whom, I wasn't exactly sure.

The blonde on the left spoke. "Good afternoon, Ms. Wertzhog. Thank you for coming back today. I'm sorry that we couldn't … visit with you yesterday, but our schedule has been slammed lately. My name is Sandra Schwartz and my colleague here is Ms. Darla Newberry."

The lady with brown hair smiled. "We're both glad you could make it today, with what must be a very busy schedule assisting and representing Mr. McInerney. We are both family social workers from the local office of Los Angeles County Department of Social Services. Each of us represents one of Ross and Salome McInerney's children, who both reside here at Valhalla. However, I'm sure you're not aware of the living situation that exists here vis a vis the children and their biological parent, Mrs. McInerney."

For the third time since age two, I had no words to speak. But that didn't matter, because neither my assent nor dissent was required. So, I became "all ears," as folks say. Here's the upshot of what each of the social workers had to say. The blonde one, Sandra, explained she was acting on behalf of one McInerney child, Ross Junior, whom she oddly described as a "pretty normal young man for his age" – at a mere twenty-six months old. The baby boy loved any and every kind of physical activity – running, jumping, even falling. (The latter never ceased to make him laugh his tushy off, so he already displayed the gift of laughing at himself, which impressed me to no end, believe me.) Sandra continued to describe Junior as "an inquisitive young man who asks questions constantly, but charmingly." She soon finished speaking, so it was the brunet's turn. Darla's "charge," as she referred to her, was "the young lady" christened Sally Amanda. The elder of the twins, Sally verbally and non-verbally reminded everyone daily that she was not only the older child, but the "leader" of the duo. As I heard this comment, I felt my mouth shift to a smile, my first facial gesture since we'd begun this exchange. Somehow, up till this moment, I'd been frozen stiff, but these new bits of information warmed my brain up and I began processing what might be going on. Darla went on to praise "Little Sal" for a variety of achievements and personal traits. Not only had the girl completed toilet training long ago, she'd devised a way to teach her brother "Little Ross" how to also use the potty properly. If that wasn't surprise enough for me, guess what jolted me more? Little Sal taught Little Ross *over the phone*. I was really being entertained by this odd story when my noodle of a brain bolted to action. *Why in tarnation was a two-year-old girl calling her also two-year-old brother every day?* It turns out that each of the twins lived on a different end of the house and was parented by a different person. (I won't type out what my brain said right then because I knew that we - Ross and I - wanted to keep the story you're reading a family story. But, feel free to use your imagination.)

Throughout the Ladies' descriptions of their respective "charges" and all the other duties they presumably needed to perform while in my presence, my head wouldn't (or couldn't) stop spinning; and I don't just mean figuratively. This weird *vertigo* began assaulting me while I sat there in the lap of luxury inside a magnificent limousine on a Hollywood estate once leased and inhabited by one of rock's biggest icons. The dizziness became so bad I had to rest my head against a side window despite the fact it had to be 95 degrees outside.

So, even though I looked and felt like "puke warmed over" – as Ma used to delightedly describe me growing up – I knew I absolutely had to remember the next few details, so I lay there propped up against that car window and tried focusing on everything being said. Throughout this ordeal, my consciousness teetered between normal awareness on one end of the seesaw and a dreamlike state in slow motion on the other that rendered everything I heard *incomprehensible.* Amidst this radical and constant shifting of my thinking, an arsenal of questions bombarded my brain. First, I wondered how twin children could be separated from one another. How could the natural mother not have custody of both kids? Why did one get to be with one's mom and the other not? And, who was the 'other woman' in charge of Junior – a court-appointed foster parent? Perhaps Delilah – Salome's friend and Ross's high-school sweetheart? Or, maybe someone I didn't know about? These and a flurry of other questions struck me head-on while I struggled to hear, comprehend, and remember all the 'facts' told me by these social workers, whom I still hadn't decided whether to trust or not. Pam's Jury was out.

Since I'd never had previous contact or involvement with the foster child system, children's protective services, or *governmental entities* of any kind in any state, I didn't pose the questions I probably should have. However, I felt like progress toward Ross reuniting with his family might possibly happen. And, guess what? Just as soon as I'd gained confidence in "the process," as both women had labeled it, Sandra announced she & Darla had enough information to proceed with their "investigation into the McInerney matter." She wrote down our hotel number and shook my hand. Our meeting had been deemed over, so Dreamy Driver escorted me the few feet to Alfie and opened my driver's-side door for me. As I started Mr. Alfie the Alfa Romeo up, I noticed Dreamy writing something in the sten pad he'd pulled out of his pocket.

As I pulled out of the space next to his limo, two thoughts struck. One, I hadn't gotten any contact information - not even a business card - from either woman. And second, I thought Dreamy Diver did something odd after I pulled away from the gate and he began to recede from my view. Call me crazy, but I believe the man blew me a kiss, although the image of him blowing me a smackaroo didn't materialize in my mind till an hour after I reached our hotel. I'd been so involved in trying to un-bumfuzzle myself regarding Ross's children it took a filled-to-the-very-brim hour to sink into my fat head that a gentleman of the real man persuasion had clearly sent a message of affection toward me with a simple, but time-tested & time-honored gesture, that always means to portray love or – at the very least – some level of infatuation.. All I could wonder was – was this sudden, expected gesture an *aberration*, an oddity, or a *harbinger* of things to come? And, Practical Pammy again knew only Father Time would know the answer.

⁂

So, things seemed to heat up after Pammy's first day as a "private dick," the job title she stubbornly insisted on calling herself. Our phone rang, Pam picked it up, and I assumed it was The Ladies, following up with a day & time for me to meet the kids, but I was wrong.

After Pam told me who it was, she handed me the phone. I spoke with Al and Stu at the same time because Stu was on their second line. Talk about Old Times Week. Oh, man. It was, in a word, awesome to speak with both of my old bandmates. I kept saying we needed to see each other as soon as possible to start the band up again, but they never responded. I was starting to feel put off, but they assured me they'd see me sometime soon, so I left it at that. But, boy, did they sound great – as though life had been a lot kinder to them than it had to me.

So, after we hung up, I tried calling my mom again. On this, my twelfth try in a week, I succeeded. "Mama- er, Mom, how are you?" is what I said after dropping & then picking up the phone. We spoke an hour and a half, but she didn't seem the least interested in the new music. "I'm looking forward to seeing you, Son, but I can't commit to anytime until after Friday night." After I asked her why we couldn't until then, she got just a little testy. "Well, I can't get into it now, Rossy, but it's not a good idea right now, Son." Strange, right? And what could I do or say about it? Absolutely nothing, so I did what I always do when I know I can't speak my mind – I bit down on my tongue. As much as things had seemed to change, they'd remained the same – at least as far as my matriarch goes. But, that's how she'd always been, and I have always loved her for being herself, even when it didn't work out as well for me.

Soon after our conversation ended, the phone rang. It was Sandra & Darla – each on a different extension. "We have good news and bad news, Mr. McInerney," Sandra began. "The good news we can report is that you will meet your wife and children very soon. And, the bad news is it won't be until this weekend sometime." The rest of our exchange consisted of them apologizing to me and then the two ladies engaging in some type of babble between them. I told them I understood all about red tape or whatever their indecipherable language was all about, but I needed desperately to speak to my wife. "We'll see what we can do," Sandra promised before hanging up.

I reasoned, "If I can go 2 1/2 years without seeing her, I can wait another day."

The rest of the week hustled by, but the highlight was Sammy the Swashbuckler calling late Wednesday night, to inform me the "special tribute concert in your honor" was only forty-eight hours hence, on Friday night. I quickly remembered the event had to be moved to a larger venue. "Who knows? Maybe it's at the 'Fabulous Forum,'" I hoped. After I really thought about it, though, I dismissed it as silly. "Who, after almost three years, wants to attend a tribute for little old me?" I wondered.

All Thursday was spent rehearsing for Friday because I assumed the person putting up all the money, Sammy the Chamois, would want me to play a song or two solo. But, in case an impromptu jam might break out, I brushed up on all three of The Talismans of Sound albums by listening to each one once. And, you know what's funny... well, 'funny-weird'? I hadn't forgotten a single song, but I had discovered - to my relief - that the music playing in my head of late was every bit as good as the old records; or, perhaps even better. As Pammy mumbles from time to time, "Only Father Time knows for sure." She's right. There's nothing I can do now to know what the future holds, but time will reveal the details. That was all I could tell myself at the time to keep from losing it altogether. The fact I couldn't find, reach, or speak to virtually everyone I knew in LA started depressing the hell out of me. And, since I'd sworn off booze and pot before my trip to Georgia, I decided to reintroduce myself to my old friend TM – transcendental meditation. Each morning & night for twenty minutes I meditated, which helped calm me and provide me faith things would work out somehow.

Chapter Sixty

Friday arrived, finally... and with it, many interesting surprises. First, some clothing designer who'd made Elvis Presley's suits visited me several days before, measured me, and returned Friday morning with not one, but two(!) outfits I could wear onstage. They weren't at all garish or flashy, but classy and borderline subtle in their design. One might technically call these ensembles leisure suits – one light green and the other dark blue – because of their jackets and matching pants, but that's where all similarity ends. These duds were the hippest clothes I'd ever worn, yet comfy and 'breathable,' meaning if I played under hot stage lights, I wouldn't leave a puddle of sweat behind when I left the stage.

Someone had taken it upon themselves to make me look good for the concert because the next person to stop by was a barber. "I'll just shape up your hair so you look like your old album covers," a bearded, long-haired guy named Tony suggested. I'm glad he was gentle with those clippers because it was the first real haircut I'd had in three years. In the hospital, my hair had barely grown, but someone (a day nurse or my night janitor friend) had trimmed my mop once.

Next, a green limousine arrived and transported Pammy Lee to some swanky salon to cut and style her hair before setting a course for Melrose Boulevard. When Pam returned, she did a runway show for me, showing off the outfits she'd been encouraged to pick out, but without being asked to pay for any of it. "I wonder who's paying for all of this fancy stuff," she said when she'd finished her fashion show.

"I have no idea, but I guess we'll find out sooner or later," I replied. After choosing which outfit we'd each be wearing that evening, Room Service brought a five-course lunch, complete with fancy china and a silver tea set. "Swanky" was all I said after two waiters brought our repast and dressed our dining table with tablecloths and flower centerpieces. I called the front desk to ask about the billing for this spread, but all they said was: "It's already taken care of."

After a couple manicurists from the salon visited, we were told the same. It was both weird and wonderful to be taken care of like this, but it especially warmed my heart to see the expressions on Pammy Lee's face whenever a new way of spoiling her was revealed. I'm pretty sure no one had ever lavished this type of service and care on her before. More than once I heard her exclaim, "I now know how those ladies on 'Queen for a Day' must feel after winning all their prizes and services. I feel as though I'm special & somehow deserving of it all." I then proceeded to tell Pammy Lee she, in fact, did deserve it all, which caused her to sob tears of joy.

When the front desk called, informing us the limousine reserved for our trip to the concert would be "on stand-by," my new friend & manager wept again. A knock sounded on the tall mahogany double doors, followed by a parade of tuxedoed waiters toting not only bouquet after bouquet of various & sundry flowers, but dozens of plants as well. Between sobs, Pammy said, "It's too bad we can't save all these wonderful plants. We must have enough here for one beautiful garden." I'll never forget the sight of all those flowers and plants everywhere, literally filling up all five rooms of our suite. The symphony of aroma generated by the hundred or more plants will undoubtedly remain in my olfactory memory so long as I possess my sense of smell.

After we'd showered, squirted ourselves with various potions & lotions, and donned our newly acquired finery, a chauffeur's assistant named Nancy escorted us to the private rear entrance of the hotel and introduced us to our driver, a man named Steven whom Pammy already knew and called "Mr. Dreamy Driver," but not to his face. Dreamy Steve greeted us and made sure we each had a glass of Poully Fuise to sip for our trip to the show. (I decided not to imbibe, but I enjoyed watching the golden bubbly affect Pammy Lee's mood and personality.) On the way, Stephen stopped at a world-famous eatery on Rodeo Drive for "an early dinner" in a private dining room usually reserved for visiting heads of state. The dinner was a blur, but I know every dish under the sun was served. There were carved meats, a medley of fish dishes, Beluga caviar, various salads and side dishes along with an entire table covered with the most delectable delights - parfaits, cakes, and cheese cake. Throughout the feast, Pammy exclaimed to me, the wait staff, and anyone she happened to see on the way to or from the ladies' room how much she loved being "Queen for a Day." It might've been the best time she'd had in her life, and it wasn't even seven o'clock yet.

After returning to the limo and settling into the luxurious black leather, Steven (aka Dreamy Driver) said: "Just sit back, you two. Worry about nothing. Anything you want or need I will personally take care of for you." So, we took his advice, sat back, and enjoyed each other's company without paying attention to any of LA speeding by. After half an hour, our cushy chariot slowed, so I looked out and saw we weren't at the venue we'd been told the concert had been upgraded to – The Long Beach Arena with 13,500 seats. Instead, we'd been somehow set adrift in a sea of autos, busses, humanity, and spirited excitement. Arriving at the largest concert venue on the West Coast, Dreamy Steve announced in a friendly tone: "Welcome to the Los Angeles Coliseum, folks." When Pammy asked her new crush how many seats the venue had, he answered: "A little north of one hundred & ten thousand for concert events."

⁂

So, I will not tell you all about our big concert experience - or at least the parts I remember. Ross can fill you in later with details I possibly missed. (Ha. I missed more than I saw.) After spending the afternoon dolling ourselves up, we were driven (by Mister Dreamy Driver, no less!) to some unnamed amazing restaurant where they ushered us into this special back room reserved for big wigs' candlelight dinners. I won't try to list all the fabulous foods we got to sample, but I did take advantage of the opportunity to have both filet mignon and prime rib. Why? Because I'd heard about both prime cuts of beef all my life, but I'd never had the opportunity to try them. I won't use up space describing the almost inexhaustible list of tastes we got to experience, but I'll summarize by saying all these foods had one little thing in common – they were all Delicious! This special 'level of deliciousness' is so intense & rare in my experience that when I invoke the word to describe the spread we feasted on that unforgettable night, I must type the word with a capital D and follow it with an exclamation point. That was how flippin' Delicious! it was. Seriously! I'm not lying at all. Todos de los comidas estan muy deliciosa! (Dolores might even approve of my Spanish.)

After leaving the private, romantic dining room outfitted like a French royal palace, we poured ourselves back into "Dreamy's Drive". (Yes, our rented limousine earned name status. I think if an Alfa Romeo can have a name, so can my crush's Cadillac.) So, Ross and I had quite a '*tete a tete,*' as the French call it. You know, it's 'an intimate type of talk between two people,' but remember, I was on my umpteenth glass of Pouilly Fuisse when we reached the concert, so I don't recall every word spoken between us, but I will describe it overall as "warm and fuzzy." And, even though that phrase captures perfectly the state of both my body & mind at that moment (warm and fuzzy), it also had to suffice as descriptions of both men – Ross Man and Dreamy Driver. Yes, they both make me feel warm and fuzzy all over - without even trying.

So, right when our conversation might've gotten too interesting for words, Ross let out a gasp. Before I could ask Dreamy what was wrong he announced we'd arrived at our destination, the

Los Angeles Coliseum – THE largest concert site anywhere west of the Mississippi River. And I didn't doubt him in the least because everywhere I looked were masses of people. Scads upon scads upon scads of people as far as my eyes could see – and every person must've been there to pay tribute to my new friend Ross Robert McInerney and celebrate the end of his absence from music for three entire years – a *veritable* eternity in the world of rock and roll.

Had I not already been floating on a cloud of French alcoholic bubbles, I'd have felt light-headed to the *Nth degree.* Luckily, Dreamy knew the ropes around this madhouse teeming with 120,000 or more humans in it, so he deposited us - without incident - to a side entrance marked "Concert Performers Only." After showing our ID cards to a Latin lady sporting a gold blazer & maroon skirt, she summoned someone on her walkie-talkie. And within the minute, three 'young exec' types (two women and a man) dressed in dark suits introduced themselves as Ann, Brian, and Cathy. "Oh, did you hear that, Ross Man? We're getting the ABC treatment," I couldn't help but say. The champagne must've kicked in because what I thought of as a classy & clever observational comment to spiff up our small talk surely sounded much closer to: "Oh, we're having the ABC's leading us around, Rossy. Ain't that cute, Babe?"

In deference to either Ross's status as rock god honoree or more likely my advanced state of inebriation, Brian got a golf cart to shuttle us over to the backstage area. With Ann and Cathy sitting in the very rear, Ross and I settled into the back seat for what proved to be a rough ride. Instead of riding, we bumped, jumped, slid, and even skidded twice over all kinds of surfaces – metal plates on the floor and ground, chubby cables running in every direction for sound and TV, and bottles or cans already littering the walkways. Soon, our cart made it down to the brilliant green turf that is the venue's historic football field and track, where the 1932 Los Angeles Olympics were held more than five decades before, way prior to either of our births. The sun had set moments before, so the smog-infused sky put on quite a display of color, shapes, and contours. It was, in a word, *resplendent*. In fact, resplendent is the word I reportedly repeated a dozen times or more as we sashayed, bumped, and sped to our destination – all lickety-split.

We soon lurched to a complete stop. I'd managed somehow to stay inside the cart, but it helped I could cling to Ross Man, of which I took complete advantage. Then, in every way, the scene changed. Word got out that the one and only Ross McInerney - "America's preeminent singer-songwriter" (according to the LA Times) - was in the house.

Everyone and their all their brothers & sisters seemed to descend on our little golf cart from all directions. At first, it was the stage crew members who'd recognized Ross Man, but then awareness of his presence spread throughout the huge oval that is the Coliseum. Then, from every corner of the Roman structure came other non-paying attendees of all sorts: ushers, food & drink vendors, sound & video technicians, and an army of media reps. I can't tell you much more of what happened during that portion of the evening's events because I passed out. Yep, I passed out directly in front of the stage. Well, that's not precisely what happened, so I'll back up & retell. What I should say is that immediately before I passed out, I did something I'd never done before – I vomited. Not everywhere, mind you, but - yes - everywhere in the golf cart in which I sat. So, that's the bad news. The only good news resulting from this barf-a-thon is that Ross didn't get hit with any of it. Aside from it possibly landing on him, I remember not caring where else my vomit flew during this flurry of yuckiness that had stricken me. After all, when one is losing one's insides, any thoughts not related to the vomiting-at-hand can't possibly break through to one's conscious mind; and I was no exception to that little-known or rarely explained law of physics. However, on this occasion all that mattered was that not one single drop of my yuckiness had landed anywhere near the raddest man alive – no, check that – raddest *person* alive at any time in history, after Jesus - the one and only Ross R. McInerney. (Just so you know I'm not being sacrilegious, let me *vehemently* state that Jesus the Christ was - or is - better than Ross Man Mac or any other mortal - by a large, perhaps infinite amount.) But, that takes nothing away from the greatness of this wonderful man's character.

So, what was the 'lion's share' of the bad news? Well, once I passed out, I stayed out; not for the whole night, but long enough to not tell you what transpired from 7:15 pm Pacific Daylight Savings Time until much later, on that stage. Since I can't tell you about that portion of the evening, I'll pass the baton & word processor to the person who knows the most about what went down that night - as it should properly be. Because, after all, this is *Ross Man's* story, y'all.

Chapter Sixty – One

We don't have much of this story left to tell, but since Pammy Lee missed out on some of the night's proceedings, it falls to me to step into the box and give you a pitch-by-pitch account the best I can. But, you must know upfront I take only three things in life seriously: music, my loved ones, and the Grand Old Game of Baseball. The American Pastime is not an area of metaphorical expression I dare to lightly enter unless I have faith I can deliver a recap of what transpired that night on not only the former, present, and future home of the city's Rams and Chargers - but more important in keeping with my motif - the local National League MLB franchise, the storied Dodgers, who played all their home games in this venue its first three seasons after deserting Brooklyn for the sun, majestic palm trees, and pile of money that help define the City of Angels.

Okay, maybe I'm getting just a touch off course, so I'll cut right to the chase and tell what happened after Pammy Lee lost consciousness. Before I could meet & greet the legion of well-wishers working the concert who'd approached, I accompanied the Coliseum's medics while they transported my friend on a device that converted from a stretcher to a gurney they rolled to the nearby first-aid station without mishap. Fortunately for us, stadium management had set the dispensary up at the left (stage right) rear corner of the stage platform – behind a series of black curtains. I stayed with Pam till an RN named Dotty Wise vowed to monitor Pammy herself. Dotty joked she would keep at least one eye and ear on my friend throughout the evening, implying she'd be training the other ear and eye on the sounds and sights of what was about to be performed on the opposite corner of the Coliseum's vast stage.

At a quarter to eight a group of several musicians whose faces I recognized visited us in the first-aid tent. After making sure Pammy Lee's condition was improving, they invited me to the venue's Green Room where they briefed me on the night's proceedings. Well, as much as they could without "giving away any surprises," to use their words.

'The leader of the pack' of musicians was my dear friend & father-in-law Pops, Julie's dad, who'd been given the multitudinous task to manage the night's performance. "Or performances, I should say," the bearded man with the twinkling eyes corrected. "I won't let you in on the nitty-gritty intel because I want you surprised by each artist, but if you look at this [set list], you'll probably figure out who's slated to play when." He then handed me a list of seventy songs or more, all of which would presumably be performed by someone on the Coliseum stage that night. The first striking element of the litany was that over fifty of the seventy-some tunes were mine, meaning I'd written them alone or with a partner. And the second was that Pops and a few guys I remembered him playing with over the years were the only musicians around, besides me. "Oh, yeah," Pops said with his signature chuckle. "You don't get to know the 'who' of this event. You're lucky we're telling you the 'what' and

some of the 'when.' The fans out there tonight are in the same boat too, R.M. So, you'll have plenty of company in that respect. Only I and a handful of others know who's playing tonight. And every ticket-buyer paid a pretty penny to be here and witness this concert, which – by the way – the critic at the Times is calling 'historic', okay? Can you believe that? And we're not just talking about an actual single penny for admission tonight. Oh, no. By my calculation, most people out there paid 2,500 pennies while the rest...... paid a whole lot more than that; some as much as 5,000 cents or fifty greenbacks." All this talk of money made my head spin even faster - if you can believe that.

Pops handed me a sheet of yellow legal paper folded roughly in half. "These are the times you'll be needed onstage, Rosso. Now, I don't want to come off rude, but to organize this thing for greatest possible impact, I have to ask you to sit over yonder until you hear your name each time." I was then escorted stage left by Ann and Cathy to a grouping of folding chairs circling a luxury reclining chair just four feet from the stage's edge. I instinctively looked for faces I'd know and then wondered what happened to the huge knot of people who'd crowded me moments before. They'd all disappeared, perhaps to keep the potential amount of surprise as mind-blowing as possible. Want to know something strange? Even though I sat in Barcalounger comfort between two equally beautiful women ('Execs A & C') on a stage facing most of the 120,000 ticket-buying well-wishers, I felt nervous and self-conscious. Most of all, though, I felt lonely... lonely as hell. Even though I'd soon be joined by the largest crowd in Coliseum history and dozens of big-time musical artists would be soon performing for no fees, (so the gate receipts could begin to pay off my legal costs), I yearned to be surrounded by the people I love most – my family... such as it is. And so, at the most inopportune moment possible, I had what one of the Coliseum's doctors diagnosed a "major panic attack."

So, back to the tent I went – this time to stabilize my breathing, mainly by blowing into a small brown bag. When I was done, A & C escorted me back to the Barcalounger. I settled in not a moment too soon as Pops stepped to the center microphone and introduced the first act. "Many of us have never heard this band before, but don't let that random fact influence you at all. Why? Because this next group played a prominent role in our guest of honor's development as a musician of not just rock, but blues, jazz, and R & B as well. Ladies and gents, please give it up for a soulful outfit from Ross's hometown of San Bernardino – The Groove Thang."

Out walked the whole Thang – Cozmo White on drums, Terrence Wolf at the piano, Bruno Carson on tenor sax, Hefty Lewis playing alto, Dorothea Durst on flute, and our 'fearless leader' Bunny Braxton singing and playing his 'harp,' a beat-up Hohner harmonica. "Hey, people," Bunny began, "you all know Ross McInerney's music with both Propinquity and The Talismans of Sound, but..." (He waited for the huge burst of applause and whistles to die down before continuing.) "But, we - The Groove Thang – have known both him and his music from the very start, so we consider the young man sitting over yonder in that comfy chair not just a former bandmate, but a brother forever." Turning to me, Bunny said: "Here's the first blues song you and I ever played together, Ross Man." Turning back to the captive audience, he explained, "This here's the oldest, most famous blues tune you'll hear tonight. It's called 'It Hurts Me, Too.'" Setting down his harp on the mic stand's base, he received a Gibson guitar and bottleneck slide from a roadie I thought I recognized. "But, one thing. Or should I say 'thang'? We need a special kind of bass on this next number, so I'll ask you - Rossy Mac - to help us out."

Before I knew how to respond, a roar erupted... everywhere. At first, I thought it was a spontaneous response to a fight or some other incident in the stands, but soon realized that the crowd's yelling, screaming, and foot-stomping were actually intended for me - an 'off-the-wall kid' whose only talents were plunking strings and writing about life in smoggy San Bernardino without any real support or encouragement from my mother or dad (a professional musical artist) who'd probably never heard me play a single note of music. And here I was, the product of that upbringing being summoned center stage to perform my second-favorite blues song , It Hurts Me Too", with a legendary band from my boyhood. I mean, wow. Talk about having a crazy childhood dream come true.

After the roar dissipated to chatter, Bunny gave a look so expressive and specific that only my Morse Code messages were more precise. "Hey, man! It's great to see you, brother. I never thought we'd play together again, but – Dude – we are jammin' and slammin'. Are you up for an encore?" I won't try to reproduce all the thoughts careening around my inner universe, but I decided to go with the flow, regardless of the invisible force of a heavy weight pressing on the top of my head. Call it what you will – a spiritual awakening, panic attack, or maybe a nervous collapse of some kind, but I'm betting the farm that the alarming sensation was directly a result of lying unconscious in a hospital bed for two and a half years. Now that I was awake in every sense, I felt like a dinghy tossed from a ship onto an ocean, set adrift, and bobbing like crazy.

However, a rhythmic, rhyming phrase repeated in my head, "Just go... go with the flow" – in a singing rather than speaking voice. I adopted it as my new slogan, which I later compared with the record of my TM mantra; and "go with the flow" stood the competition quite well.

Meanwhile, Bunny Braxton – so excited up there on that massive stage in front of a city of spectators – unwittingly changed the format for his set established by the producers by flipping it. Instead of calling me up for the finale of The Thang's set, BB drafted me for the first two numbers, so I naturally went along for the ride, to use a similar cliché. After we finished the blues standard "Sinner's Prayer," I shook the band's hands, waved to the raucous crowd, and headed back to the lounger, now nowhere in sight. In its place sat one of those construction 'cherry-pickers.' Before either of us could lodge a protest or desist, Pammy and I had been placed by some roadies on a love seat, which rose to a height I gauged to be thirty-five feet above the stage before leveling out and hovering there for the rest of The Thang's set.

So, Pammy Lee and I sat in this comfy couch together, elevated above a sea of faces moving as an ocean or other swirling, undulating body of water would. After realizing we were as safe as anyone else in that stadium, I relaxed. My entire body loosened up and began to enjoy itself; and, from the look on Pam's face, she also seemed to enjoy the heck out of floating up there like a cloud with the balmy breezes of a southern California summer evening wafting past us. Her smile reminded me of a little girl at a county fair who experiences sitting at the top of a Ferris wheel for the first time. She looked as free as... "a proverbial bird," to quote her.

While looking around the six-foot square of carpeted 'floor' and becoming oriented to our new surroundings, I saw an ice chest by my feet. Opening it, I saw bottles of Heineken beer - two of which we opened & began sipping - and plenty of food, which we dug into later.

After forty minutes, the music ceased, and we heard Bunny over the PA, "Ross Man, we're splittin' for a bit, but this band is so looking forward to jammin' with you later. How does that sound, Rossy?" Nodding my head, I held both thumbs aloft and beamed a big smile. The crowd again roared its approval. Before the next act came out for its set, I maintained my stage smile and tried to enjoy the moment, even though my heart and mind were somewhere else.

⁂

Ross and I sat way the heck up there, above that huge crowd for a long time; in fact, we floated thirty-five, forty feet in the air throughout the next act's set. I couldn't tell you their name - or any of the other bands' names either - but if you see a list of top-selling rock and R & B artists of the Seventies and Eighties, nine out of ten played that evening. Why did I not know their music? Simple: I was not only familiar with just Ross's music back then, but - frankly - I only concerned myself with his music, which represented his livelihood, financial future, and – most importantly – his well-being. Besides, in comparison with Ross's creations, everyone else's music was the supermarket variety as far as I was concerned. No one else's music connects with me like his, not even many of the songs on his Sound-About tapes. So, I can't honestly tell you who performed their music that night, but to show you the pedigree of the performers on that bill, the better question to pose would be – who *didn't* play on the Coliseum stage that night?

So, friends, I hope I didn't disappoint by not listing all the acts who performed, but - to me - that's not the most *pertinent* part. What seemed to matter to Ross was the outpouring of support from his fellow musicians, most of whom barely knew him. The fans, of course, thrilled him with their appreciation of him & the music he'd created. Every time one of his songs played, the place burst into applause, whistling, and – of course – foot stomping. (The Coliseum must be the perfect place to do the latter because once the stomping started, it sounded like a train taking a detour through the middle of the stadium. The rhythm achieved by 200,000 or more feet striking old wooden planks amplified by metal could easily substitute for a powerful coal-fed engine pulling a hundred cars at top speed.) I cannot exaggerate the noise level in that stadium, so you must believe me when I say it was so loud in that place Ma would've called it a madhouse.

When the band following The Groove Thang concluded their set, Pops announced: "The best part of this great evening is about to happen. We're calling it 'This is Your Life, Ross McInerney.' So, for us to complete all the preparations for this next segment, we're taking a longer-than-usual intermission. In the meantime, all you folks out there in the stands and down on the field: Here's your chance to stretch your legs, keep partying with your neighbors, etc., etc., etc." Pops, craning his sixty-year-old neck, directed his next comments up to the two of us perched in literal 'nose-bleed seats': "Can I ask a big favor of you, Ross? Can you and your friend stay up there and manage to relax out there in space while we finish setting up?" Ross laughed (probably at "out there in space") before raising both thumbs and beaming his brightest handsome smile. Instead of roaring its approval, the crowd of biblical proportions broke into an impromptu chant of "Ross Man, Ross Man, Ross Man" that lasted a minute or more. (I have no idea how long since I wasn't consulting my watch every whip stitch). So, my friend and I looked in each other's eyes, smiled, shrugged, and then gazed outward, at the nighttime sky - *resplendent* with skeins of white and yellow pea-sized pearls whose sparkles were – unfortunately – as scarce as hen's teeth and blurry-fuzzy, thanks to all the manmade lights burning straight ahead of us. And much worthier of the adjective 'beautiful' were the hundreds, perhaps thousands of natural lights above, in the heavens. Truth be told, we should've been able to see millions of God's night lights if human beings hadn't strung their personal or commercial lights everywhere they possibly could. But, lucky us, since we had no moon that night, there was plenty of stargazing; and we took full advantage. I felt so content and peaceful at that moment. (Sigh.)

"Why the sigh, Pammy Lee?" you might ask. You may even follow up with this second query: "Are you sighing because even though you have the greatest crush in history on this man and are surrounded by perfect romantic conditions you are fully aware Ross McInerney – *The* Ross McInerney! - is a MARRIED MAN with two children?" And then your third & final question might be – "Pammy Lee, did you sigh because you are truly concerned about the man beside you and worry what may happen if he doesn't reunite with his beautiful wife and family?" In case you didn't think the third possibility was possible, permit me to convince you. You see, Ross is as important to me as oxygen is to every living creature on Earth. So, it should logically follow that if the number-one priority in my life is the happiness and well-being of Ross, all other factors - including my own happiness - must either diminish or wait till my top priority is taken care of *completely*. Your next question might be, "Who knows how long it may take to *completely* take care of Ross properly?" And, once again, my answer is that only Father Time knows; and I don't believe the old guy will clue me in before anyone else, so I need to remain steadfast in standing for what I believe in most. And right or wrong, what I believe in more than anything is this man whose story I'm helping tell. Lastly, when this narrative ends, I hope there'll be many others who believe in Ross just like I do.

Chapter Sixty – Two

The male anchorman for L.A. CBS affiliate KNXT's news show read the following on the air the morning after the tribute: "Last night's rock concert and tribute extravaganza held for Ross McInerney at the historic Los Angeles Coliseum, home of the historic 1932 World Olympics, was quite historic itself in several ways. The lineup of musical performers was certainly historic, but also impressive, eclipsing even the lineup at the world's most famous music festival in the summer of '69 called Woodstock. To dispel any doubts veteran music lovers may have about the assertion that the concert billed "The Ross Man Rave" is superior in musical muscle to the Woodstock Music and Art Fair (Three Days of Peace & Music), it behooves me to mention that of the twenty-five different acts performing on the Coliseum stage last night, nine of them headlined the renowned New Bethel, New York festival almost two decades ago. Moreover, the paid attendance at the 100,000-seat sports and concert venue was an unprecedented 119, 475, also historic – eclipsing the previous record for attendance at a live event in a sports stadium anywhere in America. And thirdly, the total take of gate receipts and donations at yesterday's tribute to musical icon Ross McInerney attained a decidedly historic level of $6.1 million dollars. Yes folks, local boy made good and all-around positive role model for kids is also one of America's most acclaimed contemporary musical artists. Who knows what the future holds for the musical genius known as *Ross Man Mac*? However, this reporter - who's had the pleasure of observing the talented star close-up & even behind the scenes on several occasions over the years - will tell you first-hand that this man's career could well be shaping the future of modern music in the United States of America as we know it. McInerney's brilliant lyric-writing coupled with his 'McCartneyesque' flair for heartbreaking melodies and inspiring harmonies has been the magical recipe for not just excellent music, but a great American musical legacy. The global community of music-lovers eagerly awaits Mr. Mac's next musical creation."

Neither Ross nor his friend and manager Pammy Lee properly understood the depth and breadth of McInerney's influence on contemporary music genres of all stripes - in America and virtually everywhere else. To properly illustrate McInerney's influence on the music industry, coinciding with his last recording session three years ago at Capitol Records, commercial rock music has stagnated and - according to many experts - has begun the irreversible process known to botanists as *root rot*. Less optimistic observers may employ the self-destruction-associated verb 'imploded,' so it was no surprise to anyone but these two innocents (Ross & Pam) that such a mass acceptance and outpouring of love toward the event dubbed by Capitol Records as 'Ross Mac's Comeback' had been so successful. However, his fan club - declared a month ago as "anemic and in need of a transfusion" - now enjoyed membership somewhere in the six-figure range that is projected to bust through the one-millionth fan barrier in six months at the most.

What strikes many longtime music-scene observers as particularly ironic is that - as stratospheric as Ross Man's popularity climb had been since his return from Georgia and as excellent of a prospect of achieving "superstar status" as he's proven to be - Ross stood at the threshold of earning millions, and - more possibly - tens of millions, during this era of a persistent and growing demand for new, relevant music for decades to come. Of course, none of these or other prospects for great success were the man's focus. Instead, he yearned for an existence centering on his family, preferably in an atmosphere conducive to personal growth not for just his growing children, but their over-deserving parents as well.

⁂

So, after the scary, but efficient cherry-picking contraption deposited us safely on terra firma, we realized the event in full swing below our feet to be more than just the largest musical extravaganza in California since mega festivals had reached their peak popularity back in the late Seventies. A set design featuring a royal palace motif that had been conceived for the Fabulous Forum stage had been installed and now awaited Ross to sit on a throne-like platform built to accommodate a panel of guests on the adjacent dais consisting of luxury living room chairs probably borrowed from Sam the Chamois' mansion in San Marino that he rarely visited, much less lived in. Pops, acting as the event's emcee, stepped to the center microphone and announced: "And now comes the high point of the evening for not only you, Rossy Mac, but all your wonderful fans out there who want to share in the celebration of your return to

Present, and Future" in his opening comments about his beloved former son-in-law & bandmate and to kick off the evening's festivities in real Hollywood rock and roll fashion.

The highest point this night studded with highlights had to be when Ross reunited with Salome, whom he described as 'the love of my life' and embraced her until a couple of ushers seated them side by side on the theatrical thrones. Both two-year-olds scaled one of their papa's legs before reaching his lap and continuing upward to mount his shoulders. Sally Amanda (or "Salamanda" as her dad called her) clambered up to Ross's shoulder before her brother could, but only because of her prodigious head start and the well-known fact that very few two-year-olds think about climbing, much less succeed in climbing their daddy's shoulders. In fact, Ross later said about Sally Amanda: "If I had a second pair of shoulders above my first set and my head rested on top of pair number two, Salamanda would've made it all the way to the pinnacle of the mountain that would've been my body. I mean, what other kid ever did something like that?" Of course, the factual answer to that question is Ross Junior (or "R.J. Squirrel," as Ross began calling him) - partly because of his squirrelly behavior, but also due to his interest in climbing anything he can touch with any of his four limbs. Between his Alpha sister and himself, the McInerney Twins show great potential for a career as either gymnasts or - more likely - acrobats with either the time-honored, classic Ringling Brothers Barnum & Bailey Circus or the new acrobatic sensation troupe known as Cirque d' Soleil. The latter's exploits and antics at a Las Vegas Strip showroom both twins will witness in two and a half years, at age five, when they prove mature enough to appreciate the talent and majesty of the professional flying performers without demanding they be allowed to join the act in mid-show. Physically, they needed to reach age six before beginning their high-wire acrobatic training, but mentally they'd been ready since birth. "Both children," according to Ross, "were ready to fly from their mother's womb."

⁂

So, now you know what happened until the "This is Your Life, Ross McInerney" segment of the concert began. And, since I can't describe with words the effect this event had on me during the first half of the evening, I won't. But, the second half? Well, that's a 'horse of a whole different color.' Let me approach it this way: If I could capture every detail that transpired after the break, both your head and mine would be blown… to smithereens. (Not sure what they are exactly, but I know with certainty that Pammy Lee would've placed her favorite adjective 'proverbial' before 'smithereens' if she was telling this part of the story.)

Back to the concert so I can continue describing the most momentous night of my thirty-three years. When I first heard the velvety voice of my sweetheart Salome over the Coliseum PA system, my heart came to a stop and not just a 'California Stop' either. (I mean a complete halt in the function of the organ in my body most necessary for my life to continue – my heart. But when our little Sallymander bellowed out what she said, my heart not only started up, it began racing. And when Little Ross spoke? Man - oh - man.

My heart pounded like it only does when I'm pushing my body to the limit or becoming totally stoked about someone or something. But when both our little darlings crawled out from under the curtain & raced toward me with eyes full of yearning and adoration, my heart came closest to exploding in my 3+ decades on this planet. Those two tykes instantly became as important to me as my long-lost love & wife Salome.

After Salome sat, we held hands, and the twins played in my lap as if sitting in a neighborhood playground for their hundredth straight day together in the park, it hit me fully - I have a family. And my family, remarkably, is together for the very first time. And these two equally amazing human beings are playing together for the first time, too. In fact, Salome later told me about the weird arrangement she had with my former girlfriend and Sal's former best friend Delilah that kept the twins apart until the night before the show. So, big picture, what also struck me between the eyes was the realization that all four of us had been living in misery for three years, but now that we were finally together we made a beautiful image of a family; and that moment was another huge 'first.' It was the first time I had ever felt complete. To be exact, I felt complete and yet, not quite whole. I know it sounds confusing. After all, something or someone cannot possibly be both complete and not quite whole at the same time. Or, can they? Only one person holds the key to unlock that mystery. Here's your only hint: He's one of Pammy Lee Wertzhog's acquaintances. Has she told you about Father Time? According to Pammy, only he knows everything yet to happen in our future lives together or apart. I don't know if I'd want this superpower, but I would like to know what the future holds for us all – Mom, Salome, the twins, Stu and Al, and one more person. You know her – a belle from the South named Ms. Pammy Lee Wertzhog.

⁂

I'm sorry to switch voices on you so quickly, but Ross asked me to pick up the thread and weave the rest of this tapestry / story. And, as I said at the very beginning of this 'project,' if Ross asks me to do anything, I'm going to do it, even when I don't know how. (Luckily, I've caught on to this storytelling thing, so you shouldn't get too lost with me in the lead.)

The rest of the show was something else – not only mind-blowing because of the array of amazing stars of rock, country, and R&B performing that evening, but because a collection of additional "Honored Guests of the Guest of All Honors" appeared and thus took Ross by surprise. But, the next person to speak from an offstage mic was someone whose voice Ross had known longer even than Salome's. "Hi, Ross. I am so glad you are safe and sound. I prayed every day and night for the past eight hundred and ninety-six days that you would come back to me. After all, you ARE my only child; and – even today – I think of you as the little boy running around our apartment blowing on your make-believe trumpet – your hand – and singing like Louie Armstrong to the old spiritual 'When the Saints Go Marching In.'"

Pops asked Ross, "Want to take a wild guess who's lurking behind our big, black curtain?"

Smiling and laughing at first, Ross began to cry when Mary

his mother - now a bit older and slowed by sciatica and arthritis - walked onstage with the aid of her husband Rich. The three embraced while the soulful march blasting over the P.A. - "When the Saints (Go Marching In)" - inspired the crowd to stand and dance. The staff running the taped music had decided to run a loop, so it would play until it was no longer needed. After the third go-round, the conga lines began forming; and by the seventh round, there were too many lines snaking in every direction to count, so let's just say the stadium appeared from an aerial view to be a large white seashell with a hundred and twenty thousand ants inside crawling up, down, and around the countless aisles and rows of the venerable stadium.

Throughout this interlude of political convention-like dancing and prancing, Ross reunited with his mom, introduced her to her grandchildren, and then spent time with her, Salome, Rich, and the twins. What strikes me as ironic is that even though the biggest-selling musical artists in the business had been invited to play, the event's most jubilant moment happened while a loop of ancient reel-to-reel tape of Louis Armstrong and his All-Star Band played over the PA system. And though my dear friend had endeared himself to the hip world that is *Hollyweird*, the song stirring Ross the most was the first tune he remembered dancing to thirty years before. It dawned on him that life had come full circle – on so many, different levels.

Chapter Sixty – Three

The Ross Man Rave, as it became known, continued in legendary style with a lengthy list of both expected & surprise guests gracing the stage with not just their music but their love and devotion for a man whose music had clearly touched their lives. And, especially encouraging to Ross was that both his life and music had, for all practical purposes, just begun. He had arrived at the huge venue that night humbled and prepared to be forgotten or reviled. Instead, more people than he'd ever seen gathered together in one place at one time entertained him with their own love, adoration, and – most important of all – support. The latter had been lacking greatly in Ross's life until recently (when Pammy Lee entered it), but tonight – with his family, band, and friends standing together on his behalf – could be a template for his support system of the future.

And how had Pammy Lee's life progressed? Anyone following this story knows this young, vibrant woman had successfully 'flown the coop,' leaving her only home for somewhere completely foreign and different. No longer would she be ridiculed, shunned, or ignored. Instead, this attractive, intelligent woman found herself in Paradise. Not because Paradise was L.A. in the Eighties or that she'd stumbled onto a geographic area that suited her perfectly. No, she had the same 'epiphany' that Ross Man had also had; she, too, had found support and a sense of real belonging in the same place. Of course, the person they had to thank for support was each other.

It's a no-brainer to see how Pammy Lee had plucked Ross from his two-year-plus coma, but she'd also - equally importantly - freed him from a medical facility where he'd had no advocate or supporter besides the night janitor who'd stumbled across a way to communicate with him in his greatest time of need. Without her intervention, Ross languishing in that bed for the rest of his days would've been a fait accompli. Instead, as of tonight, he'd not only gained everything back – his mother, his wife and love of his life Salome, his two-year-old darlings Sally Amanda and Ross Junior, his livelihood in music, and a new lease on life – but a new person in his life who exemplifies the word 'friend' in all the best ways possible.

After the 'This is Your Life' segment had brought out the major players in Ross's life onto the stage, there were a couple influences still needing acknowledging. Pops, playing the bon vivant emcee with relish and excitement, lit up like a slot machine when asked to introduce the next person. "Ladies and gentlemen, this has been a phenomenal night. We have all become reacquainted with Ross Man, listened to groups from his childhood all the way up to the present, and before we have The Talismans of Sound come back for a short, final set, I'd like to introduce our last mystery guest. I'll let him introduce himself."

During an interlude of two minutes without anyone speaking into the offstage microphone, all that could be heard were the sounds of one person – clearing his/her throat, coughing (sometimes nervously, other times due to a chronic smoker's cough), breathing hard, and then a final medley of all three sounds. And, the voice of the offstage mystery guest began in a velvety, but rough tone that suggested its owner had decided to finally face Ross. "Good evening, Sir. Good evening to all your friends and fans." (A prodigious cheer sounded, lasting a minute before he could continue.) "I guess tonight is a night of firsts. I won't go into all of them because you've been here to witness them all, but I will say this – I should win an award tonight for knowing Ross McInerney the longest; well, the longest of any person except his mother. Your mom & I both attended your entry into this life, Rossy. Of course, she did all the heavy lifting, all the hard work, and most of the worrying the past thirty years. And although I didn't intend to leave you or your dear mother & my wonderful wife, the fact of the matter is I did. I left and stayed away… thirty long years. And though I've shown up tonight to pay tribute, this may be too much to bear…" (Another interlude of noises ensued, including sobbing, before he continued.) "Even though this must be too much for you to absorb, I want you to know I am here for two reasons: One, to show my love and admiration for you and your music and, two, to reunite with you, my one and only son - Ross Robert Padraigh McInerney."

The two special-guest chaperones, Annie and Cathy, escorted a man who looked not only to have lived sixty years, but sixty very rough years as well. He walked so gingerly it seemed the bottoms of his feet had been burned. (He suffered from an advanced case of diabetes – due to his lifestyle on the road three hundred days a year for three decades.) When the trio made it halfway to the dais, Pops continued: "Of course, our next special guest is Robert McInerney, Ross Man's father and famous jazz musician of the past forty years." This time, the audience needed a moment before deciding what to do. After all, most knew about Ross's dad splitting early and what transpired after he did; not because of a biography of Ross's or an in-depth article in Rolling Stone or any other popular publication. In fact, most of the fans knew more about Ross McInerney's life than his father. Why? Because Ross had chronicled every important event & person in his life in his songs. Stunningly apparent was the irony that everyone present seemed to know all the songs related to his parents & his upbringing in less-than-idyllic San Bernardino, California, whereas his own father knew nothing about his son's life for thirty years since leaving his three-year-old boy, wife, and the apartment he'd never paid rent on.

It could take a hundred pages to describe all the thoughts and feelings both men had as they looked in the other's direction and prepared to meet for the first time since 1957 but suffice to say both experienced the full gamut of emotions during that moment. And, it's a wonder they'd made it into each other's arms before sharing an embrace to end all embraces.

After their hug, Ross whispered a phrase into his father's ear before the elder responded with his short comment. Reports vary, according to those on stage at the time, but it's generally accepted Ross said, "I forgive you, Dad," right before Robert replied, "Thank you, Son. I am so sorry." The moment was captured for posterity by the only photog allowed onstage that night – Pammy Lee Wertzhog.

What transpired immediately after that has been greatly disputed, but consensus among the assembled fans, family, and friends is that Robert proposed marriage to Mary. And, even though she was already wed to Rich, she didn't say "no" to her former husband. What she did say was the phrase she'd used on Ross hundreds of times during his childhood, "We'll just have to wait and see."

Chapter Sixty – Four

Hi, it's Pammy again. Before we get into the post-climax *denouement* of Ross's story, I must revisit Ross's tribute concert one last time, but not for my own benefit. Perhaps you want to hear what my 'high point' of the evening was. I mean, how many high points is anyone allowed in a span of only five or six hours, anyway? Believe me, there were scads of highlights – for the audience, the performers, Ross (of course), his family and friends, and his fans. For me there was one moment of such completeness that I hoped someone or something in power would've frozen everything happening in the Coliseum and preserved it all for posterity. That moment was while Ross and band played their final song of the night. Because no other 'hands on deck' were trusted enough to watch the twins, I took them with me to the cherry-picker, where the operator simply nodded & smiled when I asked if we could go up in it. Perhaps he had no sense or couldn't care less about the welfare of a pair of two-year-olds and their back-up babysitter, but he let us board without a word. In fact, during this whole time he had a gleam in his eyes so sparkly I didn't think him human, but that's absurd, right? And later - when I mentioned the speechless, smiling stage hand - Ross said he knew him from his trip. He'd been the guy who sat in back while he, Ross, drove and chatted with the mysterious woman hitch-hiker named Vesta, who disappeared after Alfie busted through that cross-hatched fence and before Ross's 'lost years' began. I can't comment because

Ross likely sustained a serious concussion and may still suffer the effects of that trauma to his head.

So, back to the show. After the twins sat in my lap and I wrapped my arms around them, the man smiled again and asked, "All set?" When I nodded hesitantly, he said, "You're in the best hands, ma'am. In fact, you are all in the best hands now." I don't think I'll ever know what he meant exactly, but it comforted me more than any spoken word before that. Just looking in those eyes and hearing his voice was… transforming. Who knows? He might even be---

Nah… unless, of course, Ross says he is. If Mac claims the guy was an angel, who knows? He might very well be. And, just for the record, I never believed in angels – from childhood all the way up to that night; not until Ross Mac said: "Angels exist." And, as I said at the beginning of his story, I only believe things I know are right and things Ross tells me, which seem to be one and the same. (At least, so far.)

Afterword

Since Ross Man Mac asked me to finish this project, I'll do my best to dot all my I's and cross all my T's. First off, the two ladies posing as social workers were just that – poseurs. But, good poseurs. I haven't found anyone yet who knows anything about them, but I like to think they were another form of angelic being intervening on Ross's behalf. How could they not see fit to jump in, invisible wings and all, and lend Ross & his kids a hand or four? I can't think of any person living or dead, or any non-human who wouldn't want to help Ross, which impresses me most about him. Despite being a handsome, rich, talented man, Ross has a heart as big as the Great Outdoors. Which relates to his new band's name. That's right. Ross formed a new band – one with not only the four members from The Talismans, but his dad Robert as well. And, in addition to his father and Pops playing all those horns, Ross now has a second female singer who mostly sings back-up to Salome and the others but can sing lead when the need arises. No longer a self-proclaimed 'hater of music,' Mary McInerney has contributed unexpectedly to both the quality of the new band's sound and its overall morale, becoming their official tour mother and head cheerleader. And, after Rich left Mother Mary for a much younger woman and waitress, Ross's mother has begun to date Robert, on occasion. They're taking it slow & goin' with the flow, as I suggested.

Delilah, Ross's high school girlfriend and Salome's erstwhile friend and colleague, split the whole scene as soon as she heard Ross was alive and back. No one knows what kind of business she's in now, but she's way too old to be a narc and too untrustworthy to take care of children. Plus, kidnapping of a child and child endangerment are both charges that can always be pressed against her, especially if she shows her face to any member of the McInerney family again. Her days of trying to ruin Ross and Sal's lives appear to be finally over.

Dr. Regina Speckman received a great deal of bad press about her dealings with Ross. Though she didn't have her medical license revoked because of 'gross neglect,' she performed five hundred hours of community service observing other brain specialists & taking on many patients on a pro-bono basis because of her complete attitude switch. She's now in a much better place professionally than when we worked under the same roof. She claims she "lives to work and works to live," meaning – I hope – she's rediscovered her passion for caring.

Bernie Breeze, after enduring a detailed investigation into his business practices, still owns his talent agency. However, due to losing his biggest moneymaker's business, he had to vacate his palatial office complex and open a much smaller one on the Miracle Mile. Bernie left the realm of popular music and now mainly represents his old clients - aging or already aged Vaudeville and Burlesque performers - with a few break dancers and rappers thrown in for good measure. His administrative assistant and onetime lover, Mr. Minaretto, left after Bernie tossed him out for cheating on him, so they've gone their separate ways.

Which brings us back to "The Guest of Many Honors," Ross McInerney aka 'Ross Man Mac.' After Ross and Sal took a month-long trip to Tahiti with the twins, his new band – Ross Mac & the Big-Hearted Ones – commenced rehearsing their first album, which they recorded at Capitol with their supportive, amiable producer Fred. And though not every cut was recorded on the first take, their debut album "Ross Mac & the Big-Hearted Ones" is a bona fide 'Number One with a Bullet,' shooting straight to the top of The Billboard 100 and staying there the past couple months. Pretty good for a 'debut double album,' but then that feat is not a first for Ross, whose musical vision continues to explore & expand. And when Ross isn't working on his music or hanging out with his family, he attends at least two of the twins' acrobatics training every week. Word has it they will begin working at age twelve for Cirque d' Soleil.

And lastly, there's little old me. (Grammatically, it should be 'little old I' because it's an elliptical phrase with the 'I' understood, but the fact of the matter is 'I' doesn't sound half as good or correct as 'me.') After living for six months at Valhalla with Ross, Sal, and the kiddos, I bought a little parcel on Pacific Coast Highway an hour away. Because I had no house I wanted to live in more than my lifelong friend and sister-in-arms Rose' Residence, Ross and Sal paid for little Rose' to be disassembled and transported to the

California Coast. And, yes, I finally had her painted – with all the colors of the rainbow.

I still manage Ross & the band but insist on staying 'up the coast' and only making my twice-weekly trips to Hollyweird to either work or catch up with the McInerneys, who've adopted me as Aunt Pammy or Sister Pammy, depending on which McInerney is addressing me.

Mr. Dreamy Driver visits me at least weekly, sometimes insisting on wearing his uniform and driving me and "Big Black" around Santa Barbara, Ventura, Carpinteria, and anywhere else our hearts desire. Although we're considered an 'item' by Ross and family, we too are taking it slow & going with the flow. But, who knows where it will all lead or end? Only one 'person' knows how that will all turn out; and his initials are F.T.

All I can say to properly wrap this project up is to state what may be obvious to some, but something I nonetheless must leave you with, and it is this: We never know everything about a person we either meet once or even see on a regular basis. But, maybe - just maybe – that person or *personage* might instead be … a true-blue friend or an angel of good. Or, both. And, I'm not only referring to Ross. Our lives and the world we inhabit is populated by not only real friends, but real angels. All we need to acknowledge & welcome the second group is faith - simple faith that good will usually prevail over evil.

When I think of angelic beings, I remember their main purpose is to play music & sing praises to their boss continuously.

So, like their human counterparts on Earth, we all need music to bless not only our own lives, but the lives of others, too. Or, as a musician once observed so succinctly & correctly: "You can change someone's life in three minutes with a song."

Ross McInerney changed – no, *metamorphosed* – my life with one Sound-About tape that was the soundtrack of his first thirty-three years. Of course, I would've never communicated with this amazing-beyond-words man if it hadn't been for my Girl Scout training in decoding & transcribing Samuel Morse's famous, but rarely-used-anymore code. And so, every time Ross and I meet, we exchange the same greeting with a few taps on the other's arm.

No, I won't reveal our four-word messages, which have nothing to do with romance but everything to do with friendship & admiration. I will, however, give you this hint - our messages both end in 'angel.' If you've been following this story, you should figure out the rest. Oh, and one last thing: Ross presented me with a tape he said I can play anytime on his Sound-About. It's labeled "Pammy Lee's Story" and features nothing but positive songs, all with angel themes, which is what I wished for when Ross insisted I add my own goal to our Trident Mission – to be somebody… not just in someone else's life, but in my own life as well. And, *that* is what I think is the perfect ending to Ross's story… and my own, too: a gift of music that describes who we are and what our mission here is supposed to be all about - love.

My Own Musical Journey

My first connections with music were all based on other peoples' musical tastes – my parents and their generation, disc jockeys, TV and movie soundtracks, commercials, etc. My father was a genuine "Music Man," in that he founded and directed a boy's drum & bugle corps through St. Mary's Catholic Church in Palmdale, California, introducing dozens of fresh-faced, eager young men to the marches of John Phillip Sousa. Dad would assign kids to various instruments – piccolos, flutes, trumpets, bugles, snare and bass drums – that he, of course, would teach them to play. In fact, Dad insisted everyone learn two instruments, so the band would always be ready for any disasters, such as occasional outbreaks of measles, mumps, or chicken pox. I only listened to these fresh-faced ones because I was even more "fresh-faced" at ages four to six. However, when we moved back to Palmdale and Dad resurrected the church's corps, he began teaching me percussion. So, when he left this world three months short of my ninth birthday, I didn't lose just my father, I lost my band instructor and drum teacher, too. After that, the corps ceased to exist. No one else, it seemed, had the passion, the blood, the verve Robert E. Rowlee had for performing music, especially parade-ready military marches. And *that* is the kind of passion I have for music of most kinds, but – alas – as a listener & student rather than a practitioner of one of the dozens of various & sundry instruments available.

My musical journey continued through the medium of my trusty beige General Electric transistor radio tuned to 500-watt Palmdale-based radio station KUTY (1470 on your AM dial), which introduced me to rock & roll, especially the British Invasion variety. My first concert was in sister-city Lancaster, at AV College, where I saw the legendary Animals in '68. When I first heard B. Mitchell Reed on KMET (94.7 on your FM dial) speaking like a normal person who clearly possessed a huge love for music, I secretly aspired to virtually any job inside the world of rock & roll – local disc jockey, station manager, rock critic for the Los Angeles Times and/or Rolling Stone Magazine, host of nationally syndicated radio and TV programs, and author of rock-related biographies & research materials for the more serious rockers.

While in college, I experienced a wide array of local radio as I picked up my desert roots and moved to northern California in '72, and Long Beach & Costa Mesa, where I resided from '73 through '77 studying for my degree in English literature and teaching credential. The very best DJs or radio personalities were in plentiful supply during this time, especially in the Los Angeles market. Talented music purveyors and all-around genius comic announcers all, my favorites were Jimmy Rabbitt, Stephen Clean, B. Mitchell Reed, Paraquat Kelly, and – of course – the king of all rock jocks, Shadoe Stevens, first on KMET, then KROQ. After deciding not to throw caution to the wind and become a rock concert stringer, I entered the field of California public education, where I spent the next thirty-six years of my days. But music NEVER left my side. I navigated the Seventies thanks to The Beatles, The Who, CSN&Y,

Neil Young & Crazy Horse, Stephen Stills, Bruce Springsteen; the Eighties because of Tom Petty & The Heartbreakers, The Bo Deans, U2, Los Lobos, Jackson Browne, The Blasters, Paul Simon; and on & on. Today, I've expanded from listening almost solely to old rock & blues to following artists such as Bruno Mars, My Morning Jacket, Imagine Dragons, Coldplay, Mavis Staples, Melody Gardot, REM, and Keb Mo.

I've shown you a couple, three glimpses of my musical background, but there's so much more to the journey than just our own favorite singles, bands, artists, albums, downloads, etc. No, as we traverse this trail of tears & giggles called Life we are fortunate to hear others' musical favorites and sometimes we bond over the experience. Other peoples' musical tastes have been so instrumental in my own love for music that I want to give a few examples of friends who "introduced" or "turned me on" to various musical sensations. Here are just a few musical acknowledgments: My sister Diann's astounding collection from multiple record club memberships, causing me to "discover" Bob Dylan, Janis Joplin & The Holding Company, The Ike & Tina Turner Revue, and Three Dog Night. Classmate Joseph Potter Davies III – for jazz guitar greats Django Reinhardt and Wes Montgomery. My brother Gene Kennedy's love for jazz and R & B, especially Herbie Mann, Stan Getz, Chick Corea, Ray Charles, Keith Jarrett, and The Modern Jazz Quartet. My little sister Baby T for her devotion to Bobby Dylan, Elton John, and a host of others. Cedric Abriam, high school chum – The Electric Flag; Ernie LeBlanc – Santana, Neil Young, his cousin Clarence White of The Byrds, Kentucky Colonels; and bluegrass music in general, etc.; Vicki Hoff – Neil Young & Crazy Horse and Crosby, Stills, Nash & Young; Chad Fjeld – Manassas, latter-day Beach Boys ("Holland" album – California Saga); Gary Armstrong – Earth, Wind, and Fire; Little Feat, Frank Zappa & the Mothers of Invention, and Captain Beefheart & His Magic Band; My other brother Keith Kennedy ("The White Miles Davis") – classic jazz, but mostly his own original compositions with his bands The Looneytoons and Rattlesnakes & Eggs; Gene Briggs – British blues rockers Ten Years After, Savoy Brown, and Fleetwood Mac (original version); my wife Linda – Southern Gospel artists JD Sumner & The Stamps, The Blackwoods, Oakridge Boys, Jake Hess & The Statesmen, The Happy Goodman Family, The Carter Family, and so on.

There are songs I hear that immediately transport me back in time, usually to my childhood, back to memorable events and relationships. I can tell you the favorite songs and groups of every girlfriend, guy friend, or relative I've ever known. But, so what - right? I tell you this not to magnify myself, but to instead support this amazing creation called music and demonstrate how music relates to us in so many ways and with so many people, mostly people we love the most. Music is the glue of intimacy that binds like beings together. If you love the top ten artists of, say, an anonymous person, you might very well become close friends with that person based on sharing musical tastes. I believe we humans learn, create, and perform better at most tasks if we have music along for the ride.

Yep, music is *the roadmap* of the journey that is our life. Without it, we'd lose our bearings and eventually lose our way altogether and not reach our respective destinations. Music is *that* vital. It is - at least for me - the very essence of life, love, romance, and relationships. I hope that this power of love will continue to grow; and as it grows, draw humanity closer together than anything else possibly can. Not religion, not race, not geography. The life blood of any evolved society is its enjoyment of its own music. I believe this life blood has a healing power stronger than just about anything or anybody else. Without this nectar of musical gods, I'm not sure life itself would be worth living.

Acknowledgments

This project, probably the most detailed and daunting of "my babies", is - like Ross's music – a collaboration of more than just one lone voice (mine). The people whom I wish to thank for a plethora of reasons are many, but each of them had their part in The Talisman Effect's inception, development, and/or birth.

First, I must acknowledge my three familial musical influences: My father, Rowlee Emerson Rowlee, for his "Music Man" persona & lifestyle wherein he founded my first and only band, St. Mary's Drum & Bugle Corps; my sister Diann, "the first flautist," who impressed me with her own musical journey of playing the flute for five or six years of our childhood. And last, my brother Keith Kennedy – otherwise known as "The White Miles

Davis" – whose musical skill and prowess are still discussed in our once-small hometown of Palmdale, California, where Keith played his horn (cornet) alongside many talented, even legendary musicians in our area. His former bandmates have played with and/or supported such musical artist greats as Frank Zappa, various incarnations of the Mothers of Invention, Don Van Vliet (Captain Beefheart & His Magic Band), Bruce Hornsby, Sparks, Eric Clapton, Roger Waters, Pete Townshend, Jeff Beck, and several others. Also, John Drumbo French, DJ Kevin KB Smith, Ralph Molina, Jason Scot Cacciacarne, and Marty Prue – for your kind words in support of this book.

After my family, I'd like to thank Andrea Danehower – for cover design, technical assistance, overall moral support, and genuine friendship. Muchas gracias para su ayuda, Bertha Briseno.

And lastly, my wife Linda Woods Rowlee for her undying support of me, my writing projects, and pretty much everything else in which I am involved.

Thank you, all.

Made in the USA
San Bernardino, CA
14 July 2018